A Fiancée's Guide to First Wives and Murder

Dianne Freeman

KENSINGTON
PUBLISHING CORP.

www.kensingtonbooks.com

KENSINGTON BOOKS are published by

Kensington Publishing Corp.
119 West 40th Street
New York, NY 10018

First Kensington Hardcover Edition: August 2021

ISBN: 978-1-4967-3166-1 (ebook)

ISBN: 978-1-4967-3163-0

First Kensington Trade Paperback Edition: June 2022

10 9 8 7 6 5 4 3 2 1

Printed in the United States of America

Books by Dianne Freeman

A LADY'S GUIDE TO ETIQUETTE AND MURDER

A LADY'S GUIDE TO GOSSIP AND MURDER

A LADY'S GUIDE TO MISCHIEF AND MURDER

A FIANCÉE'S GUIDE TO FIRST WIVES AND MURDER

A BRIDE'S GUIDE TO MARRIAGE AND MURDER

Published by Kensington Publishing Corp.

A Fiancée's Guide to
First Wives and Murder

Chapter One

⟐

November 1899

Life has an unerring way of balancing good and bad, rather like math. For every positive, there's a negative; for every gain, a loss; for every plus, a minus. The plus on this occasion was that my mother, who'd been living in my house since my sister's wedding last month, was about to leave for a holiday in Paris.

Huzzah! Dare I hope peace would reign in my household once more?

During her stay, she'd disrupted our lives with a constant critique of everything from the staff, the décor of her room, and the newspapers I took, to things that were entirely out of my control, like the weather. As I shivered on the wet pavement beside her hired carriage, enveloped by the damp air of a typical November morning in London, I could hardly fault her for that one.

A ray of sunlight broke through—at least in my mind—as my eight-year-old daughter, Rose, skipped down the walk to the carriage, her dark curls bouncing against her shoulders.

Nanny followed in a more sedate manner. She, too, had had just about all she could stand of Mother's interference, particularly with Rose's routine. Nanny set specific times for meals, lessons, recreation, and sleep. Despite my insistence she adhere to Nanny's schedule, Mother had one of her own—whenever she was in want of company, Rose should be made available. My daughter loved it. Nanny did not.

I wasn't exempt from my mother's judgment, either. Still, not only had she brought me into the world, but she'd also saved my life just a few short weeks ago, so I felt I owed her some degree of latitude.

Rose kissed Aunt Hetty, then came to me for one last hug before the groom handed her up into the carriage. She settled in next to my mother, fairly humming with excitement. That was the minus in this otherwise favorable equation—Rose was leaving, too.

The groom closed the carriage door, and I leaned through the open window. "Mind your grandmother, Rose." I turned to my mother. "And you don't give in to her every whim." This was a definite possibility as the only person safe from my mother's criticism was Rose. In her mind, Rose could do no wrong, which led my imagination to run rampant about their week ahead.

"We'll be fine, Frances." Mother batted away my concern as a mere trifle. "If you are so worried, you should join us."

If only I could. The three of us had planned to take this trip together to order gowns for my upcoming engagement party given by my fiancé's sister. But then the Romanovs had arrived in London: Grand Duke Michael Mikhailovich and his wife, Sophie, Countess de Torby. The elite of society had received invitations, or commands, to attend various events honoring them this week. That included me, the Countess of Harleigh, and my fiancé, the Honorable George Hazelton. Despite all my admonishments to my mother not to give in to Rose's whims, I had done just that, allowing her and her grandmama to go to Paris without me.

With the jingle of a harness and the shuffling of hooves, the carriage pulled away from the curb. I clutched Hetty's arm with one hand and waved with the other, while my heart sank to my toes.

Hetty brushed away a tear from her cheek. "Cheer up, dear. Little Rose has a good head on her shoulders. She'll keep your mother out of trouble."

Nanny let out a grunt as we trudged back to the house under the heavy gray sky. "I can still see them," she said. "It's not too late to call them back."

"My aunt is right, Nanny." I lifted my chin. "We are worried about nothing. Between the servants, the hotel staff, and my mother, Lady Rose will be fine. After all, my mother raised me, and I turned out well enough."

Her lips compressed as she eyed me, clearly unimpressed.

"At least I came to no harm." I picked up our pace. "You must be eager to be off on your holiday. Visiting your sister, are you not?"

Nanny grumbled something unintelligible, bobbed a curtsy, then stomped down the stairs to the service entrance.

Hetty and I exchanged a glance as we stepped through the open front door to the entry hall. "Honestly, you'd think Rose was her daughter," Hetty said.

"She may not be Nanny's daughter, but she is her little girl. Still, I thought she'd be happy for a short break."

Hetty and I wandered into the drawing room off the hall and settled ourselves on the sofa, part of a cozy conversation area around the tea table. It was not an expansive room, just an ordinary rectangle, with a card table near the front windows, this grouping near the fireplace, and a cabinet against the wall between them that held a few sentimental treasures and a cache of spirits and wine. To me, it was a warm and welcoming place.

"I suspect the real problem is the changes we're making to the household," Hetty said.

"We're only asking her to move next door, but I suppose I know what you mean."

George and I had yet to set a date for our wedding, but we had been making plans. I'd move into his home next door with Rose, Nanny, and my maid Bridget. Hetty would purchase the lease to this house and retain the rest of the staff. It was a sensible plan. My gaze traveled the length of the cozy room. But this was the first home that belonged solely to me, and though I'd lived here only six months, I'd miss it.

This was where I first met George. No, that wasn't true. I first met him years ago, when I made my London debut. That was before I married Reggie and became Countess of Harleigh—before I spent nine years married to the philandering cad, followed by a year mourning his death. Then I moved to this darling little house in Belgravia and learned George Hazelton was my neighbor. It was as if fate had played a role.

"It's a little soon to be looking so nostalgic, Frances." Hetty's voice drew my attention back to the present. She smiled. "You haven't even left yet, and when you have, you're welcome to visit anytime you like."

"You may depend upon that. The gate George installed between our gardens was not just for our convenience. It's so Rose and I can visit easily when this becomes your home. How will you like living alone here?" I paused as a thought struck me. "Will this be the first home you've owned?" Hetty lost her husband to influenza back when I was just a child. She moved in with our family and became something of a second mother to me and later to my sister, Lily, after I left New York for London.

A smile crept across her face and crinkled her eyes. "This will be my first home—at the age of fifty, can you believe it? I suppose I was comfortable living with your parents and never thought of a home of my own. Now that I have, I find it very exciting."

"Well, if I must give it up, I'm glad you'll be taking it over. I couldn't wish for a better neighbor." I had a difficult time thinking of Aunt Hetty as fifty. Unlike my mother, who spent hours on her beauty regime, Hetty had an energetic nature that made her seem younger. I hoped I would age as well as she had. We were both tall, though her figure was fuller than mine. Her brown eyes were framed by a few lines at the corners, but her square jaw would likely never sag, and so far, her dark hair hadn't so much as a strand of gray.

As I studied her, something behind me caught her attention. I glanced over my shoulder at the window. "Are you already contemplating a change to the draperies?"

"Perhaps, but right now, I'm trying to determine whose carriage is out front."

I slipped over to the window and peeked out as a slight, redheaded woman emerged from the carriage. "It's Alicia Stoke-Whitney. What could she want?"

"Do you wish me to stay with you?" Hetty asked.

I strode to the mirror over the drinks cabinet and adjusted the dark curls on my forehead. I'd always liked my blue eyes, but now they were tinged with red from crying over Rose's departure. So was the tip of my nose, and my cheeks were pale. As I pinched them, I caught Hetty's eye in the mirror, and her question sank in.

"What? No, no. I'm sure I'm up to any business Alicia might have to discuss." I winced as the doorbell rang.

Hetty pulled me around by the arm. "Which is why you're suddenly so concerned over your appearance?"

Any meeting with my late husband's lover had the effect of making me question my appearance. It didn't help that Alicia, somewhere in her mid-thirties, seemed to grow more beautiful with each passing year.

"I'm just straightening myself after having been out in the wind," I said. "I appreciate your concern, and you're welcome to stay if you like. But it truly isn't necessary."

Hetty pursed her lips. "I'll forgo the pleasure if you don't mind."

I followed her to the hall and watched her slip up the stairs as Mrs. Thompson arrived to answer the door. "That will be Mrs. Stoke-Whitney," I told her. "Will you show her into the drawing room, then arrange for tea?"

I stepped back into the room and took a bracing breath. Alicia and I weren't friends, but my husband's death had forced us to share a secret. We could hardly let the world know Reggie had died in her bed, so with the assistance of the ever-chivalrous George Hazelton, we had relocated dear Reggie. The subterfuge had created something of a bond between us. It had been aided by the need to behave cordially toward one another in public to quell the rumor that she and my husband had been lovers. I suppose if one pretends to like someone, one may actually come to do so—to some degree, anyway.

The door opened. "Mrs. Stoke-Whitney, my lady." Mrs. Thompson moved aside to allow Alicia to enter, which she did with the grace of a swan. If she'd been born into another class, she might have been a dancer; she was so slender and graceful. With her red hair and green eyes, she would likely have been a star. Instead, she was the third daughter in a family with great prestige and little money. She had no choice but to marry well. I had never considered it before, but she was the female version of my late husband.

Alicia removed her coat, revealing a cunning walking dress of gray and pink, which matched her hat beautifully. "Frances," she said, heaving a theatrical sigh. "I'm simply devastated and in need of your help."

"Do come in, Alicia." I gestured to the seating area.

Mrs. Thompson took Alicia's coat and left to see to the tea. Alicia and I perched on either end of the sofa.

"Arthur is being such a beast," she said, tugging her kid gloves from her fingers.

"Is he indeed?" Arthur Stoke-Whitney was her husband and her escape from genteel poverty. He was a good twenty-five years older than her, and there had never been any pretense that their marriage was anything more than an alliance. He already had an heir and a spare from his first marriage. After a few years as a widower, he had decided to look for a beautiful woman with a good pedigree to grace his table and aid in his political career. He was wealthy enough not to require a dowry. Alicia had fit the bill perfectly.

"He's banishing me to the country," she said. "I'm to be stuck there until he allows me to return to town."

I raised my brows, and I must confess it was difficult not to smirk. "An indiscretion, Alicia?"

At that moment, Mrs. Thompson entered with the tea tray, forcing us both to be discreet until she left and quietly closed the door behind her.

Alicia threw me a glare. "I was discreet. The gentleman in question was not."

I handed her a cup of tea and drew back as she stirred in a spoonful of sugar with enough vigor to whip an egg. When I stilled her hand, she collected herself.

"I shall never choose such a young man again. They simply must boast." She shook her head when I offered her a delicate plate with a selection of sweets. "Of course, word got back to Arthur, and he was absolutely furious."

"No doubt," I said. Stoke-Whitney didn't care what Alicia did, or how many affairs she conducted, so long as nary a hint of her improprieties became public. He was a member of the House of Commons and had elections to think of. His wife didn't have to be above reproach, but she must give the appearance of it. He was a stickler for appearances.

I suppose I understood their marriage a little better when I reminded myself that he was a politician and something of a courtier. The queen could not abide a whiff of scandal among the aristocracy or her members of Parliament. I took a sip of tea. Her Majesty was frequently disappointed, but never by Arthur Stoke-Whitney, at least not yet.

Alicia patted an errant curl back into place. "Yes, yes. It's understandable but terribly inconvenient."

"Have you considered ending your dalliances altogether? You place yourself, your husband, and your family in an awkward position and risk all your reputations for what is nothing but a momentary thrill." I dipped a bit of scone into the clotted cream on my plate and popped it into my mouth, waiting for her to defend her actions.

Instead, she gave me a pathetic look. "I do believe it's time to consider that possibility, but don't lecture me, Frances. I've come to you for help."

That was intriguing. "How can I help?"

"Well, as I said, Arthur is furious, and I expect my stay in the country to be longer than usual. He won't get over this in a month or two. He's already told me I should not bother with a new wardrobe for the season."

"I find that hard to believe. With all the entertaining he does, he'll need you."

Alicia lifted her chin. "He said if he needed a hostess, he'd call on his sister."

I gasped and nearly choked on another bite of scone. A sip of tea set me to rights. "Surely you don't mean Constance?" A foolish question, as she was his only sister—a woman whose only social skill was hunting. Her lack of manners and even the most rudimentary grasp of precedence was one of the reasons

Stoke-Whitney had married for a second time. She was an abysmal hostess.

"Of course I mean Constance, and I see you grasp the magnitude of my problem."

"Indeed, but I still don't understand how I can be of help."

"That's right," she said. "I missed an important point. Our daughter will turn eighteen in January. Harriet should be presented to the queen and make her debut this spring. When I reminded Arthur of our responsibility to her, he said Constance could handle that little matter."

My heart went out to Harriet. A presentation to the queen was an inspiring but formidable undertaking for a young woman, even under the best of circumstances. With someone like Constance guiding one through the complexity of a presentation, well, disaster became inevitable.

"Surely he wouldn't do such a thing to his own daughter?"

Alicia twisted her cup until I thought it would crack. She set it down. "His sons are everything to him, but Arthur barely recalls that he has a daughter, so I cannot take this threat lightly. The only way to avoid complete humiliation for Harriet is if you agree to act as her sponsor."

"Me?"

"Yes, you." She lifted her brows. "That's what you do, isn't it? You sponsored your sister and that other American girl, and they both had successful seasons. You wouldn't turn up your nose at my daughter because she's not American, would you?"

"Of course not."

She clapped her hands in delight. "Then, you'll do it?"

"I'm still not convinced I'll be needed. And will Mr. Stoke-Whitney approve?"

"Approve that Frances, Countess of Harleigh, is willing to sponsor his daughter? Arthur will be beside himself with glee. He may even see Harriet in a new light. And I promise I will call on you for this favor only if I'm still in exile come March."

"Then, yes, I shall help Harriet. Though I don't believe you'll be in exile, as you call it, for that long. He will need you sooner rather than later."

"I do hope you're right. And you've given me another idea. I'm to remain in town until after our reception for the Romanovs this week. Perhaps, if I'm on my very best behavior and help him with that miserable speech he's presenting in the meantime, I can convince him to change his mind and not send me away."

"Is he speaking in the House?"

"No. This is a speech for some ladies' society hard at work for the preservation of morality in politics. I don't know what they call themselves—something, something, public corruption." She waved a hand. "They supported Arthur in the last election."

I could only imagine what sort of help Alicia might provide for this speech. "Perhaps you could just remind him how awkward Constance would be around the Russians and the Prince and Princess of Wales."

Her eyes locked on mine. "Very good. I'll remember that." She picked up her gloves from the table and came to her feet. "I must thank you, my dear. You've given me a reason to hope again."

I rang for Mrs. Thompson and walked Alicia out to the entry hall, where we waited for my housekeeper to bring her coat.

"I neglected to compliment you on your beautiful engagement ring." Alicia eyed my ring while she pulled on her gloves. "Hazelton has splendid taste in jewelry." She lifted her gaze to meet mine. "I haven't seen him out in society lately. How is he faring?"

"He couldn't be better or happier, so don't get any ideas." I opened the door and signaled to her carriage driver.

Alicia smirked. "As if I would. Anyone can see you two are a love match." She tossed her head, then peered through the doorway and pointed out to the street. "Haven't I seen that man before?"

"Probably just our neighbor's butler. We call him the gossip of Chester Street. He spends far too much time watching the comings and goings of each of us."

"This man's no butler." She tipped her head. "Isn't he the policeman who helped me with my stolen bracelet last spring?"

I stepped around the door and peered out just as Mrs. Thompson arrived with Alicia's coat. Inspector Delaney was indeed outside, and he had a young woman with him. He had just walked from George's door to the pavement and appeared to be at a loss, looking up and down the street.

As Alicia had donned her outerwear, I stepped outside with her. Delaney must have been looking for George, who was currently at his club.

We strolled toward the pavement while Alicia's driver pulled the carriage around the corner and up to the house, drawing Delaney's attention. When he caught sight of me, his face took on a horrified expression. He took a step backward, but the young woman approached us eagerly. Delaney reluctantly followed.

"Good afternoon, Inspector," I said. "Are you here to call on Mr. Hazelton?"

He pulled off his hat, revealing the gray and brown bramble that was his hair. "We were, indeed, Lady Harleigh. Sadly, he's not available."

Delaney's companion stood with a fist on her hip, eyeing me with an insolent gaze. "Do you know Hazelton?" Her French accent came as a surprise.

"Of course. I am his neighbor."

"And his fiancée," Alicia added.

The woman narrowed her eyes. "Are you indeed? Imagine that." She turned to Delaney. "Did you know this?"

Delaney pressed two fingers to his temple.

Such impertinence. "And may one ask who you are, miss?"

"Mrs." Her lips tipped up to one side. "I am Mrs. George Hazelton."

I blinked. What had she just said?

Behind me, Alicia drew in a breath. "My, my," she said, leaning close to my ear. "And I thought I had problems."

Chapter Two

꩜

Somehow, with Delaney directing our small procession, we made it into my house. Tantalized by the scent of scandal, Alicia tried to linger, but he set her firmly in her carriage and waved the driver on his way. When the carriage moved, I spotted Jackson, the nosy butler from across the street, taking in all the activity with raised brows and a pinched expression. *Lovely.* Now we were presenting a spectacle for my neighbors. I took the little baggage by the arm and preceded Delaney into the house.

The next thing I knew, I was handing a note to Mrs. Thompson, to be delivered next door, urging George to call on me immediately upon his arrival at home, to settle a delicate matter.

Mrs. Thompson took the note from my shaking hand and, with a cautious glance at the others, retreated from the drawing room. By this time, the shock had worn off, leaving me a bit disoriented and positively enraged. How dare she claim to be married to George? My George! What manner of game was she playing?

I took a calming breath before turning to my "delicate matter," who had made herself far too comfortable in one of my chintz-covered chairs. She presented a sensual and exotic sight. Her few hairpins did little to contain the masses of dark waves that tumbled past her shoulders. They framed a pale oval face with dark eyes and brows that slashed upward. She'd removed her coat to reveal a gauzy tea gown, the likes of which should never have left the privacy of her own drawing room. Yet she and her gown were draped over a chair in mine. I disliked her from pure instinct.

"Where is my husband?" Again, I was taken aback by the French accent in her husky voice. I glanced at Delaney who had taken the matching chair beside her. His head tipped down, he made a show of reviewing his notes, giving me a view of only his wiry salt-and-pepper hair and his rumpled brown suit.

I turned back to the woman. "If you're referring to Mr. Hazelton, I've sent him a message. He'll come here as soon as he arrives home. In the meantime, perhaps you'd care to tell me what your business is with him? I don't for a moment believe you're his wife."

"Perhaps you don't know the man as well as you think."

"I beg to differ. I know him better than anyone. We are betrothed."

She gave me a Gallic shrug. "That may present a problem. I don't think British law allows for more than one spouse at a time."

As we spoke, I'd moved closer, until I was fairly towering over her. Delaney must have thought I posed a threat, for he took to his feet and directed me to the chair on the opposite side of the table before resuming his own seat

"Who is she, Delaney? And wherever did you find her?"

"Why don't I begin with telling you what I know and why I brought the lady here?" he said.

I gave him a grudging nod, and the woman waved a hand, as if she really didn't care what either of us did.

"I was at my precinct when a constable brought her in." Delaney glanced at the little notebook he always carried. "She'd been apprehended outside of Marlborough House. It appeared she'd attempted to attack Grand Duke Michael Mikhailovich."

I don't know what I'd expected to hear, but it certainly wasn't this. "You attacked the grand duke?"

"Whoever said that has made far too much of the matter. I merely wished to speak with him." She tossed her head. "He would not listen. He could not be bothered."

"Is there some reason he should bother himself to speak with you?" I asked.

"He is my cousin."

I huffed. "I see. Hazelton is your husband, and the grand duke is your cousin." Egad, the woman was delusional. "I suppose you're related to the queen, as well?"

Her expression grew thoughtful. "Why, yes, though it's a distant connection. I'm pleased I can credit you with more intelligence than the policeman who arrested me. At least you understand a simple statement."

I gaped at Delaney, who looked as flustered as I. "There's nothing about your relationship to the grand duke in the report," he said.

"I suspect the constable didn't believe me."

"That's understandable. Your identity papers are French. They state your name as Irena Teskey, aged twenty-four." He glanced up from his notes to the young woman and raised a brow. "Don't know much about Russia and the royal family, but I believe their surname is Romanov. Teskey isn't Romanov."

"Neither is it Hazelton," I said, feeling a little better by this point. Both Delaney and I leaned in toward her. Let's see her talk her way out of this lie.

"Teskey is a name I use for professional reasons. Like a writer has a nom de plume."

"You're a writer?" I asked. That could explain her vivid imagination.

She placed a hand to her throat and threw her head back. "I am an actress." With a glance at our blank expressions, she dropped the pose and sighed with impatience. "And I own a theater here in London."

Delaney and I stared in mute astonishment.

I recovered first. "Let me see if I understand. You are a French actress who is cousin to a grand duke of Russia and wife to the very British Mr. Hazelton. Oh, and you also own a theater here in London. Does that sound right?"

Her eyes narrowed. "Now you sound as if you don't believe me."

"At least there's nothing wrong with your hearing."

"How dare you? You, who are clearly an American, claim to be a British countess, and I don't doubt your honesty. You also claim to be betrothed to a man I know to be my husband, and I don't cast aspersions on your integrity."

"Because I am telling the truth."

"As am I!"

"Ladies!" Delaney came to his feet. "Please. I ask you to keep this discussion civil."

Miss Teskey and I settled back in our seats, hostility fairly sizzling between us.

He gave each of us a warning look, then consulted his notes once more. "Miss Teskey, you say you arrived in London three weeks ago. Why did you not seek out Mr. Hazelton at that time?"

"It never occurred to me. I came here for business—to open the theater with my new partner. We've been very busy hiring actors, advertising, staging the play itself." She raised her hands. "It is all a great deal of work. Our opening night was just two days ago. Since I planned to make London my home, there was plenty of time to contact Hazelton once everything settled down. Besides, I wasn't sure where he lived."

"Indeed? Just how did you happen to lose track of him?"

Delaney groaned. "Lady Harleigh, I beg you."

I understood Delaney's frustration, but this charade had gone on long enough. "How on earth did you even meet Hazelton? And how did you come to be married? And if you were husband and wife, why did you separate? For goodness' sake, you live in two different countries, with a body of water between you."

"You are not entitled to know everything about me, Lady Harleigh, but suffice it to say, Hazelton came to my rescue a few years ago, when I had been abducted by some horrible men."

I hadn't thought there was anything she could say to make her story more ridiculous. I was wrong. "Abducted?"

"By some horrible men?" Delaney's expression showed the same incredulity I felt.

"Yes." She sighed. "It's not something I care to elaborate upon."

I groaned. "Yet I have a sense you are about to do just that."

"It was a most heinous experience." She rose slowly to her feet, her gaze fixed on something off in the distance. "I had just arrived in Paris and was strolling in a park, rehearsing some lines for a play in which I hoped to obtain a role. In the blink of an eye, a man slipped from the woods and whisked me up in his arms as if I were no more than an armful of flowers." The tiny sprite made a show of looking me up and down, as if gauging my weight. "He carried me to a waiting carriage and spirited me away. We drove for hours, until I had no knowledge of my surroundings."

She returned her attention to us, her audience of two. "I don't know how Hazelton ever found me."

"Or why he bothered." I returned her snarl with a sweet smile.

She frowned in concentration, creating a small furrow between her brows. "I believe my father sent him—or perhaps it was Edward, the Prince of Wales."

And now the heir to the British throne had been dragged into her story.

"Whoever sent him, he was my savior. He rescued me and returned me to the little village near Trouville, where I used to live with the Teskeys."

Delaney's gaze sharpened. "Teskey? Is that your family?"

She gave a little shake of her head and sank back into her chair. "They are the people who raised me. Hazelton must have sensed I needed loved ones nearby. He's so considerate in that way. However, the distance of the trip meant we were forced to spend a night on the road. We came to know each other very well." At this, she cast a little sneer my way.

"Of course, he did the honorable thing and married me. It was at a charming chapel in our little village. So romantic." She snuck a glance at me from under her lashes and caught me gnashing my teeth. "But love does not solve all problems, does it? He had to return to his duties here in London. For some time, I waited patiently, but then the stage beckoned, and I returned to Paris. Not long ago, I heard Mr. Gilliam was seeking partners in his theater venture. We met, discussed terms, and, voilà, here I am, right next door to my husband. Is that not the very essence of romance, Countess?"

"Just like a fairy tale." I struggled to keep the words as light as possible, but even I could feel the chill in my tone. "And it's just as unbelievable."

"You don't *want* to believe me, or that Hazelton deceived you. I'm sorry, my dear Countess, but your fiancé happens to be my husband."

"Your story doesn't even make sense. Why would Hazelton have been sent to your rescue?"

She narrowed one eye. "I couldn't say with any certainty, but doesn't he do something for your government?"

I only just managed to restrain a gasp as a chill overtook me. She'd bumped right up against the truth with that comment. He did do "something for the government." Another truth she'd spoken was that I didn't want to believe her story. That would mean George had deceived me. But I couldn't believe it of him. He would never have asked me to marry him if he wasn't free. I hated to admit it, but much of my anger at Miss Teskey had arisen from fear—that she was telling the truth.

Upon the heels of that acknowledgment, the drawing room door opened, and Hetty popped her head inside.

"Ah, there you are, Frances. Look who I found in the back garden." She pushed the door open to reveal George beside her. Dressed impeccably in a dark blue morning coat and tie, he looked every bit the dashing man about town. But the smile he gave me brought to mind the charmer, the silly boy, the unassuming yet sometimes dangerous man I also knew him to be. Indeed, the man I might be about to lose.

Hetty pulled up short. "Inspector Delaney. A pleasure to see you here, but a surprise, nonetheless. Is there some trouble afoot?" She chuckled.

Delaney made a shallow bow. "Good day, Mrs. Chesney. Just a small matter we wished to consult with Mr. Hazelton about."

Miss Teskey brightened at the sound of Hazelton's name. Her back was to the door, and the chair kept her hidden from their view. Before she could rise, I came shakily to my feet.

"We have another guest," I said, sweeping a hand toward Miss Teskey.

I held my breath and watched George's face as she stood and turned toward him.

Everyone seemed to freeze for the space of a breath. Hetty

frowned as she perceived the tension. "Won't you introduce us, Frances?"

But I could see no introduction would be necessary for George. Recognition, shock, and confusion played across his expression.

"Hazelton," Miss Teskey said, "you are here at last."

"Irena?"

Fearing my legs would fail me, I sank back into the chair. If there were ever a time I could wish to be a woman who fainted, it would be now—anything to take me out of this moment.

Chapter Three

Panic tightened my throat and froze me in place as their re-union played out in front of me. Miss Teskey slipped around the chair and threw herself at George. Easily a head taller than the young woman, he caught her at arm's length and kept her there, his face still revealing nothing but astonishment.

"What is wrong?" She took a step back and dropped her hands to her hips. "Aren't you pleased to see me?"

"*Surprised* might be a better word." His wary gaze fell on Delaney, then me, as if he was asking for some explanation. When neither of us produced one, he returned his attention to Miss Teskey. "Tell me what the devil you're doing here, and I'll let you know if I'm pleased or not."

Hetty eyed the woman with suspicion. "Has she something to do with the small matter you mentioned, Inspector?"

Delaney shifted his weight, cleared his throat, then pulled his notebook from his pocket and flipped through the pages. "Miss Teskey landed herself in a spot of trouble at Marlborough House this morning."

"I simply wished to speak to my cousin." She lowered her head and looked up at George like an innocent lamb.

He frowned. "Your cousin? Ah, that's right. The grand duke and the countess are visiting."

Thank goodness I was seated, or I might have fallen over. The grand duke truly was her cousin?

"I didn't realize they were staying at Marlborough House," he said. What sort of trouble did you cause?"

Miss Teskey waved her hand. "It was nothing. Do not concern yourself."

"She threw a rock at their party as they walked from the carriage to the house."

Three of us gasped at Delaney's pronouncement. Miss Teskey pouted. George rounded on her.

"A rock? What were you thinking?"

"It was an impulse of the moment. I was passing Marlborough House, and by coincidence, a carriage arrived. I saw Michael and Sophie emerge and thought to speak with them." Her face took on an angry expression. "I called out to them and approached, and then a groom took hold of my arm and pulled me away. They took no notice of me, as if I were no one. When the groom let me go, I picked up the tiniest of pebbles." She whirled her dainty hand in the air. "And I may have thrown it at them."

The woman was demented. Truly demented.

Delaney cleared his throat. "The size of the rock wasn't noted in the report, but I'll add that the Prince of Wales was a member of their party, and the sentry at the gate did not take kindly to Miss Teskey's actions. A constable was summoned. He collected her and brought her to my precinct."

George cut a horrified glance at the woman. "Gad, Irena! Next time write the man a letter."

"As I said, it was just an impulse. I was angry Michael Mikhailovich wouldn't acknowledge me."

"Did he even know who you were? After all, he would have no expectation of seeing you in such surroundings."

She shrugged.

George released an impatient huff and turned to Delaney. "I understand why she was arrested, but how does she come to be here? What has Lady Harleigh to do with this?"

"That's a bit of a story."

My stomach was in knots. I couldn't look at either man. I dropped my face into my hands, silently urging Delaney to ask the question.

He cleared his throat. I peeked through my fingers. "I was at the precinct when they brought the young lady in," he began, "and when I heard her mention your name—"

George's eyes widened. "*My* name?"

"I thought it best to take control of the situation and brought her to your house."

"*My* house?"

"For heaven's sake!" I rose to my feet. "Is she your wife?"

"My *what*?" George jumped away from Miss Teskey as if he'd been burnt. "Gad, no!"

Hetty let out a gasp. "Frances, where did you come by such an idea?"

Delaney and I turned our gazes to Miss Teskey, who stared up at George with her arms crossed, her haughty exterior crumbling just a bit. In a blink, her hand shot out and thumped him in the chest. "What do you mean, 'Gad, no!'"

"Did you tell Inspector Delaney we were married? You and I? Together?" The pitch of his voice rose with each word and held a distinct note of hysteria.

"And what is wrong with being my husband?" She stabbed her finger into his chest again and again. Hetty scooted aside as George retreated.

"What's wrong with it? This for one thing." He caught her finger in his fist. "Stop poking me."

By this point, my emotions had been put through a mangle

and were now stretched and limp. Enough of this confusion. "Are the two of you married or not?"

He jerked his head up, our gazes locked, and it seemed he finally noticed my anguish. His expression softened as he crossed the room to me and, with no regard for anyone else, placed his palm on my cheek. "My dear Frances, there has only ever been you for me. I'm so sorry this misunderstanding has caused you distress, but I can assure you, Irena and I are not married."

It felt as if I had been pulled from a raging sea and my feet set on solid ground again. I found myself in desperate need of the arm he slipped around my waist.

Across the room, my rival stamped her foot. "Yes, we are."

"This is all very confusing," Hetty muttered.

"Some further explanation does seem to be in order," Delaney added.

As much as I hated to lose the sanctuary of George's arms, I stepped aside and settled myself on the sofa, bringing him with me. Miss Teskey had shaken me to the core. I, too, wanted an explanation. As this was my home, I supposed I should take charge of the situation. Perhaps with George here, we could make some sense of her story.

"Aunt Hetty, Miss Teskey, please join us. We'll all have some tea and talk this out civilly."

"We'll need something stronger than tea, my dear." Hetty ambled over to the drinks cabinet and pulled out a bottle of brandy. "This should do."

"There is nothing to talk out. Hazelton is my husband, and I will not sit and chat with people who refuse to believe me." With a scowl, Miss Teskey crossed her arms over her chest, as if daring anyone to make her speak.

George took the dare. "Irena, you spoiled child, you've already caused enough trouble for these good people. Come over here this instant and explain yourself."

"I won't!"

Hetty stepped up to the tea table with a tray of glasses, all filled halfway with brandy. None of us would make any sense once we finished these. Delaney declined the brandy and took a chair at the end of the rectangular table. Hetty glanced over her shoulder at Miss Teskey who stood stubbornly apart from us. "If you'd like some refreshment, dear, I'll leave it for you here on the table." She gave the woman a nod and set the glass in front of an empty seat.

Miss Teskey squared her jaw and pushed her hair behind her shoulder. "Thank you. I believe I will." She took the chair and swept up the glass. After swirling the liquid under her nose, she took a sip and glanced at Hetty. "A very good vintage."

"Well, of course," Hetty replied. "Drink up, dear."

How had I ever thought I had control of this situation?

George slipped forward on the sofa and rested his elbows on his knees. "Let me see if I understand how this all came about." He turned to Delaney. "After Irena was arrested, you heard her say she was my wife, so you brought her to my home to verify her claim with me. Is that correct?"

"And to put a stop to any gossip as quickly as possible. You are not exactly unknown to the Metropolitan Police, and neither is your engagement to Lady Harleigh. I could imagine the rumors spreading."

"Thank you for that. I only wish I'd been at home when you called." He drew my hand from my lap and caressed it. "I'm so sorry you've been imposed upon in this way."

"It was distressing, but I feel much better now. Can you explain why she claims to be married to you?" I lowered my voice to a whisper. "Is she insane?"

I glanced up in time to see the woman in question glaring at me in haughty disdain. "So, you've had a difficult morning, have you? How do you think mine has been? And the two of you are not making it any better. Why do you comfort her while I am sitting right here? I, your wife. Remember me?"

"I remember you perfectly well, Irena." George held firmly to my hand. "I also remember you were a child when we met. No one would have married us, and I would have been a cad to have attempted it."

"She said you rescued her from an abductor."

He nodded. "Indeed. It's a poorly kept secret that Irena is the daughter of Grand Duke Alexei Alexandrovich. Living in a small village, with only the Teskeys for protection, she was subject to abduction with alarming frequency."

Hetty sipped her brandy and frowned. "I can't keep all those Romanovs straight. Which one is he?"

"Brother to the last czar. Uncle to the current one," George said.

"Why should there be any secrecy involved?"

Miss Teskey gave her a long look. "You British would say I am his natural daughter."

"I'm not British, my dear, but—oh—I see." Hetty hid her pinkening face behind her glass.

"Isn't Alexei the naval commander?" I asked.

"He is," George said. He could hardly raise a child on board a ship, but he became responsible for her when her mother passed away."

"She was murdered," Miss Teskey added, swirling the liquid in her glass.

George pressed a hand against his eyes. "She died in child-birth, which is bad enough. No need to make it more dramatic."

"I heard her husband murdered her in a jealous rage," she insisted. "The Teskeys told me this."

"I'm not sure the Teskeys were the best of guardians."

Considering she'd been subjected to several abductions, I was inclined to agree. I was also inclined to feel a slight twinge of sympathy for her, raised without a father or mother, part of a royal family, but forced to remain outside of it due to her illegitimacy.

Then I recalled the way she had tortured me over the past hour, trying to convince me she was George's wife, and I hardened my heart. "She said the two of you spent a night on the road together. That's why you married."

George released a tsk. "That story and the marriage exist only in her imagination. The criminal left a trail any fool could follow. He was holding Irena in a small cottage in the same village where she'd been living."

Miss Teskey frowned, as if giving this some thought, then shook her head. "No, that is not how it happened at all."

"Before we go into all that, I'd like to determine what we are to do about her attack on the grand duke." Delaney had been quietly listening for so long, his words came as a surprise. "If Miss Teskey is his cousin, and it appears that she is, why did he allow her to be arrested?"

The young woman examined her fingernails. "It's possible he didn't know who I was."

"Have you ever met one another?" George asked.

"Many years ago. Long before you and I met." She gave him a sweet smile. "He wouldn't have known my face, but he would have recognized my name had I been given the opportunity and the common courtesy of an introduction. That guard overreacted." She gestured to her admittedly small person. "Do I look as if I could hurt someone?"

George rubbed his chest. "You do have dangerously sharp fingers."

"And you did throw a rock," I reminded her.

"A small stone, a mere pebble." She sighed. "I simply wanted the man's help. I was threatened, and I hoped he would offer his protection."

"Protection? Never say someone is trying to abduct you again?" Hetty leaned back to take the woman in.

"No." She paused, placing a slender finger to her lips. She looked the picture of innocence. "But someone has threatened my life. I have letters."

Delaney pinched the bridge of his nose. He must have thought he was on the verge of escaping this situation. Unfortunately, it did nothing but grow more complicated with each passing minute. "Why did you not mention this when you were at the police precinct? Do you have the letters now?"

"They are at the theater." She tipped her head, her gaze drifting upward, as she thought. "Or I may have left them in my rooms."

George broke in. "Why would you leave them at a theater?"

"Not *a* theater," she corrected. "*My* theater."

"She's an actress," I said.

"And I own the theater." She shrugged. "With a partner."

"Let's return to the threatening letters," Delaney said. "Do you know who they're from?"

She shook her head. "They are unsigned, but recently, I noticed a man following me. Perhaps they are from him." She paused, her glass poised before her lips. "Or maybe they came in the post."

For someone who'd gone to such lengths to obtain assistance with this matter, she seemed wholly untroubled by it now. George and I shared a glance as Delaney continued with his interview.

"What sort of threats were they, and when did you receive them?"

"A week or two after I arrived in London, I received the first one. It hinted that it wasn't safe for me to be here. The next one came the following week. It said, 'Go away, or you will die.'"

I stared, wondering if this was another of her fairy tales.

Hetty looked incredulous. "And you never went to the police?"

Again, she shrugged. I couldn't discern if she was genuinely unconcerned or if that careless shrug of hers was just a habit, like a tic or a twitch.

"Seriously, my dear," Hetty continued, "you are taking this far too casually. The only help you sought was from your cousin, and as a result of that encounter, you were arrested?"

"Exactly. This is what happens when I ask for help." With a sigh, she tipped her head back and drained her glass.

Delaney opened his notebook to a blank page. "What do you know of the man who was following you?"

She spread her hands. "Nothing."

George released a groan. "He means, what did the man look like? How long has he been following you? Where have you seen him?"

"Why are you snapping at me? I am the one who was threatened. I am the innocent party."

"Forgive me for snapping, Irena, but will you please answer the questions?"

"I'm not sure I can. I've seen him around the theater, but there are always men milling about backstage, and I can't tell one from the other. He was just an average man. Will that do?"

"There you go, Inspector." George's words were clipped. "Simply arrest every average man in London."

I touched his arm, hoping it would remind him to moderate his tone. With a glance at me, he added a note of concern to his voice. "What made you feel threatened by him? Did he say anything to you? Did you see him anywhere other than the theater?"

She seemed to have a difficult time recalling. "Perhaps. Why don't you go to my rooms and look around for him?"

George bounced his palm on the arm of the sofa. "Capital idea. I should have no trouble recognizing him with the vivid description you've provided."

She narrowed her eyes. "You are not being kind."

"I'm not feeling kindly at the moment." He leaned forward.

"You say someone has been following you, but you did nothing about it until you learned your cousin was in London. Are you just trying to gain your father's attention again?"

"Hardly. My father is fully absorbed in his own life. Between his loves and his travels, even his son cannot obtain his attention, and I don't even bother. I tell you I have been followed and threatened. Check the theater or my rooms. You'll find the letters."

"All right." Delaney abruptly came to his feet. "Before I can investigate your claim, I need to find out if the Crown plans to file charges against you."

"Against me?"

"Once I explain who you are, I suspect none will be filed."

"You tell Michael Mikhailovich I expect some assistance from him." She tapped her finger on the arm of the chair as she issued the order.

"I'm not likely to see him face-to-face, ma'am, to convey your message. I'm also afraid you'll have to return to the precinct with me until we get this cleared up. Once we do, I'll investigate those threatening letters."

Outrage surged into her eyes. The breaths she drew were probably meant to calm her but served only to fan her anger, until she slammed her palm on the table. "I refuse to go with you. You wish to lock me up, and I have done nothing wrong."

"He cannot take you back to your rooms and leave you to your own devices," I said. "Besides, if you really are being followed, you won't be safe."

She turned her wide eyes to Delaney. "But didn't you bring me here to release me into the custody of my husband?"

"Don't start that again." George came to his feet, shaking a finger at her. "I'm not your husband."

"You are my husband, and you will take responsibility for me, or I'll make sure every policeman at this prison knows you are abandoning me."

"I'm not taking you to prison, ma'am."

If Miss Teskey had heard Delaney, she gave no sign of it. "Once I am released from prison, I will go to the papers and tell them you and my cousin have both turned your backs on me."

I groaned. Once a story like this took hold, it could take weeks before the truth came out, and even then, the stench of scandal could linger indefinitely.

"Irena, you know you are not my wife."

"I know nothing of the sort. Either I stay with you, under your protection, or I tell all of London society that *my husband* is betrothed to the Countess of Harleigh."

Chapter Four

George pinched the bridge of his nose. "Irena, Irena. I'd forgotten how exhausting you can be." He dropped his hands to his sides. "Fine. If Inspector Delaney is willing to leave you in Lady Harleigh's custody, you may stay."

"I beg your pardon?" I gaped at him, resentment stiffening my spine. What was he thinking? "Have you just invited your wife to stay in my home?"

The little baggage preened. "I believe he did."

"You're not my wife. She's not my wife and—" With a sound of exasperation, he took hold of my wrist and drew me to my feet. "If you'll all excuse us, we need a moment in private."

"I should think so." Aunt Hetty returned to the drinks cabinet for the brandy bottle as George led me from the drawing room out to the hall. With a self-satisfied smirk, Miss Teskey watched us leave until he closed the door on our audience and turned to face me. I met his gaze with a very cold one of my own.

"You cannot mean for that woman to stay in my home."

"Considering the alternative, that's exactly what I mean. You don't know the trouble she can cause for us. I do. When she says she'll go to the press, she will."

I planted my hands on my hips. "You may recall I have some personal experience with the press. Anyone from Delaney's precinct may have already sold this sordid little story. A reporter might even have been there when Delaney brought her in. Odds are the newspapers will find out all about Miss Teskey and her claims with or without her assistance."

"Perhaps, but without her confirmation, or mine, the most the papers can do is report that a woman calling herself Mrs. Hazelton was arrested. It can easily be put down to a misunderstanding, and the story squelched in a day. If Irena talks to them, there's no telling what sort of tale she'll concoct. The scandal will spread all over town." He placed his finger under my chin, then tipped my head up to meet his gaze. "You've never been the subject of scandal, and that's what this would be. To all of society, you'd be engaged to a man with a living wife."

"And just how would it look having her move in with me?"

"It's likely to give lie to the rumor, if one ever takes hold."

I stifled a groan. I couldn't deny his point, but the prospect of that woman living in my house was untenable. "Do you really think she'd follow through on her threat?"

"Without a doubt. Irena's a scandal waiting to happen. She's the most impetuous, impulsive person I've ever had the misfortune to deal with. Do you remember I said she'd been subject to abduction a number of times?"

I nodded.

"I believe she arranged at least one of them herself."

"She arranged her own abduction?" The woman was absolutely mad.

"In some ways, Irena is to be pitied—no mother and an absent father. But since her father and the Teskeys have always given her anything she's ever asked for, she's really little more than a spoiled child and can be difficult to reason with."

"Yes, I'm coming to see that." I pressed my fingers against my temple to slow the throbbing there. "Do you believe her life was really threatened?"

"Instinct tells me she's merely seeking attention. She was going blithely about her life until she learned her cousin was here." He snapped his fingers. "Suddenly she is being followed and her life threatened. She has no idea what the person looks like or where the letters came from. It's highly suspect, but it's best to humor her. If I conduct an inquiry, she may be more inclined to drop her claims to being my wife."

"And that's another thing. Why would she make a claim that can so easily be disproved?"

"In my brief acquaintance with her, I've noticed she has a capricious attitude toward the truth."

"I can't make out which of her stories are true. Is she an actress, or does she own the theater? Was her mother murdered, or did she die in childbirth? Is she being followed? Has her life been threatened?"

"The only point I can answer for certain is that she is definitely not my wife. She couldn't have been more than fifteen when we met. I would never have married her." He sighed. "She doesn't appear to have changed much since then, either. I know it's a lot to ask of you, Frances, but I think it's best if she stays here with you and your aunt while I investigate her claim and Delaney finds out if charges will be filed."

So I was to host that woman in my home. I'd rather jump into the Thames or move back with my brother-in-law or, worse, host my mother permanently. Heavens, my mother! "If I agree to this, she must be gone before my mother returns. There is no possible way to explain this to her, or to Rose, for that matter, so you had best investigate with all due haste."

He pulled me into a hug. "I promise to end this as quickly as I can, but I won't be able to do anything tonight, as I have plans to attend the opera with my fiancée."

"That's right. I'd forgotten." I leaned back and gave him a chilly smile. "Will your wife be joining us?"

Fortunately, Aunt Hetty had been liberal with the brandy, and by the time George returned to take me to the opera, Miss Teskey was reclined on the sofa, snoring softly, under Hetty's watchful eye. How had I come to find myself in this awkward situation? I was sneaking out of the house with George, while the woman who claimed to be his wife was sleeping off the effects of too much brandy in my drawing room. I could only imagine the scene she'd make were she awake.

I suppose we were lucky Delaney allowed her to stay with us, though I believe part of the reason was that he didn't want to take the responsibility for her onto his own shoulders. The risk of leaving her with me was small. George had confirmed she was the grand duke's cousin, and as such, His Imperial Highness was unlikely to file any charges against her.

I pushed all thought of Miss Teskey from my mind, determined to take advantage of the lull in this latest bit of insanity and enjoy something as simple and normal as an evening out with my fiancé. He barely noticed my newly refurbished gown, cut rather daringly low, as he plunked my cloak on my shoulders and nearly shoved me out the door.

"Goodness, why are you in such a rush? We're in no danger of being late."

"No, but I fear we're in danger of someone detaining us."

Indeed, someone did—our temporary neighbor, Mrs. Chiswick. A middle-aged widow, she was visiting London from Chelmsford and staying at her brother's home across the street while he was away on a spot of business. I'd experienced only one short coze with Mrs. Chiswick, and I had to congratulate Colonel Perkins on having the good sense to invite his sister to visit when he was out of town. A bit of gossip now and then is all very well and fine, but she enjoyed it far too much and seemed to relish the nastier variety.

A glow of excitement lit her vulturine eyes as she approached us on the pavement, having just disembarked from her own carriage. I leaned a little closer to George, who tipped his hat to the lady. "Good evening, Mrs. Chiswick. Returning from an outing, I daresay?"

"Indeed I am." She bestowed a smile upon us that actually made me shiver. "And clearly, you and Lady Harleigh are about to embark on one of your own."

"The opera," I said, wondering why I felt the need to explain.

"I won't keep you. I just wondered what happened out here this afternoon. Jackson told me there was quite a commotion right in front of your house."

Jackson, the colonel's nosy butler. He and Mrs. Chiswick must get on like old friends. "A simple misunderstanding," I assured her. "Nothing to worry about."

"I'm afraid we must be off now, madam, or we will surely be late." George took my arm in one hand and opened the carriage door with the other, then urged me inside, leaving Mrs. Chiswick on the street, watching us with a tight expression. It might have been a breach of good manners, but the last thing we needed at this moment was a gossipy neighbor.

George was feeling the strain of our situation, as well. He held my hand as the carriage traveled swiftly through the night, but we kept our thoughts to ourselves and watched the landscape change through the windows as we passed Hyde Park and St. James's Park, on our way to Covent Garden. It seemed only minutes had passed before we arrived at the Royal Opera House.

He reached out to open the door, then sat back, turning his gaze to mine. "You do know how much I love you, don't you?"

And just like that, my worries grew lighter. I couldn't stop the smile that crossed my lips if I tried. "Oddly enough, considering the circumstances, that was something I never doubted. Heavens, confidence like that smacks of egotism, doesn't it?"

"It most certainly does not. I hope I never give you reason to lose that confidence in me."

"We will handle this together."

With a grin, he leaned in for a kiss. Unfortunately, one of the horses grew impatient and lurched, nearly throwing us both off the seat. "We had best go in, or we shall miss the overture." He climbed out and handed me down. "What are we seeing, by the way?"

"*Eugene Onegin*. Fanny Moody plays Tatiana."

He released a snigger. "Russian opera. How appropriate."

We were alone outside the building. It seemed we'd dallied too long, after all. We'd have to head to our seats directly, without the usual socializing. After dashing up the grand staircase, past the Ionic columns and Grecian lamps, we made it to our box just as the houselights dimmed, leaving us finding our way in the dark. We were using George's brother's box, as the earl was in the country, and though it seated six, it appeared we'd have it to ourselves. We settled into our seats just as the curtain rose and the first strains of Tchaikovsky filled the theater.

"It's been some time since I've been here," I said, "but I don't remember it being so dark once the performance begins. Perhaps because I was already seated."

He leaned in close to me. "I recall my mother being quite put out when they installed electric lighting. She resented the fact that one can neither see nor be seen. And wasn't that, after all, the point in attending the opera?"

I smothered a laugh and rested my head on his shoulder.

Though my eyes had become accustomed to the darkness by then, anything farther away than my hand was little more than a vague shadow. I knew there was only a partial wall separating our box from its neighbor, but it felt so much more private when I couldn't see the occupants. "Personally, I rather like it."

George sighed, pulled me close to his side, and we settled in to enjoy the performance.

A few minutes before the interval, a servant slipped into our box. He bowed, handed a note to George, murmured something to him in a low voice, then retreated. It all took place in less than a minute.

"What was that about?"

"His Royal Highness requests our presence in his box at the interval."

"*Our* presence?"

"I have no intention of going by myself, so don't think you're getting out of it."

"Don't tell me you fear facing him alone? Are you expecting a reprimand of some sort?"

"What I fear is this is about Irena. In fact, I'm certain of it. Somehow, he wants to make me responsible for her. I want you there to remind him I am a man engaged to be married and cannot take custody of another woman."

He looked so earnest, I almost giggled.

"I'm serious," he said. "We must present a united front."

"And so we shall. We are partners, after all."

Applause filled the theater as the lights came up and the low buzz of voices and movement came from the audience. I blinked in the sudden brilliance and in a realization. "How did the prince even know you were here? He couldn't possibly have seen us."

"No idea." He took my hand and led the way out to the passage. "Perhaps he didn't know and only sent the footman to check."

We wended our way through a trail of other patrons. The royal box was on the other side of the theater, and we did not wish to keep the prince waiting, so we did our best not to catch anyone's eye, lest we be forced into a lengthy conversation. Finally, we arrived at our destination, which, though larger, looked exactly like our box. I'd expected something more regal. We waited at the entrance until the liveried servant notified the prince of our arrival, and he turned to acknowledge us.

"Hazelton. Lady Harleigh."

I swept a curtsy. "Your Royal Highness."

Bertie had grown stout since I'd first met him ten years ago. He was also in possession of significantly less hair, and what he retained, particularly his beard, had largely turned to gray. What had been a dour expression lightened as he greeted me. When he took my hand, I rose, noting his eyes held some of the sparkle I remembered.

"What a treat to see you again, my dear. It's been far too long."

"Indeed, sir. I believe the last time we met was at Floors Castle, and that's been at least six or seven years."

He chuckled, possibly at the memory of a week's delight with whichever lady had taken his fancy at that time. "Ah, yes. A fine visit that. I was expecting only Hazelton tonight, but of course, now I recall you are engaged. May I extend my congratulations? And, of course, my sincerest regrets on Reggie's passing."

"Thank you, sir." I had no doubt his regrets were sincere. My late husband had spent a great deal of my dowry entertaining the prince and his friends.

He released my hand and turned to greet George. "A bad business this morning, Hazelton. Had no idea Miss Teskey was even in London. A policeman called on my secretary today to explain it was she who caused the ruckus outside Marlborough

House. He mentioned Lady Harleigh had taken custody of the gel, and that you were looking into some trouble she'd run into. He also mentioned you'd be here tonight."

"The inspector mentioned a great deal," I muttered to George.

"It sounds as though he was quite forthcoming," he agreed.

"Gave us all the pertinent details, I believe," the prince continued. "Of course, the grand duke won't pursue charges, but have you any idea what the incident was about?"

"She claims she's had a threat to her life, sir," George said. "She was hoping to speak to the grand duke about it but couldn't gain his attention."

"Well, that's a dodgy way of obtaining it."

"I agree, sir."

"Any truth to her claim?"

"I don't really know."

The prince heaved a sigh. "A bad business all around. Last I heard of her, she was living a rather bohemian life in Paris. Alexei should have married her off by now and had her living quietly somewhere in the country. Every time I hear something of her, it's that she's causing more trouble. This little incident made the papers this evening. Embarrassing to the Romanovs. I wouldn't blame her father if he sent her to a sanitorium after this."

He paused for a moment and stroked his beard. "Still, someone should check into this threat on her life. Can't have someone threatening a member of the Russian royal family on British soil, even an illegitimate member. I'll leave that to you, Hazelton."

"Thank you, sir."

Poor George. This was exactly what he'd feared. Well, perhaps not exactly. He'd already intended to look into Miss Teskey's claims.

"And keep an eye on her. Make sure she gets up to no more trouble while the grand duke and the countess are visiting."

"Yes, sir."

All right, *now* it was exactly as he'd feared. The prince dismissed us, and we left, keeping our thoughts to ourselves and uttering not a syllable until we rounded the curve along the back of the theater and were well out of earshot.

"Why you?" I asked him, taking care to keep my voice low. "Are there not hundreds of investigators with the police who could be trusted to deal with this?"

He blew out a breath. "The prince knows I've dealt with her before, but my guess is he thought of me because he somehow heard she was claiming to be my wife. Perhaps Delaney mentioned that detail, as well. That would lead him to assume I also have a stake in obtaining her good behavior."

"Does this mean she'll be staying with me longer than planned?" My feet suddenly stopped propelling me forward. "If he heard of her claim, do you think anyone else has?"

We wandered over to the saloon, crowded with patrons in need of refreshment during the interval. "I think it's likely anyone who's been in company with the prince or the Romanovs will have heard about it. Shall we have a glass of wine? I could use one."

He stepped away to see to our refreshments and left me with my disgruntled thoughts. A glass of wine was not likely to help us with this problem.

"Frances."

A gloved hand was raised in the crowd, its long, tapered fingers wiggling over coiffed heads. A bejeweled bracelet glittered on the wrist below it. I watched it move closer, until I saw it was attached to the arm of Alicia Stoke-Whitney. Another minute and her full person moved into view, and much to my surprise, she had her husband in tow. Such a rare occurrence to see them together. Then I recalled her determination to work herself back into his good graces. There was always a purpose for Alicia's actions.

The diamonds around her throat glistened as bright as her smile when she greeted me. "You remember my husband, don't you?"

"Of course, though it's been some time since we last met."

Arthur Stoke-Whitney was the perfect foil for his flamboyant wife. Just as his stark black evening attire showed off her bright pink gown, everything about him, from his thinning fair hair and beard, both flecked with gray, to the stern lines of his face, his square shoulders, and, well, a bit of a paunch, contrasted with the petite, effervescent redhead.

He took my hand and bowed ever so slightly. "Enchanted, Lady Harleigh. You are looking lovely, as always."

"Ever the politician, Mr. Stoke-Whitney. I'm well aware I could be standing here in sackcloth and ashes and you would say the same."

His brown eyes crinkled as he laughed. "Either you are trying to wound me or urge me to a greater compliment."

I retrieved my hand. "Neither. I'll accept the one you've offered with somewhat belated good grace."

"You needn't be suspicious of Arthur's compliments, my dear. You are definitely in good looks tonight, and you know I wouldn't say that if I didn't mean it."

That was certainly true.

"I'm so glad I caught sight of you. Arthur was determined to talk politics with some of his cronies." She cast a sweet smile at her husband. "And while I admire his dedication to queen and country, it's good for him to take part in some light conversation, as well."

"How flattering that you think of light conversation when you think of me."

Alicia didn't attempt to contradict me, though her husband smothered a laugh.

She glanced around the lobby. "Is Hazelton with you this evening? Have you two resolved the matter of that young woman?"

I shot her a glare and was about to respond that this was not the time or the place to discuss the matter when George stepped up and handed me a glass of wine.

"Evening, Stoke-Whitney, Mrs. Stoke-Whitney. Enjoying the performance?"

"Man snubs girl, shoots friend, decides he wants girl, after all." Alicia feigned a yawn. "The music is splendid, but I'm enjoying the interval more."

"Ah, then you must be discussing something interesting."

"Indeed. I was just asking Lady Harleigh about the woman who claimed to be your wife."

Both men coughed, as if their wine had gone down wrong.

George recovered first. "Mrs. Stoke-Whitney, this is hardly the subject for discussion in a crowded room. And certainly not when you use such a strident voice."

She jerked back, as if struck. "My voice is never strident."

"It certainly was just now," I said. "And I'll thank you to keep it lower when discussing my private affairs."

While we bickered, George spoke quietly with Mr. Stoke-Whitney, who paled to the point of looking positively ill. I guessed George was explaining the situation. The look of concern the other man gave me told me I'd guessed correctly.

"Hazelton, you must nip this in the bud before a scandal erupts. Make sure this girl retracts her statements. Better yet, send her back where she came from."

"She looked like trouble, if you ask me." Alicia was enjoying this far too much.

"The prince agrees with you both," George said. "He considers her to be trouble and asked me to ensure she modifies her behavior."

"Never say she's the chit who threw the rock at the grand duke?" Arthur's expression was now horrified.

"The very same."

Her name is Irena Teskey, is it not?" At George's nod, he pursed his lips and seemed to be considering the matter. "Interesting that the prince has entrusted you with the task of reining her in. Let me know if I can be of any assistance."

"Good of you to offer, but I'm sure I'll manage."

And I was sure Arthur was relieved with George's answer. This situation was a bit too scandalous for his comfort. Though, as a politician, he might see this as a chance to do a favor for the prince. Before I could give it much thought, I noticed an addition on the periphery of our little group. "Mr. Bradmore. What a surprise to find you here."

George cast a quick glance at me, then followed my gaze to the large blond man standing just behind Alicia. He gave him a polite nod, but I noticed his lips compress, leading me to assume he hadn't forgiven Bradmore for his subterfuge a few weeks ago, when George and I were dealing with a spot of trouble in Hampshire. Bradmore had made matters even worse by being less than forthcoming with us. Though I understood his need for secrecy, his actions had only added to the chaos we were experiencing at the time. I'd never trust the man again, and it appeared that George felt the same.

Bradmore seemed not to notice George's cool welcome and joined our small group, so introductions were necessary. I had to admire Alicia's self-control. She cast one look of longing at the newcomer, then inched closer to her husband. She must be determined to show him she could control herself. Under normal circumstances, she'd flirt with any man under fifty. Percy Bradmore was well under that age and quite attractive into the bargain.

Stoke-Whitney studied the younger man. "I believe I've heard you've recently been named heir to Baron de Brook."

"That's correct," Bradmore said. "My uncle finally came to the conclusion he would have no children of his own, so the title must move to my branch of the family."

"One would think he'd have noticed it thirty years sooner," Stoke-Whitney said with a snigger.

Bradmore raised his glass. "Hope does spring eternal."

I considered Lady Esther's advanced years and agreed. This was a hope that should have been dashed long ago.

Bradmore turned his attention to George. "I believe I heard you speaking of someone by the name of Irena Teskey a moment ago."

"Have you some interest in the lady, Bradmore?" George eyed the man with suspicion.

"I have a slight acquaintance with her and should like to renew it, if you could inform me of where she can be found."

Alicia let out a titter. "Why, she is stopping with Lady Harleigh, if you can imagine that." She clamped her lips together and shot a glance at her husband, who must have given her some sort of signal to hold her tongue. I gave him silent thanks, as I was certain she was again about to announce Miss Teskey's claim to be George's wife.

Bradmore didn't notice the exchange and turned to me. "Is she indeed? Would it be acceptable if I called on her?"

"Of course you may. I'm not certain of her immediate plans, so you would be wise to pay that call soon."

An attendant warned us the interval was nearly over, drawing our attention back to the opera. Bradmore quickly agreed to call on Miss Teskey tomorrow, and after polite farewells, we all returned to our seats. George seemed to be brooding once the performance started.

"What's troubling you? Bradmore?"

"Just wondering how he knows Irena."

"You need only to be at my house tomorrow, and I'm sure he'll enlighten you."

He took my hand and laced our fingers together. "Oh, I definitely intend to be there."

Chapter Five

◆

Since everyone was abed by the time I returned from the opera, except for my maid Bridget, of course, I rose early the following morning, eager to learn if Hetty had extracted any more information from Miss Teskey. Happily, I discovered Hetty alone in the dining room, reading the morning papers while enjoying her coffee.

"Good morning, Frances." She folded the paper and set it aside upon my entering the room. "How was your evening?"

I poured myself a cup of coffee from the pot on the sideboard and joined her at the table. "It could have been better. The prince has officially requested that George take charge of Miss Teskey. He's to keep her out of the public eye while he investigates her claim that someone is threatening her." I lifted my cup to my lips, then froze in mid-motion. "She is still here, isn't she?"

"Oh, yes. Toddled off to bed a few hours after you left." She gave me a sympathetic look. "The prince's request isn't that much of an imposition, is it? After all, Hazelton had already planned to investigate."

"I suppose it's really no more than he expected, but that's not all that happened. We bumped into the Stoke-Whitneys during the interval, and Alicia, in a booming voice, inquired about the woman who claimed to be Hazelton's wife."

Hetty let out a tsk. "What is wrong with that creature? Did anyone hear her?"

"I don't know about anyone around us, but her husband certainly did." I twisted and turned the cup in my hands, imagining it was Alicia's neck. "It would serve her right if Stoke-Whitney rejected her request for me to sponsor her daughter."

Hetty gave me a blank stare.

"Due to the rumor of my fiancé having a wife."

"Yes, yes, I understand that, but why did she request that you sponsor her daughter? Why wouldn't she do that herself?"

"That's right. I forgot you slipped away when Alicia visited yesterday."

Hetty parted her lips to protest but stopped herself when Mrs. Thompson came in, bearing a tray for the sideboard. The aroma of eggs, tomatoes, and toast wafted toward me as she passed, and I found myself filling a plate before the house-keeper had even left the room. Hetty followed close behind me.

"As to Mrs. Stoke-Whitney's visit, you said you didn't need my presence."

"I didn't. Alicia brought no trouble to my door, at least not for me." I returned to the table and dug into my meal. "The trouble was all hers and of her own making, if you ask my opinion on the matter." I relayed the story of Alicia's impend-ing banishment from London mere months before her daugh-ter's presentation to the queen.

"Forgive me for being blunt," Hetty began, "but the man must be a complete fool if he's only just discovered the shenani-gans his wife gets up to."

"He's not a fool. I believe he finds it convenient to pretend he doesn't notice. Alicia fills all the requirements for a politician's wife. She's the perfect hostess and campaigner. She's also a favorite of the prince, and no one would appreciate that more than Stoke-Whitney. From his point of view, there are more positives to their marriage than negatives." I shrugged. "They can't all be love matches. Chances are he has a mistress tucked away somewhere, so he can hardly make a fuss if Alicia enjoys the company of other men."

Hetty returned to the table, her brow furrowed. "If her infidelity doesn't trouble him, then why does he plan to banish her to the country?"

"She broke the most important rule of managing one's liaisons, Aunt. She was indiscreet, and people began to talk. A group of high-minded, influential ladies championed Stoke-Whitney in the last election. If they learn of Alicia's misbehavior, he could lose their support. He can't ignore her indiscretion if everyone is talking about it, so he hopes to sweep her out of sight and out of the general conversation."

"I don't like these modern marriages." Hetty set her plate on the table with a thunk.

"Nor do I." I took a bite of toast and washed it down with coffee. "But I also wouldn't call it a modern viewpoint. Marriages like that have been around for ages, particularly among the upper crust. Let's not forget my late husband."

"I'd like to forget him, if you don't mind."

"Well, if I had to put up with his philandering, at least he was discreet. I rarely heard even a whisper of it. The point is, if one plays that game, one must play by the rules, and Alicia broke them."

"You don't expect Hazelton to act in the same manner, do you?"

I recoiled and let out a gasp. "He had better not even consider it. I refuse to share him with anyone else."

"That's reassuring. You sounded so calm about this sort of arrangement, I began to wonder."

"It's easy to be calm if the arrangement doesn't affect me. I want my marriage to be a true one, and George completely agrees. That's why this business with Miss Teskey is so upsetting. I hope he can prove her claim is without merit. And quickly, before any gossip starts." I dipped into my egg. "That reminds me, how was your evening with Miss Teskey last night? Did she give you any trouble?"

"None at all. She slept on the sofa for most of the evening." Hetty grinned. "The result of the fine brandy, I assume. She asked for Hazelton when she woke, but I sent her up to her bed, telling her he'd call in the morning. I hope he plans to do so."

"He'll be going to her rooms at Brown's Hotel first to gather some of her belongings, the so-called threatening letters, and anything else he thinks might be helpful. He planned to go first thing this morning, so he could be here at any time."

"I missed much of the conversation yesterday between the three of you, and I'm not entirely sure I understand her story. Hazelton rescued her from an abductor. She says they married at that time. He says they didn't. Since she didn't come to London in search of him, why is she here?"

"You aren't alone in your confusion. I'm not certain Miss Teskey understands her own story. As to why she's in England, it has something to do with the theater. Either she's an actress or she owns a theater."

My expression of soured misery was what greeted Miss Teskey as she stepped, or rather stumbled, into the dining room. She spared me a glance as she sank into a chair opposite me at the table. "*Mon Dieu*, you look as wretched as I feel."

"I have no wish to compete with you on that front." Indeed, her eyes were puffed and shadowed, and her face was drawn, and if she'd even attempted to pull a comb through her hair, I assumed it was still stuck somewhere amid the dark tangles. How much brandy had the woman consumed?

"I believe your evil friend here tried to poison me with that vile drink."

"Vile? That was a superb French brandy, and you found it very much to your liking last night." Hetty lifted her chin. "Perhaps a little too much."

Miss Teskey ignored Hetty and turned her ghoulish face to me. "Is there any coffee to be had?"

Unwilling or not, I supposed I was the girl's hostess. I poured a cup from the pot on the sideboard and placed it in front of her. After dumping in several teaspoons of sugar, she took a deep drink and released a sigh. "Perhaps it was not poison, after all."

"I should say not," Hetty said.

"But I had far too much."

"As to that, we are in agreement, but you seemed determined to finish the bottle, and I didn't have the heart to stop you."

"It was a difficult day. I came here seeking help from my husband, only to find he plans to marry another woman. And it was an excellent brandy. I'm sure I'll recover soon." She planted her elbow on the table, then rested her chin on the back of her hand. Her gaze locked with mine. "Tell me, Lady Harleigh, did you and my husband have a pleasant time at the opera last night?"

I pasted a smile on my face. "My fiancé and I had a delightful time. Thank you for asking."

"Did you speak to my cousin?"

"We did not. He wasn't in the royal box, so I doubt he attended. We did speak to the prince, though. He informed us that there would be no charges filed against you."

She released a little snort of contempt. "As if they would. I should be able to call on my own cousin in my moment of need."

"I'd wager it wasn't the calling that disturbed them, but the rock throwing."

Hetty clapped her hands together, drawing both our gazes. "The point is," she said, "you won't be arrested. Isn't that good news?"

"That is no news at all." Miss Teskey swept her arm as she spoke, playing to the back of the house. "What about my plight? I thought Hazelton would speak to my cousin about the threats to my life. He promised he'd help me. Where is he? What is he doing? Has he left me to the tender mercies of you ladies? One of you who plies me with drink and the other who hates me. I may be no safer here than out on the streets of London."

"Aunt Hetty did not make you drink, and I don't hate you. Well, not precisely. At least not yet. If someone is threatening your life, then you are indeed safer here. You could certainly hurry things along by providing more information. You've been far from forthcoming, and every story you tell goes in circles, with each fact contradicting another. How on earth are we to help you when we can't even keep up?"

Her eyes welled up with tears. Now, what had I started?

"You don't hate me?"

That's what she was crying about? I glanced at Hetty in an appeal for help, but she seemed as confused as I. "No. I wouldn't say I hate you. At least, not exactly."

"My dear Countess, you are all that is kind." She dashed away a tear from her cheek and grasped my hand. "We shall be good friends, no?"

"I don't think I'd go that far." I squeezed her hand and tried to extricate mine, but she held fast. For such a little wisp, she had quite a grip. "But we can work together to solve your problems."

And get her out of my house and away from George.

"I will settle for no less than friendship," she said. "You will be like my older sister."

It was on my lips to decline the office, but she wore such a wistful smile, I held my tongue.

"As long as I can remember, it has only been me, on my own—my mother dead, my father out to sea or traveling in some faraway land. The Teskeys had no children of their own. I was always lonely."

"How did you come to be with them?" I asked. "I would have thought your mother's people would be determined to hold on to you after having lost her to childbirth."

"I suspect they were eager to be rid of me. Their daughter was dead, possibly at the hands of her own husband, all because of me."

Hetty tutted, and Miss Teskey finally released my hand to shake a finger at her. "Yes, it's just a rumor, but rumors often have some connection to fact."

"How did you come to hear it?" I asked. Who would tell a child such a thing?

"I *over*heard it." She shrugged. "Ten years or more ago. Right after the first time someone tried to abduct me. *Oncle* thought I should be returned to my mother's family, and *Tante* said, 'To the man who murdered her mother?' *Oncle* just grumbled and said she couldn't be sure of that, but Tante gave him a look like she knew. And they never spoke about sending me back again."

"While that sounds rather damning, it could also mean that Mrs. Teskey was prone to exaggeration or hysterics," Hetty said. "If that's all you have, I'd say it's likely she died of natural causes."

"Did anyone ever tell you who your mother was?" I asked.

"All I know is she was English and a lady. That makes England part of my heritage. I wanted to see if I felt any sense of kinship here."

"Russia is also part of your heritage. Why did your father not settle you there with his family?"

She spread her hands. "Who explains to a child what is happening to her? From what I understand of my Romanov relations, they are in and out of favor with each other as often as you might change your gown. Perhaps my father was not on the best of terms with his family when I was born. By the time I became aware of my circumstances, the arrangement was a settled matter. The Teskeys were happy in our little seaside village. My father spends very little time in Russia, after all. In France, at least he would visit now and again."

Well, that explained how everyone found out Alexei was her father. Though it seemed she was well taken care of, I felt rather sorry for the girl and wondered how things might have been different for her if her mother had lived. Regardless of the affair, her mother's husband would likely have called the child his own. She would have grown up in England, surrounded by family. Though had those events taken place, she would never have known her real father.

Mrs. Thompson tapped on the door at that moment and stepped inside. "Mr. Hazelton, my lady."

As he stepped around my housekeeper, George took in the scene with a wary eye. "Everything all right here?" I suppose he thought we'd be at daggers drawn by now.

Miss Teskey visibly revived and scurried toward him, her arms open wide. "Husband, you have returned."

He recoiled as she approached, causing her to stomp her foot. "You must stop doing that," she said.

"I will when you stop attempting to throw yourself at me."

"If you fear Lady Harleigh's reaction, you mustn't. She and I understand one another and are good friends now."

He gave me a wary glance. "I'm not certain that bodes well for me."

"Both of you come and sit down." I assured George we were all managing and poured him a cup of coffee as he settled in next to me. Miss Teskey returned to her seat across from us.

"Mrs. Thompson has taken your things up to your room," he said. "I did not close your account with the hotel, but you are all but moved out."

"Thank you, my dear." She rewarded him with a glowing smile. "Did you find the letters?"

"I did not. Are you certain they were in your room?"

She busied herself with her coffee. "No. Maybe they are at the theater, or perhaps I left them back in Paris."

"I thought you didn't receive them until after you came to London." I couldn't help the note of irritation that crept into my voice. How quickly I'd gone from sympathy to exasperation, but for heaven's sake, this ever-changing story was maddening.

"Yes, that's right. If they aren't in my room at the hotel, they must be at the theater. I'm certain I didn't destroy them."

And now I assumed she must have destroyed them—if they ever existed in the first place.

"Tell me about the man you believe was following you," George said with an edge to his voice. "You must have noticed something about him."

She stared into the depths of her cup. "He wore a hat and overcoat."

"It's November. In London," I said. "If one is out of doors, one is wearing a hat and overcoat."

George placed a hand over mine. "There was a man in the lobby at Brown's Hotel who struck me as suspicious. He didn't seem to be occupied with any business, yet he was there both when I arrived and left. Was the man following you a bit older, perhaps fiftyish, my height or taller, and bulky? The man I saw had a rather spectacular beard and wore a homburg."

She gazed up at the ceiling, as if she were pondering the matter. "That sounds like Igor," she said at last. "The poor dear must be waiting for me."

He drew a deep breath and released it slowly before turning a deadly glare on her. "Who is Igor?"

Hetty and I leaned forward, poised to stop him from doing her any harm in case he was as angry as he looked. Miss Teskey either didn't notice or ignored it.

"Igor? He's been with me for five or six years now. My father sent him to watch over me after the third or fourth attempted abduction." She sat back and bobbed her head. "It was probably Igor you saw."

The muscles in his jaw clenched. It was my turn to pat his hand, which had curled itself into a fist as he pushed up from the table. "If you had an attendant who, I assume, is on hand to protect you, why have you dragged me into your troubles?"

"Because you are my husband." Her expression said she thought him a complete simpleton. "Igor would have been no help with the police. Why, he barely speaks English. I needed you. Since you are some sort of investigator, and my husband, you are the perfect person to track down the man who is threatening me and have him arrested."

"Your logic would be fine except for the one little detail you have wrong. I am not your husband." He threw himself back into the chair and folded his arms, possibly to keep from shaking her. "Whatever put that notion into your head?"

Miss Teskey squared her jaw. "Our wedding. If I have to return to Paris to retrieve our marriage certificate and wave it in your face to make you believe me, I will."

So engrossed were we all in the conversation, none of us had

noticed Mrs. Thompson enter the room until the scuffle between her and a guest drew our attention. The housekeeper was
clearly trying to push a gentleman back out to the hallway, and
he, in turn, appeared unwilling to leave.

"I say," he called out. "I believe I can clear this up."

I recognized that voice. "Mr. Bradmore, is that you?"

With that, Mrs. Thompson relented and allowed Bradmore
to move around her. He did so, pulling off his hat, and then
nodded to each of us. "I do beg your pardon," he said. "But I
couldn't help overhearing a bit of the conversation. I think I
can help sort things out." He moved toward the table under the
weight of George's glare.

"Do you have some information on the matter, Bradmore?"
I asked.

"Indeed, Lady Harleigh. I do." He turned his gaze to Miss
Teskey and waved his fingers at her. "Irena, you seem to have
mistaken Hazelton for someone else. He is not your husband.
I am."

I glanced from one man to the other. George was tall and
lean, with dark hair and eyes—one had to be very close to see
they were actually green. Bradmore, on the other hand, was tall
and broad, with tawny blond hair, a short, upturned nose, and
light brown eyes. How one could be mistaken for the other was
beyond my comprehension.

Miss Teskey examined him through narrowed eyes. "You?"

"Me."

"You do look familiar."

"That is gratifying, as it's been a good six years since we've
seen each other."

"The two of you are married?" George seemed to be having
as difficult a time taking this in as Hetty and I. And Miss Teskey, for that matter.

"We are," Bradmore confirmed, twisting the brim of his hat.

"In fact, I have been searching for Irena for the past month. I owe you a debt of gratitude in finding her for me."

"You have been looking for me?"

"Indeed. This is somewhat awkward, considering I've just reintroduced myself as your husband, but I'm afraid I must ask you for a divorce."

Chapter Six

❧

The room grew quiet enough to hear the ticking of the clock in the entry hall—counting down the seconds until Miss Teskey released an explosive shriek that broke the silence and caused each of us to cringe.

"How dare you?" Her sinewy motion as she came to her feet, the narrowed eyes, and the flashing teeth all brought to mind the image of a venomous snake after a sharp poke from a stick. I'll admit to some relief, I wasn't the one to poke her. "Who are you to come here and ask me for a divorce? You beast!"

Bradmore strode toward her and dropped his hat on the table in one impatient motion. "Who I am is the only man who could make such a request. And don't act as if you are crushed by it. You didn't even know who I was until I informed you."

Glancing around the table, he took in the image of the three of us reeling from astonishment. It must have taken him aback, as he squared his shoulders and held out a hand to her. "Let us go into another room and discuss this like civilized adults, shall we?"

Foolish man. He'd get nowhere with that condescending tactic.

Miss Teskey lifted her chin, her eyes flashing. "I will go nowhere with you and will discuss nothing. I do not want you for my husband. Hazelton was much better. At least he doesn't want to divorce me."

"Only because he's not married to you, you little baggage."

"Bradmore! That's uncalled for." As this was my home, I felt the need to step into the fray. "Miss Teskey, I agree it would be best for the two of you to retire to the drawing room and discuss your situation privately."

She shifted her gaze to me, her eyes filling with tears. "You can suggest this? You who profess to be my friend?"

Bradmore angled a glance at me. "You want to be her friend?"

"I never said—"

"No. This is too much." Brushing past Bradmore, she fled the room and, judging from the sound of her heels on the steps, took to her bedchamber for sanctuary. Bradmore dropped into her empty chair.

"Well done, old chap." George allowed a sardonic tone in his voice. "If your intention was to chase her off, that is."

Bradmore raised a brow. "I could just as easily have left the girl to believe you were her husband."

"Yes. Well, I suppose I should be grateful for that."

"Yes, you should," I said. "But he's right, Mr. Bradmore. You might have used a bit more delicacy when you requested a divorce."

"What I'd like to know is how on earth you came to wed the girl." This was not the first time I gave thanks that Aunt Hetty had no qualms about asking questions I might find too indelicate. Now that it had been asked, however, I didn't hesitate to prod him.

"How did that come about?"

"Let me take a guess." George leaned over the table. "You rescued her from an abductor?"

Bradmore stared. "You too?"

"That's how she got you two mixed up," Hetty said.

I gaped at her. "That's absurd. Yes, they performed the same service for her, but how did she fail to notice that they look nothing alike or that they have different names or that she married one and not the other? The woman may be a bit cracked, but I believe she has the use of most of her faculties."

"She may not have had use of them at the time," Bradmore said.

"Opium?" George asked.

Bradmore nodded. "She was living in Paris, trying to become an actress. Her cohorts may not have even been aware of who her father was, but they could tell she came from money. They sent the ransom note to the Teskeys' home. Irena was so far gone by the time I arrived, I don't even know if she realized she was being held prisoner."

"How did you free her?" I asked. "She couldn't have been much help in that condition."

"None at all. Thank heaven I wasn't trying to arrange a rescue. My orders were simply to pay the ransom and take charge of her. That was difficult enough. She was largely incoherent when I moved her things into my lodgings. I couldn't let her go back to her own rooms for fear her abductors would strike again. Finally, once she had recovered well enough to pay attention, I removed her to the Teskeys', back at the coast." He heaved a sigh. "She was nothing but trouble."

"Yet you decided to marry her," I said.

"That's the sticky part. I had hoped simply to put her on the train, but I couldn't convince her that leaving Paris was in the interest of her safety. She pestered me until I agreed to escort her to the station, then on to Trouville. As we traveled, I suppose she wormed her way into my affections. She teased me into escorting her on to the Teskeys' cottage, and before I knew it, I found myself escorting her down the aisle of some village church."

George was eyeing him with skepticism, and I, too, assumed he was glossing over some significant elements of the story. I had never really trusted Bradmore. "So, she just charmed you into marrying her?" I suggested. "You were helpless to resist?"

"My dear." George gave me a wink. "I think at some point on this fateful trip, our friend discovered Miss Teskey has many charms—many thousands of charms."

Bradmore crossed his arms over his chest and sank back in the chair. But I doubted he could deny the charge. I let out a tsk and shook my head. "A woman should never discuss her fortune with a single man. They can't help but imagine themselves in charge of it."

"She might not have done so, Frances." Aunt Hetty was grinning at Bradmore's discomfort. "He might have assumed her father would be generous to her husband. Just think of what he'd save in ransom payments."

"Har, har, har." Bradmore twisted his lips in a sneer. "I'm delighted I could provide your amusement for the day."

I brought my cup to my lips to hide my grin.

"Yes, the thought of her fortune did sway me," he continued. "It was no secret her father was generous to her, and I had no real prospects at the time. So, why not, I ask you? What I did not consider was the possibility that her father might object. Irena informed me after the ceremony that he fully expected to choose her future husband. She warned me not to let on to the Teskeys that we were married until she'd had a chance to write to her father."

This sounded to me like one of her embellished stories. Alexei may have paid for his daughter's keep, but he was hardly a doting or even present father. I'd have wagered good money that she simply regretted her impulsive marriage.

"That must have come as something of a shock." George struggled to contain his amusement. "To learn a royal duke of the Romanov dynasty might just take offense at your unauthorized marriage to his daughter. He might actually think you took advantage of her, considering the distressing circumstances she'd just endured."

"The thought did cross my mind," Bradmore muttered.

"Not surprised you ran."

"I didn't run. I returned to England and kept in touch with Irena through correspondence up until nearly a year ago, when she stopped responding. At the first opportunity, I paid a visit to Trouville and found her and the Teskeys gone. Neither could I locate her in Paris after an exhaustive search, so I returned home."

"Now that you've found her, why the change of heart?" I had a feeling I knew the answer.

He had the decency to look embarrassed. "Well, as you know, my circumstances have recently improved. I'm my uncle's heir now. It's not as if Irena and I ever lived as man and wife. Please forgive the indelicacy, ladies, but there must be some sort of amnesty or discharge after all this time, wouldn't you think?" He reddened. "The woman vanished on me. Isn't that a good enough reason?"

"Who am I to say?" I leaned in and examined him. "But I think the real reason is that you need a suitable wife now that you are to be a baron. And you don't find Miss Teskey suitable."

"Oh, Mr. Bradmore." Aunt Hetty gave him a disapproving look.

He slapped his hand down on the table. "She's an actress. She is far too fond of opium. And she abandoned me. I stand by my decision."

"It's certainly your decision to make," I said with a note of appeasement. "Though this may not be the best time to discuss it with her." I told him about the threatening letters she had claimed to receive. "Hazelton plans to look into the matter. Why don't you two pool your knowledge of Miss Teskey back at your house?" I touched George's hand. "Hetty and I have a luncheon to attend this afternoon. Before we leave, I'll check on her and send word if she's willing to speak with Bradmore."

Miss Teskey was not willing to speak with Bradmore. At least that was the impression I gained as she wailed through the locked door about all the things she'd like to do to the man.

Painful things.

None of them involved talking.

I'd have made more of an attempt either to reason with her or to comfort her, but Hetty and I were in danger of being late to a royal appointment, and one did not keep a princess waiting. On our way, we were further frustrated by the tangle of carriages along Pall Mall, all headed to our destination—Marlborough House.

"How long do you suppose we'll have the pleasure of Miss Teskey's company?" Hetty asked.

I blew out a breath. "I wish Bradmore didn't want a divorce. Otherwise, he could take the woman off our hands right now. Since that's not possible, I hope he and George can make some headway regarding the threatening letters, find the culprit, and have him arrested so she can return to her own rooms. Tonight would not be too soon."

"Don't you find her to be a strange creature? I really don't know what to make of her."

"Nor do I. She had an unusual upbringing, to be sure, which might explain her need for connections—to her cousin, to Hazelton, even to me. But can that account for not knowing whom she married?"

Hetty gave me a sidelong glance. "It sounds as though opium can account for that."

"I suppose so."

"Strange, too, that she started receiving threats right after coming to England. Who here would know her?"

"Her business partner? Another actress? Do people in the theater move around much? If so, it might be someone she knew in France. Perhaps even this Igor person." My mind boggled at the dozens of possibilities. "Whoever it is, I have faith that George and Bradmore will find him out—assuming there is anyone to find."

The carriage turned, and Hetty glanced out the window. "I think we've arrived."

"Along with everyone else," I said, glancing at a cluster of carriages on the drive and in the courtyard.

"This is grand, isn't it?" Hetty murmured, marveling at the guarded gate, the surrounding walls, and the many outbuildings. "More of an elegant fortress than a home."

"That's right. You haven't been here before." I'd grown so used to my aunt's company and her natural way of adapting to her surroundings, I often forgot she'd been in England less than a year.

"Reggie used to be part of the prince's set, though I don't know how much time they spent here. The prince counts on his friends to entertain him, and Reggie put on many an expensive dinner at Harleigh House during our early years together. Even given his love of extravagance, and willingness to empty his pockets, he finally saw we couldn't afford to continue the practice."

"Hmm, I'd never given Reggie credit for much sense," she said. "Perhaps I was too hard on him."

"No, you were right." As our carriage finally passed under the arched entry, I indicated the courtyard and the façade of the redbrick house for her perusal. "Reggie pushed it as far as he possibly could, but the thought of leaving himself short was too much to bear. Ultimately, he learned how to tag along and enjoy the largesse of Jennie Churchill or Daisy Greville, both of whom were more than willing to spend until it hurt. Not that it ever would."

Hetty turned away from the carriage window. "When you say they entertained the prince, do you mean . . . ?" She rolled her hand in the air.

"I don't know, and I don't wish to." I batted the idea around a bit. "Well, it's rumored that they did, but that's just rumor. It's possible. Probable? In any event, Daisy is out of the picture now, and I'm not certain who has taken over entertaining the prince." I raised a brow on the last words. "All I know is this is only the third time I've been here, and on those prior occasions, like today, it was at Princess Alexandra's invitation."

The driver opened the carriage door and dropped the steps before assisting Hetty, then me to the pavement in front of the entrance. As we alighted the stairs, she gave my arm a squeeze. "I'm looking forward to meeting the princess."

"You do know she's quite deaf, don't you?"

Her brow furrowed. "I have heard that. Can she hear at all? Should I raise my voice?"

"I believe she can hear a bit, and she's quite good at reading lips, but you shouldn't expect a long conversation with her."

Hetty's disappointment faded when we entered the house and she took in the grandeur of the hall. It was an impressive sight, with the gilding, the paintings on the walls and ceiling of the first duke's battles, not to mention the murals completely surrounding the staircase.

We crossed the gray-and-white marble floor to greet our hostess and her guest of honor. I always found Alexandra to be the perfect image of a princess. Her height, bearing, and calm demeanor quietly commanded attention, while her eyes and smile spoke of kindness. She bestowed one of those smiles on me as I introduced Aunt Hetty. After a few pleasantries, we moved on to Sophie, Countess de Torby, who was under siege by a talkative guest. She made a helpless gesture but appeared to need no rescue, so Hetty and I stepped past her and into the saloon, where there were yet more battle scenes and a few ladies who had drifted in from the hall. We'd all await the princess's signal before entering the dining room.

We were just looking for a seat when Fiona slipped around a potted palm and touched my shoulder. "We need to talk," she whispered, her expression unusually serious.

Hetty waved us off. "Go on, then. You needn't worry about me. I see plenty of my acquaintants here."

Fiona gave me no chance to demur. She linked her arm with mine and led me back to the hall, smiling and nodding as we passed a cluster of chatting ladies, and around the corner to a deserted area near the staircase, where she rounded on me. Her eyes looked positively frantic.

"Fiona, what's wrong?"

Her brows inched even higher. "That's exactly what I want to know. What is wrong with you and my brother, and what is this ridiculous story of a prior marriage?"

A jolt ran from my neck to my toes, as if every inch of me were electrified. "How did you find out?" I whispered.

Fiona gulped air into her lungs like a woman drowning. "Do you mean it's true?"

"Of course not. How can you even ask? As you said, it's nothing more than a ridiculous story, but what exactly did you hear, and from whom?" Fiona was always in possession of the latest gossip, but it shocked me to think Miss Teskey's claims had already *become* gossip.

"Jonesy, my maid, told me."

"Your maid? Where did she hear it?"

"Jonesy has a brother with the Metropolitan Police. He told her of a woman who had been arrested and was about to be locked up until she claimed to be the wife of George Hazelton. At first, he thought nothing of it—people make absurd claims all the time in the hope of avoiding arrest—but the inspector actually took the woman to Hazelton for confirmation. When he returned alone, Jonesy's brother assumed the woman's claim was true."

I stretched a hand to the banister to steady myself. "A police officer telling this tale to his sister is one thing, but I wonder how much farther the story has circulated."

"Difficult to say. He told Jonesy because he knows George is my brother. For that very reason, she threatened him with dire consequences if he ever breathed a word of it to anyone else." She shrugged. "Thus, it depends on how much this man fears the wrath of his sister."

"That's not very comforting."

"I fully appreciate that. I'm sure he wasn't the only one to overhear the woman's claim, either."

And the more people who heard it, the faster this would spread. I was beginning to rue the day I ever met Miss Teskey—or, more to the point, the day George met her.

Fiona pulled my hand away from the banister, forcing me to stand up straight. "Since I've already heard the rumor, why don't you tell me the facts? Perhaps I can help."

It took a good ten minutes to relay the details of the previous day and this morning. I paced the confined area while Fiona listened in stunned silence until I had covered everything, from Miss Teskey's arrival at my house to Bradmore's revelation that he was her husband.

Her expression brightened. "Then this is no more than the ravings of a madwoman."

That sounded a bit extreme now that I knew Miss Teskey better. "Perhaps more the ravings of a confused woman."

"Anyone who could confuse those two men must be mad." She gave my arm a comforting squeeze. "Should this rumor slip out to the public, that's how we must rebuff it. You can depend on me to do just that."

"Thank you, Fi. I still have hope it won't be necessary, but it's reassuring to know I can count on your help in squelching any future gossip."

"Piffle. I adore you, and my brother, and I refuse to let anyone ruin your happiness." She held up a finger and, leaning back, glanced around the wall. "I thought it was too quiet in there," she said. "They've already gone into the dining room."

We scurried across the hall and sagged with relief when we saw everyone was still finding their seats. It would have been a horrible breach of etiquette to arrive once the meal had begun. I pushed thoughts of Miss Teskey from my mind and prepared myself for the usual conversation about Princess Alexandra's various and many charities. If one weren't paying rapt attention, one could find oneself in charge of a committee or handing over a large bank draft. My worries about gossip would have to wait.

Lunch was lavish and long, and if that wasn't enough, tea was set up in the saloon, where I noticed Aunt Hetty at a table, in conversation with the princess. I found myself in the company of our guest of honor, the former Sophie of Merenberg and now the Countess de Torby, an interesting woman. She and Grand Duke Michael Mikhailovich had married almost a decade ago. Unfortunately, he had neglected to ask his cousin, the czar's permission, and that had set off a minor disaster in the Romanov family. He had been stripped of his military rank and had been banished from Russia. He hadn't even been allowed to return for his own mother's funeral. Some said her death had been brought on by the announcement of his marriage, but I've often observed that people who make such cruel remarks rarely have proof to back them up. Obviously, he had been removed from the line of succession, and Sophie would never have the title grand duchess.

Fortunately for the couple, the czar was not angry enough to cut off the grand duke's income from the estates he could no longer visit or from his factory. They were understandably insulted, perhaps bereft to be parted from his family, but they lived a happy life. They spent summers in Germany and departed for Cannes every winter, where Sophie was one of the brightest lights of society. They had three healthy children, and Sophie's uncle had bestowed upon her the title Countess de Torby.

I hardly thought they'd be happier freezing in Saint Petersburg and living under royal protocol, but who was I to say?

The countess herself was lovely. Her no-nonsense features—high cheekbones with just the slightest curve to the cheek, straight nose, and brows—were transformed to beauty by the softness in her blue eyes and the cloud of brown waves surrounding her face. She turned that softness on me just as the elderly woman beside me excused herself, allowing Sophie the seat next to mine.

"We spoke earlier, did we not?" she asked. "When Her Royal Highness made the introductions?"

"Indeed, we did," I replied, though indeed we had not. I had hoped for the chance to speak with the countess, and her ploy had saved me the task of finding someone of higher rank to introduce us. We were both countesses, but her husband was a grand duke. Still, hers was a foreign title, so I might have outranked her, but who knew for certain? The pretense that we'd already spoken meant we could dispense with the formality.

She took a surreptitious glance around the immediate area. We were seated on a curved velvet settee, which backed up to its twin, currently occupied by the princess, Aunt Hetty, and an older matron. "Have you seen the Indian Room?" Sophie asked.

"Why, no. I haven't." My answer was true, but I would have said the same had I seen the room hundreds of times, as it was clear the countess wanted to speak with me privately. "Perhaps you'd care to show it to me?"

She came to her feet with alacrity. "Of course. I'm sure you will find it most delightful."

I allowed her to lead me along the perimeter of the saloon and into another room, which did have an Eastern décor, though the chairs had a more modern and comfortable look to them. My shoes were beginning to pinch, and I looked to the chairs with longing, but she looped her arm through mine, and we wandered through the room instead.

"I understand you are hosting a relative of my husband at your home."

"Yes, I am. Are the two of you acquainted?" It would be extraordinary among the aristocracy for legitimate family members to be on friendly terms with illegitimate members, but one never knew with the Romanovs—or any royalty, for that matter.

"Not at all. My husband met her long ago, and since she is Alexei's child, I know of her." She led me toward a large window overlooking the courtyard. "Apparently, she was raised as a hoyden. Did you hear what she did?"

We paused when we arrived at the window, and acted as if we were enjoying the view. "Are you referring to the rock-throwing episode?"

She released a mirthless laugh. "Yes. At least she lives up to her heritage. The Romanovs are all barbarians." Her gaze narrowed in assessment—of my discretion, perhaps? "With some exceptions, of course."

"Of course." I readily conceded the point. Her husband was a Romanov, after all. "I formed the impression Miss Teskey had little supervision in her youth and was largely left at liberty. Now that she has gained her majority, she is very much on her own. I'm not sure she's so much hoydenish as untutored."

"Hers is an unfortunate situation, but in this case, I'd have to say Alexei has done his best for her." She leaned in, as if sharing a confidence. "It would have been better for all if he'd left the girl's mother alone in the first place, but it's absurd the husband didn't simply claim the child as his."

"I understand the mother died in childbirth." Unless one chose to believe Miss Teskey's story of murder. I set that thought aside. "Perhaps the husband couldn't afford to house and feed another child, especially one he hadn't fathered."

Sophie drew back and gazed at me in surprise. "Perhaps if this were some middle-class family, but my understanding is that was not the case. These were British aristocrats."

A fine pedigree didn't always come with wealth, but I didn't correct her. "Do you know her mother?"

"No. Alexei keeps that information very much to himself. But he referred to the husband as an aristocrat, which is why he kept their identities quiet. Now tell me, wouldn't a typical British lord simply accept the child as his own?"

"As long as he already had an heir, then, yes, that would be the normal course of action. I suppose that is the whole point of men having affairs with married women. But British men are positively fastidious when it comes to making sure their heir is really theirs."

"And in Britain, they are also particular that their heirs be male, so that hardly applies in this case." She waved a hand, as if it were a minor detail she didn't think worth discussing. Quite honestly, it astonished me that we were having this conversation at all. What was she getting at?

"No matter. I think the husband put Alexei to a great deal of trouble all these years and denied the girl a real home." She let out a little tsk. "The prince tells us she has made some trouble for you and your fiancé."

I nearly choked. *Some trouble? Yes, one might say that.* The countess waited for my reply. "She was under the mistaken impression that Mr. Hazelton was her husband. We have since made her aware of her error."

"Thank goodness for that. And just what did she wish so desperately to speak with Michael about yesterday?"

"She says she's received threats to her life. She sought her cousin's protection, but the prince has asked my fiancé to investigate claims." I gave her a sharp look. "Of course, if your husband wishes to speak with her, we can make the arrangements."

She waved a hand. "No, no. I'm sure he's more than willing to let Mr. Hazelton handle things. The prince says he is very capable."

"Of course." I couldn't help my disappointment. Her taking me into her confidence had made me think she actually wanted to take some action regarding Miss Teskey. Instead, she had simply wanted a report and seemed content to leave the matter in George's "capable" hands. Since it was the prince who had arranged George's involvement, there wasn't much I could do. I had had quite enough of this conversation and took the first opportunity to excuse myself and find Aunt Hetty. The gathering was beginning to thin, and I was ready to leave.

"I tell you she was positively gleeful to drop everything in George's lap. All she could say was how inconvenient Miss Teskey was for poor Alexei."

Hetty and I had just arrived at home and handed our cloaks to Mrs. Thompson. For the first time since my aunt had arrived in London, I was the first to head to the drinks cabinet. *Whiskey would do*, I thought. I poured us each a splash before continuing my tirade.

"And isn't that just like royalty? Always expecting someone else to handle their problems." Hetty, seated on the sofa, eagerly relieved me of one of the glasses. She took a sip while I proceeded to pace in front of the tea table. "And how cruel of me to speak of Miss Teskey as a problem. She is, rather, but she's also a person. A person given over as an infant to strangers to raise and care for as if she were a pet." I stopped my pacing and glanced belatedly around the drawing room, hoping Miss Teskey wasn't nearby.

"I wonder if she's still in her room." I rang the bell. Mrs. Thompson would know where she was.

Hetty glanced at the mantel clock. "We've been gone for several hours. Even in her condition, that's a long time to sleep."

Mrs. Thompson opened the door wearing an inquiring gaze.

"Have you seen Miss Teskey since this morning?" I asked.

"No, ma'am. She hasn't left her room, even when the gentleman called for her."

"Mr. Bradmore? She refused to see him?"

"She told me to send him away. That was shortly after you and Mrs. Chesney left for your engagement."

I turned to Hetty when Mrs. Thompson had left. "I suppose I should try to speak to her, don't you think?"

"She'll have to face Bradmore sooner or later. He is her husband."

I drained my glass, and thus fortified, I headed upstairs to knock on Miss Teskey's door. There was no answer, but the door was unlocked. I pushed it open and peeked inside, only to find the room empty. Mrs. Thompson must have been mistaken, but where was the woman? I headed downstairs. I knew she wasn't in the drawing room, and it was unlikely she was in the dining room, so I headed for my library. Perhaps she'd lost herself in a book.

But that room, too, was empty. I stood near the desk, wondering where I would be if I were Miss Teskey. She'd refused Bradmore an audience when he called, but I couldn't ignore the fact that she still held George in high esteem. Left alone for the past few hours, she might very well have gone next door to visit with him. I clenched my teeth to suppress my irritation.

With Bradmore now in the picture, I'd hoped she'd release her claim on George. Still, Miss Teskey was a stubborn young woman, and in asking for a divorce, Bradmore had not endeared himself to her. Well, I had no intention of leaving her alone with George.

Since I was already at the back of the house, I could cut through my garden and slip into his through the new gate in our shared wall. I walked around the desk and opened the door to my back garden and immediately wrapped my arms around myself. I'd forgotten how chilly it was out here now that the afternoon was waning and the garden was mostly in shade. It was that shade that made me take a second look at the rosebushes or, more particularly, the bench next to the rosebushes. Was that shape a person?

I moved closer. It was a person. In fact, it was Miss Teskey, reclined against the arm of the bench. Heavens, if she'd fallen asleep out here, she must be frozen. I recalled George had said she had a taste for opium. Though I didn't know where she might obtain it, that was the only reason I could imagine for her sleeping in this chill.

Leaves crunched under my shoes as I approached her. "Miss Teskey, you must wake up." When my voice didn't rouse her, I ignored the sense of dread tickling the back of my neck and touched her arm. I jumped back as her head lolled to the side, revealing angry red marks on her neck—her eyes wide open and sightless.

Miss Teskey was dead.

Chapter Seven

Instinct urged me to action—scream, run for help, check for a heartbeat. Yet my feet had taken root. I blinked away my tears and forced myself to slow my breath. In and out. The marks on her neck suggested she'd been strangled. My hand shaking, I placed my fingers on her neck. *Please let there be a pulse.*

No pulse.

I snatched my hand back and bit down hard on my lip. *Control yourself.* Somehow, I managed to stumble into George's garden and tapped on the window of his study. From his desk, he took one look at me and nearly knocked the chair over in his haste to reach the door. I leaned against the house until I heard the crunch of his shoes on the path and felt his hands on my shoulders.

"My dear Frances. What happened?"

He looked me over for signs of injury. His hands ran down my arms, then drifted to my waist with the lightest touch to avoid hurting me further. It was too light a touch and landed on a bundle of nerves that had me jumping away with a squeal.

Very inappropriate for the occasion. He stared in shock as I slapped his hands away.

"Stop it, stop it. This is no time to tickle me."

"That wasn't my intention." He took hold of my arms, examining my face. "Are you all right, then?"

Indeed, I was. The physical jolt broke me out of my stupor. "There's nothing wrong with me. It's Miss Teskey," I said. "I found her in the back garden."

"I wasn't aware she was missing."

"She's worse than missing. I'm afraid she's dead."

He jerked back, his grip on my arms tightening. "Dead? Are you sure?"

"She has no pulse. There are marks on her neck. I think she's been strangled."

His brows drew together in a sharp line. "My God! Did you see anyone about?"

"No, but I didn't stay around to conduct a thorough search. After checking her pulse, I came here. Mrs. Thompson said she hadn't seen Miss Teskey for hours, so it's likely this happened some time ago."

He blew out a breath. "That poor girl." After wrapping an arm around me, he led me into the house. "I'll place a call to the police right now, and we'll go back to your house together before someone else stumbles into your garden and right into the crime scene."

He seated me in a comfortable wingback chair before he telephoned the police. Out of his warm embrace, I began shaking again and found myself repeating George's words. *That poor girl.* She was both infuriating and pitiful, and I definitely wished she'd never entered my life. I certainly hadn't liked her, and now I felt guilty about that, which was foolish, but true all the same. My ill will had never extended to wishing her dead, and even if it had, a mere wish wouldn't have caused her end.

But I had left her alone, even after she'd told me someone had threatened her life.

Of course, I hadn't believed her. I suppose that's where the guilt came from.

George touched my arm and roused me from my brooding thoughts. "Are you ready to go back home?"

We took the garden route, examining every shrub and pebble along the path as if we were frontier trackers. Sadly, if someone had left traces of their passage, I'd probably obscured them when I came stumbling through.

I left him in my garden while I hastened inside to inform Hetty of Miss Teskey's murder, ask her to watch for the police, and tell the staff what had happened. I was sure they'd be questioned later. When I returned, I found George examining the gate that opened to Wilton Mews along the side of my house.

"It's unbolted," he said. "Is that normal?"

"No. Ever since that footman was murdered and left here last spring, we're careful to keep it bolted." I closed the door behind me and joined him by the gate. "Mrs. Thompson opens it for coal delivery." I pointed to the chute at the corner of the house. "Otherwise, it stays locked."

He straightened and walked carefully along the stone path that wound through the garden. It was littered with leaves from the overhanging trees. Moss filled the spaces between the flagstones. "Well, unless the coalman or Mrs. Thompson murdered her, it looks as though Irena opened the gate herself and let her murderer in."

"Then it must have been someone she knew, or at least someone she didn't fear."

"Bradmore left me several hours ago, intending to call on her." George was bent over, examining the flagstones, or perhaps the moss or some other such thing that looked to him like a clue.

"He did call, but Mrs. Thompson said Miss Teskey sent him away."

"Where was she at the time?"

"In her bedroom. When Hetty and I returned home, Mrs. Thompson told me she was in there still, but clearly, she left it at some point. It's possible she changed her mind, came down here, and left through the gate, looking for Bradmore."

He straightened and gazed up at the house. "Hmm. Does her window face the street?"

"It does. If she were looking out, she might have seen him at the door. Are you suggesting Bradmore murdered her?"

"Not necessarily. The only way that's likely is if she instructed him to meet her in the garden. She could have opened the window and called down to him."

"But why ask him to meet her in the garden when he's standing at the door? Why not just go downstairs and let him in?"

"Because it's Irena and she's a complicated little wretch—or she was."

I tsked. "It's just as likely she went out to the garden for some air, walked a bit outside, and left the gate unlatched. Someone might have been waiting for her. But other than members of my household, you, Bradmore, and Delaney, who else knew she was here?"

He twisted his lips from side to side. I'd come to learn that meant he was mulling something over. But what? There really was no one else. . . . Wait, yes, there was.

"For heaven's sake, you aren't considering Bertie or Michael Mikhailovich, are you?"

George chuckled. "I can't imagine the prince doing something like this, but Romanov knew she was here. I don't know that he has any sort of motive, but I wouldn't rule him out." He pointed to the path. "Do you see how the moss has been disturbed? Someone's been walking over this path."

"Rose plays out here from time to time. She left yesterday, but it takes more than two days for moss to grow back in those cracks. I wouldn't consider that as evidence."

"Good point." He smiled, making me realize what a good choice I'd made. Imagine a man not minding when you tell him his evidence is faulty.

"Since I don't suppose Miss Teskey strangled herself," he continued, "we must assume someone else entered the garden, either through the house or the gate. Mrs. Thompson is not the only one to answer the door, is she?"

"No. If she was busy, Jenny might have answered it."

"Do you mind sitting in on the meetings when the police question the servants? That will help us get a better feel for everything that happened here while you were gone."

"Of course."

George led me back to the door to the library, but instead of going inside, as I'd expected, he turned me around to face the garden. "This may be our last chance to view this before the police arrive and tromp all over. Do you see anything out of place, anything that doesn't belong?"

I took a few steps forward and started with the left side of what was a very small area. My gaze fell on the wall separating George's garden from mine and the new addition of the narrow gate. That side of the space received the most sun and was covered with the trailing branches of wisteria, its blooms either long past or far in the future, depending on how one considered the matter. Between the wall and myself was the open lawn. The table and chairs that usually graced the area were now tucked away below stairs for the winter. As my gaze traveled to the right, it landed on the hazel tree, the dozen or so nuts littering the ground, the bench under its canopy, the rosebushes behind, and the unfortunate Miss Teskey. I did not allow my gaze to linger there.

Moving to the right, more vines covered the back wall, and I began to consider the benefits of a gardener. The flagstone path bisected an open area where Rose might play and the coalman had room to turn his cart. The street wall, unadorned with vines, the gate, and the back wall of my house followed. Nothing seemed out of the ordinary.

George gave me a nudge. "Anything?"

I sighed. "Only a young woman, who ought to be alive."

Inspector Delaney was assigned to the case. Finally, a piece of good fortune. He arrived with a constable and the coroner, and as George had predicted, by the time they were through with the garden, they'd tromped over everything. George, Hetty, and I waited in the drawing room for them to finish their work and remove Miss Teskey's body.

"What do you suppose will become of her?" My query was met with two baffled gazes. "I mean her remains. Her father is off somewhere in the American West. The only relations she has on hand are Michael and Sophie." I grimaced. "Should we contact them?"

"Somebody will have to make arrangements for her. Since they are family, I'd say we should leave it in their hands. Perhaps, Delaney plans to contact them." He nodded toward the doorway as the inspector strode in, his long-legged gait leaving his constable trailing behind.

"I'd be grateful for any information you can provide regarding the young woman's family," he said. "And yes, we will want to contact them."

George and I exchanged a glance. Delaney could hardly imagine a family like Miss Teskey's.

He came directly to me. "Lady Harleigh, if it meets with your approval, I'd like Constable Martin to interview the staff, while I speak with the three of you."

George flashed me a warning look. Though I hated to delay the inspector's investigation, it was a necessary evil. "I'm sorry, Inspector, but I'd like to be present when the constable interviews the staff."

"I assumed as much, ma'am." His smile took me by surprise. "I'll just speak with you after the constable is finished."

Goodness, no argument? Was he allowing me to sit in on the staff interviews? But now I'd miss anything George or Hetty had to say. Dratted man. George gave me an infinitesimal nod, so with a sigh, I led the constable below stairs, to the room off the kitchen that served as a sitting room. My two maids were waiting for us, cups of tea at the ready, while Mrs. Thompson worked on tonight's dinner just a few steps away.

I introduced Constable Martin, and he assured them his questions were just routine, an assurance neither woman needed. Bridget, whose bouncy blond curls surrounded a heart-shaped face, might make a man wish to protect her, but a sharp mind and a spine of steel hid behind her sweet smile. Jenny, a plucky eighteen-year-old country girl, gazed at the constable, her brown eyes untroubled. They'd both been through this before.

Constable Martin and I took a seat at the worktable, across from the maids. His questions were slow and plodding while he laboriously wrote down each word the women said. As dull as this was to sit through, I had to admit, if I worked for Delaney, I'd pay close attention to detail, as well. The recitation of Bridget's day seemed uneventful. Though she had assisted Miss Teskey in dressing this morning, she had spent the rest of the day mending one of my gowns and cleaning my shoes. The constable moved on to Jenny.

"Wait," I said, turning back to Bridget. "Did Miss Teskey have no conversation with you this morning?" That would have been beyond extraordinary. Bridget was capable of dragging even the smallest detail about anything from me while she attended to my toilette.

"Yes, my lady. She told me I could ask a much higher wage if I worked in the theater." She gave me an impish grin, the little wretch.

I wasn't amused. "Did she? I suppose that means she had a dresser. Apparently, one who is well paid."

"Actually, ma'am, it means she was looking for one."

"Are you telling me she offered you a position?" How dare she! I forgot momentarily the woman had been murdered.

"Not outright, ma'am, and maybe not at all. She was just talking about the theater and telling me what such a position would be like. Though she said it meant working with a lot of actresses. She said some of them weren't very kind and none of them could be trusted. She sounded as if she had gone sour on the whole business of acting."

The constable frowned. "Because she had to deal with actresses who weren't trustworthy?"

Bridget puckered her brow while she considered the question. "No, more like she was disappointed with the theater. She expected it would be all applause and accolades, but there was a lot of business involved, lines to learn, and people with petty grievances, I think she called them."

"Did she mention anyone by name?"

"No, ma'am."

"Did she say anything about Mr. Bradmore?"

"She sounded pretty sour on him, too," she said with a firm nod. "Said he'd never get away with leaving her. Said her father would stop him."

I wasn't so sure her father would stir himself to come to her aid as far as Bradmore was concerned, but Bridget's account confirmed my impression of her state of mind regarding the man. "Anything else?"

Bridget replied in the negative, and the constable wrote furiously in his notebook. Once he finished, he glanced up to see the three of us waiting for his next move. He cleared his throat, thanked Bridget, and told her that would be all. Then he quickly glanced at me and raised his brows.

"I can't think of anything else, but Bridget will be here if you find you have further questions," I said.

Bridget pulled a face, but Constable Martin looked relieved, and as she left, we moved on to Jenny.

"Did you have any contact with the deceased, miss?"

"She was in her room when I straightened it this morning." Jenny twisted her fingers together.

"Did you speak to her?"

"Just to say good morning."

"Jenny, Mrs. Thompson told me Miss Teskey had a caller, somewhere around noon, and she refused to see him. Are you aware of that call?"

"Only because Mrs. Thompson told me. I was cleaning the back rooms at the time."

Interesting. "The dining room and the library? Did you happen to notice anything in the garden?"

Jenny chewed on her lip. "I saw Miss Teskey go out to the garden when I was cleaning the dining room. I'm not exactly sure when, but it was probably about half past noon. I heard steps in the hall, and when I looked out, I saw someone walk into the library. Since I was to clean there next, I peeked around the doorway to see if anyone was settling in, but I saw her, Miss Teskey, that is, go out to the garden, so I went back to finish the dining room."

"Did you see her come back in? Perhaps when you moved on to the library?"

"I didn't make it to the library. As soon as I took the dishes back downstairs, Mrs. Thompson told me the laundress had delivered the linens, and I spent the next hour or so refolding them and putting them away." She lowered her voice, as if speaking in confidence. "She doesn't fold them at all proper.

After that, I moved on to the drawing room and forgot about the library. I'll get to that right now if you like, ma'am."

"It may be better if you don't." I addressed the constable. "My aunt and I returned home about four o'clock, and I found Miss Teskey's body within fifteen or twenty minutes of that time, when I noticed the door from the library to the garden was open. Since she left through that door, you might wish to inspect the library for"—I raised my hands helplessly—"clues?"

"I'll make note of that, ma'am. Is there anyone else I should speak with?"

I led him a few steps away into the kitchen, where Mrs. Thompson turned over the task of stirring a pot emitting a savory aroma to the kitchen boy. The lad said he'd never left the servants' quarters all day, and Mrs. Thompson vouched for him. Given the chores he had, he wouldn't have had a chance to leave. She tapped a finger against her chin as she considered her own day.

"Well," she began, "after preparing and delivering breakfast, I visited the market this morning. I barely got my coat off when someone rang the bell. It was that Mr. Bradmore. I trotted upstairs and spoke to Miss Teskey through the door. She told me to send the gentleman on his way, so I did. Then back down here where the laundress was waiting for me. Once I attended to her, I set about cutting up vegetables for the soup and preparing a leg of lamb for the oven."

I simply must raise her wages.

Once Constable Martin decided she had no further information, he and I returned to the drawing room, where Delaney waited alone.

He instructed the constable to return to the precinct, promising to join him there shortly. "I have only Lady Harleigh left to interview."

"What have you done with my companions, Delaney?" I

joined him in one of the wingback chairs at the tea table and widened my eyes. "Don't tell me you've arrested them."

He tipped his head to the side. "Is there any reason I should arrest them? Is there something you'd like to tell me?"

"Of course not. You know very well I was making a joke. I had assumed they'd both still be here when I returned."

"Yes, I'm sure you did, but I wanted to speak with each of you separately." He raised his brows. "You have no problem with that, do you, Lady Harleigh?"

"Well, I'm not pleased with the implication that we might coordinate our statements, but as Miss Teskey was murdered here, I can understand your need to treat us as suspects."

"Then let's begin."

I walked Delaney through the events of my day, from my conversation with Miss Teskey at breakfast to George's arrival, where we learned he hadn't found the threatening letters, to Bradmore's revelation that he was Miss Teskey's husband. I proceeded to describe the luncheon and the Countess de Torby's attitude about her husband's cousin, then finished up with our arrival back here and the discovery of Miss Teskey's body.

Delaney jotted down the facts in his notebook, then looked up and gave me a penetrating stare. "How did you feel about Miss Teskey?"

The question took me by surprise, as I assumed it was meant to. "What do you mean by that?"

"A strange woman shows up in your life, essentially on your very doorstep, and claims to be your fiancé's wife. Your fiancé arrives, denies the claim, but he obviously knows her, and as an added insult, he asks you to allow her to stay with you." He leaned closer. "Come, come, Lady Harleigh, that could hardly engender any kindly sentiments."

What? Was he accusing me of murdering her? "The state of

my emotions regarding Miss Teskey makes no difference, Inspector. As you will learn when you speak to your constable, she was alive and well when I left, with my aunt as a witness, to attend Princess Alexandra's luncheon. While I was there, many more witnesses saw me and conversed with me. And by the way, while at Marlborough House, I learned one of your constables was speaking out of school. He was in the precinct when Miss Teskey was brought in, and he relayed to his sister that she claimed Hazelton was her husband."

"I'm sorry that got out, ma'am. Do you know who the constable is? I'll ensure he doesn't breathe another word of the incident."

"I know only that he has a sister with the surname of Jones who works for Lady Fiona Nash."

He nodded and jotted down another note. "All right, then. After the luncheon you returned home, I take it?"

"Yes, in the company of my aunt. We returned home and found her body."

His eyes narrowed. "Your aunt was with you when you found the body?"

These questions were beginning to grate on my nerves. "No. Hetty stayed in the drawing room, so I was alone then."

"And what did you do when you found her?"

"At first, I thought she was asleep, so I touched her arm to wake her." I drew in a long breath as the memory assailed me. "I also checked the pulse in her neck, and when I determined she was dead, I went through the garden to Mr. Hazelton's home to call the police."

"Once that was done, Hazelton returned here with you? You came directly into the house, where someone saw you?"

"I came in to tell Aunt Hetty what had happened, then returned to the garden."

"Where you had left Hazelton . . . alone?"

"He wanted to view the area before the police and coroner tromped over everything."

He cocked one bushy brow. "Or perhaps he wanted to remove some evidence."

"Now you imply Mr. Hazelton murdered her? You know us, Inspector. You know neither of us is capable of murder."

"Lady Harleigh, you must be aware I hold both you and Hazelton in high regard, but my line of work has taught me anyone can be capable of murder. All that's needed is the right motivation. So perhaps you'd like to answer my question now. How did you feel about Miss Teskey?"

I lowered my head, blinking back a tear. Then I realized that would make me look doubly guilty and turned to face him. His eyes softened. It must have been hard to push me for an answer. And was he wrong, really? My extremely limited experience with murder had shown me that people I never would have suspected were capable of taking a life. However much I disliked it, Delaney was simply doing his job.

"When I first met Miss Teskey," I began, "I assumed she was a liar and up to some sort of trickery. As I came to know her in our very brief acquaintance, I felt at turns sympathetic and irritated with her. She was a lonely young woman deprived of a family. I think the embellishments to her stories comforted her in some way, made her feel less alone."

His brow lifted a bit higher.

"For Miss Teskey, the truth was bleak. I didn't hate her. I didn't want her dead. Bradmore confirmed she was married to him, not Hazelton. I think she was being honest and simply didn't know the difference between one man and the other, and it appears she may have been telling the truth about her life being threatened."

Delaney closed his notebook around the small pencil and stuffed it into the pocket of his coat. "I'll check with this Bradmore chap and, of course, see what the coroner has to tell me about the time of death, but until I learn more, I have to consider you, Hazelton, and Mrs. Chesney as suspects."

He came to his feet as I sputtered random words of denial.

"You all had motive and opportunity. I can't rule any of you out yet."

Chapter Eight

I found Hetty and George waiting for me in the dining room after Mrs. Thompson informed me dinner was ready. I was surprised so much time had passed, and I ought to have been hungry, but Delaney had successfully ruined my appetite. However, now that I knew marketing and cooking had taken up much of Mrs. Thompson's day, I'd eat every bite if I had to choke on it.

Hetty had found time to change into evening wear, but I had no intention of asking the housekeeper to wait dinner even longer while I did the same. As George was still dressed for the business of the day in a wool suit, I saw no reason why my afternoon gown should not suffice.

Now that I thought about it, I wondered why he was here at all. As we moved to the table, I asked him. "I'm surprised to see you here. Didn't Delaney send you home?"

No sooner had we seated ourselves at the table than Mrs. Thompson brought in the soup.

"Didn't he tell you? As a suspect who'd been alone with the deceased, I might have taken some evidence and hidden it away at my home, so of course he must search it. I suspect he's there right now."

"Enough of that talk. You'll frighten Mrs. Thompson off, and however will I replace her?" Mrs. Thompson ladled a rich vegetable broth into my bowl. "Please say it's not becoming too much of a trial working here, Mrs. Thompson."

The housekeeper clucked her tongue. "Miss Teskey's murder is a sad state of affairs, my lady, but at least I didn't discover the deceased this time. And I know very well no one in this house is a killer."

George stood and took the soup tureen from her. "If everything is ready, why don't you and the maid bring the dishes up and lay them on the table? We're just a family party tonight and perfectly capable of serving ourselves."

Mrs. Thompson looked to me for confirmation, and when I nodded, she left to find Jenny. George returned to his seat on my right.

"That was an excellent idea," I said. "As soon as the table is laid, we are free to talk without frightening the staff."

In fact, none of us spoke a word until Mrs. Thompson and Jenny left the room, now filled with the enticing aroma of rosemary, thyme, and garlic emanating from the covered dishes at the end of the table. Perhaps I did have an appetite, after all.

"I, for one, am completely incensed that Inspector Delaney has accused all three of us of murder." Hetty's jaw was tight, and her words were clipped. She was usually such a calming influence. How odd to see her more ruffled than I.

"Did he provide any explanation as to how you might have murdered her?" I asked. "You were never alone in the garden with her."

Hetty pressed her lips together. "You underestimate how swiftly I move, Frances. When you went upstairs to check on Miss Teskey, I had all of five minutes to learn she was in the garden, strangle her, and return to the drawing room."

I stared at her as I lowered my spoon to the bowl. "Are you joking? Did he actually say that?"

"Not in so many words, but no other time was possible. Perhaps he thought I had ten minutes." She picked up her spoon and dipped it into her soup.

"In your case, Mrs. Chesney, it's likely Delaney believes you might be willing to aid Frances or me in the murder of Miss Teskey, due to your affection for us. I doubt he thinks you'd murder her yourself."

"That's all well and fine, but how can he suspect you or I would do such a thing?" I asked.

"Love. Jealousy. He likely believes Irena stood between us and our future happiness." George got up and nosed around the dishes at the end of the table, tipping the covers up just a bit and peering under them. He made a happy noise of discovery upon finding the roasted lamb and brought the dish to our end of the table.

"You're missing my point. I understand the typical motives involved in these circumstances, but Delaney knows us. How could he think I'd be so overcome with jealousy that I'd murder Miss Teskey?" I snatched the soup bowl from George's plate before he could serve the lamb in it. He gave me a look of suffering but added his portion to the correct plate. Hetty handed me her bowl, and I set them all aside.

"Both of you are taking this far too personally," he said.

Hetty and I first turned to one another, then back to George before attacking him in unison.

"How do you suggest we take it?" I asked.

"It feels quite personal to me," Hetty agreed.

"Delaney is looking at this case objectively, dispassionately, and disregarding any relationships he has with any of us. It's the only way he can do his job and solve the crime."

"Are you saying it does not trouble you one whit that you've been accused of a crime?" Hetty looked incredulous.

"I am *suspected* of a crime. There's a big difference. And no, it doesn't bother me, because I didn't murder Miss Teskey, and any motive Delaney thinks I . . . we have will disappear once he speaks with Bradmore."

"But I already told Delaney that Bradmore was Miss Teskey's husband."

"He needs the man himself to confirm it. In fact, he needs to confirm that not only do you know that now, but you also knew it this morning." He shrugged. "Delaney has to follow procedures. He can't just take your word for it."

Hetty frowned. "That should serve only to make the inspector transfer his suspicions from us to Mr. Bradmore." She paused. "What about the letters she is supposed to have received? They don't sound like something Mr. Bradmore would have sent her. 'Go away, or you will die!' "

"That's true. Bradmore said he had been trying to contact Miss Teskey. If he realized she was in London, he would have sought her out, not chased her away." I turned to George, who was applying himself to his lamb. "Shouldn't Delaney be looking for someone else? Someone who might have sent those letters."

"What letters?" he asked, gazing longingly at the remaining dishes.

"Take your plate and serve yourself something of everything. You needn't wait until Hetty and I are ready for the next course." I turned to my aunt. "And we should eat, as well. If we send this food back, that may just be the last straw for Mrs. Thompson. If she leaves, good luck to you in finding another housekeeper who also cooks and puts up with murders in the back garden."

Hetty blinked. "That's right. It will be me she's leaving."

She turned her attention to dinner, so I prodded George, who'd just returned to his seat with a full plate. "What do you mean, what letters? The threatening letters Miss Teskey received."

"I didn't find any letters, and it's definitely possible they never existed."

"If not, that does make Bradmore a more reasonable suspect. What did he tell you about their supposed marriage? What was his state of mind?"

"I don't know any more about how he got himself into this mess than he told us this morning. I suspect, in addition to opium, copious amounts of cognac were involved. At least enough to make him think marriage to Irena was a good idea. But his state of mind today was that he wanted to be free of her."

I pondered Bradmore's situation. It didn't paint him in a favorable light. "I don't know how much cognac he'd need to convince himself Miss Teskey was a desirable match—at the time, that is. He had no real prospects of his own, and Miss Teskey had a blood connection to the Romanovs, one of the crowned heads of Europe. It's possible he expected her father to provide her with a fortune, allowing him to lead a life of leisure."

"Then he learned her father might not approve." Hetty's tone made it clear she didn't.

"And his own prospects improved." I tsked. "There's a name for men like that."

"Cad," Hetty muttered.

"I was thinking opportunist, but I can't argue with cad. What about you, George?" I was stunned to see he'd consumed the small mountain of food he'd piled on his plate. Mrs. Thompson should be satisfied that we'd done justice to her meal.

He took a sip of his wine and followed my gaze. "I haven't eaten since this morning, what with running after Irena's things, then taking charge of Bradmore, then . . . Well, you're aware of everything that happened this afternoon."

"Yes, yes. Please eat as much as you like, but tell me if you consider Bradmore as Miss Teskey's murderer."

"He didn't strike me as that desperate. He'd barely spoken to her and had no reason to suppose she'd refuse him a divorce."

"But what if she did?" Hetty asked.

"He told me he'd start divorce proceedings, regardless. He might have a case for abandonment."

"From where I sit," she said, "it looks more as if he abandoned her."

"He left at her urging, then corresponded with her until she disappeared." George tapped his fork against his plate to emphasize each point. "He would have preferred that she just go along with the divorce, but if she didn't, he was prepared to take a legal path. He had no reason to murder her."

"Now that you've pled his case," I said, "please tell me you can do the same for us. From Delaney's point of view, we would be the next most likely suspects."

"Not once Bradmore tells him that we all knew Irena was his wife."

Hetty frowned. "This is rather perplexing. We know none of us murdered her. If Bradmore didn't, either, then who did? Are you certain those letters don't exist?"

"Certain? Not at all. I just wouldn't be surprised if they existed only in Irena's head. But you make a good point. If not us, then who?"

"I fear it was Bradmore." I told them what Jenny had told me about seeing Miss Teskey go through the library and out the door to the garden. "She said it was somewhere around noon, and according to Mrs. Thompson, that's when Bradmore called."

George frowned. "I thought she refused to see him."

"She did, but she then left her room for the garden, where she obviously came across someone. Bradmore was nearby."

"And because the gate was unlocked, it would appear she let the killer in," Hetty said. "If it wasn't Bradmore, it must have been someone else she knew."

George leaned on the table and rested his chin on his open palm. "I don't know Bradmore very well, but I'd wager my last shilling he had no intention of killing her." He straightened. "And he would have required some intent. Irena was strangled with a rope or cord. He would have had to bring it with him."

"Perhaps she wore a scarf," I suggested.

"I didn't bring her a scarf from her hotel room, and it's not as if he could have found something in the garden. You didn't have rope lying around, did you?"

I envisioned my garden. "There was nothing like that. But Bradmore did have something with him. He could have used his necktie."

Aunt Hetty brightened at the idea, but George drew in a breath and rubbed his hand over his eyes. "He might have done, but then we must make one of two assumptions." He held up his index finger. "Bradmore came here planning to strangle the girl and so removed his necktie before meeting her."

I pondered the possibility. "That sounds unlikely. As you said, he hadn't really had a chance to speak with her about the divorce. She might have agreed to it. I would have thought he murdered her in the heat of anger."

"All right, let's say he didn't come prepared. He spoke with her. She wouldn't agree to the divorce. He became angry, positively enraged. Is that more or less how you envision it?"

I eyed him suspiciously. "More or less."

"In that case, you have to assume that while his rage is bubbling up, Irena is patiently waiting for him to untie and remove his neckwear." He pantomimed struggling to a ridiculous degree to remove his own, while pretending to choke for good measure. "This is something of a complicated knot, you know. Doesn't just slip open."

"Fine. I see your point. You may cease with your theatrics."

"I found it rather amusing," Hetty said, earning her a warm smile from George. "But here is another possibility for your consideration." She raised her brows suggestively. "What if she removed his tie? What if he asked her again for a divorce, and she tried to change his mind by seducing him? A few kisses, some sweet nothings whispered into his ear, she removes his tie . . . Well, I'm sure you can envision it for yourselves."

"I can envision it perfectly," I said. "Two people shivering on a damp wooden bench on a cold November afternoon, in what is essentially a stranger's garden." I shivered at the image and glanced at George, who stared at Hetty as if he'd never seen her before.

"Perhaps that was a bad idea," she said, poking at a roasted potato on her plate.

I turned to George. "It's possible Bradmore left, defeated, and, after some thought, decided to come back and murder her."

"In that case, we're back to imagining he's a cold-blooded killer, and I find that hard to believe."

"It sounds as though you simply don't think Bradmore is guilty of this crime." I pushed my plate away and came to my feet. "But if he didn't do it, then someone else had to enter the garden and strangle her. Probably right after he left. She had no wrap, so I doubt she planned to stay out there very long. Mr. Bradmore might well be the last person to have seen her alive. I think you should speak to him."

George studied me over the rim of his wineglass. "You just suggested he might be a cold-blooded killer, and you want me to pay a call on him?"

"You just declared that he's not."

"I only said it was hard to believe." He set down his glass and came to his feet. "But for you, my dear, I'll talk to him."

I gave him a smile. "You aren't fooling me. You're as eager as

I am to find out what he knows. And if he has an alibi." We both knew if Bradmore had an alibi, we would come under much greater scrutiny.

"Clearly, I've become predictable. I also hope speaking with Bradmore will help to fix her time of death. With any luck, that could exonerate all of us." He reached into his pocket, retrieved a card, and gave it a glance.

"Bradmore's calling card?"

He nodded. "Complete with his direction, so I'll take my leave of you ladies and go there now."

"Shall I go with you?" My curiosity in the matter was overwhelming. I'd hate to wait for information until he returned.

"I'd prefer that you look about her room and through the things I brought over this morning." He shrugged. "Perhaps I missed something."

I sighed. "Very well."

"Wait just a moment." Hetty had been quietly observing the conversation, but now she squirmed and fidgeted, as if she were uneasy. "I'm not sure this is such a grand idea. Didn't the inspector tell us all to stay put?"

"No, no," I said. "He only meant we shouldn't leave town."

Hetty narrowed her eyes. "Is that so?"

"I'm sure he'd like us to stay put, Mrs. Chesney, but he has no power to make us do so. At least not until we interfere with his investigation."

"Isn't that precisely what you're doing?"

"No." We answered in unison, both looking at her, aghast. George and I had investigated a few crimes together, but while Aunt Hetty had occasionally provided information or assisted here and there, she had never fully taken part. She also had only a vague idea of George's expertise in this field.

"Delaney will generally allow interference up to a point," I said. "We do our best not to go beyond that point."

When George made his farewells and departed for Bradmore's lodgings, I suggested that Aunt Hetty and I check Miss Teskey's room.

"But wouldn't the police have locked the door?"

"Oh, good thinking. I'll get the key from Mrs. Thompson first."

"Don't you suppose Delaney locked the door to keep us out?"

"I'm certain of it, but if you want to investigate a crime, you can't allow such trifling matters to stop you. Need I remind you we are all suspects?"

As I drifted past her for the bellpull, I noted the look of surprise on her face and was rather proud of myself for having put it there. When Aunt Hetty had first come to London, I believe she considered me quite the little mouse. No, that wasn't fair. She thought me the dutiful daughter, wife, and mother—prepared to do what was expected of me and not much else. And so I was, but that was before George entered my life and I learned how much one could accomplish when one took a risk and did the unexpected.

Once I had the key from Mrs. Thompson, Hetty and I did our duty and searched Miss Teskey's room. Since she had only the clothing and toiletry items George had brought, it took less than thirty minutes. As expected, he had missed nothing. He had set us to this task only to give me something to do and keep me out of trouble. There were no threatening letters, no marriage certificate with Bradmore's name on it, nothing that would help prove our innocence or lead us to the murderer.

Then I checked a pocket of Miss Teskey's coat. My fingers closed around a key. I held it up, letting it dangle from a narrow red ribbon, for Hetty's inspection.

"She gave Hazelton the key to her hotel room," she said.

"Yes, which makes me wonder what this one opens." I handed the key to Hetty and reached into the other pocket, then pulled out a card. "It seems she had calling cards made since her arrival in London." I flipped the card over. "Ah, this is a good find."

She took it from me with a frown and inspected it. "Hmm, apparently, she really was an actress, at least so her card says." She lifted her gaze to my face, and her frown deepened. "Why are you so pleased about this?"

"Because the name and address of the theater are on the reverse side."

She flipped the card over and took a look. "I'm afraid I still don't understand. What does this mean?"

With an arm about her shoulders, I led her from the room. "It means we must change our clothes, Aunt, and quickly. We are going to the theater tonight."

Chapter Nine

A cab had set us down outside the Hanover Theater in Piccadilly at precisely nine o'clock. We just had time to leave our coats with a checker before an attendant showed us to our seats in a private box that was as yet unclaimed. Aunt Hetty looked utterly breathtaking in a gown of deep red silk shot with velvet that molded itself to her statuesque figure. It made me miss the days when I could buy a gown without any thought for its price.

I was wearing blue velvet embroidered with silver throughout. The gown was two years old but had been brought up to date by the very skilled modiste Madame Celeste. It was flattering and suitable for the occasion, so what was I pining for? Returning to the old days meant returning to the days with Reggie, and I'd never wish for that. As for spending money without thought, I sincerely doubted I could do that anymore, even if I had it to spend. I pushed the idea of extravagant clothing from my mind as the attendant pushed aside the curtain to our box.

Hetty swept in beside me. "How did you know we'd be able to purchase tickets on such short notice?"

"This theater opened only two weeks ago, after having been closed for several years. New owners refurbished the whole theater, and news of the opening was in all the papers. Unfortunately, so were the reviews of their debut performance."

Hetty quirked a brow. "I take it they were not favorable."

"Dismal. The theater was praised, but the performance . . . Well, let's just say I suspected there'd be a box or two available."

As I spoke the words, I took the opportunity to look around ours. "It appears the new owners spared no expense." In fact, the box was a study in luxury. The seats were deeply cushioned and upholstered in crimson velveteen. The curtains behind us were heavy and sure to block any noise from the hallway. I took my seat and glanced around the theater, noting that every surface that could be gilded was. "Quite showy, don't you think?"

Hetty settled in next to me. "I haven't yet taken the time to absorb everything, as I'm still trying to determine why we're here."

"We're looking for Miss Teskey's threatening letters."

"Why do you suppose they'd be here?"

"Because they weren't in her rooms at the hotel. She was an actress here, so one assumes she had a dressing room. There must be someplace for her to store her belongings." I'd have continued my explanation, but Hetty was staring at me in amazement. "What is it?"

"Just how do you propose we gain access to her dressing room? And if that is the point, why sit through a play that is reportedly terrible?"

"Because we need something to do until the performance is over. Then we'll go backstage, speak to the manager, and ask him for access. People rarely say no to a countess."

Whatever Hetty was about to say was silenced by the overture. We turned our attention to the stage as the curtain rose and the performance began.

Whoever had called this play dismal had to be the crankiest of cranks ever to review a play. It might have dragged a bit toward the end of the first act, but it was terribly amusing, and the cast was wonderful. There was just no accounting for taste, but I was glad we managed to see the show early, as the theater was certain to be sold out once a proper review was written.

When the houselights came up, everyone applauded loud and long. The attendant arrived with our coats, but before we donned them, I asked if he could take us to the manager. He suggested we wait there, but after a bit of back-and-forth, my insistence won out, and he escorted us to the office of one Herbert Gilliam. If I remembered correctly, Miss Teskey had mentioned his name as one of the owners.

Our guide suffered a moment's confusion when Mr. Gilliam was not in his office. Hetty and I agreed to wait in the busy corridor until he could be located. Unfortunately, that was all too soon. I had barely turned the handle of his office door when the man stepped out of a room down the hallway. The attendant pointed to us and led him our way. *Bother. No chance for snooping.*

Herbert Gilliam was about forty, with dark, closely cropped hair. He was tall, with a sturdy build, which showed to advantage in his formal attire. When he spoke to the attendant, his voice carried down the hall, making me wonder if he was a former actor who had turned his hand to business. His waxed and curled mustache tweaked upward when he smiled at us, giving him a jovial countenance. He approached and greeted us. I made our introductions.

"I understand you have some business to discuss." He gestured to the door. "Would you care to step into my office?"

We agreed it would be best to hold our conversation in private, and Hetty stepped aside, allowing the manager to open the door and usher us inside. His office was small, simple, and utilitarian, a stark contrast to the flamboyance of the theater itself. But it was tidy and comfortable. I gave the man credit for having the good sense to know where to spend his capital. He rounded the desk and we all took a seat.

"I hope you enjoyed the performance this evening?" He smiled and rested his gaze on both of us in turn. "Perhaps you're interested in a subscription?"

"We did enjoy the performance, and now that you mention it, a subscription might be in order. We can discuss that another time. At the moment, we have a less congenial purpose for speaking with you."

He rested his elbows on the desk, then clasped his hands and leaned forward. Only a slight narrowing of his eyes countered his calm composure. "Indeed?"

"I believe you're familiar with Irena Teskey?"

Both his shoulders and mustache sagged as his former good spirits seemed to drain from his face. "I'm very familiar with Miss Teskey and have been wondering what's happened to her. She's missed two performances now, with nary a word to explain her absence." He glanced between the two of us. "I wasn't aware she had any acquaintance in town. Is she in some sort of trouble?"

Well, this was awkward. I'd assumed Delaney would have been here already to deliver the news of Miss Teskey's death. I debated what to do with my advantage. This definitely crossed the line of interfering with his investigation, but I could hardly walk away now.

"We've only recently become acquainted with Miss Teskey, but before I go into that, you should prepare yourself for some distressing news."

"What has she done?"

"I'm afraid she's died."

He bounced back in his chair as if he'd been struck. His eyes widened. "How? What happened?"

"She was murdered," I said.

"Good Lord!"

"I'm sure this comes as a shock," Hetty said.

"A shock and something of a disaster." He shoved himself away from the desk, scraping the chair across the floor. "Are you sure she was murdered?"

"I'm afraid so," I said.

"How? Who? Why? I can easily believe she could aggravate someone enough to *want* to murder her, but my brain is having a hard time taking in the fact that someone actually did it."

"I hesitate to say more, sir, as the inspector in charge of her case will want to discuss those questions with you. I may already have brought some trouble upon myself by informing you of her death, but I'd assumed the police would have been here by now. Perhaps they didn't know where Miss Teskey worked. I'm sorry to be the bearer of such bad news and terribly sorry for your loss."

Hetty murmured her condolences. "I'm sure she was a friend as well as a colleague."

The mustache drooped as he frowned. "She was a pain in the backside is what she was. But I don't know how I'm to make a go of this place without her."

"Was she one of your best performers?" Hetty asked.

"Irena? She was a terrible actress. Couldn't learn her lines to save her life. Never here on time. Always in a dispute with the other actors. The woman was nothing but trouble." He sighed. "Sometimes I wish I'd never met her."

It seemed Miss Teskey evoked the same sentiment from all her acquaintances. "Why didn't you just dismiss her?"

He gave me an incredulous stare. "Dismiss her? She was my partner. I would have had to buy her out, and I don't have that sort of money at hand."

Well, for heaven's sake. Miss Teskey was telling the truth about that, as well. She did own this theater, at least in part. "How did you come to meet her?"

His eyes grew wary as he drew his chair back to the desk and drummed his fingers on its polished surface. "Not to be rude, ma'am, but just what is your interest in all this? How do the two of you know Irena, and why are you here asking questions, instead of the police?"

"There's an interesting story to that." He raised his brows, and I continued, hoping Hetty wouldn't correct me. "Miss Teskey was at my home when she was murdered. She claimed to have received some threatening letters and asked my fiancé to help her. Under the circumstances, she didn't want to return to her hotel room, so she stayed with me. Though I'm sure the police will pay you a visit in the coming days, Miss Teskey herself authorized Mr. Hazelton to investigate on her behalf." I couldn't help preening a bit. "Right now, he is speaking to a witness, so I offered to come and search for the letters here, perhaps in her dressing room."

"With all due respect, ma'am, that sounds like a lot of humbug."

Was he calling me a liar? No one had ever called me a liar before, at least not to my face. How dare he? I opened my mouth to protest, but he spoke first.

"I'm willing to believe your man's an investigator, but that he'd let you involve yourself in a murder investigation? A countess?" He narrowed his eyes. "Does he even know you're here?"

"Whether you believe me or not is your choice, Mr. Gilliam. Whether or not Mr. Hazelton knows of my whereabouts is none of your business. But since this is your theater, I do need your permission to look for the letters."

He studied me a moment. "If your story is true, you may be able to help me. Irena's death presents a problem. I need the police to solve this case as soon as possible, and I don't have much faith that they will."

"Indeed?" Hetty leaned forward.

He sighed. "Irena was my partner. She was an atrocious actress and had no head for business, but what she did have was money. We had a contract, so she couldn't just walk away, but if anything happened to her, I'd lose this theater." His gaze shifted from Hetty to me and back. "So, I had her life insured. The insurance people won't pay me until the police have a nice, tidy report and, hopefully, an arrest. However, the Metropolitan Police are a busy lot. I don't see them caring much one way or the other about who murdered a Frenchwoman. I could be waiting a long time for my money, unless your investigation proves fruitful."

"Insurance companies can be difficult." Hetty blew out a breath. "You seem to have a good business sense, sir. I believe we can help you. As Lady Harleigh said, Mr. Hazelton is currently with a witness, but we could get the investigation started if you'll allow us to search for the letters and perhaps speak with her associates. She may have mentioned these threats to one of them."

Good work, Hetty. I forged ahead. "She never mentioned anything of this nature to you?"

He pursed his lips. "I fear this won't paint me in a favorable light, but Irena had an endless array of complaints and grievances, which I simply didn't have the time or inclination to address. She may have mentioned those letters among them, but I confess I stopped listening after a week or two."

"I see. She also suspected someone was following her—someone unknown to her. Have you noticed anyone new around the theater?"

"Everyone's new. Just a few hands came here with me from Paris. The rest we hired on over the past month."

"Is Paris where you met her?"

"I own a theater there, as well. Irena had a small part in one of the productions. When she heard I was looking for a partner to renovate and reopen this place, she suggested herself for that office. I thought she'd simply provide funding. I didn't expect her to show up here a few months later and demand a starring role in the production, but by that time, I'd used her capital. What was I to do?"

I could think of one thing—murder her and collect the insurance payment. Now I understood the horrible reviews I'd read of this play. Miss Teskey had been in the leading role. If she was as bad an actress as her partner claimed, I could see how the production would be ruined.

Hetty let out a tut-tut. "Partnerships can be so difficult to manage."

"That they can," he replied. "But if one wants to expand, partners are a necessary evil. I'm an ambitious man who loves the theater. I hope to own several before I end my career, but capital is tough to come by. Even when the production is small, the necessary crew is costly. Dressers, seamstresses, ticket sellers, attendants, gasmen . . . I could go on and on."

Hetty nodded her agreement and launched into a discussion of board meetings she'd attended back in New York, presumably to provide him with the investors' point of view. Or perhaps to bore me to tears.

Gilliam appeared fascinated. "Now, see, that's too complicated for the likes of me. I know my business, and I don't want a contingent of investors telling me what to do or an enterprise so large, I can't have a hand in the day-to-day operations."

"With one theater in Paris and another in London, you can hardly be managing daily operations of the two you own now," Hetty countered.

"True, not day to day, but I can travel back and forth easily and often enough."

"You won't likely be allowed to do so this week if we don't

begin our investigation immediately," I said. "The police may ask you to stay in London."

He gave me a sharp glance. "Where would you like to begin?"

"Her dressing room, perhaps?"

"She shares with the other actresses, and they're likely still in there."

"Perfect." Hetty spoke up before I could even decide if this was wise. "Perhaps we can ask them a few questions?" She glanced at her velvet reticule and sighed. "That is, if you happen to have a pencil and paper."

Gilliam gave her a smile, opened the desk drawer, and rooted around for the requested implements. "Good luck getting anything out of that lot."

I wasn't sure conducting interviews was a good idea now that I knew the police hadn't been here yet. Delaney was bound to be angry that we had nosed around without his knowledge. I could just imagine his reaction once he learned we'd interviewed Miss Teskey's colleagues, too. But who knew when we'd have this chance again? Just as well to be hanged for a sheep as a lamb, I supposed.

Gilliam rounded the desk and handed Hetty pencil and paper. "If you'll follow me?" He opened the door for us to precede him and gave Hetty a warm smile as she passed. She blushed prettily. I'd have to remind her the man might be a killer. We followed him a few yards down the hallway before stopping at a room just before the turn that led backstage.

The manager banged on the open door, facing away from it. "Everyone in there decent?"

Several female voices made negative replies, including one that called, "As if we ever were." I was sure my face burned as red as Hetty's.

He gave us a cheeky grin. "You ladies are on your own, then. I'll wait for you out here."

As we were about to pass by, he stretched out an arm, blocking our entrance. "Irena's dressing table is against the far wall, and I'll ask you not to remove anything. If you find something of import, we'll notify the police."

"Fair enough," I agreed. He let us pass.

The women in the dressing room, in various stages of dishabille, some with freshly scrubbed faces, others still in full makeup, were watching the door with curiosity when Hetty and I passed through. The space was rectangular and about as large as my dining room. To our left, a shelf about chest high ran the length of the wall, with five or six mirrors spaced out above it, each surrounded by lights. A rack of gowns and robes filled the right side of the room, and against the far wall stood a single dressing table, supposedly Miss Teskey's. Yet it was occupied by a dark-haired woman industriously applying some sort of cream to her face. She alone had no apparent interest in us.

The other five women in the room more than made up for her indifference as they stared at us in open curiosity. "Who's this you're sending in here, Gilliam?" one of them inquired.

He must have stepped away from the door, as there was no reply. We were indeed on our own. Perhaps we might be able to do more than just search her dressing table. But where to begin?

I cleared my throat. "Pardon us for disrupting your toilette, but we're here about Irena Teskey."

"You mean Her Majesty?" One of the women in full theatrical makeup chuckled at her own joke. "Why wasn't she here tonight? Tea with the queen?" This brought snickers from everyone.

"Sadly, no." I glanced back at the door to see Gilliam was still missing. "Unfortunately, it's been left to me to inform you of Miss Teskey's death."

Each face registered some variation of surprise. Even the

woman at her table stopped and turned her cream-covered face to us.

"Here, I didn't mean no harm." The fair-haired woman who'd called Miss Teskey "Her Majesty" stepped forward in her own defense. "Are you friends of hers?"

"Not exactly. We met only yesterday. She came to us with a request for assistance. It seems she knew her life was in danger."

"Wait just one minute." The woman at the dressing table left her seat and strode toward us. Even through the cream, I recognized her as the lead actress in the play, Sally Cooper. "Are you saying she was murdered?" A collective gasp spread through the room when I nodded. "And she knew it was coming?"

"She had reason to be concerned," I said. "I was hoping she might have mentioned something to one of you. As colleagues, I'm sure you're together for more than just the performances. Perhaps she took one of you into her confidence."

The lead actress made a noise of derision. "Her? She was too far above us for any sort of confidences. All she ever talked about were her connections—to the prince, to the queen, to some Russian royalty. As if we'd believe that." She wagged her finger at me. "If she's related to half the royalty in the world, what was she doing here? That's what I want to know."

"What happened to her?" This came from a fresh-faced young woman already dressed in her street clothes.

"She was strangled," Hetty said.

I gave her a nudge. Had she already forgotten we weren't to reveal too much? Perhaps pressing her to accompany me had been a mistake.

Miss Cooper turned to Hetty. "By who?"

"That's what we're attempting to find out," I said before Hetty could start naming suspects. "If she didn't mention her fear to any of you . . ." I let the sentence hang and glanced at each face for confirmation. "Did you happen to notice a strange man hanging about the theater lately? Someone who might have seemed to have an interest in Miss Teskey?"

A flurry of responses attacked me from all directions.

"Might this not be better if we speak to each of you one at a time?" Hetty asked.

I thought this a good idea, but another wave of dissent rose from the ladies. The short of it was that they wanted to go home. As I was not the police, I couldn't force them to stay and talk to me. Neither did I want to antagonize them. I was certain Delaney and his men would be here themselves by tomorrow, and I'd like to stay as vague and unmemorable to these ladies as possible.

"Very well, we'll speak to you all at once, and I'll do my best to be quick about it." Hetty took a seat along the wall, ready to record anything of import that might be revealed, and I brought the ladies back to some order. I addressed the fair-haired actress first. "Did you ever see anyone following Miss Teskey?"

"Not following, exactly. There was someone new hanging about the place, a Russian chap, but she talked to him now and then, like they were friends." She glanced around at her companions, who nodded in agreement. Perhaps this was the man, Igor, Miss Teskey had mentioned.

"How do you know he was Russian?" I asked.

"His accent, I reckon. Irena said she was Russian, so since he had an accent I didn't recognize, I assumed he was, too."

"You spoke with him?"

She bumped her forehead with the heel of her hand. "Right, right. That's how I pegged him for Russian. If I left before her, I might see him in the hall. He'd ask for Irena Alexeievna." She wrinkled her nose. "That's Russian, isn't it?"

"I believe it is. Did you see him last night? Or today?"

This brought on a bit of debate. It seemed Igor, if that was who this was, had become something of a fixture the actresses had stopped noticing. They eventually came to the conclusion he'd been backstage yesterday evening, but no one had noticed him today.

"But I only ever saw him when I was heading home," said the woman I'd started thinking of as the young one. "He may be out there now, for all we know." She gave me a pointed look. "We're a little behind our usual time."

I took the hint and moved the conversation forward. They gave me a description of Igor: tall, stocky, dark hair, with some debate over the amount of gray, and a very full beard. All the ladies agreed there was no one else they'd seen backstage or at the stage door who hadn't been around from the beginning. He was also the only one who had paid particular attention to Miss Teskey.

"I'd like to go through her dressing table, if I may." I looked at Miss Cooper when I made the request.

She shrugged. "Her Majesty's table is right there."

"Go on, Sally," said the blonde. "You shouldn't talk about her like that."

"Why not? Speaking ill of the dead is no different from speaking ill of the living. Besides, I'm not saying anything I wouldn't have said to her face." She turned to me. "She bought her way in here. Took the plum parts she hadn't the talent for."

Miss Cooper was a pretty young woman, with ice-blue eyes that struck a startling contrast to her dark hair. Her only imperfection was a slight twist to her left front tooth, which made her upper lip protrude the tiniest bit. I doubted she ever lost a role to another actress before Miss Teskey came along.

"You played her role tonight, didn't you?" I asked.

"And did a lot better job of it."

I nodded. "And now you're using her dressing table."

With a huff, she turned away from me, snatched a towel from the table, and swiped at the cream on her face. I moved around her to the table and began opening the small drawers.

Nothing but greasepaint, hairpins, brushes, and combs. When I'd returned everything to the drawers, Miss Cooper sauntered over to me, one hand on her hip.

"It's fair enough to say I didn't like her," she said. "But that doesn't mean I'd want to hurt her. I only had to bide my time. Soon enough, the empty seats would push Mr. Gilliam to get her off the stage and put me in her roles."

She had a point. "He was in an awkward position, wasn't he? If he wanted her as a partner, he had to accept her as an actress."

She let out a snort. "Irena wasn't much of a partner either, from what I could see. For all she had a fancy office, she only showed up here in time for rehearsals. I don't know why she even used the dressing room, except to rub our noses in the fact that she was the lead."

I suppressed a groan. Gad, I was a fool. "She had an office?"

Her scowl turned into a smirk. "If you're looking for anything she left behind, you should probably start there."

She pointed us in the direction of the office, but I had a feeling we were too late. If Miss Teskey had left anything there, we'd given Gilliam plenty of time to go through it.

Chapter Ten

❧

We had to pass Gilliam's office on the way to Miss Teskey's. Through the corner of my eye, I saw him at his desk, in conversation with another man. I pretended not to hear him call out to me as I rushed Hetty past the open door and down the corridor. The door to Miss Teskey's office was closed and, as I found when I tried the handle, locked. So much for my plans to search without the watchful eye of the manager.

He was at my shoulder by the time I turned around. "I was searching for the spare set of keys while you were talking with the girls, but nobody seems to know where we keep them."

"You haven't been in here, then?" Perhaps luck was with me, after all.

He laughed. "Doors and doorframes are expensive items, Lady Harleigh. I don't break them down without first determining if I must. Even though I couldn't find the duplicate, I held off in the hope that you had Irena's key."

His expression gave nothing away, which didn't necessarily mean he was telling me the truth. In his business, people lied for a living. If he was lying, I couldn't discern it. Either he hadn't entered her office or he wanted us to think he hadn't. I didn't trust him, but I was inclined to reserve judgment.

I pulled her key from my bag. "I don't know if this is it or not. Shall we try?" I pushed the key into the lock and turned. It moved stiffly, but it did move. The three of us crowded in the doorway as I pushed open the door. The dull, workaday office, much like Mr. Gilliam's, came as a disappointment.

"Odd. I expected it to be more exotic." Hetty echoed my sentiments.

The office was off an interior hallway, so there were no windows. Shelves lined the far wall, behind a desk that faced the door. An electric lamp, a pencil, and a bound stack of papers, which I thought might be a script, covered the desktop. I turned on the lamp, the better to see what was on the shelves— several recent newspapers, a stack of writing paper, and a lot of dust.

Behind me, Gilliam stepped up to the desk and thumbed through the papers. "Well," he said, "it seems she actually was attempting to learn her lines."

"Her colleagues don't seem to think much of her talent," I said, turning back to the desk.

He smirked. "I'd wager it was Sally who gave you that impression." At my nod, he continued. "Sally had the lead in this production, but when Irena came along, I had to give it to her." He blew out a breath. "For obvious reasons."

"Otherwise, you'd be short one investor?"

"Exactly. I hate when people put conditions on their money, but at the time, I thought she had at least a bit of talent."

Hetty pulled the chair from behind the desk around to the front and seated herself. "Did you actually see her perform when you were in Paris?"

"I did." He took a few steps toward Hetty. "It was a small role, and she performed it well. I found out too late that the more lines she had, the worse she performed. It's bad enough having to feed an actor his lines, but Irena would panic when she forgot one. She'd lose her connection to the character and, in turn, to the audience. The performance would slowly fall to pieces. It was a difficult thing to witness."

I casually ran my fingers over the desktop. Since there had been nothing of import at her hotel or in her dressing table, this was the last place to search. But I felt that as soon as I opened the drawers, Gilliam would be looking over my shoulder again. As if Hetty sensed this, she kept him talking—and facing away from me.

"Miss Cooper seemed to think all she had to do was wait, and eventually, you'd have no choice but to put her back in the leading role." Hetty made the statement sound like a question.

"She was hoping for that, but she might have had a long wait. Irena was adamant about the acting part of our agreement."

"But if you didn't replace her, you would surely begin to lose revenues. Patrons don't want to buy a ticket for a shoddy performance. Don't you think even Miss Teskey would have seen that, eventually?"

"I'm not so sure. She craved an audience." He paused. "No, not just any audience, an adoring one. Maybe after some time, she would have seen that they did not adore her, but for now, she was willing to pay me for the privilege of a stage on which to perform."

Hetty sighed. "That's unfortunate. One always hopes that business partners are of the same mind. In your case, the two of you were working at cross-purposes."

My aunt, with her usual flair for business, had identified the professional issues Mr. Gilliam and Miss Teskey had faced. Their conversation had me wondering if Gilliam had given up on waiting for his partner to come around to his way of thinking. He had an insurance policy on her life. She was causing unrest among his cast and costing him money in the form of lost revenue. Might he not be better off with Miss Teskey out of his life?

As they were deep in conversation and ignoring me, I took

the opportunity to slide open the center drawer of the desk. The first thing I saw was an account book with a sheet of blank bank drafts tucked inside. Leaving it in the drawer, I turned back the leather cover and goggled at the numbers on the page. The woman was as wealthy as a robber baron. Or the average Romanov, I supposed. Unsure if I'd made any noise when I saw this, like a gasp or a choking sound, I glanced at my companions. They paid me no heed.

So, Miss Teskey was worth a great deal of money. What did that mean? Bradmore couldn't have known, or he'd never have asked for a divorce. Or, as her husband, would he inherit her wealth? That complicated the matter. I shook my head and pushed the problem aside. Right now, I needed to dig a little deeper into this drawer. I composed myself and took another peek at Mr. Gilliam and Hetty.

"I don't suppose you'd be open to an investment in my little theater venture, would you, Mrs. Chesney?"

Hetty visibly drew back from the man. "I make it a habit to invest only in business I understand, sir. I know nothing about the theater."

"But you did mention your interest, Aunt Hetty." Her expression of shock said she wasn't following me. "Don't you recall, at the interval, you said you'd love to understand the working of the theater."

"Perhaps I did. That doesn't mean I intend to invest in one." She threw me a glare, which I answered with a bob of my head toward Gilliam.

"I'd be delighted to take you for a tour at any time, ma'am," he said. "Obviously, I'm in need of a new partner, and I'd consider myself lucky indeed to find one so knowledgeable as you, but I promise not to pressure you to make any decisions. I'd be grateful if you'd just consider it."

As Gilliam faced Hetty, he couldn't see me frantically nodding at her. She flashed me a scowl but twisted it into a smile for the man. "Very well, sir. As long as you have no expectations of me, I'll be happy to let you try to convince me to invest in your theater. But you should know I am no easy mark."

"That's all I can ask," he said. "Let me just fetch my schedule so I may take you around at your earliest convenience." With no further thought of Miss Teskey, he dashed out of the office, leaving me alone with my furious aunt.

"You know I don't want to invest in a theater."

"Before you rail at me, you must see this." I handed her the account book. "And it's not as if you have to go through with it. You can always send word to him later that you've changed your mind, but for the moment, I needed a distraction."

"Well, I'm not sure I want to be a distraction, either . . ." Her words trailed off as she took in the numbers. "That's quite a healthy bank balance." She returned the book to the desktop and watched while I rummaged through the drawer. "I hadn't expected her to be so well off."

"Neither did I. It looks like Alexei didn't stint on her allowance." I found two sheets of thick paper folded and wedged in the back. With a little force, I pulled them free. "At least I assume that's where the money came from. She wouldn't earn that much acting."

"What are you looking for?"

"The letters, of course. And I think I've found them." Sure enough, a brief perusal was all it took to see the words *Leave London*. "Watch for Gilliam, will you? I want to read these, and I don't want him to see them."

"Why not?"

"He might be their author."

She scurried over to the open door. "You should slip them in your coat. He'll be right back."

"They're evidence. I can't take them."

"He's coming." She made a shooing motion. "Just take them. We can turn them over to Delaney later. If you leave them here, they may disappear."

I pushed the drawer closed with my hip and, against my better judgment, stuffed the account book and the letters into a pocket of my coat, which I hung over my arm. Thank goodness Gilliam was brimming over with excitement at the prospect of Hetty's money, or he'd have seen the guilt on our faces. He headed straight to her.

"If you have some free time tomorrow, around noon, I can make myself available to show you around the place. I'd be happy to share my plans for the theater, the financials, whatever you require."

Hetty threw me a glance, and I pressed my hands together in prayer. Resigned to her fate, she forced a tight smile and managed to make him believe she was enthusiastic about the idea. Good on her. I rounded the desk and took her by the arm.

"Thank you for allowing us to search Miss Teskey's office. A wild-goose chase, I'm afraid."

"That's a shame. Perhaps she destroyed the letters."

"I suppose that's a possibility, but I feel better for having looked at least. Now, we've taken enough of your time, so we'll be on our way."

He nodded. "Let me see you out and find a cab."

As it happened, a cab was rolling down the street out front as we left the theater. Gilliam hailed it, and we waited for it to approach.

"May I assist you with your coat?" I felt it slide from my arm into his hands and snatched it back.

"No, thank you. I'm fine. A rather warm evening." I willed myself not to shiver as I gave the driver my direction and allowed Gilliam to hand us into the cab. The door had barely closed behind us before we were off.

Hetty blew out a breath. "My word, I've never been so nervous."

"You played your part well, I must say."

She rewarded me with a beaming smile.

"Do be careful around that man, though. He has more

charm than the average Englishman. Perhaps from living in France. In fact, you might want to send a note tomorrow morning to cancel."

"Are you suspicious of him?"

"He was surprisingly willing to allow us to investigate. Willing enough to make me wonder if he expects us to make a hash of it and make things more difficult for the police. And he does have an insurance policy on her life."

Hetty shook her head. "That's not so very unusual among business partners, but you make a good point."

I dug into my pocket and removed the letters. Far too dark to read them now, but at least I could put on my coat. I shimmied around, hunting for my other sleeve, until Hetty assisted me.

"I thought you were too warm?"

"That was for Mr. Gilliam's sake. If he'd taken hold of my coat, he'd have felt the account book."

"When did you become so cunning? I don't know whether to be shocked or proud."

It was very late when the cab dropped us off at my door, so I was surprised to find George waiting in my drawing room, sipping a glass of whiskey and reading the *Times*. Hetty claimed exhaustion and retired to her room, leaving the two of us alone for the first time in what felt like days but was actually just early this afternoon. Given all that had happened since then, I doubted this would be a romantic interlude.

I joined him on the sofa and turned to drop a kiss on his lips.

"Bradmore's done a bunk," he said, his words more growling than conversational.

Yes. Well, romance would have to wait. "Are you sure? Were his rooms cleared out, or was he just not at home?"

"It turns out he has not been at home for weeks. Someone else lives there now and has no idea where Bradmore might have taken himself off to."

"Yet he said Miss Teskey abandoned him."

George raised his brows.

"He claimed he kept up a correspondence with her until she ceased to write. When he traveled to her former home, she'd moved on, and he couldn't find her. It sounds as though he did the same thing. Did you look anywhere else for him?"

"I looked everywhere else for him." He placed his glass on the table and rubbed his eyes with the heels of his hands. "As my search turned up nothing, I stopped at the Home Office, hoping to call in a favor—to no avail. Apparently, Bradmore did not inform his superiors of his change of residence. When I explained my problem, my contact offered to put me in touch with a gentleman who keeps a close eye on the Russians."

I frowned. "What purpose would that serve?"

"Probably none. He ought to be able to tell me about Irena's relationship with the Romanov family, though." He shrugged. "I suppose there's a remote possibility one of them might be tired of her antics or of supporting her. And at the moment, I'll take all the information I can get. I put the meeting off for a couple of days, thinking Bradmore will turn up on his own before that."

"Did you consider that he might be at his uncle's estate in Hampshire?"

"I did, and toward finding out, I paid a visit to Lady Esther."

"You poor dear." Lady Esther was Bradmore's aunt, and one of the most peevish women I've ever tried to avoid. "Did she know where he was?"

"No, but she gave me an interesting piece of news." He tipped his head to look me in the eye. "Bradmore is not just hoping to marry. She believes he has already proposed marriage to—I'll quote her here—a prominent young woman in society."

"He really needed that divorce." I shook my head. "This isn't looking very good for him."

"Yes, that's my opinion, as well, but looking at the situation from Delaney's perspective, it doesn't look any better for either of us."

"How so?"

"He only has our word that Bradmore was ever here, let alone that he was married to Irena."

I gave the matter some thought. "He has our word and that of the servants, who will state that not only was Bradmore here, but he also called on Miss Teskey just before she ended up dead in my garden. Since the man has now vanished, that should be enough to make Delaney suspicious."

"But until he finds Bradmore, it's not enough to remove us from suspicion." He picked up his glass and took another sip. "And speaking of suspicion, where did you and your aunt Hetty get off to? I thought you intended to stay home and sort through Irena's belongings."

"We did." I gave his shoulder a nudge. "Your plan to keep us occupied and out of your way worked." I told him about the key and the calling card I found in Miss Teskey's coat pocket that had led us to the Hanover.

His face grew more concerned as my story unfolded. "You mistook my point. It was not to keep you out of my way but to keep you out of trouble. Gad, Frances, what if the murderer was one of the theater crew? And in you waltz, on your own, asking a lot of intrusive questions."

"First of all, I wasn't waltzing."

"You know what I mean."

"I do, and you should know I'm not so foolish as to go there alone. I took Aunt Hetty with me."

He raised his brows. "I gathered that much since you returned together, but I don't count her as protection."

"As it turned out, she wasn't my best choice. She let slip a considerable amount of information. When Delaney interviews them, he's bound to learn I was there." I gave him a sheepish smile, which did nothing to improve his humor. "But mistakes aside, I did learn a few things."

"Such as?"

"There are two people at the theater who had a reason to want her out of the way." I told him about the actress Sally Cooper, who, if not for Miss Teskey, would be playing the leading roles, and about the owner, who would be selling far more tickets. "Mr. Gilliam has an insurance policy on her life," I added.

"Really? I wonder if that's normal for partnerships?"

"Aunt Hetty thought it wasn't uncommon, but with Miss Teskey dead, he no longer has to deal with a troublesome partner, yet he'll still have the money she provided."

"The best of everything. I wonder how Irena came by the money to buy herself a partnership."

"Her father, I assume."

"You suppose he gave her that much?"

"That much and more. I found her account book. She's very wealthy, which puts Bradmore in a suspicious light. As her husband, I'd say her wealth gives him a good motive for murder. He would inherit, wouldn't he? I mean assuming he got away with her murder."

"Under most circumstances, the husband would inherit, yes." His mood seemed to have brightened with this news. "I'm still not sure Bradmore's our man, but you've also brought two new suspects to light, and managed to come home unharmed. That's a good night's work, my dear."

"Why, thank you, but there's more."

He chuckled. "Must you always outdo me?"

I fluttered my eyelashes. "I do try. But to continue, I found the threatening letters Miss Teskey spoke of."

"Indeed? What do they say?"

"Let me get them." Hetty and I had let ourselves into the house, and I'd left my coat on the entry table. I retrieved it and pulled my cache from the pocket. My hand froze in place when I glanced up to see George beside me, staring in horror.

"Frances, why did you take these things? What were you thinking?"

"I know I should have left them, but time was short, and I had to make a quick decision. Before you scold me, you may as well review them." I handed him the account book.

He tutted as he examined the pages. "This does make Bradmore look like a profiteer."

"He admitted he expected Alexei to keep her in funds, but look at these." I pushed my coat aside and spread the letters on the entry table. The first was not particularly threatening.

You are not safe in London. Go back to France.

The second was a bit more explicit.

*Leave London immediately. What you seek
here is not worth your life!*

Both were written on expensive vellum, in black ink, with a firm, upright hand.

"Do they tell you anything?" I asked.

"Not much. It's quality paper, but any of our suspects could have purchased it. The handwriting tells me only that they weren't written by either of us." He squinted. "It almost looks like Fiona's hand."

I swatted at his arm. "Stop joking. They really offer no clues?"

"There's value in knowing they exist and weren't some figment of Irena's imagination. Otherwise, all they tell me is the person was literate and could get straight to the point. I'm surprised you didn't just read them and put them back."

"I barely had time to do more than find them while we were

in her office. I didn't want Mr. Gilliam to know, in case he was the one who wrote them." I bit my lip. "Also, I'd agreed to leave anything I found for the police."

"Which is exactly what you should have done. Delaney will surely go to the theater tomorrow, looking for the very evidence you've taken. As we're under suspicion ourselves, he's not likely to appreciate that."

I sighed. "Yes, I see now it was a bad idea, but I had to act quickly, and once the manager returned to the room, there was no changing my mind. I'd hoped I could just hand them off to Delaney."

"We don't want Delaney to know you ever had these in your possession. He'll be angry enough to learn you were there at all. We can't let him know you also walked off with evidence." He released a dramatic sigh and shook his head. "There's only one thing to do. Take everything back tonight." He flashed me a grin. "Fancy another visit to the theater?"

The Hanover Theater was shrouded in darkness when we returned a little over an hour later. George's driver let us off at the corner, and we made our way to the back of the building and the stage door. Jack was instructed to circle around the neighborhood and return for us in twenty minutes. Not a great deal of time, especially if George kept fumbling in the dark, as he was now.

"Got it." He turned the handle on the door and pushed it wide before ushering me inside.

"Goodness, you impress me to no end. I never thought you'd be able to pick that lock in the dark."

"It's all a matter of feel," he whispered as he moved in front of me. Once the door was closed again, I noticed a light coming from the end of the hallway, where it turned left just past the actresses' dressing room. Eventually, the hallway led to the stage, but I didn't know what was just around the corner.

"Her office is the first door on the left, but it looks like someone may be here." I pointed toward the light.

"It could be that someone's simply left a light burning. I've heard they do that in theaters. Regardless, let's try to get in and out without giving ourselves away."

I nodded, and we crept forward, careful of any squeaky floorboards, until we reached Miss Teskey's office. I'd neglected to lock the door when Hetty and I had left. At the time, I hadn't thought it mattered, since we had all the important material. Now I was grateful I wouldn't need to fit the key in the lock in the dim light.

We crept inside. The distant light in the hallway made the interior of the office seem even darker. George leaned in close. "I'll keep watch at the door while you return everything to its proper place. Can you see well enough?"

"Barely." I was grateful for the spare furnishings. There was nothing between me and the desk, which I found when I cracked my knee against its edge. I let out a slow hiss as I moved around the side, keeping my hand on top. It was the work of a moment to slide the center drawer open, stuff the letters in the back, and place the account book on top. I closed the drawer and tiptoed back to George.

"Don't you want to look around?" I whispered.

"I trust you've already found anything of value."

My heart swelled at this vote of confidence.

"We don't have much time left, and I'd like to spend it in Gilliam's office. You didn't have a chance to search it, did you?" he added.

"No, but do we dare? His office is that way." I nodded toward the lit end of the hallway.

"I haven't heard a peep from down the hall since we arrived," he said. "I don't believe anyone else is here." He felt for my hand and closed his fingers around it. "Come on. It's too much to resist."

Holding my breath, I followed him two more doors down the hallway. I stopped when we reached Gilliam's open door. Lights left burning. Doors left open. Gilliam's security was rather lax, in my estimation. We were closer to the light source, but it was still dark as pitch inside.

"I'll need a light to search properly. Let me find the lamp first, then be ready to close the door, so I can turn it on." He bumped into a guest chair on his way to the desk, then almost knocked the lamp over before settling it back on the desk and turning up the gas. I swung the door against the jamb, allowing just a fragment of light to escape into the hall.

I stepped over to the desk, where he leafed through a stack of papers. Miss Teskey's name jumped out at me from the print. "This must be the insurance policy he mentioned." I stopped his hand from pushing it aside.

His lip quirked upward as he scanned the document. "He will be the beneficiary of a tidy sum. If she was his financial partner, having insurance on her life doesn't seem like an outrageous act, but now that she's dead, he does look suspicious. Particularly since this is dated just a few weeks ago."

"Their partnership was only a few months older than that. Hetty didn't think the insurance policy was unusual, but it does mean he benefits from her death." An idea struck me. "Look for something with his handwriting on it, not just his signature. We could compare it with the threatening letters."

The drawer squeaked when he pulled it open. As we cringed at the noise, the office door swung open.

"Here! What are you doing?"

A charwoman stood in the doorway, holding a mop aloft, ready to strike. There was something about housekeepers and cleaning women that made them ever ready for battle. It did not do to cross one when she was poised to attack. I would never understand why our military regiments weren't staffed with them.

"Terribly sorry to disturb you." George's voice was calm and smooth. "Had we known you were still at work, we'd have let you know we were here." He raised his brows and looked as innocent as a child. "I do hope we didn't alarm you."

She gave him a smile and tucked blond curls back into her cap. Lowering the mop to her side, she dripped dirty water onto the floor. I released my breath, grateful she hadn't decided to use it as a weapon. "Not usually anyone around by this time, even me. I got a late start, but what's kept you here so long? It's gone past one."

Heavens, she thought we were actors.

George tipped his head in my direction. "Frannie here wanted to learn some new lines. The leading role might be open." He frowned. "Did you hear Irena Teskey died?"

With a gasp, she set the mophead on the floor and leaned against the handle. "No! She was a young thing. Wot happened?"

Her ease and willingness to gossip with two strangers who had absolutely no business being in the owner's office well after hours took me aback. Somehow, after a single look at us, she had managed to suss out that we were not here to steal anything or do her any harm. Amazing.

George drew a finger across his throat, and her eyes widened. "Murdered?" She leaned forward eagerly, then froze. "Not here, was it?"

"No, not here. They don't know who did it, though. Can you think of anyone here who'd want to kill her?"

She waved a hand at him and laughed. "You know I don't mix with your lot. Only see you when I'm here early. Otherwise, it's just Miss Irena and Mr. Gilliam." She narrowed her eyes and gave us a knowing nod. "But I don't think you players had much use for her. Look at you." She tipped her chin in my direction. "I bet she's not cold in her grave, and here you are, learning her lines."

I sputtered some inanities.

"Oh, I know how it is, dearie. Dog eat dog and all that. Not saying you killed her, mind."

"Thank you for that."

"But if you want the lead, you'll have to fight that Sally for it."

"Sally wanted the role, did she?" George said.

"As if you didn't know it."

He cocked a brow. "I'm just surprised you know."

"Like I said, you players are usually gone when I get here, but a few times that Sally's been here, right in this office, with Miss Irena and Mr. Gilliam. The three of 'em fighting like cats in an alley, I'm sure, wot with the shrieking and shouting. No love lost there."

"Well, Sally had better watch her step." He shot me a glance. "And we had better watch the time. Are you ready to leave?"

"Indeed. It's far later than I thought. We should be off."

The charwoman took me in with a head-to-toe glance. Her lips ticked upward. "Well, la-di-da," she said. "You might have a chance at that part, after all. Your posh talk is a lot better than Sally's."

Chapter Eleven

~⸎~

After such a long day and my late-night activities, I'd asked Bridget to let me sleep a bit longer the following morning. It still felt far too early when I heard her open the draperies. The heavy brocade had kept the room beautifully dark, and the stark light breaking through told me it must be later than my usual time.

I stretched and rolled my head in a circle to ease the stiffness in my neck. "Is it still morning, Bridget?"

"Nearly ten, my lady." She retrieved a tray she'd left by the door, and placed it on the bedside table. The aroma of coffee wafting toward me was the perfect inducement to open my eyes.

"I hesitated to let you sleep any longer. Lady Fiona already called once and said she'd be back soon."

"Fiona, so early? Did she say what she wanted?"

"No, ma'am. Only that she was going next door for breakfast with her brother, and as it's Lady Fiona, you know that won't take long."

Actually, we had much more time than Bridget suggested. It

was a well-known secret that Fiona was always reducing. Not that she was prone to putting on weight. She had a fine figure, but of course, that might be due to her endless reducing plans. But one thing known only to a select few, myself included, was that when she breakfasted at her brother's table, she made the cook proud. George would be lucky to get a scrap for himself.

As it turned out, I had time to bathe, dress, eat a light breakfast, and see Hetty off for her tour of the theater and Gilliam's accounts. I was to allow no more than two hours before calling for her, just in case the manager became too pushy.

I assumed Fiona had arrived when the bell rang, but it was followed by my housemaid, Jenny, with a telegram. As it was from my mother, I opened it with more than a little anxiety. She and Rose had been in Paris for less than two full days. What could have happened to warrant a telegram? As I unfolded it, I found the telegraph company's form appended to a second page of close writing. Though my eyes boggled at the preponderance of words, my heartbeat slowed as I read the opening.

> *Don't be alarmed, dear. Rose and I are perfectly well.*
> *We're comfortably established at the hotel and have*
> *already begun our shopping.*

I stopped reading and slumped against the chair. Well, that settled it. Mother had lost her mind. While I was relieved the purpose of this message wasn't to inform me of some tragedy or accident, didn't she realize that was what telegrams were for? At least they ought to convey information of some urgency or import. But this—I continued reading—this entire message, which must have cost her a pretty penny or, more accurately, many francs, consisted of detailed descriptions of two fabrics, both of which she adored. She planned to have one of them made up as a gown for me. *How lovely!* She couldn't decide which, so I should reply with my choice. Or I could allow Rose to choose.

As both fabrics sounded beautiful, I was perfectly content to let Rose decide. I'd just put the telegram aside when Mrs. Thompson led George and Fiona into the dining room.

It wasn't until Fiona kissed my cheek and I turned to George that I realized they both looked somewhat unsettled. I urged them to join me at the table. "What is wrong?"

Fiona slipped into a chair. George pulled one next to mine and seated himself facing me, his knees touching my legs. "Why didn't you tell me there's been talk about Irena and me?"

Flustered, I threw a glance at Fiona. "Isn't it just your maid and her brother?" I turned back to George. "The brother is a constable from Delaney's division. I told Delaney about it, and I trust he will make sure the young man doesn't mention it again."

"The story's spread farther," Fiona said. "You left the luncheon before I did yesterday. Somebody asked me if it was true Irena was George's wife." She made a painful grimace. "A Mrs. Chiswick. Rather a nobody, if you ask me, but George tells me she lives across the street."

"She's Colonel Perkins's sister, and yes, she's staying in his home while he's away." I drummed my fingers on the table. "She's a terrible gossip, and if she was invited to luncheon with the Princess of Wales, she is not a nobody."

"True, but I don't think anyone else heard her. I told her in no uncertain terms she'd been misinformed."

George scowled at his sister. "Why didn't you tell Frances?"

Fiona gaped. "This was my first opportunity. For heaven's sake, it happened less than twenty-four hours ago."

"Frances's reputation could be ruined by this rumor."

I placed a calming hand on his arm. "Don't scold her. She addressed the matter with Mrs. Chiswick, and I'm grateful she's telling me now. Once Delaney speaks with Bradmore, the story will come out that he was her husband. My reputation will be fine."

"That's assuming Delaney can find Bradmore. I'm not feeling very confident about that."

I was struck with an idea. "What if Delaney has already arrested Bradmore? Perhaps that's why you couldn't find him at the clubs."

He settled back into his chair with an expression of relief. "I hadn't considered that possibility, but we'll find out soon enough. I plan to call on the inspector this morning." He consulted his pocket watch. "Right now, in fact. If he hasn't arrested Bradmore, I'd like to see if he knows where the man has got to. And if he isn't aware of Irena's involvement with the Hanover Theater, I'll make sure he becomes aware." He raised his brows. "Plenty of suspects right there."

"There, you see? Things are not so bleak."

George came to his feet. "Meanwhile, it might be best if you stay close to home, or at least avoid any social gatherings."

I released a sigh of suffering patience, and he took my hand. "Please take this seriously. We've announced our engagement. If people start putting it about that I'm not free to marry, and you haven't denounced me, it won't go well for either of us. You have never been shunned by society, and I don't want to be the reason it happens now."

"How could I hold you responsible when you are as much a victim as I?"

"It doesn't matter. It doesn't even matter what Delaney learns about Bradmore. Until he finds Irena's killer, this is too titillating a story for people to ignore. If he doesn't find the culprit soon, society will condemn us both."

Though I felt he was taking this a bit too much to heart, I could see he was in earnest. "My only engagement is to collect

Aunt Hetty from the theater in a little over an hour. Is it possible for you to take a cab to the police precinct so I might use your carriage?"

He frowned. "Why is she there again?"

"Actually, I'm surprised she didn't cancel. I'd asked her to go along with Mr. Gilliam's obvious interest in her as a partner, so I could search Miss Teskey's desk while he checked his schedule. Who knew she'd go through with it? Perhaps she's interested in investing in the theater, after all."

"Certainly you may use the carriage, but try not to linger very long. I wouldn't want Delaney to find you there and become even more suspicious. And remember, the owner is a suspect."

"I'll attempt to be quick, but I would like to pry just a bit into those arguments between Mr. Gilliam, Miss Cooper, and Miss Teskey—" I cut myself off when he glared at me. "Fine. Only if time permits and the opportunity arises."

With an unintelligible grumble, he bid us goodbye.

Fiona visibly relaxed. As I poured each of us a cup of coffee, concern clouded her expression once more. "He's right, you know," she said. "About your reputation, that is. Only half of society will condemn George, while the other half will call him a dashing devil of a man. You, on the other hand, they will tear to shreds." Which was precisely what she proceeded to do to a slice of toast.

"Didn't you breakfast with George?"

She pulled a face. "No. He became upset when I told him about Mrs. Chiswick, and I couldn't eat with him railing at me."

My plate held only a few scraps from my own breakfast. "I'm sorry, dear. Would you like me to ring for something?"

She brushed off my concern with a flick of her fingers. I blinked as crumbs flew my way. "No, no. It's no matter. I'll just have this toast. I do hope Bradmore owns up to his responsibilities and takes you and George out of the fire."

"We don't know that he murdered her."

"I'm not worried about that. I just want him to proclaim himself as her husband." She cut her gaze toward me. "Do you consider the people at the theater more likely suspects?"

I told her about Gilliam and Sally Cooper, as well as the arguments the cleaning woman said she'd overheard. Fiona looked unimpressed. "The insurance policy might raise a few questions, but otherwise they sound like any group of people working together. My staff likely has as much motive to murder one another as these players."

"Neither of them struck me as dangerous." I paused as the truth of my words hit home. I wasn't even worried about Hetty being alone with Gilliam. "But then, I'm not interfering with their flow of income. Miss Teskey gave them both motives for murder."

She sniffed. "My money's on Bradmore, though it's odd the man she had working for her has vanished."

"Isn't it? Igor, I believe she called him. He was hired by her father as a sort of bodyguard, so you'd almost expect him to be searching for her and asking questions around the theater. He should at least have checked with the police."

Fiona gave me a pointed look. "Unless he already knows what happened to her. Perhaps Alexei has had enough of a daughter who won't stay quietly in the country and do as she's bid."

I contemplated the theory of her father as the culprit. "It didn't sound as though he bid her to do anything. Of course, I gained that impression from Irena." I paused, wondering when I'd begun thinking of her as Irena.

"Not a particularly reliable source. It sounds as though her life was a fairy tale woven from her own imagination."

"That's what the Countess de Torby implied. I don't think she has much use for Miss Teskey. She and the prince are of the opinion that Alexei should just marry her off to someone." Both of us rolled our eyes at the idea. "But as far as fabricating stories, I must admit, most of what she told me, however implausible it sounded at the time, has turned out to be true."

"I refuse to believe she and my brother were married."

"Of course not. She did marry someone who rescued her. It just wasn't George. Mr. Gilliam confirmed she was both an actress and a partner in the theater. And the fact that Alexei takes care of her indicates he is her father."

She looked doubtful. "He takes care of her?"

I shrugged. "Financially. She has quite a plump bank balance."

"Do you suppose Bradmore knew that?"

"That's difficult to say. He was worried about her father disapproving of their marriage. To me, that sounds as though he was afraid of Alexei cutting them off financially. If he knew she had independent means, why worry?"

"Will he inherit her fortune?"

"He is her husband."

Fiona raised her brows. "One hates to make a hasty judgment, but that man looks as guilty as sin."

Fiona stayed another half hour, at which time I had to excuse myself to meet Hetty at the theater. As my travels went smoothly, I arrived twenty minutes ahead of schedule. No one stopped me, so I made my way right into the theater, where the players were rehearsing. I saw no sign of Hetty or Gilliam, but as luck would have it, Sally Cooper was seated in the third row, watching the actors on the stage. She glanced up, then scowled as I slipped in next to her.

"You again."

"With all that grumbling, Miss Cooper, you're leading me to believe you don't care for my company."

She made a rude noise. "Perish the thought."

"My aunt is in some business discussions with Mr. Gilliam. I'm here to collect her." I kept my voice low so as not to disturb the performers on the stage. It was odd watching them from this angle after becoming accustomed to sitting above the stage in a box.

"They took their tour and should be in his office by now." She raised her brows. "I'm sure you know where it is."

"Left you in charge, has he?"

"Yes, and I'm afraid I'm far too occupied to chat right now. This is an audition for my previous role, and I ought to be paying attention. So, if you don't mind?"

"Of course not. I find this fascinating. I'd love to find out who will fill your shoes now that you have Miss Teskey's role." I settled into my seat. "You'll never even know I'm here."

She made that unpleasant noise again—half sigh, half growl—and came to her feet. "That will do, Caro. The rest of you, take a break." The players left the stage, except for the woman I assumed was Caro, the blond actress I'd met last night. She hovered uncertainly, but Miss Cooper paid her no heed and turned to me. "Just what do you want from me? I didn't kill Irena. I had no reason to."

"I understand the two of you had some rather loud arguments. What did you disagree about?"

She gave me a smug smile. "Her talent. She thought she could act. I disagreed. Any more questions?"

"Just one. Where were you yesterday, at about noon?"

Her eyes widened. "Are you accusing me?"

"Of course not. I'm certain you'll be able to account for your whereabouts. Won't you?" There was absolutely no reason for her to answer me. I had no authority in this matter. But the way her color heightened when she glanced around, as if seeking help, I was sure she'd attempt to come up with something.

"Caro," she said at last, latching on to the name like a lifeline, and causing the actress on the stage to jump. "We had rehearsal in the morning, and then Caro and I took a meal together during our break." She gave me a firm nod. "Then costume fittings in the afternoon."

"You see? I was sure you had nothing to do with this horrible crime. You were with Caro." I eyed the other woman. "And where was that?"

Her glance flitted from me to Miss Cooper and back. "The pub around the corner?"

"I see. Would you recommend the fare?"

"Too plain for your taste, I'd reckon," Miss Cooper said, just as the other actors returned to the stage. "If you're through here, we need to get back to work."

"And I should find my aunt. Thank you, Miss Cooper, Miss . . . Caro." I nodded at them in turn. "You've been very helpful." I slipped out of the row and made my way for the exit, certain of two things—Sally Cooper was lying, and Caro would definitely get the part.

I took a few wrong turnings but found my way to the right hallway. I passed the ladies' dressing room and heard a hearty laugh from the manager's office. When I rounded the door and popped my head inside, Hetty, wearing an enormous smile, blotted a tear with her handkerchief. At the same time, Gilliam released one of those long sighs one heaves after a bout of laughter.

Well, well. Hetty needed no rescue, after all. I tapped on the open door. "It sounds as though the two of you are getting along swimmingly," I said. "I almost hate to interrupt."

Gilliam jumped to his feet. "Lady Harleigh. Though I'm delighted to see you, I fear this means Mrs. Chesney is about to leave me." He rounded the desk and extended a hand to Hetty, who allowed him to assist her to her feet.

She looked at me, slightly bemused, as she tucked the handkerchief into her bag. "My goodness, is it time already? I apologize for running off, Mr. Gilliam, but we have that"—she rolled her hand—"thing."

"Appointment," I said at the same time. For some reason, Hetty found this amusing and smothered another laugh with a hand over her lips.

"I completely understand. You have a busy schedule, and I will simply have to content myself with seeing you again on Thursday." He delivered her to the door, where I waited, and bid us both good day.

"I look forward to it," Hetty replied.

After threading my arm through hers, I gave her a tug, and we made our way to the side exit, where the carriage awaited. "That was a friendly tête-à-tête," I said while Jack, George's driver, jumped down from his perch and lowered the steps.

"He's a friendly man." Hetty threw the words over her shoulder as she climbed inside. "And amusing, too." I seated myself next to her, then gaped as she reached for the newspaper.

"No, no, no." I pushed her hands and the paper to her lap. "I must insist on knowing what happened to the woman who reminded me three times this morning to rescue her from what would certainly be a tedious meeting and an attempt to part you from your purse."

She folded the newspaper and tucked it away, smiling, as if she had a secret. Finally, she faced me. "It turned out rather differently."

I leaned closer. "In what way?"

"Well, I found him to be an honest, intelligent businessman, with a pleasant disposition and a sharp sense of humor."

"But is he attempting to take possession of your purse?"

"I'm sure he'd like to, but I explained I'm not one for partnerships. The stock market is more in my line."

"He didn't look like a man who's given up hope."

"I gave him no reason to pin that hope on me." She shrugged. "He may not even need a partner, after all. Depending on how the investigation turns out, he may receive a payment on his insurance policy."

I narrowed my eyes. "What is to happen Thursday?"

"Thursday?"

"You both said you were looking forward to Thursday."

Hetty fussed with her gloves. "He is taking me to the Savoy for dinner."

Dinner? That complicated matters. Hetty was nobody's fool, but I'd recently had some experience with a confidence man, and it struck me that Gilliam might be playing that game. He was younger than my aunt by ten years or so. Did he plan to flatter her and woo her into a financial partnership? She'd never succumb to such tactics. But there was that smile on her face. He'd worn a rather sappy grin, as well. Perhaps this was truly a budding romance. *Interesting.* Of course, one could not forget he was a suspect in a murder investigation.

Yes, that definitely complicated matters.

"May I assume you accepted his invitation because he has an unimpeachable alibi for the time of Miss Teskey's murder? Please tell me you thought to ask him before you became so friendly."

Her head snapped around. "Of course, I did. He was in rehearsal all day. It is not the perfect alibi, because they broke for lunch for a good hour, but it sounds as though he was in the company of some person or another all day. Something Delaney can check on."

"Well, I certainly hope he does so before your dinner engagement. I'd hate to see you involved with a murderer."

"You are making far too much of a simple dinner. I won't be *involved* with him. Mr. Gilliam and I have interests in common. He is a pleasant man."

"Yes, you mentioned that."

"He has a good sense of humor."

"So you said. I could see you were clearly entertained."

"And I enjoy his company." She held up her index finger before I could speak. "I'm well aware he'd like me to make an investment, but I flatter myself that the reason he extended the invitation is that he enjoys my company."

"It appeared to me he does. I have no fear of him swindling you, Aunt. You are far too intelligent for that. My concern is that a potential murderer is attracted to you."

She choked on a laugh. "I don't flatter myself to that extent. He is far too young for me, and I'm far too old for romantic attachments." She waved a hand. "We may become friends, but nothing more."

Aunt Hetty was just fifty. Were I her age, I might feel the same. Yet it distressed me that she considered herself too old for romance. Before I could voice my opinion, she touched my shoulder and directed my gaze to the window. "Who are all those people?"

We'd just pulled up to my front door, where at least half a dozen men milled about, a few with cameras on stands, pointed at the carriage. Cameras could mean only one thing—these were "gentlemen" of the press. I stepped out when Jack opened the carriage door, and they crowded around us in a very ungentlemanly manner.

"Lady Harleigh, did you know about Mr. Hazelton's wife?"

"Did Hazelton have anything to do with her death?"

"Lady Harleigh, may we interview you for our paper?"

Wretched reporters! How had they caught wind of this news? And what would it take to make them go away?

Hetty scrambled out to the pavement and wrapped a protective arm about my shoulders. "She has nothing to say to you." She guided me swiftly to the door, where Mrs. Thompson rushed to let us inside. I took a glance around before closing the door and caught sight of Mr. Mosley from the *Daily Observer*. Perhaps he could tell me how this had come about. I caught his eye and tipped my head toward Wilton Mews. Hopefully, he'd understand and meet me there.

Hopefully, the others wouldn't.

Chapter Twelve

~⌘~

I leaned back against the door, as if those clamoring wolves outside were about to break it down. Hetty's hand shook as she gave her coat to Mrs. Thompson.

"How long have they been out there?" I asked.

"Have to be less than an hour, ma'am. That's when the first one knocked at the door and asked for you. I turned him away, of course, but if I had known they were growing and gathering out there, I'd have chased them off."

It was times like this I wished I'd employed a footman. A very large one.

The housekeeper reached for my coat, and I handed it over along with my hat and gloves. "I'll just put these away and go shoo them off, my lady."

"Thank you, Mrs. Thompson, but they seemed quite ravenous for information. I don't know if they'll leave so easily."

She turned to me in surprise. "They'll go, all right, or they'll feel the wrong side of my broom up against their heads. That should teach them not to plague a good, honest woman." With that, she stomped off, leaving Hetty and me staring at each other.

"Do you think she'll successfully chase them off?" she asked.

"I don't know, but just in case she needs assistance, would you slip next door and borrow George's footman? I have to go out to the gate and see to Mr. Mosley." I waved a hand at her inquiring gaze and headed down the hallway. "I'll explain later." Hetty had never met Mosley, but I'd worked at his paper for a short time not long ago. Well, it wasn't actually his paper, but he was the editor.

Once in the library, I had to steel myself to open the door to the back garden. The last time I'd done this, I'd found Irena's body. I hurried along the path, rubbing my hands along my arms, covered only in the fine wool of my gown. Why had I relinquished my coat and gloves? Sometimes I had no foresight at all. After turning the bolt, I opened the gate just enough to peer out. Mr. Mosley waited on the pavement, arms crossed over his chest.

"Come in, Mr. Mosley." I opened the gate wide. "In fact, come into the library. It's too cold to be chatting out here, and I'm not dressed for it."

"Good afternoon, Lady Harleigh. Thanks much. I'd be happy to warm up a bit." He glanced around the garden as he followed me to the house. "The paper said the sun would pop out today, so I wasn't expecting it to be so cold and damp."

I stood aside as we stepped through the door and waved him in. "Perhaps you should sue someone at the paper for printing false statements."

He let out a bark of laughter. "We don't make the forecasts, ma'am. We just report them. Poor sods would just do better to report clouds with a chance of rain every day. They'd have a better chance of being right." He waited for me to take a seat before settling his considerable bulk into one of the armchairs on the guest side of the desk. His brow furrowed as he took in my agitated state. "Now, what's all this about Hazelton and a wife? Didn't take him for a man to play with a woman's affections. Or her reputation, for that matter."

"You're right. He's not that sort of man. He and Miss Teskey were never married, and neither of us had anything to do with her death."

He took a labored breath and reached a hand to his head, as if to scratch it. Finding his hat instead, he yanked it off. "That's no more than I'd expect to hear from you, ma'am, but do you have any evidence?"

I blinked. "Do you have any evidence to the contrary?"

"No, but rumors don't work that way. They're just whispered from person to person, and if anyone hears it more than once, they consider it fact. People don't need any proof to decide what they believe, but if you want to change their minds, you need evidence."

Though it was lamentable, he was absolutely right. "Do you know what stage this rumor is in at the moment?"

"First whispers."

"How can I keep it from growing?"

"What really happened?"

I gave him the full story, from the moment Irena arrived on my doorstep to finding her body in the garden. "Inspector Delaney may be with Bradmore as we speak. I can't say that he murdered her, but it was he, not Hazelton, who married her."

"Do you know where to find the man?"

"I'm afraid the direction he gave to Hazelton is outdated. He no longer lives there. Delaney was eager to find him, so my best guess is the police precinct in Chelsea."

Mosley nodded. "I'll start there, but I'll take that old direction all the same. Neighbors might know a thing or two about where he went." He pressed his lips together. "I won't print a word about you or Hazelton, but in return, I'll ask that as you learn more, you'll share it with me, and only me."

I'd expected nothing less. "I have no interest in or intention of speaking to any of those other newspapermen. You may rest assured you will have your exclusive report, and I dearly hope to provide you with evidence as soon as may be."

"If the police arrest someone else for the crime, that will do, but until then, I'll thank you for keeping me up to date. I'll try to word my stories in such a way as to draw suspicion away from you. That way, the other fellows will think I know something, and they'll start nosing around other possible suspects."

"I would be forever grateful."

"You're doing me the favor, ma'am, so I'll do my best to help you, but keep in mind, misdirection will throw them off the scent only for so long. A few days at most. I hope the police will make an arrest or you'll have some solid evidence before then."

"You can't wish it any more than I, Mr. Mosley."

I let Mosley out the gate to Wilton Mews and plodded back to the house. How could one ugly rumor cause so much trouble? Back in the library, I rolled my shoulders and checked my hair in a little mirror I kept in the drawer, tucking in some loose strands. Between Mosley's misdirection and Delaney's investigation, perhaps we could quell this rumor before it took on a life of its own. I slipped the mirror back in the desk. As much as I'd like to hide here for the remainder of the day, it was time to see what was happening in the rest of the house. Perhaps Mrs. Thompson had managed to rid us of the reporters. One could hope.

I found Hetty in the drawing room, peeking out at the street from the window.

"Have they gone?"

She threw a glance at me over her shoulder. "Oh, yes. Mrs. Thompson sent them scattering." She let the curtain fall and joined me on the sofa. "She was quite ferocious with that broom of hers, but I doubt they'd have done more than fall back if Hazelton's footman, Frederick, hadn't arrived and posted himself outside the door. With his arms crossed over his chest and a deadly look in his eye, he intimidated the lot of them."

"Good. With any luck, we won't see them again."

"Reporters weren't the only ones out there. That butler from across the way was peering from around the service door, then stepped right out and goggled while Mrs. Thompson chased the reporters off."

"The man is such a nosy parker." I pressed my fingers to my forehead. "But I can hardly blame him. We are certainly putting on a fine show for our neighbors. He will undoubtedly report it to Mrs. Chiswick, and then who knows how far the story will spread? Hopefully, Mosley can contain the gossip." I told her about my arrangement with the newspaperman.

"Sounds a bit like extortion to me. As long as you provide him with exclusive tips and ultimately the whole story, he'll print nonsense to lead his readers and the other publications in the wrong direction. Is that about it?"

"Extortion implies that I'm not willing. As for nonsense, if Mosley's story is based on information I've given him, he'll be more likely to print the truth than any of the other reporters. They just want a sensational story. It doesn't matter if it's factual. Mosley's doing me a favor."

"And selling newspapers at the same time."

The sound of voices outside kept me from arguing with her about Mosley's motives. "Another reporter, do you think?"

"I doubt it," she said. "Not with Frederick at the door."

We were not left in the dark for long. George's footman

tapped on the drawing room door before opening it a crack and squeezing his enormous bulk inside. "The Earl of Harleigh to see you, my lady. Are you at home?"

Bother. What could Graham want? I glanced at Hetty.

"One would assume it's important, since he didn't send a message first," she said.

"Send him in," I said to the footman. "And thank you for assisting us today."

He flashed me a grin and slipped out, to be replaced with the more compact form of my brother-in-law, the Earl of Harleigh. Though next to Frederick, anyone would appear small. Graham was roughly my height, putting him at about average for a man. *Average* was actually a good word for him. His hair was somewhere between light brown and dark blond. His eyes were brownish; skin was fairish. If he'd had the inclination, his looks would have made him a good spy. Nothing particularly stood out. In fact, it took a few minutes for me to notice he'd grown a mustache.

He chose to forgo the usual pleasantries in favor of a simple nod to each of us and seated himself in the chair closest to me. "I came as soon as I heard," he said.

Hetty and I exchanged a glance. "What exactly did you hear?" I asked.

"What did I hear?" He gaped in astonishment. "Why, that Hazelton's wife surfaced a few days ago and was subsequently murdered. Of course, the paper didn't dare mention you, but everyone who knows of your engagement can have nothing but sympathy for how you were duped."

I narrowed my eyes, somehow thinking if I focused harder on him, what he was saying would make sense.

Hetty took a more direct approach. "Duped? What are you going on about? In what way was Frances duped?"

He leaned forward, as if the problem was that we simply

couldn't hear him. "By Hazelton, of course. But she was hardly alone. We were all under the impression he was free to marry."

"For heaven's sake, you read that in the newspaper?" she asked. "And you believed it?"

He backed off, as if affronted. "Well, yes. Why shouldn't I?"

This was worse than I'd feared. How could any reputable newspaper have gone to print with this story without any sort of confirmation from Hazelton or me? "What paper was it, Graham? You didn't happen to bring it with you by chance?"

"Are you quite serious? I burned the dratted thing." He frowned. "Not sure where I saw it. I take the *Times* and the *Gazette* in the morning, but it might have been last night's paper."

I rose and stepped over to the card table, where the afternoon papers waited. "Thank you for your outrage on my behalf, but it would have been good to know whom I needed to contact to file a complaint."

"You can't think to contact any of them." He followed me to the table. "Newspaper people are a dodgy lot, scurrilous liars every one of them."

I wondered what he'd think if he knew I'd been one of them for a short time. He'd probably disown me. A tempting possibility. Leafing through the pages of one of the papers, I glanced at him over my shoulder. "If you consider them all scurrilous liars, why would you believe them when they wrote such nonsense about Hazelton? He was never married to Miss Teskey, and he had nothing to do with her murder."

"Loyalty will not serve you well in this, Frances."

"For goodness' sake." Hetty stalked over to us, shaking a finger at Graham. "It has nothing to do with loyalty. It has to do with truth."

He blinked. "It isn't true?"

"Not a word," I said. "And I'm terribly disappointed that

you would so easily believe Hazelton to be a scoundrel and me a fool."

Graham drew himself up, regrouping for another attack. "They couldn't have made up the story in its entirety. There must be some thread of truth."

I gave up on finding the right paper and herded both of them back to the sofa and chairs. "There really is a Miss Teskey," I said. "She did have an acquaintance with Hazelton, but she was actually married to a gentleman named Bradmore."

"Why hasn't this chap come forward?"

"Bradmore came forward to us. We passed on the information to Inspector Delaney, who I hope will soon confirm it with the man himself."

"Was the woman really murdered?"

"Sadly, that part of the story is true. She was strangled in the back garden."

"Here?" His voice rose to a shriek. "In your garden? What was she doing here?"

Goodness, I was really mucking this up. "She was staying with me as she had nowhere to go."

"One presumes she had a home. Why didn't she go there?"

"She'd received some threatening letters and asked Hazelton to investigate them. Until then, she was afraid to go home."

"Why on earth did she ask him? Why not her husband? Why not the police?"

"It is somewhat complicated, Graham. She couldn't produce the letters, and she didn't know Bradmore was her husband at the time."

"She didn't—" He gaped. "How is that possible?"

"I will never be able to tell this story properly if you keep shouting questions at me. Forget all the whys for the moment. Here are the facts." I proceeded to give him the details of the past two days. "Inspector Delaney is investigating and looking for Bradmore," I continued. "As soon as he is able to say publicly that he was her husband, there will be no more gossip."

Hetty was giving me a dubious look, and Graham shook his head the whole time I was speaking. "The newspaper report made much more sense," he said.

"I'm afraid the truth often makes little sense."

Graham lowered his gaze and drew a deep breath. "Do you have any idea when the police or Mr. Bradmore will come forward with the truth?"

"Soon, I hope, but I'm afraid I don't know."

"It may be wise for you to retire from society until they do," he said.

"Hide, do you mean? Won't that make it appear as though I believe the rumors?"

"Perhaps, but it will also take you out of the line of fire. Society hates a vacuum. In the absence of facts, everyone trusts the rumor. Then they repeat it and elaborate on it. I don't think you're aware of how ugly this story could become."

"It will do so even if I'm at home, hiding."

"People will whisper behind your back, to be sure, but that's just gossip. It's relatively harmless. They can always deny later that they ever put any stock in it. But if you appear in public, they will assume you are throwing your scandalous behavior right in their faces. They will stop whispering and will freeze you out. Many will have nothing further to do with you. It's very difficult to recover one's reputation once that happens."

I knew his advice was sound, but it felt so cowardly. "But don't I have to choose a side? I am not the subject of this scandal, just an object. If I don't show my loyalty to Hazelton, won't I be adding fuel to the fire?"

"Possibly, but he is a grown man and can take care of himself. I'm not worried about his reputation. He's not likely to receive the nastiest edge of society's scorn."

"Why should I receive it? I did nothing wrong."

"You were engaged to a married man."

"I am still engaged to him, and he is not married."

Graham placed a hand to his forehead. "They"—he waved vaguely at the outer wall—"do not know that. Until they do, you should not go out in society, or they will push you to disavow him. If you do go out in his company, they will think you have no morals, and their anger will fuel their suspicion that Hazelton murdered the woman."

"But the people who know us—"

"Will be forced to choose a side." He was looking at me, not unkindly. In fact, this might be the most compassion I'd ever seen Graham show—surprising in this situation. If my reputation suffered, so would his. We were family, after all.

Hetty, sitting next to me, gave me a nudge. I looked up to see George in the doorway, Frederick beside him.

"Mr. Hazelton, ma'am." The footman intoned the words and backed away.

"Sorry to intrude," George said as he stepped forward. I could see from the shadows in his expression, he'd overheard some of our conversation.

Graham realized it, too. He came to his feet and offered his hand. "Apologies if I've offended, old chap, but I'm only looking after Frances's interests."

George shook his hand. "I understand, and I can't argue with your advice."

"I can," I said, feeling oddly as if George had betrayed me.

"Then I shall leave it to Hazelton to convince you and be on my way. I do wish you the best, Frances, whatever happens." He took his leave, closing the drawing room doors behind him.

I turned to George. "Please tell me Bradmore has made a full confession to Delaney."

"I'm afraid not. Delaney has been no more successful in locating him than we were. Well, he managed to find his latest lodgings, but no sign of the man himself."

Hetty rose. "I should leave the two of you to discuss this together." She reached out and squeezed my shoulder. "Whatever you choose to do, I will stand beside you."

I watched her leave, wondering what would happen next. "I don't think it will be quite as bad as Graham describes."

George settled in next to me. "I think it will be every bit as bad, if not worse."

I looped my arm through his and dropped my head on his shoulder. "No, no, no. I will not allow you to sink into despair. Bradmore running off must make him look much more guilty to Delaney than you ever did."

"It certainly makes him look guilty to me. Hard to believe he might have killed her."

"He had the opportunity, but I suggest we find him before we jump to any conclusions. Mr. Gilliam didn't have much of an alibi, and Miss Cooper's was a complete fabrication." I told him what Hetty and I had learned at the theater today.

"Delaney was headed there when I left him. He should be able to sort out the alibis, find the threatening notes and the insurance policy. I'm glad we were able to put them back, as he warned me against interfering in his investigation. He reminded me that I'm a suspect, and it wouldn't look good if I were thought to be tampering with evidence."

"I'm relieved he didn't catch me there today, but I'm sure someone will mention my visit."

"You don't carry the taint I do. I just hope that charwoman doesn't mention the two actors she chatted with last night."

"With the gossip rising, he can hardly expect us to sit quietly at home. The least he can do is report that there are other suspects." That reminded me of Mr. Mosley, and I told George about my arrangement with him.

"Frederick told me he was assigned to chase away any reporters. I'm sorry they were here pestering you."

"It's not your fault. And you should know I don't subscribe to Graham's opinion of hiding in the house until this is all over. If Mosley prints a story suggesting there are other suspects, no one in his right mind would believe it was you who murdered her."

"Right minded or not, there are plenty of people who will believe it was me."

"Then they are fools, and I refuse to allow them to dictate my actions or rule my life. Besides, the fact that I am seen in society with you should tell everyone it's a lot of nonsense."

"I can't agree with you there. Those same fools can ruin your life. For now, let's wait and see what the *Daily Observer* reports. If Mosley can help exonerate me in the public eye, then perhaps your reputation will be safe. If not, we shall have this discussion again." He cocked a brow. "Are we in agreement?"

"I agree we can have this discussion again, but not that I will change my mind. In fact, I'm supposed to be informing Mosley of any progress in the investigations. Should I tell him about Bradmore running off?"

"I hate to point a finger at a man who may be innocent."

"But running off is rather damning. He was in the middle of a crisis. He needed a divorce, and he needed it soon. Then his wife is murdered, and he disappears. Should we assume he suddenly remembered a pressing engagement?"

"My point is though he looks guilty, we have nothing concrete. We need more information, or we will just be providing Mosley with gossip to circulate. The fact that it's gossip about Bradmore rather than me doesn't make it better."

"Point taken. How do we get more information?"

He gave me a sheepish look. "I have his new direction."

"Delaney just warned you against interfering in his investigation, yet he gave you Bradmore's direction?"

"Of course not. I took advantage of a moment alone with the file and made note of it."

I sat back and stared at him. "Am I to understand you are contemplating searching Bradmore's lodgings?"

"I'd have to be awfully devious to do that, wouldn't I?"

I grinned. "Don't be so modest, dear. You'd be wonderfully devious."

Chapter Thirteen

George had the carriage brought round, and we were on our way in no time at all. In fact, it seemed far too early for my comfort. It was still daylight, not the best time for housebreaking.

"Do you intend to access Bradmore's lodgings by force, or have you a key?" I asked.

"I have nothing more than an address on Brook Street. I don't even know what type of dwelling it is, if he lives alone or with a bevy of relatives. My understanding is this residence is only lately acquired. I suspect he relocated sometime after his visit to Fairview last month."

That's where we first became acquainted with Bradmore. My sister's wedding was held at Risings, the Hazelton family home in Hampshire. We were gathered there for the festivities while Bradmore visited his aunt at Fairview, a neighboring estate. It currently belonged to his uncle, the Baron de Brook, but as Bradmore was the heir, he would one day inherit it. He gave us plenty of reason to mistrust him then, and I couldn't help but wonder just what he was up to this time.

I turned my head to see George watching me with a benign

smile on his face. "You are trying to sort this mess out, aren't you? I can see it in your eyes." He took my hand in both of his and let them rest in his lap. "Tell me, Lady Harleigh, however do you keep yourself occupied when you are not investigating crimes and chasing after suspects?"

"That does seem to be chief among our activities, doesn't it? Do you suppose if not for the criminal behavior of others, we might not be together? Are we bucking the moral assumption that nothing good can come of bad behavior?"

He held my gaze while shaking with suppressed laughter. Affronted, I tried to pull my hand away, but he held fast. Once he had gained control of himself, he raised his brows. "I live next door to you. I'm confident we'd have run into one another at some point."

"But without these challenges, we might not have become so close."

"Perhaps not so quickly, but I missed my chance with you once. I was determined that would not happen again. Now, do you intend to answer my question?"

"What do I do with myself? Well, for a while, I entertained my aunt and sister. I recently planned a wedding for said sister. Currently, I'm missing my daughter, who is enjoying a shopping trip with my mother in Paris."

"Any word from them yet?"

I chuckled. "My mother sent me the longest, most costly telegram in history, all about fabric for a gown she plans to have made for me."

"Oh? Would there be a special occasion for this gown?" He sidled closer, one finger tracing the high collar of my cloak, barely grazing my neck.

"Very special. It's for my engagement party. You see, I'm to be married." I tipped my head aside to catch his eye. "So you might want to return to your side of this seat. I daresay my fiancé would not like you sitting so close to me."

"I can guarantee you he approves." He nuzzled my ear. "He definitely approves."

Conversation was forgotten for the next few moments, until I realized the trip to Bradmore's residence likely wouldn't take long. Sensing the change in me, he pulled away, taking several pins from my hair with him. I sighed as I heard them hit the leather seat and put a hand to my hair to assess the damage. At the same time, I studied George.

"Did your question tend toward anything more than the obvious? Do you feel you don't know me well enough?"

"Not anywhere near as much as I'd like to, and I hope to spend a lifetime discovering new aspects of you."

A charming answer, but it felt incomplete. "And?"

He grinned. "Right. I believe you happen to know me all too well. I've been trying to determine what to do with myself once we are married." He caught my look of surprise and continued. "Professionally, I mean." He sighed and ran a hand through his hair. "After what happened at Risings last month, I've come to the realization that I must be more particular in the cases I choose to take." He paused. "Or perhaps not take them at all. I don't want to bring danger to you or Rose or any future Hazeltons."

What had happened at Risings was that a killer had joined us there, had laid traps that caused several injuries and even a death. I had never been so happy to see my daughter ill, but it had kept her in bed and out of danger through the worst of it. Still, I couldn't see George giving up his investigations.

"You love what you do."

"And I must do something. You and I could live off my investments, but for any of the niceties, and if we expand our family, I must work."

"Well, another little thing I do is to sponsor young ladies making their London debut. It's not particularly lucrative, but it does help. I may be sponsoring Harriet Stoke-Whitney this spring."

George blinked. "Why you?"

"Because Stoke-Whitney has threatened to banish Alicia to the country for a long stay. If I didn't agree to sponsor her, his sister would take up the task. Can you imagine her at a presentation?"

He laughed at the image I'd created. "No young lady deserves that."

"No, and Harriet is a sweet girl. It will be no hardship to help her."

"But you're also helping her mother."

I grinned. "Hard to believe, isn't it? I don't often sympathize with Alicia, but I can understand her feelings in this situation. I know what it is to be an inconvenient wife—hidden away in the country, out of sight and out of mind."

"You need never worry about that again."

"I should hope not."

"I only hope sponsoring young ladies still leaves you with some time to help me with my investigations."

I suppressed a whoop of joy. "You don't know how happy it makes me to hear you say that. I was hoping you'd let me lend a hand on occasion."

"Is there even a remote possibility I could stop you?"

The question sobered me. We were both well aware that a husband had the power to stop his wife from doing anything, just like my late husband and Arthur Stoke-Whitney. I had the greatest faith that George would not be that kind of husband. "Thank you for seeing it my way."

"As if I'd ever want to dim that light in your eyes." He chuckled as he caught me glancing out the window. "Look at you now—checking the streets, trying to determine if we're close to Bradmore's lodgings."

"The only reason you aren't doing the same is that you already know where it is."

"We should be close. The house number is near Bond Street, and I believe that's where we are right now." He took on a pensive look as he gazed at me. "I've asked Jack to set us down a few doors away from Bradmore's residence so we can walk by and observe it first. Now I'm not certain that's wise."

"It sounds like a good plan to me."

"I realize you feel strongly about this, but I'd hate for you to be the subject of any loose talk." He tipped his head toward the window. "I wasn't expecting so many people out on the street. They're just salivating for a juicy bit of gossip. You and I strolling along Brook Street could provide them with exactly the story they're looking for."

"You're right. I do feel strongly about this. I won't abandon you."

"You wouldn't be abandoning me. This isn't a social event. I'm simply walking down a street alone." He raised his hands, as if to ask, "Do I need to say more?"

I saw his point but still hated to be left out. "I brought a veil."

"Unless you brought a second one for me, that would look all the more obvious. I'm not exactly unknown, you know."

"Fine." I hated when he was right, and nearly growled the word as the driver pulled out of traffic and came to a stop. "I suppose I must wait in the carriage?"

He stared at me in mock amazement. "You mean I've won this point?"

"You had better move quickly, before I change my mind."

"I'll have Jack pull across the road from Bradmore's house, so you'll be on hand if I come to any trouble." With a quick kiss, he slipped out of the carriage and gave instructions to his driver.

I caught only a glimpse of him striding away before the carriage moved back on the street. We traveled around the block, almost making a full circle, and finally stopped across from a block of houses on Brook Street. In the short trip, I recognized several people of my acquaintance. If they had heard the rumors, then saw George and me together, they would fall over each other in an attempt to spread the word.

It took a full minute, perhaps even two, before I grew restless. I tried to take in my surroundings while staying back against the seat to avoid prying eyes. It was a reasonably broad street, with a mix of residences, clubs, and a hotel, with the shops around the corner on Regent Street, along with flocks of shoppers. There were fewer pedestrians here. One of them approached Jack, the driver. I heard him rather than saw him, as I drew back into the seat. They exchanged a few words I couldn't make out, and the man moved on.

Or so I thought. A tap on the door startled me. I looked out to see Delaney standing just outside the carriage. He did not look pleased.

"Now, how did I know I'd find you here?" he asked. "Or if I'm honest, I expected you to be in the house. I suppose that's where Hazelton is." He took a step back. "Let's check on him, shall we?"

Without allowing me to answer any of his questions, he opened the carriage door and held out a hand to help me step out. What else could I do?

"I assure you, Inspector, we have no intention of disrupting your investigation."

He took my arm and led me across the street. "As much as I appreciate your assurances, my lady, it's your actions, not your intent, that disturb me. Do you not recall my telling you to stay put?"

I had to scurry to keep up with his longer strides, wondering if my hat would stay pinned at this pace. "Of course I remember. I only thought you meant we shouldn't leave town."

"I meant stay put, which is not an invitation to break into the theater, search the offices, and question the actors."

"It didn't happen exactly that way. One thing just led to another."

We stopped at the main door to the building. Delaney thrust his hand into his coat pocket and pulled out a key on a ring. He held it up. "Observe how this works. I've been given the authority to enter this building, so I have the key. If you don't have a key, you should stay out."

I'd never felt so chastised. Nor had I ever seen him this angry, at least not with me. "You must see that Hazelton and I have a stake in this investigation. We must prove our innocence."

"Then it may surprise you to hear your actions make you appear precisely the opposite." Delaney unlocked the door and pushed it open, then turned his angry glare on me and waved me inside. I stepped around him into the building.

"It's not as if we took anything," I lied.

The building had been divided into flats. One flat per floor, with a staircase running along the left-hand wall. Delaney used the key to unlock the door to our right. He opened it and stepped inside. "Find what you were looking for, Hazelton?"

Still in the hallway, I peeked around Delaney and through the doorway into a dimly lit room with sparse furnishings. No sofa or chair before the fireplace. A single lamp in the corner, alongside a few framed paintings leaning against the wall. Bradmore might have been here only a short time, but wouldn't he have furnishings from his previous quarters? This looked like the home of someone trying to leave his past behind.

I spotted George on the far side of what must be a drawing room, seated at a desk and wearing a look of utter surprise. I raised my hands helplessly.

Delaney instructed me to take a seat in the chair next to the desk, and then he paced across the rug in front of us. "This time we got here before you. At least I believe so. This isn't your second trip, is it?"

George shook his head. Like me, I was sure he realized any explanation would only make this worse.

With a huff, Delaney came to a stop and glared at us both with his hands on his hips. "If you were anyone else, I'd have arrested you already. But there's really no point, is there? Your friends at the Home Office would come charging to your rescue. I doubt you'd be in a cell for more than a day."

He loomed over George, who appeared remarkably calm, one arm draped over the back of his chair. Delaney held up his index finger. "Once more, Hazelton. You interfere once more, and I'll take that day. At least I'll know where you are and what you're up to for twenty-four hours."

"As for you." He turned his head, and I was struck with the full intensity of his glare. "I expect you to talk sense into this man. You're not doing yourselves any favors when witnesses tell my constables they've been questioned by Lady Harleigh."

That had to be Sally Cooper, the wretch.

"Or when the charwoman describes the actors she found in Gilliam's office, and they bear a striking resemblance to you two."

"You're right, Inspector," I said. "It's much better if you arrive at the scene first."

"Keep that in mind next time. I'm probably just wasting my breath here. You can't keep your noses out of this investigation any more than I can, but try to remember that I am the only one authorized to investigate. When you get ahead of us, I have to worry that you're tampering with evidence."

"For the record, Inspector," George said, "you are not the only one authorized to investigate. And it won't be the Home Office coming to my rescue, but the Prince of Wales himself."

Delaney swung around to face George, who raised his hands helplessly. "If you hadn't told his man we'd be at the opera, he wouldn't have had the chance to ask me to investigate the threats Irena received."

"Surely he didn't expect you to investigate her murder?" De-laney's tone had changed from heated to merely peevish.

"You have only to arrest me to find out. I don't think His Royal Highness will take it kindly."

Delaney swept off his hat and ran a hand through his hair. "Well, did you find anything we missed?"

"Bradmore has a good claret in the next room."

"Let's have it, then. Lord knows I've earned it."

George gave me a wink and stepped through an open door-way. I glanced tentatively at Delaney. "You don't really believe either of us murdered her, do you?"

"I'm fairly certain you didn't, but when you or your names keep turning up in the investigation, people do begin to wonder."

George returned with an open bottle of claret in one hand and three glasses in the other. Delaney pulled up a chair, and we all used the desk as a table. Delaney finished off his drink in one long gulp.

"Whoa there, Inspector," George said, filling the glass once more. "You're hardly doing the stuff justice when you gulp it like that."

"I'm not worried about justice for a glass of wine." His gaze traveled back and forth between us. "Tell me what you think of that lot at the theater."

"That would be Lady Harleigh's report." George gave me a smile. "I never spoke to them."

Relieved Delaney wasn't slapping us in irons, I responded eagerly. "Sally Cooper and Herbert Gilliam both had motives."

"Her partner, eh? Why him?"

"As part of their agreement, Miss Teskey insisted on playing the lead role, and from all reports, she was a terrible actress. If she continued to star in the productions, the theater would never survive." I took a sip of the claret. "And I assume you found the insurance policy."

He nodded. "What about the actress?"

"Same circumstance except for the insurance. Miss Cooper had the talent and should have played the lead. Now that Miss Teskey's gone, she has the part she always deserved. She also lied about her whereabouts at the time of the murder. According to her, the only time she wasn't at the theater with the rest of the cast was when she and another actress, Caro, shared a meal at the local pub. Caro was clearly surprised to hear about that."

Delaney chuckled. "She was a little more inventive with my constable, but it was a cock-and-bull story if I ever heard one."

I felt a little better that she'd lied to the police, as well.

"We'll get to the truth eventually," Delaney continued, "but I have two problems with your suspects. They were on the other side of Mayfair from your house. They broke for lunch at a busy time of day. They had only an hour to travel across town, find Miss Teskey, strangle her, and return to the theater. And everyone in the cast agrees they were both there for the afternoon rehearsals. I'm not saying it couldn't be done, but they'd have to move quickly."

"They'd also have to know where to find her," George said.

Delaney lifted his glass in a mock toast. "That's the other problem. How would they know where she was?"

"Miss Teskey sent no messages when she was at my home, but what if one of them had been following her when she was arrested? She did say someone had been following her."

"They might have seen her arrested, but then what? Did they wait outside the precinct while constables came and went? It was a good hour before I brought her to your home. They'd have looked too conspicuous."

"Yes, and once you and Irena left in a hack, they'd have lost you," George added.

I couldn't entirely agree with either of them. The streets of London were never empty, and as theater people, they'd have known how to blend into a crowd. They might well have heard

Delaney give the direction to the driver. My theory was too weak to propose, but I wasn't ready to take Gilliam or Sally Cooper off my list.

"What about the man she mentioned?" George asked. "Igor? The one who's supposed to be a sort of bodyguard for her."

"Poor sort of bodyguard, if you ask me," Delaney said. "How did he manage to lose track of her?"

I'd forgotten about Igor. "Perhaps he didn't lose her. Maybe he was just keeping his distance."

Delaney drained his glass, then placed his hand over the top when George offered to fill it. "Bradmore's my prime suspect right now, and I have a good idea where to find him."

We both turned inquisitive eyes to him.

Delaney lifted his fuzzy brows. "I'm keeping that information to myself. That's the benefit of finally having arrived and searched this place before you. I know his whereabouts, and you don't."

"I wasn't aware you had such a cruel streak, Delaney," George said. "You dangle information in front of us, only to snatch it back."

"I can just imagine what would happen if I told you. You'd be off like a shot. But . . . ," He left a long pause. "Since the two of you are so interested in this investigation, there is something you could do." He shrugged. "Just to keep you busy and out of trouble."

"We're listening," George said. Indeed, we were on the edges of our seats.

"I'd like to find out more about her family situation. Her relationship with the Romanovs and the people who raised her. The grand duke refuses to talk with the police. Claims he has nothing to offer. If you could get some information from him, well, I might be willing to overlook this bit of housebreaking."

"I'm sure I could do that," George said. "But you don't think her father's family had anything to do with her death, do you?"

"Who can say? She was kept out of the way, in the country by a sort of foster family. She was a wealthy woman playing at being an actress. Maybe she was an embarrassment to the family."

"They aren't an easy family to embarrass, but I see what you mean. I can't promise results, but I'll have a go at it."

"Good enough." Delaney put on his hat and made as if to leave. "And if you happen to run this Igor fellow to ground, I'd like to talk with him, too."

Chapter Fourteen

❧

The next morning brought another lengthy telegram from my mother. I certainly hoped George or Hetty or perhaps my father was invested in the telegraph company. As long as Mother was in Paris, it seemed they'd do a booming business. As no one waited for a reply, I ignored the missive while Hetty and I enjoyed a peaceful breakfast.

"Ah, here's the story you were expecting from the *Daily Observer*."

I turned to Hetty with interest as she shook out and refolded the broadsheet.

"Let's see . . . The Metropolitan Police have a new suspect in the Irena Teskey murder."

"That isn't much help," I said. "Readers might just assume I'm the new suspect."

"Not as long as you remain in town, dear. It says the suspect led the police on a merry chase to the Continent."

"Much better. In fact, I quite like the idea that the culprit is no longer in London. I'll have to give Mosley my compliments. Anything else?"

Hetty scanned the paper. "It just goes on to state who Miss Teskey is. At least there's no mention of where the murder took place, or of you or Hazelton."

"That's a relief."

Hetty folded the paper and placed it next to her plate when Jenny brought in a note from George. "I'll leave you to your correspondence, dear, as I have some to attend to myself."

Since I'd finished my breakfast, I moved to the library, where I opened George's note first. It was to inform me he'd obtained an appointment with Grand Duke Michael Mikhailovich that very afternoon and to invite me to come with him. I loved that he had thought to include me. Next, I turned to the telegram.

> *Greetings, my dear, or as they say in Paris, bonjour! The weather here is rather dreary, but since I suspect yours is likely worse, I won't complain. Rose is doing well, and her French is progressing, which is fortunate for us, as everyone here speaks French. I'm aware that sounds non-sensical, but when you and I were last here, it seemed English was spoken all over Paris. That has certainly not been my experience on this trip. Whenever I request something, they look at me as if they have no idea what I'm saying. Except at Worth, of course. Rose chose the em-broidered silk for you, and it should be ready in three days. Do let me know if the engagement party has been canceled.*

I shook my head and took a sip of my coffee. Would she never give up? She'd been less than thrilled at my choice to marry a man without a title, and a third son at that, but I thought she'd come to accept George as her future son-in-law.

> *I ask because there was a disturbing piece of news in the London paper today about a woman who was*

arrested during a kerfuffle outside Marlborough House.
She identified herself as Mrs. George Hazelton. She could
not have meant our Mr. Hazelton, could she?

Blast! The last thing I needed was for Mother to get wind of this nasty rumor. I'd have to reply to this and give her the truth before she read any more London newspapers. Perhaps I could refer her to the *Observer.*

I returned to the telegram. There was one more paragraph.

> *We came across Mr. Percy Bradmore in our travels yes-*
> *terday. Do you recall he'd been staying with Hazelton's*
> *neighbor in the country last month? I invited him to dine*
> *with us this evening, but he declined. Apparently, he's*
> *here only for a brief visit. Such a charming man, and in*
> *line for a title.*

I fanned myself with the telegram until my heart returned to its normal rhythm. Thank heavens he had declined her invitation. Perhaps there was no proof Bradmore was a murderer, but I still didn't want him anywhere near my daughter.

Once I calmed down, I gave Bradmore's travels some thought. How interesting that he'd left London. Just like the story in the *Observer.* Either Mosley was prescient or he was a better reporter than I'd given him credit for. I wondered if Bradmore had told Mother his stay was to be short, or if she just assumed it. Where would he be off to next, and would Delaney catch up with him? Whatever his plans, I needed to convey this information to George.

I penned a short note to George to accept his invitation and to inform him of Bradmore's whereabouts. Then I spent the next half hour composing a telegram that would convince my mother to ignore anything she read in the papers about George. Since everything either was or would soon be resolved, I assured her the engagement party was still planned. Then, without actually calling Bradmore a murderer, I indicated he was up to some mischief and she should take every care to avoid him if they happened to cross paths again. Mother hated scandal, so my hints should keep her and Rose safely out of his way.

I was just handing the message off to Jenny to deliver for me when Mrs. Thompson stepped into the library to announce that Mrs. Stoke-Whitney had arrived. Odd to see Alicia so frequently, but perhaps there'd been a change in circumstance regarding her banishment. I had Mrs. Thompson put her in the drawing room and handed Jenny the second note, to be delivered to George as soon as may be.

As I was still dressed for morning, I debated changing my gown. It would serve Alicia right to make her wait while I did so. We were not exactly the type of friends upon which one could drop in unannounced at such an early hour. Then I felt petty and decided to greet her as I was, and even instructed Mrs. Thompson to bring tea when I met her on my way to the drawing room.

Alicia awaited me in one of the chairs at the tea table, impeccably turned out, as usual. At least I thought so until I drew closer and noted the pallor behind her rouged cheeks and the riding gloves she wore with her carriage dress.

"Good morning, Alicia. You seem a bit out of sorts today."

She raised her hands. "Do you mean these? I was in a hurry to be off this morning and couldn't wait for my maid to find the right gloves."

"I've never known you to be in a hurry. What is wrong? Has your husband not succumbed to your plans?"

"He is proving to be stubborn." She cocked her head and met my gaze with a smirk. "You seem chipper for a woman whose fiancé is the talk of the town."

I seated myself in the chair opposite hers. "I was chipper until this moment. How fortunate I am to have you to remind me of my problems."

"When last I saw you, it was my understanding you and Hazelton had this entire Miss Teskey debacle under control. But it's only grown larger and more scandalous. What do you intend to do about it?" She tapped her gloved finger on the tea table like an irate customer at a shop.

"Good heavens, Alicia. You forget yourself. How dare you come here making demands? The situation gained momentum when the poor girl was murdered. How could we have foreseen that?"

She sat back and placed a hand over her mouth, as if she was shocked, but I wasn't finished. "When did you become the arbiter of good behavior, anyway? And how is this any concern of yours?"

To my amazement, she managed to squeeze a tear from her eye that trailed down her cheek. Even Sally Cooper would envy Alicia's skill. Before I could call out her fakery, Mrs. Thompson entered with the tea things. Alicia turned her head and blotted her eyes, causing the housekeeper to cast a wary glance my way. *Lovely.* Now my housekeeper thought I had brought the woman to tears.

When Mrs. Thompson left the room, I poured the tea and handed a cup to Alicia. "I'd still like an answer to my question. How do my problems affect you?"

"Have you forgotten your promise to sponsor Harriet this spring?"

"Of course not, but I thought you were using your wiles on your husband to convince him to allow you to remain in town. Has your plan gone awry?"

She heaved a sigh and took a sip of tea. "Arthur has become as immune to my wiles as you seem to be. He's determined to send me to the country." She shook her head. "I suppose I should be grateful he's not trying to send me to a convent somewhere, but my banishment is a certain thing. Which is why your problems, as you call them, are affecting me. He has concerns about asking you to sponsor Harriet."

"Truly? He has some cheek to judge my behavior."

"That's not it, Frances. You know how he is. You and Hazelton could have murdered the woman and buried her in your garden for all he cares."

"I'm growing weary of repeating this, but we had nothing to do with her death."

She waved a hand. "That's not the point. I'm just saying as long as there was no scandal attached, he wouldn't care what you got up to. But now there is a scandal. People are whispering that Hazelton was married to Miss Teskey. How on earth did you let that get out?"

My fingers dug into the padded arm of my chair, and I must be forgiven if, just for an instant, I wished it was her neck I was squeezing. "We didn't let it get out, and unless one constable at the Chelsea precinct has a multitude of sisters in service throughout the neighborhood, my guess is *you* let it slip."

Her eyes rounded. "Me? I never engage in gossip."

"I beg to differ with you. It was you who brought her up when we were at the opera. Mr. Bradmore was standing behind you and heard you mention Miss Teskey's name. Any number of people might have overheard you."

She opened and closed her mouth several times before releasing a groan of frustration. "Well, you must do something to rein this in before it's too late."

"I assure you I'm as concerned about this scandal as you are, and we are working to put an end to it. There was a story in the *Daily Observer* this very morning indicating that the police are investigating another suspect in the case—one who is no longer in town. I happen to know Delaney is searching for the man. The truth should come out soon. Everyone will learn Hazelton wasn't her husband, and he didn't murder her. What more am I supposed to do?" I ended with my hands in the air, wondering why I was defending my actions, or lack of them, to her.

"If, after all this, your husband still doesn't want me to sponsor Harriet, then you'll simply have to find someone else," I added.

Alicia set down her cup and moved to the edge of her seat. "That's not as easy as you make it sound, Frances. No other lady in town would make any effort to assist me." She frowned. "I don't get on with other ladies at all. Not like I do with you."

Perhaps if she didn't try to entice their husbands away, they might feel more kindly toward her. "I can't imagine why," I said.

"Neither can I, but whatever the reason, you are my only hope. I cannot let Arthur's sister manage Harriet's presentation."

I'd forgotten about the presentation. *Poor Harriet.* "If you can't convince your husband, how do you suppose I can help?"

"He's much more likely to believe you than me. He'll just assume I'm telling him what he wants to hear. Sometimes that works, but not now." She made a beseeching gesture. "Please, Frances, if you'd just send him a note assuring him all will be put to rights shortly, I'm sure he'll relent."

Though I felt ridiculous pleading Alicia's case to her own husband, I agreed to do it. "As soon as I find the time. I do have my hands full at the moment. In fact, I must make myself ready for an appointment."

"I have to be going, as well. I'm to deliver an invitation to Mrs. Chiswick, and I hope to simply leave it with the butler, along with my card. If I don't make haste, I may be forced to speak with the lady herself."

"Mrs. Chiswick? Colonel Perkins's sister? The woman across the way? You are inviting her to the reception?" And Fiona had thought her a nobody.

Alicia heaved a sigh. "She's a constituent—an important one. Do you recall that ladies' society I mentioned? She's head of the regional group back in Chelmsworth. Her counterpart in London is Lady Pettipiece. She's been very vocal in support of

Arthur." She gave a weary shake of her head. "It's not likely to change anything about elections, but it should be a feather in his cap. He called on Mrs. Chiswick the other day and informed her I'd be delivering an invitation." She shrugged. "So, here I am. Are you acquainted with her?"

"As much as I care to be. She makes it her business to know everything that happens on Chester Street, and I'm sure she judges all of us as not living up to her standards. If you do happen to speak with her, for heaven's sake, don't mention anything about Miss Teskey."

"Duly noted, my dear."

She thanked me profusely as I walked her to the door. I had to feel sorry for Alicia. After all, I barely tolerated the woman, and she considered me her only female friend. Or did she? As I saw her out, I noted the lift in her spirits and wondered if it was due to having successfully manipulated me. Perhaps I wasn't immune to her wiles, after all.

George came to collect me two hours later. I'd like to say I made good use of that time, but in truth, Bridget and I spent at least an hour arguing over what constituted an appropriate ensemble for the occasion.

"You're going to Marlborough House, my lady. You might see the prince or princess. That calls for formality." Bridget pulled out the gown of her choice.

"That's practically a presentation gown," I said. "This is an early afternoon call on the grand duke. He's sure to have his own suite of rooms, and I have no expectation of seeing either of the royal highnesses. An afternoon dress will do just fine."

It took several selections to come to a compromise, but the battle was worth every minute when I saw George smiling up at me as I descended the stairs. "Every time I see you, I'm reminded of what a lucky man I am," he said, taking my hand and tucking it into his arm.

Bridget coughed from the landing above me, as if it were all her doing, and we left for the carriage.

"Did you read my note?" I asked when we set off for our meeting.

He tipped his head to the side, giving me a bemused expression. "That's another thing. How did you manage to learn where Bradmore snuck off to?"

"Did I neglect to mention that? Perhaps I should keep my source a secret."

"You are not allowed to keep secrets from me."

I chuckled. "Very well. My mother told me." I watched his brows shoot up. "She and Rose came across him somewhere on the streets of Paris. She invited him to dinner."

He drummed his fingers on the seat. "Is she still holding out hope that you'll change your mind and marry him rather than me?"

"Not that it matters, but I'm sure she'll change her mind if he ends up being charged with murder, don't you think?"

"Ordinarily, I'd say yes, but as she's so disapproving of me, she might think a murderer the lesser of two evils."

I patted his arm. "She's coming round to my way of thinking about you. She's buying me a gown for our engagement party, after all."

"She knows you're engaged to me, correct?"

I gave him a stern look. "She does. I sent her a reply and warned her I'd heard Bradmore was involved in some trouble, so she ought to keep her distance from him."

He groaned. "And I was imagining Delaney arresting the man at your mother's dinner table. How cruel of you to spoil my fun."

"I'm practicing for when we're married."

While he mulled over my words, the carriage drew up to Marlborough House, and the driver stated our business. We were greeted at the door by a steward, who guided us through the palatial halls to the Romanovs' suite. Sadly, I would have to inform Bridget that we ran into neither the prince nor the princess. The steward left us in a private sitting room where we remained standing until His Imperial Highness, Grand Duke Michael Mikhailovich joined us twenty minutes later.

He was quite tall and, with his military bearing and lean form, cut a dashing figure. His dark whiskers covered his chin in a neat V, while his hair, just beginning to sport a bit of gray, was clipped very short, giving him a pronounced widow's peak and narrowing his face. I could easily imagine him in uniform, but as he'd been stripped of his rank by the czar, that was not to be.

When he acknowledged us, George bowed and made the introductions. I executed a deep curtsy and wondered how we were to question this man while observing the protocols his status required.

I needn't have worried. He took a seat on a velvet settee and invited us to be seated. "Let us dispense with formalities," he said. "I understand you have questions for me."

"First, may I offer my condolences on the death of your cousin?" George began.

Michael Mikhailovich nodded, a smile quirking the side of his mouth. "Perhaps I should be the one offering them to you, as she claimed to be your wife." Before George could respond, he laughed and held up a hand. "I know she was mistaken. As for me, I accept your condolences on behalf of my family. Though she was my uncle's child, I haven't seen her in years."

"She resided not far from your home in Cannes." I left the question unasked.

"Yet we, the two exiles, never visited. It seems strange, now that you mention it, but it never occurred to me. Cut off from my family in Russia, I thought only of my wife and children."

"Will there be any sort of funeral service for her?" George asked.

"Her remains will be taken back to France, and the Teskeys will see to her burial. They raised her, and I understand they were close." He nodded approval of his own plan.

It seemed a rather sad plan to me. "What of her father?"

"We sent Alexei word, but he is in America, exploring the wilderness of the West. I don't know how long it will take for the news to reach him. We thought it better to proceed than to wait for his instructions."

I hoped at least the Teskeys would mourn her.

"Then let's go back to earlier days," George said. "Why did your cousin settle her in France rather than Russia?"

"You would have to ask him. I don't even know why she didn't live in England. Her mother was English."

"But her mother died."

"Yes, when Irena was born. I can only guess Alexei didn't know what to do with the child. He was only rarely in Russia himself. Since he was more frequently in France, it makes sense he would set up her household there. I know he visited her from time to time."

"So, he was fond of her?" I asked.

"Ah!" With a smile, he threw back his head and gazed at the ceiling. "You are looking for a suspect for this crime." He brought his gaze back to me and shook his head. "I have no idea how my cousin felt about his daughter. He took care of her, so one would assume . . ." He shrugged. "But Alexei is not in England, and he hasn't been here for some time. He could not have done this."

George leaned forward. "You understand why we must ask, of course. The police are investigating her murder, and they have to check every possible connection. Family is the closest of connections."

"Sadly, I am cut off from my family. There is little I can tell you of my cousin and his affairs."

"Have you any idea who her mother was?" I asked. This

earned me a look of surprise from George and a curled lip from Michael Mikhailovich, as if I were the lowest of gossips. It was all well and fine if Alexei fathered a child out of wedlock, or two, if I remembered correctly, but how crass of me to inquire about it.

"Is that important?" George asked.

"I'm not entirely certain, but through her mother, Miss Teskey was half English, and though she lived in France all her life, she suddenly arrived in England." I glanced up to find two blank faces gazing back at me. "What if she was here to find her mother's people? And what if they didn't want to be found?"

Understanding dawned in George's eyes. "The threatening letters."

"What you seek here is not worth your life," I quoted. "Go back to France."

This aside left the grand duke confused, so George explained about the threatening letters Irena had received. Though he had no knowledge of the identity of Irena's mother, he agreed to send another cable to Alexei to inquire.

"It might be faster to gain that information from his family in Russia," George suggested.

"I'd be surprised if anyone in the family can enlighten you. Alexei kept her name to himself." Michael Mikhailovich let his gaze linger on George, narrowing his eyes. "You should speak to Igor Petrov. He was close to Alexei before taking up the task of guarding Irena. He might be able to help you."

"We'd welcome a chance to speak with Mr. Petrov," George said, "but we've been unable to locate him. Do you know where he is?"

"He was here to see me just yesterday." He gave us a humorless smile. "Everyone thinks I know what is in the family's heart and mind. Ironic, is it not? I, the outcast. However, he told me where to find him. I will send him to you."

He came to his feet, and George and I followed suit. Was this interview over already? It took me longer to dress for it. I could tell George wanted to know where to find Igor Petrov, but it was clear the grand duke had no intention of telling us.

The gentlemen shook hands, and the grand duke brought my hand to his lips, fairly towering over me. Before I knew it, we were back in the hands of the steward and escorted to our carriage.

"Do you think he'll send Mr. Petrov to see you?" I asked George.

"He's left us with no choice but to wait and see."

Chapter Fifteen

George brought me home, and after he instructed Jack to stable the carriage and horses, we both retired to my drawing room. The ride home had been quiet. For my part, I had been wondering just where we were in this investigation.

"The grand duke was not much help, was he?" I took a seat at the card table and pulled out a sheet of paper and a pencil from a small hidden drawer.

George sighed and sank into the sofa. "I doubt Delaney expected much from him. Romanov wouldn't implicate his own family in a crime. However, if he sends Igor Petrov to us, I'd consider that helpful."

I jotted names in a column on the page. Bradmore, Romanov, Gilliam, Cooper. "You don't suppose Mr. Petrov might have murdered her, do you?"

"Right now, Petrov is just a shadowy figure in Irena's life. I couldn't say what he might be capable of until I learn more about him. I wouldn't rule him out, but right now, Bradmore is our best suspect. Gilliam and that actress—"

"Miss Cooper."

"Yes, her. They may have motives, but I can't see how they'd have done it."

"But . . ." I dragged out the word while I assembled my thoughts. "Miss Teskey did say someone was following her, and as she was unable to give us much of a description, it could have been Gilliam or even Miss Cooper." I looked up to see him watching me over the back of the sofa. "The threatening letters implicate them, in my opinion. At least more so than the rest of our suspects. Both of them would have been better off if she had returned to France."

The more I pondered it, the more I liked the idea. "Even if Bradmore lied when he said he didn't know where Miss Teskey was, he had no reason to write the letters. If he truly wanted a divorce, why scare her away?"

"If he was courting another woman, he certainly wouldn't want Irena to show up at some society affair and declare herself his wife."

There was no arguing with that. I let the idea of Bradmore as Miss Teskey's killer simmer for a bit. "He said he'd been trying to locate her, and he did seem genuinely surprised to find she was in London. He had a motive, he had an opportunity, but if he murdered her, I don't understand the threatening letters. I don't think they're from him."

George rubbed his head. "Who else is on your list?"

"Petrov and Romanov."

"If it was the grand duke, then he would have been taking orders from Alexei or some other member of the family. Perhaps they'd had enough of her abductions. But if Michael Mikhailovich was involved, he would not have murdered her himself. He'd have passed the order on to Igor Petrov or some other minion to carry out the dirty work."

"If Igor had been following her, as a good guard would, he might well know she ended up here. But if he killed her, why the threatening letters?"

"Perhaps the person who wrote the letters had no intention of killing her."

"'What you seek here is not worth your life' doesn't leave much room for ambiguity."

"It could be a helpful sort who is aware of the danger and wants to warn her." He stood up and strolled over to the table. "Or someone else we know nothing about."

"Like her mother's family. Perhaps Mr. Petrov can enlighten us."

"Maybe. Right now, I should send a message to Delaney to tell him what we've learned."

"That will be a short message."

"Yes, sadly." He put a hand on my shoulder. "Do you recall we have an engagement tomorrow evening?"

"Of course. The Stoke-Whitneys' reception."

"Do you still wish to go?"

I placed the pencil on the table and gave him my full attention. "This reception is the reason I didn't go to Paris with my mother and Rose. It was something of a royal command. Besides, I sent my acceptance weeks ago. How could I not attend?"

"I meant, do you still wish to go with me? I'm sure your brother-in-law would be happy to escort you."

I came to my feet and turned to face him. "Stop that. You are my fiancé, and I love you. We will face any gossip together. Besides, we will have allies there—your sister and brother-in-law will defend us. The prince and princess might come to our aid, as well. They both know you were not married to Miss Teskey. We will be fine."

"I wish I could believe that, but you seem to have a higher opinion of human nature than I do. The prince, in particular, hates to be in the presence of scandal. I don't see him coming to our defense. We could lose what little support we have if we flout the rules of society."

"And those rules say you must hide and I must disown you?"

He placed a hand on my cheek and gave me a sad smile. "I know this goes against your principles, and if we were closer to finding the murderer, I wouldn't suggest it. But as things stand, it might be best if we play the game. You need not disown me. I'll become ill and stay at home. As long as people don't see us together, we won't be adding fuel to the fire."

I leaned back to study him. He dropped his hand to my shoulder. "We'll uncover the truth soon," he said. "But in the meantime, at least for this reception, we need to keep our heads down and keep the gossip at bay."

"I don't like this one bit."

"Neither do I."

"But I do see your point, so as it's only one reception, I'll agree, but I promise you, I won't enjoy it at all."

I continued playing with my list after George left. Surely, the answer would present itself if only I could arrange the names, motives, and opportunities in the right order, rather like a puzzle. It didn't happen, and I was just about to abandon the project when someone rang the bell. I tucked the paper back into the drawer and made myself ready for a visitor.

Indeed, Mrs. Thompson opened the doors to the drawing room in a matter of minutes, but she wore a look of surprise upon seeing me. "So sorry, my lady. I didn't know you were in here."

I addressed her before she could back out. "Hasn't someone come to call?"

"Is that Lady Harleigh?" Mr. Gilliam peeked over the housekeeper's shoulder.

"Mr. Gilliam?"

"He's come to call on your aunt, my lady."

"Please let her know, Mrs. Thompson. I'll entertain the gentleman in the meantime."

Gilliam pushed forward, handing his hat and coat to Mrs. Thompson before she backed out. "That's very hospitable of you, my lady."

"Please have a seat." I directed him to one of the chairs near the tea table. "Does my aunt expect you?"

"Not at this very moment, she doesn't." Once we seated ourselves, he laced his fingers together in his lap and gave me a pleasant smile. "We have plans for tomorrow evening, and I wanted to make sure my arrangements met with her approval."

"That's right. It's Thursday, isn't it? You are taking her to dine tomorrow, and you've found time to drop by now. It's good to see you are not a slave to your theater."

His smile never wavered. "Not at all. I'm fortunate in having a good director for this production."

"Do you? I had no idea."

"Perhaps you should have brought Mr. Hazelton with you the other night, to interview the male performers and staff."

"If you recall, my intention in visiting the theater was to look for the letters Miss Teskey spoke of, not to interview—"

His eyes twinkled with amusement.

"Are you laughing at me?"

"Never, my lady. It's just that I now understand why you were so diligently investigating on Irena's behalf. It was imperative you find another suspect in order to take suspicion off yourself."

I sputtered a moment before finding my voice. "I am not a suspect in Miss Teskey's murder."

He gave me a knowing look. "The newspapers may not have mentioned you by name—they wouldn't dare unless they had absolute proof—but they did mention Hazelton. They questioned if he was Irena's husband, and mentioned the two of you are betrothed. Well, it didn't tax my brain overmuch to trace the connection from one to the other, and the line circles right around you."

"How dare you come to my home and accuse me of murder!" I came to my feet and loomed over him.

"You came to my theater and accused me of murder." Gilliam rose until we were nose to nose. "I'd say we're even—except I really don't think you did it."

"Well, I . . . What?" Once again, I saw the glimmer of mischief in his eyes.

He spread his arms wide. "I was just trying to illustrate how easy it is to implicate anyone with a connection to Irena as a suspect in her murder." He twisted his lips in a grimace. "She had a gift for pushing people too far. Though I doubt she'd gotten to you yet, you have a stake in finding the culprit if you wish to take suspicion off Hazelton."

I took a step back, watching him warily, trying to determine what game he was up to. A part of me believed he wasn't playing at all, just speaking his mind—not something I was accustomed to. Nobody of my acquaintance ever said what they actually meant. Well, close friends did, but I couldn't count Gilliam as one of those.

"I still think you were laughing at me," I said.

"Not you. Your methods, perhaps."

I raised my chin. "My time with your cast was limited, due to their eagerness to leave for home. My method was to use that time to the best advantage. I couldn't question all of you, and I knew the police would come to question everyone I'd missed." Since my goal in the first place had only been to search Miss Teskey's office, I didn't know why I was defending myself. The man could think what he wished.

He grinned. "Of course."

"Fine. Call me inept if you must. Just don't call me a murderer. Nor should you consider Hazelton one."

"Then you should do something about the newspapers. I've seen nothing new today, but yesterday they were spreading innuendo as thickly as marmalade."

"Today the *Daily Observer* indicated the police had a new and more likely suspect, someone outside of London." I returned to the sofa, watching him for a reaction.

"Did they? I don't read that paper. No theater reviews, and it seems they largely deal in gossipy, sensational stories."

"Well, that should bode well, don't you think, Frances?" Hetty said, slipping in through the half-open doors. "If they deal in gossip, one would assume all the gossips read it."

"That is the audience I'm hoping to reach."

"Did you have something to do with that article?" Gilliam examined me through one narrowed eye.

"Of course not." Hetty spoke up first, joining us at the tea table. She shooed him back to his chair and took a seat on the sofa, observing the empty table. "No tea?"

"Forgive me, Aunt Hetty. My manners must have taken their leave while Mr. Gilliam and I were accusing each other of murder."

"I'm not stopping long enough, Mrs. Chesney." Gilliam's smile for Hetty was quite tender, and I had to remind myself to be suspicious of him. "I'm not certain we agreed on a time for me to collect you. I also wanted to assure myself that you would be comfortable with our mode of transportation."

Hetty looked like a child anticipating a sweet. "Our mode of transportation? How intriguing. Are we to take bicycles?"

He chuckled. "Not bicycles. I believe the weather will be a bit too cool for that."

She lowered her eyelids and sent him a sultry glance through her lashes. "Perhaps the Underground. Doesn't that have an exotic sound to it?"

He stared at her, completely transfixed. "It does when you say it." He cleared his throat. "Do you wish another guess, or shall I tell you?"

"Oh, do tell us, Mr. Gilliam," I said.

"No, let me make one more guess." Hetty leaned back and

examined the man with a lingering gaze. "You are a man of the times. Rather an adventurous one at that. Do I dare guess that you will be collecting me in a motorcar?"

"If that is your guess, you would be correct. And it sounds as though you might just enjoy such an adventure."

Gilliam beamed. Hetty sparkled. I dearly hoped this man had not murdered Miss Teskey.

"I would enjoy it very much indeed," she said, smiling prettily.

If I remembered correctly, Hetty's opinion about motorcars was that they were completely unreliable. Of course, she also thought she was too old for romance, and that was utter rot.

While I observed their flirtations, Mrs. Thompson opened the door and nodded to me when she caught my attention.

"There's a gentleman calling for Mr. Hazelton, ma'am. I was about to send him next door but thought I might check to see if he was here first." She went on to mumble something about Mr. Hazelton popping up unannounced, probably referring to the way we traveled from one house to the other through the garden.

"He's not here at the moment, Mrs. Thompson." Then my curiosity got the better of me. "Who's calling?"

The usually stoic housekeeper scurried forward and lowered her voice. "A Mr. Petrov, ma'am. An imposing figure of a man." She lowered her voice even further. "I don't think he speaks much English. I already tried directing him next door, but he only became agitated."

Petrov! Well, now I was intrigued. "Why don't you show him in and send Jenny to fetch Mr. Hazelton. I'm sure he won't mind."

Mrs. Thompson looked relieved and returned to the hall.

"Have you met Mr. Petrov?" I asked Gilliam.

He tore his gaze from Hetty. Really, the man's infatuation could not possibly be pretense. "Petrov?" he said. "Irena's man? A time or two. Haven't seen him around lately, though I suppose that's only natural now she's gone."

He was still speaking when Mrs. Thompson brought Mr. Petrov in. I could easily see why she'd been intimidated. Like Michael Mikhailovich, he was tall, certainly over six feet, and his hair was clipped short and showed some signs of silvering, but that was where the similarities ended. His beard, a rich brown, was magnificent, covering his lower face and extending to his shirt front. And while the grand duke was lean, this man was heavily built and muscular. In other words, the perfect candidate for Irena's protector. Alexei had done well. Who would dare abduct her with Igor Petrov around?

He became even more fearsome when he lunged at Gilliam. The jovial grin vanished from the man's face, to be replaced by shock as he jumped over the back of the sofa, placing it between him and his adversary. Petrov took a step back and spat at Gilliam.

Heavens, now I'd have to have Jenny clean the sofa.

"Please, sir! I will not allow such behavior in my home." I tugged on the man's arm with both hands until he backed himself against a chair. At the same time, Hetty was apparently checking Gilliam for signs of injury—at least I think that was what she was doing. I returned my attention to the Goliath at my side.

"You!" He pointed a meaty finger at the theater owner. "You kill Irena." He spat—again.

"Mr. Petrov, if you persist in doing that, I will have to ask you to leave."

He gave me a blank stare. I had no knowledge of Russian, but I recalled the man had been residing in France. "Would you prefer to speak French?" I asked him in that language.

"*Oui*," he said and proceeded to speak at such a speed, he quickly lost Hetty. Gilliam, too, looked confused. *Wonderful.* I'd have to act as translator. Once he finished, I convinced him to sit. I faced the others.

"I doubt his dislike of you needs any translation, Mr. Gilliam, but it seems he bases his accusation on your treatment of Miss Teskey. He feels you lacked the proper respect."

"What rot! I've never disrespected a woman in my life. How dare you, sir?"

"He said the two of you argued incessantly, in raised voices."

"Yes, I suppose that's well documented." He looked a bit disgruntled by his inability to deny the charge. "Repetition didn't work with her, so I hoped increasing my volume would do the trick. She shouted right back at me. It was hardly one-sided. Our disagreements were always of a business nature, nothing personal."

I wondered if Mr. Petrov understood that Irena was a partner in the theater venture and not just an actress Gilliam argued with. I explained as best I could and asked him if he ever saw Gilliam threaten her safety in any manner. He grudgingly replied in the negative. He also slowed his speech enough for my companions to pick it up.

"Why don't you ask him where he was when Irena was murdered?" Gilliam spoke in English. "He was always at her side. He'd have known to find her here. Perhaps he's the murderer."

I stared at him. "Are you quite mad? You want me to ask this bear of a man if he's a murderer? Hetty and I just barely stopped him from tearing you apart."

Gilliam's answer was forestalled by George's arrival. He'd shown himself in, so I assumed he'd taken the garden path. Mrs. Thompson would be miffed. The smirk he wore indicated he'd heard me, but I had the last laugh when I introduced him to Mr. Petrov. His eyes rounded as the other man stood, displaying his vast proportions.

Nonetheless, he offered the giant man his hand. Personally, I'd be afraid he'd rip it off and throw it back at me. Fortunately, Mr. Petrov was more civilized than I'd given him credit for— spitting notwithstanding. The scowl remained in place, but he did shake George's hand.

"Perhaps you should take over," I said. "So far, each man has accused the other of murder, but both claims seem to be unfounded." I lowered my voice. "Neither holds the other in much regard."

George raised his brows. "And the other half of this argument is?"

"Forgive me. I'd forgotten you haven't met Mr. Gilliam. He owns the Hanover Theater. Mr. Gilliam, this is Mr. Hazelton."

The two men shook hands, and George returned to Mr. Petrov. "Why don't we start with when you first lost track of Irena?"

I stopped him with a hand on his arm. "First of all, you should speak to him in French. Mr. Petrov doesn't speak much English. And secondly, you might want to rephrase your question. It sounded too much like an accusation." I sidled up to him and lowered my voice. "He has a bit of a temper."

He replied in the same manner. "You think I'm afraid of him?"

"I think you're too intelligent to ask for trouble."

"Well, in that case." Facing Petrov he switched to French. "When did you last see Irena? How did you become separated?"

"Three days ago," the Russian said. "She asked me to collect something from her hotel room. While I was gone, she slipped off to talk to the grand duke. She knew I wouldn't approve. This was just her way to get around me. I didn't know this at the time, of course. She never came back to the hotel, so I checked at the theater and learned she'd missed the performance."

"That's confirmed by two of the actresses I spoke to the other day," I said. "They told me they saw him backstage that evening, looking for her."

"Where did you go when you left the theater?" George asked.

"There was a restaurant she frequented. I checked there. When no one had seen her, I returned to the hotel for the night.

The next day, I went to Michael Mikhailovich to ask if he'd seen her. He told me what had happened, but he didn't know where she was. I assumed the police had her. I didn't know what to do, but the grand duke told me to go back to her rooms and wait." His features softened as he glanced at me. "She was here all that time, wasn't she? Was she murdered here?"

"I'm afraid so." I glanced from Petrov to Gilliam. "Miss Teskey told me she thought someone was following her. Did either of you happen to notice anyone?"

Gilliam gave a quick denial, but Petrov grew thoughtful. "There was a man," he said. "I don't know that he was following her, but I noticed him at the hotel because I had also seen him at the theater." He gave me a close look. "Was she in danger from him?"

"We're not sure," George answered for me. "Did you get a good look at him? Was he an older man?"

"He was a bit older than me," Petrov said. "Near sixty. I saw him at night. He just looked like most of the theatergoers. He wore a hat, a coat with the collar turned up. He was built like you. What I could see of his hair was gray. He was clean shaven, with a pinched look. I would know him if I saw him again."

"Well, now that you describe him, I might have seen the same man." Gilliam spoke up from his seat next to Hetty. "Didn't think anything of it at the time. Must have been a week or more ago. A man, well dressed, aged sixty or so, bumped into me outside the theater after a performance." He glanced up at the ceiling, as if remembering the scene. "I begged his pardon, even though he was the one not watching where he was going. He took a step back and looked me over. Asked me if I was the manager, and I admitted I was. He told me I should replace my lead actress. Then he simply walked off, just like that."

Gilliam shrugged. "Can't say I disagreed with him, and he

might not be your man. But if he is, I can add that he was definitely upper class—had the tone and drawl."

"Is this man her killer?" Petrov asked, still speaking French.

George moved to the back of the sofa to pace, something he liked to do when he was pondering a problem. "Until now, I'd have said the man was a figment of Irena's imagination. Indeed, he still may be, but it is possible he's responsible for the threatening letters." He glanced across the room at me. "It's also quite possible he murdered her."

Chapter Sixteen

~⚬~

I woke the following morning feeling quite sorry for myself. I'd done nothing to bring these troubles to my door, yet they seemed to be mounting daily. Despite Inspector Delaney's warning against interfering in his investigation, George planned to return to the theater, in the hope of learning something more about the man who'd been following Miss Teskey. He'd asked both Gilliam and Petrov to look out for the man before they left my house yesterday.

Meanwhile, I was left with nothing more productive to do than to bide my time until one of them solved the mystery of who had murdered her. Worse, I had to do that without George. It just wasn't fair.

My gloomy attitude persisted while Bridget helped me ready myself for the day. What difference did it matter what I wore? I had no plans. Neither did I have any patience for conversation, and I was far too fidgety to sit still while she dressed my hair. By the time I made my way to the dining room, wearing a tea gown and my hair pulled back in a ribbon, I was thoroughly sick of myself.

I could only imagine how Bridget felt.

Hetty had already left on some errand, so I broke my fast alone. I poured a cup of coffee and thumbed through the post. Nothing of particular interest except a note from Mosley, asking for further information. Unfortunately, I had nothing to provide him. I should send a message to Graham, asking if he'd escort me to the reception this evening, but I couldn't bring myself to do it. I wanted to attend with George, not Graham.

Just as I was bemoaning the absence of a telegram from my mother, I took myself in hand. Enough was enough. I was in danger of drowning in all my self-pity. Perhaps there was nothing I could do at this very moment to move this investigation forward, but I had to do something to relieve my mind of its current misery before I went completely mad.

Fiona was the only person I could call on so early, and without warning, so my decision was easy. I returned to my bedchamber and rang for Bridget. Fortunately, she was understanding of my earlier ill temper. She was so eager to move me on my way, I found myself in a hired hackney within the hour, and in Fiona's drawing room a mere twenty minutes later. Fiona joined me just as a maid brought in the tea service.

She was still dressed for a morning at home, as I had been an hour ago. After a hug, she looked me up and down. "Would you prefer coffee? You seem a bit out of sorts."

I assured her tea would be fine, and we seated ourselves at either end of the sofa.

"Trouble with the investigation?" she asked.

"We're at an impasse at the moment. Delaney has located Bradmore and gone to fetch him, and he warned George and me to stay away from the investigation. Of course, George thinks that order applies only to me, so he's gone to the theater to ask more questions." Her eyes filled with sympathy, and I succumbed. "The worst part is he has decided to cry off the Stoke-Whitney reception, and I am to attend with Graham."

"Oh, my dear." She reached across the sofa and squeezed my hand. "I understand how galling that must be, but he is only trying to protect your reputation."

"It just feels like we're giving up and letting society dictate our actions."

"It's awful, and it's wrong. Usually, I would be in favor of directly confronting those who would judge you."

"I knew you'd see it my way."

"But not this time." She averted her gaze. "In this case, I fear the scandal about my brother and Miss Teskey has already grown roots."

"Have you heard something new?"

"In a manner of speaking. I've been meaning to talk to you about your engagement party." She gave me a tentative glance, her fingers fidgeting with her pendant. "I've received nothing but regrets in the past two days."

Her eyes held so much misery, I wanted to console her. "Poor Fi. I've been so wrapped up in finding Miss Teskey's killer, I hadn't even thought of the engagement party. Of course people are sending their regrets. If they believe George already murdered one wife, it's no wonder they hesitate to celebrate our engagement. Should we cancel it?"

Fiona took me in with a glance. "I think you're taking this far too lightly."

Her sharp tone came as a surprise. "Forgive me, dear. I know you've gone to a great deal of trouble, but right now the opinion of a handful of society matrons matters less to me than the opinion of Inspector Delaney."

She waved a hand. "My trouble has nothing to do with it. The opinions of those society matrons matter a great deal. They will determine what sort of life you and George will have in the future. Whether you're accepted or isolated. And that will be true for Rose and any future children."

"Fiona, you are not cheering me up."

"I'm hoping to wake you up. If you plan to be part of London society, you must play by its rules."

"I understand, but appeasing a lot of gossips is not a priority at the moment. I won't have any part in society if George finds himself in Newgate Prison."

She scoffed. "Surely it isn't that bad? Didn't you say Delaney's coming back with Bradmore?"

"That doesn't mean he's the murderer."

"But he might have more information, don't you think?"

"I certainly hope he does. Information seems to be our biggest stumbling block. We know virtually nothing about Miss Teskey, except that anyone she came into contact with for more than a day had a motive to murder her. Even her husband spent only a few days with her, so I don't know how he can enlighten us."

Fiona poured more tea as I pondered this. Miss Teskey had actually given me a great deal of information about herself, most of which I had discounted as nonsense. What if the key to finding her killer was somehow tied up in the complicated story of her life? Perhaps we weren't at an impasse, after all. If I could reconstruct the woman's story, it might lead me to the author of the threatening letters or the person who had been following her.

I felt a glimmer of hope.

"I'm confident everything will be resolved in time for the engagement party." Fiona gave me a crooked smile. "But until then, I have to agree with my brother. It's best if you aren't seen together. I wonder that you haven't heard from the Stoke-Whitneys—some discreet suggestion that you might prefer to stay home this evening."

"Indeed?" I raised my brows. "Arthur Stoke-Whitney should welcome us with open arms. If his guests are talking about George and me, they won't be talking about Alicia's latest indiscretion."

Fiona chuckled. "You make a good point, but right now, I think it's best if you don't give the gossips anything to talk about."

If she continued, I didn't hear her. Her last words had given birth to an idea. The more I considered it, the more I liked it. Yes, I could go to the reception with Graham, and George could stay home. The gossips would still talk. But what if I could give them something different to talk about? Could I take charge of the gossip? Perhaps. But I would need assistance.

Fiona jumped when I suddenly reached out and hugged her. "Thank you, Fiona. I knew you would help me."

She gave me a wary look. "What have I done?"

"You've given me an idea. A marvelous idea." I came to my feet and headed for the door. "But to put it into effect, I must pay a call on my brother-in-law."

"Graham? Why?"

"You'll find out this evening." I turned back when I reached the doorway. "I shall see you at the Stoke-Whitneys'. And George will be with me."

After I left Fiona, I paid a call on my brother-in-law. Graham was surprisingly in favor of my scheme. He also volunteered to deliver my request to the Countess de Torby in person. If she agreed, this could work, but I wouldn't know until this evening.

I chose to be optimistic, and as a result, my mood was vastly improved by the time I returned home a few hours later. I now had two plans. If they worked, one would help us find Irena's killer and the other would put an end to this annoying gossip. I alighted from the hack with a new bounce to my step and reached up to pay the driver. I tucked the change into my bag and wondered if I should knock on George's door to see if he'd returned from the theater yet.

"Lady Harleigh."

I jerked around as a youngish-looking man stepped away from the wall between my door and the service stairs. He touched his fingers to his homburg, and—of all the cheek—did he wink at me?

"Beg yer pardon, my lady, but I'm hoping for just a moment of your time." He sauntered toward me, gnawing on the end of a cigar.

I squeezed the handle of my umbrella and straightened my back. "I don't think you could have any business with me, young man, and I'll have you know, I'm very adept with this." I raised the umbrella in what I hoped was a threatening manner.

He stopped a few paces away, holding his hands out wide. "Just want to give you a chance to tell your side of the story, ma'am."

"My side?" Too late, I realized who he was. The hack pulled away, leaving me alone on the street with a newspaper reporter. One who stood between me and my front door.

"Yes, ma'am." He removed the cigar and pointed it at me. "I hear the police brought that poor lady to your very door, once they heard she was Mrs. Hazelton."

"She was not Mrs. Hazelton."

"Tried to get a comment from Hazelton himself earlier today, but, ah, he wasn't in the mood to talk. Thought you might have something to say." He tipped his head to the side, examining me. "Did you try to buy her off? Was that the idea?"

"Buy her off?" The suggestion that my meager funds might be enough to tempt Miss Teskey of the Plump Pockets to do something she didn't want to do was so absurd, I couldn't hold back a snort of laughter. Once it had escaped, more bubbled up behind it. I clapped a hand over my mouth, but it was no use. I was overcome with unrelenting giggles. This entire situation was beyond ridiculous.

"Here now. It's not impossible. Isn't that what you posh folk do?"

He looked so offended, it made me laugh all the harder. Tears streamed down my cheeks, and I struggled for breath. With a wary look, he took a step back and, in doing so, appeared less of a threat. Young and brash, this man would ruin my life in a heartbeat if it might advance his career. But absent knowledge of what had actually happened, he made it up as he went along.

I took a deep breath to regain control of myself and took a step forward. "Do you really suppose an inspector from the Metropolitan Police brought a woman he'd arrested to my house so that I could bribe her? That's what you plan to print?"

"That's what I heard. Why don't you tell me what really happened?"

It was the smirk, not his words, that offended me. His source had to be Jackson across the street. He didn't want my side of the story. He just wanted to goad me into saying something quotable.

"You are just guessing. You hope if you throw out some theories, I'll react and confirm one of them for you. Well, here's my reaction." I poked him in the chest with the umbrella. "If you want to find out what Inspector Delaney did and why he did it, you will simply have to ask him yourself."

I poked him again, and he backed away. "Here now, I'm just trying to get to the truth."

Anger made me poke him again, and once more, until I'd maneuvered him away from my door. "You just want to sell papers. You don't care if it's true or not. You don't care if it ruins someone's life. I worked very hard to jolly myself out of the doldrums today, and you are spoiling . . . My. Good. Spirits." I tapped the umbrella against his chest with each word. "Talk to the police and leave me alone."

I stomped up the steps to my door, which, thank goodness, was unlocked, and stepped inside, slamming it behind me. Let him make what he would of both my outburst and my fit of laughter. He'd likely print I was a raving lunatic, but who, after living through my past three days, wouldn't be a lunatic? A woman claiming to be my fiancé's wife. A murder in my own garden. My fiancé accused of this murder and, worst of all, a nosy butler across the street making up stories for the reporters. Well, I was just guessing at that last bit, but I wouldn't be surprised if it was true.

It was beyond enough. I moved to the drawing room to peek out the window. The young man was nowhere in sight. *Good.* It was time to take my bad mood and direct it where it belonged.

I stalked to the door, determined to alert Mrs. Chiswick to the harm Jackson was causing with his spying and gossiping. She simply must put an end to it. Hopefully, she'd take the hint and curtail her own busybody instincts. I threw open the door to find Mrs. Chiswick herself tottering on my doorstep, her hand raised toward the knocker. She flailed her arms, attempting to regain her balance, and I instinctively grasped the small woman's shoulders to steady her as she stumbled forward.

"Goodness me," she said. "Forgive my graceless entry. I'd just taken hold of the knocker when the door opened." She massaged her fingers.

I stepped aside and gestured for her to come in. "I hope you're not injured."

She wiggled her fingers experimentally while I closed the door. "No, they appear to be fine. It was just a clumsy accident on my part, and I owe it to my anxiety to find out if you are well or if that awful man upset you."

"Do you mean the reporter?" Had she watched the entire exchange from her window? She and Jackson were certainly a pair.

"So distressing." She clucked her tongue and placed a hand on my arm. "But I see that you withstood his harassment, as the true lady I always knew you were."

I raised a brow. "Indeed?"

"Of course, my dear. I'll admit until recently I was concerned that you'd be swept up in this horrible scandal with
Hazelton. I was much relieved to see you separating yourself
from him. It's one thing to be deceived by a rake, but quite another to continue the relationship once the deception has been
exposed. One cannot be too careful with one's reputation."

How does one even begin to respond to such a load of pop-
pycock? "You must know—"

"I do know," she said, as if taking a solemn vow. "You are an
innocent party caught up in this heinous crime. Jackson and I
discussed the possibility of my counseling you to extricate
yourself from this situation. I'm pleased to see you've done so
on your own initiative."

"About Jackson. I've been meaning to speak with you—"

"If you'd like him to keep a watch over your household, I'm
sure he'd be willing."

"Actually, I believe he already does keep a close watch over
my household."

"He worries about you. We both do. Living alone as you do.
Perhaps you should come to one of our meetings. You do
know I'm the chair for the Ladies' Society for the Preservation
of Public Morality, do you not? The meetings are very uplift-
ing, and practical, as well. For example, we would certainly ad-
vise you to seal up the passage between your garden and his."
She jerked her head in the direction of George's house. "While
you have taken the first steps to rid yourself of the man, temp-
tation is likely to hover over your shoulder."

With each passing minute, this day just kept growing more
ridiculous. Perhaps I was still asleep and merely dreaming all
this nonsense.

As she parted her lips to blather some additional platitudes, I
raised my hand to stop her. "Mrs. Chiswick, you are speaking

as if I have broken with my fiancé. I don't know how you came to that conclusion, but you are mistaken."

"But you drove off today in a hackney, when you generally use Hazelton's carriage."

I sent up a prayer for strength or patience or whatever would keep me from throttling her. "No one could fault your powers of observation, Mrs. Chiswick, but you have drawn the wrong conclusion. Mr. Hazelton is an innocent party in all matters involving Irena Teskey, and it pains me to hear you condemn him unjustly."

She blinked. "But—"

"The police are working to bring this case to a speedy conclusion, and when they do, you will find I speak the truth. Until that happens, I can only hope that you and Jackson will keep your speculations to yourselves."

Mrs. Chiswick drew in such a great gasp, I feared her imminent explosion. "I do not gossip, Lady Harleigh," she said at last. "Such a scandal as this takes on a life of its own. One cannot keep it a secret, as you will undoubtedly learn." She snapped around and jerked open the door. "I came here out of concern for you and your reputation. I now see that concern was misplaced."

I closed the door behind the awful woman and stomped up and down the few paces of my entry hall. How does one become so sanctimonious? On the flimsiest of evidence, she had George tried and convicted. I was now convinced that staying away from him didn't help me so much as it hurt him.

My mind made up, I took the garden path to George's house and let myself in his drawing room, where I found him reading a book. He jumped to his feet as I stormed into the room.

"Frances, what's wrong?"

"This." I spread my arms wide, as if to embrace everything. "What we're doing is wrong. Keeping my distance from you is wrong, or at least it just isn't working for me. We shall have to adopt a different plan."

His brow furrowed. "A different plan?"

"What I mean is we are both going to the Stoke-Whitney reception this evening. Together." I gave him a sharp nod. "You may call for me at eight."

Chapter Seventeen

Of course, it wasn't that simple. I hesitated to tell him about my plan, in case the countess denied my request. Instead, I resorted to persistence and persuasion. Some might call it badgering. In fact, George used that word several times, but I finally won him over with a simple truth—no one would believe he was ill. They would say he was hiding and would assume the worst. If he stepped boldly into society, obviously in no danger of imminent arrest, those same people would begin to doubt the rumors whispered into their ears. I was not entirely sure if I convinced him or if he just grew weary of arguing with me, but he agreed to attend the reception.

My powers of persuasion had their limits, however. They failed me when it came to Aunt Hetty. Though I'd spent far more time working on her, Hetty stuck to her plan of a drive to the outskirts of the city with Gilliam, followed by an intimate dinner. She even used the same argument I'd used with George—that the man shouldn't have to prove his innocence.

The lateness of the hour forced me to give up and ready myself for my own evening events. I was still in the midst of preparations with my maid when Hetty came to my room. She was dressed, coiffed, and ready to leave, though it was a full thirty minutes before Gilliam's expected arrival—in an automobile, no less.

"Will this do, do you think?" Hetty did a slow spin beside my dressing table, while I strained to see her from the corner of my eye. Bridget was pulling my hair upward and had it in a grip so tight, there was no moving my head. I caught a flash of black with silver and white and knew which gown she wore.

"Why black? Are you in mourning?"

"Only for my lost youth."

I jerked my head around instinctively, only to hear a loud sigh of exasperation behind me as my hair fell about my shoulders. "Apologies, Bridget." I faced the mirror once more and addressed Hetty. "What on earth do you mean by that?"

Hetty waved a hand and stationed herself next to Bridget so we could see each other in the mirror. "Nothing really. I just need to remind myself that I am much older than Mr. Gilliam, and I shouldn't become carried away by his attentions. I'm sure he's just hoping I'll become his next partner."

It took all my discipline not to jerk around again. "Surely you don't still believe that? The man is completely besotted with you."

She huffed. "How ridiculous." She paused, but before I could speak, she added, "Do you really think so?"

"Indeed. At first, I thought he was just trying to entice you to open your purse, but after seeing him with you yesterday, I've dispensed with that theory. The man might have the theater in his blood, but no one is that good an actor."

"He's not an actor at all. What gave you that idea?"

That made me pause. "I suppose just his line of business. How did he become involved in the theater?"

"His father designed and built them, well, not theaters exclusively, but when he had his first commission for one, Gilliam was just a young man. He and his father visited every theater in Paris, judging the acoustics, the structure, and the materials. Gilliam became entranced with the idea of staging productions. The theater he owns in Paris is one his father built."

Let that be a lesson to me not to make assumptions. "Apparently, your conversations have been about more than just business."

Hetty stopped me from speculating further with a wave of her hand. "My conversations with Hazelton have been about more than business, too, as they've been with Lord Harleigh, for that matter. I don't fancy that they have any designs on me." She frowned. "I don't want to imagine an attachment where one doesn't exist. Gilliam and I are friends. My hope is that we can remain friends when I tell him I won't be his partner."

And I hoped he wouldn't be charged with murder, or there might be prison visitations in Hetty's future. She made a sensible point, but it seemed to me she was ignoring a few details. The Hanover was his second theater. Irena contributed her funding, but she didn't pay for everything, so one would assume his Paris theater was successful. He should have no difficulty finding a partner. It was clear to me it wasn't Hetty's money he was after, but Hetty herself. How could she not see that?

I decided to keep the thought to myself for the moment. While it seemed Hetty had become familiar with his background, there was still one more objection—Gilliam may have murdered his partner. My suspicion of his guilt was waning, but I feared that was simply because I was coming to like him— not a good reason to remove a suspect from the list.

I tilted my head to steal another glance at her in the mirror and made one more attempt to change her mind about her dinner plans. "Perhaps black is a good idea, after all, considering all the smoke and debris a motorcar spews."

She smiled. "You can't frighten me, dear. Gilliam is bringing me a motoring coat and goggles. I'm looking forward to a thrilling ride."

"Not too thrilling, I hope."

"Do you think it wise for your aunt to be alone with that man?"

George and I were in his carriage, wending our way to the Stoke-Whitney home in Mayfair.

"I tried to talk her into canceling, but to no avail. Besides, I thought you agreed with Delaney that Gilliam was an unlikely suspect."

"He's not a very good suspect, but I thought you weren't convinced of that."

"I'm not completely convinced, but Aunt Hetty is a grown woman and entitled to do as she pleases." I released a weary sigh. "She's not willing to admit it, but she and Gilliam are in the midst of a budding romance."

George laughed. "I could hardly help but notice that yesterday."

"The more I see of him, the more I come to like him." I tipped my head toward George, giving him a pleading look. "Therefore, I want to believe him innocent of any wrongdoing. I could use some convincing."

"All right, then. How could he have known where Irena was staying?"

"You'll have to do better than that. If he's the man who was following Miss Teskey, he would know she ended up at my house."

"Both Irena and Petrov identified the man as older. Gilliam is somewhere around forty. That hardly counts as old."

"He has an entire theater at his disposal. He could easily have donned a costume."

George drummed his fingers on his knee. "Do you really think he's a danger to your aunt?"

"I don't. No matter what he may have done, he has no motive to harm Hetty. I'm more worried about them driving around town in his motorcar."

He gave me a sympathetic smile. "As you said, she's a grown woman."

"Well, then, to take my mind off my aunt's potential death by motorcar, let's consider our other suspects. Mr. Petrov, for example."

"There are several things about Petrov that make me wonder. He'd been with Irena for years. He was used to finding her, so there's a good chance he was lying when he said he didn't know where she was. However, I must ask myself what he would gain if she were dead." He looked to me for the answer.

"Maybe he was tired of guarding her."

"It's possible. I'd like to ask him some questions. With both Petrov and Gilliam in the room yesterday, I couldn't question either of them as much as I'd have liked."

I raised a brow. "So, Gilliam remains on your list of suspects."

"Well toward the bottom."

"Who is at the top?"

"As much as I hate to say it, Bradmore is still the most likely. He had a reason to want Irena out of the picture. He had an opportunity to meet with her in your garden. And now he's disappeared."

"If he didn't murder her, it was certainly a mistake for him to run."

George took my gloved hand and laced his fingers with mine. "I love these romantic conversations with you."

"I'm afraid it's imperative we have this one."

"All right, then, who is at the top of your list?"

"My list? If the man who sent the threatening letters is also the man who was following her, then he is at the top of my list."

"I take it you don't think Bradmore sent her the letters."

"Not if someone was really following her."

"That could be Bradmore."

"He's not an old man. Yes, he could have donned a disguise, but he could hardly make himself appear lean. He doesn't fit the description."

"You make a good point, but considering the description we've been given, I don't know how we'd ever find this man. Although another conversation with Petrov might help."

"He probably knows her better than anyone else." I told him about my theory that if we had a better understanding of Miss Teskey's life over the past few years, it might give us some insight into the threatening letters and who sent them.

George brightened. "That's a good idea. Due to the nature of the threats, I tend to believe the man is someone she knows, or at least someone who knows her."

"Someone who doesn't want her in London. The letters were telling her to leave. Someone also tried to jeopardize her position in the theater by telling the owner she was a liability to his production. I still wonder about her mother's family. If she was looking for them, perhaps she mentioned something to Petrov."

"An excellent notion, but one we'll have to consider later." He brought my fingers to his lips and gave them a gentle kiss. "We've arrived, and right now, we must attend a reception. Unless, of course, Stoke-Whitney turns us away at the door."

"He's far too diplomatic for that. In fact, he's probably delighted with us. The more people talk about us, the less they'll talk about his wife."

George stared a moment, until he realized what I referred to. "I'd forgotten all about Mrs. Stoke-Whitney's scandalous affair."

"And I'm sure Mr. Stoke-Whitney hopes you won't be the only one to do so. Thus, I believe we've done him a favor and he should welcome us with open arms."

"I won't hold my breath for that."

"We'll never know if we stay in this carriage. And we should not keep our hosts waiting. Are you ready?"

He grinned. "With you by my side, how could I not be?"

The reception in honor of Grand Duke Michael Mikhailo-vich and Sophie, Countess de Torby, was something of a crush, at least for November. Though they were exiles, and of little use politically, the Prince of Wales wanted some sort of fuss made for his friends. Other politicians might not have troubled themselves, but only one person understood the currying of favor better than Alicia Stoke-Whitney, and that was her husband. He would make sure the prince felt indebted to him for this grand gesture.

We ascended the stairs to the ballroom, and George handed our invitations to the butler. While we waited to be announced, I focused on the room rather than the occupants. Alicia had chosen a single color for her decorations again. This time everything was pink: the flowers, the draperies, and possibly even the glass globes on the chandeliers, as the high coffered ceiling seemed to have a rosy glow. When the butler intoned our names, I forced myself to lower my eyes and take in the crowd.

Every species has a way of culling the herd. In the British aristocracy that method was scandal. Anyone not rich, power-ful, or clever enough to survive a scandal would be discarded, left behind, culled. It happened all the time. I wasn't rich or powerful, but I'd like to think I was clever. At least clever enough to find powerful allies. As I looked out at the cream of society gathered in this glittering ballroom, I knew just our ap-pearance here was a dare, and if I didn't play my hand carefully, George and I would find ourselves culled.

Arthur Stoke-Whitney stepped away from a group near the doorway upon hearing our names. Though he approached us with a smile, George bent to whisper in my ear, "He's going to throw us out."

Instead, he greeted us both pleasantly, then lowered his voice. "Have you had any success in finding that woman's killer?"

"Not as of yet," George replied.

"He's still investigating," I added. Though I'd been sure Stoke-Whitney would be happy to see us, I had not expected to receive any particular attention from him. This was going better than I'd hoped. "The fact that we know almost nothing about Miss Teskey is proving to be a problem. It's difficult to know if someone from her past is involved, when we know nothing about that past."

"What of her present? Do you know why she was in London?"

Stoke-Whitney did have a tangential interest in clearing George's name, and thereby mine, but his questions were a bit annoying.

While I debated what to tell him, George spoke up. "She was part of the new management at the Hanover Theater. And an actress, I understand."

Stoke-Whitney curled his lip. "Theater people. A bad lot. That's where you'll find the culprit, I'd wager."

Since my aunt was currently alone with one of them, I hoped he was wrong, but I conceded the possibility.

"You must do something quickly," he continued. "Put an end to the rumors. My offer still stands. If you need assistance, I'd be happy to make some inquiries."

"Thank you. I may take you up on that."

With a nod to both of us, he moved on. I led George in the opposite direction.

"Would you really let Stoke-Whitney assist us?"

He grinned. "Probably not. I was just dazzled by the fact he was willing to be seen with us. It appears you understand the workings of society better than I."

"I don't for a moment believe everyone will be so obliging, but here are two more friends now." Fiona and Robert Nash approached through the crowd. *Bless them.*

Fiona bussed my cheek and drew me aside. "Nash, dear, why don't you and George find us some refreshments. Frances and I need to catch up."

Nash, looking bemused, gestured to the footman, not two feet away from him, and soon had us supplied with champagne.

Fiona flashed him a smile. "Thank you, dear, but we still need to catch up."

Not really wanting to lose track of George until we had tested our reception with the rest of the room, I allowed her to lead me only a few steps away. "How bad is it?" I whispered.

"We've been here only a short time, but so far, two people have asked me if it was true George was married. I set them straight, of course."

"It's to be expected, I suppose, though I had hoped the report in the *Observer* today would put an end to some of the speculations. Have you seen my brother-in-law?"

She blinked. "Yes, I have. He gave me a message for you. Just what is going on between you two?"

"He's part of the plan I devised today. What did he say?"

"He said to tell you everything is set. What does that mean?"

"You'll find out soon. In the meantime, George and I must simply brazen it out and hope for the best."

George and Nash stepped closer.

"If that's our plan," George said, "shall we put it into action now? Let's make a circuit of the room. We might as well find out who is with us and who is against us."

The four of us strolled through the glittering crowd, pausing here and there to sip our drinks and speak with anyone who appeared willing to be seen with us. No one deliberately cut us, but many seemed on the verge of approaching Fiona or Nash, then nearly injured themselves in their haste to back away once they caught sight of George and me.

"You'd think we had some sort of contagious disease," I said. I didn't count any of these people as my particular friends, but it hurt, nonetheless.

"We do," George whispered. "It's called scandal, and they want no part of it."

As we reached the far side of the ballroom, about halfway through our circuit, the gentlemen became caught up in a side conversation, and Fiona and I stood alone. The exchange with Arthur Stoke-Whitney had fortified my confidence somewhat, but it was not to last.

"What is *he* doing here?" The question came from behind me, delivered by a female voice I couldn't quite place. It was followed by a nasty laugh. "I can't imagine Stoke-Whitney invited him. Must be Alicia's doing. She likes to take risks. Perhaps she has her eye on the wife killer."

"I know Alicia's reckless in her affairs, but what of Lady Harleigh? What makes her think he'll stop at murdering one wife?"

Fiona clutched my arm before I could turn around. "Don't do it," she whispered in my ear. "It's just a silly girl trying to act grown up. Let it pass." She gave me a little shove when I hesitated. "Most of the people in this room are on your side, even Stoke-Whitney, but they won't be if you cause an embarrassing scene. Let's move on."

I saw the wisdom in her counsel and did as she instructed. Thank goodness George hadn't been close enough to hear. So it went for the remainder of our promenade. Some people turned sharply away upon seeing us, a few greeted us warmly, but the rest were the ones who had me on edge—the ones I couldn't read. If I chose not to speak, would I appear to snub them? If I did approach them, would they snub me? The anxiety was nearly paralyzing.

Within an hour of our arrival, Michael and Sophie opened the dancing, and the focus of attention moved to them. It might well have been my imagination that it was ever focused on us, but even so, I managed to relax a bit. George and I danced together first then he took the floor with his sister, and I danced with Nash. When the dance ended and he brought me back to the side of the room, I noticed Graham standing nearby. He was in conversation with Mrs. Chiswick and Lady Pettipiece. He caught my eye and made a discreet gesture for me to join them.

So, he planned to tackle the highest sticklers first, did he? I'd have preferred an easier audience.

"Frances," he called.

Taking a deep breath, I made my way to his side, where he reached for my hand and smiled in a way I had never seen before. My staid, often contrary, and frequently grumpy brother-in-law looked positively delighted. "Frances, my dear sister."

It was likely I looked every bit as shocked as the matrons beside him. I had had no idea Graham was such a good actor.

Lady Pettipiece shrank back and clutched Mrs. Chiswick's arm. "Is this the creature you were telling me about? One would think he'd cease to claim her."

"On the contrary, I've never been more proud to have her in the family."

I had no idea what their reaction was, as Graham swept me out to the dance floor and into a waltz.

"The old cows," he muttered.

"Well done, Graham. I've never seen you willing to offend anyone, and certainly not a grande dame such as Lady Pettipiece."

"She's a small-minded, stupid old cow," he repeated. "Mrs. Chiswick's been making snide comments about you and Hazelton, and Lady Pettipiece was happy to lend her an obliging ear, the useless article."

"I never expected everyone here to approve of me."

He smiled at a nearby couple who'd been staring at us.

"I must thank you for agreeing to my plan. Knowing my

family stands beside me will make everyone think twice before condemning George."

"You needn't thank me at all. I'm only sorry I didn't think of it myself."

"What exactly did Mrs. Chiswick say to you—to everyone?"

Graham pursed his lips, as if the topic wasn't suitable for a woman.

I let out a tsk. "It pertains to me. Don't you think I have a right to know what a large portion of the room has been told?"

"It's not so much what she said, but that she claims it's first-hand knowledge." He huffed. "A woman who spends all her time in Chelmsford."

"She currently resides in Colonel Perkins's home, just opposite mine." I responded to his obvious surprise with a grim smile. "She and her butler spend the day watching out the window."

"That's neither here nor there, because she claims someone here this evening gave her the details firsthand." He frowned. "I suppose that makes her information secondhand."

I noticed he managed to avoid providing the actual information. "Was she told that George was married to Miss Teskey or that he killed her?"

"Both."

"Who was her source?"

"She wouldn't say, which makes me wonder if she simply made it up." He made an abrupt turn. "Ah, here is the countess, and it looks as though she's ready."

He drew me out of the flow of dancers and pulled me up next to the Countess de Torby, whose smile glittered almost as much as the diamonds about her neck. "Is it time?" she asked. At his nod, she linked her arm with mine. "I will take custody of Lady Harleigh while you find her partner. I think he is smoking in the cardroom."

Graham departed, and Sophie gave my arm a tug. "Smile,"

she said. "As if you have no care in the world. You are supposed to be enjoying yourself." She glanced around the room. "Now, where is that fiancé of yours?"

I pasted on a smile and fell in beside her. "Do you mean Hazelton?"

She raised a brow. "Do you have more than one fiancé? That would be a scandal, indeed."

I gave her a genuine smile. "It's very kind of you to help us."

"Nonsense. I am no stranger to scandal myself. But you are clever to seek out allies before you do battle." She patted my hand. "After all, you could say it was our family who started all your problems. Irena was family, after all. It seems only right we should come to your defense."

She stopped and nodded to her left. "Here comes Hazelton now, and your partner is with him. How convenient."

I turned to see George strolling toward us with the Prince of Wales at his side. "My goodness, I thought your husband was to dance with me."

She raised a brow. "It seemed best to go straight to the top."

I instantly regretted everything I'd ever said about her high-handedness. She'd fallen in with my plan graciously. If my family, a guest of honor, and now the Prince of Wales approved of George and me, how could anyone else question our behavior?

Their actions would go a long way toward bolstering our sagging reputations, but if we didn't find Irena's killer soon, that cloud of suspicion would come back to haunt us.

"How did you orchestrate that display of support?"

We were in the carriage on our way home. It was barely midnight, but we had stayed as long as either of us could bear it, and just long enough to avoid a breach of good manners.

"I didn't manage it on my own. I had a coconspirator—well, two if you count Sophie. I had only intended we'd dance with the guests of honor. It was she who brought the prince into the scheme."

"It was an ingenious scheme."

"Since I convinced you to brazen it out with me, I thought it best to have some people in our corner. The more influential, the better."

"I'd say we have at least half of those in attendance on our side now. Well done." He leaned back into the leather cushions of the seat and pulled me against him. "Who was the other partner?"

"Graham. Can you believe it?"

He thought a moment, then shook his head. "No. Are you certain it wasn't someone impersonating him?"

"Quite certain. I imagine saving the family name was uppermost in his mind, but I won't quibble over his motive when his deeds were so effective. And he was very gracious about it."

"Now that you've taken care of society so handily, it should be a simple matter to find Irena's killer, don't you think?"

"Graham told me something that has me wondering about that very matter." I moved away so I could see George's face. "Our temporary neighbor, Mrs. Chiswick, told him she not only heard you both married and murdered Miss Teskey, but also that her intelligence came from a reliable authority at the reception."

"We didn't win over everyone tonight. Plenty of people were talking about the murder—and me."

"Yes, but who among them would be a reliable authority? I wonder if someone there felt it necessary to spread the story and give it more gravitas. Who would have more need to do so than the guilty party?"

He blew out a breath. "If that's the case, you have removed nearly every one of our suspects from the list. It couldn't be Bradmore, Gilliam, Petrov, or Miss Cooper." He frowned. "Is there anyone left?"

"The grand duke? He wasn't very helpful yesterday. If you were found guilty, there would be no need to scrutinize her relationship with the Romanovs."

"And we gave him reason to believe that's exactly what the

police would like to do. Did Graham ask how Mrs. Chiswick came by this tidbit?"

"He did, and she wouldn't say. I don't think she's on gossiping terms with anyone at the reception except Lady Pettipiece. She has a slight acquaintance with Arthur Stoke-Whitney and an even slighter one with Alicia. Neither of them would want to stir up our scandal." I considered my own actions this evening, stopping near groups and picking up bits of their conversations. "She might simply have been eavesdropping."

"Let's put Mrs. Chiswick aside for the moment. If you believe Irena's killer is tied to the letters and the man following her, and I think that's a good possibility, it couldn't be Romanov, since that all happened before he arrived in London."

My shoulders sagged. "You're right."

George blinked and cupped a hand to his ear. "Could you say that again?"

My thoughts were spinning too fast. I had to slow them down before I could possibly explain them. "You're half right."

"No, no, no. That's not what you said."

I placed a hand on his arm. "Stop joking and hear me out. Do you recall Gilliam saying the man who told him to rid himself of Miss Teskey was a gentleman? What if he was at the reception tonight? He would certainly benefit by making you appear guilty."

"It's possible. Unfortunately, we don't know who that is. I think your notion to learn more about Irena's life and her connections is our best course of action. It may help us learn who would want her to leave London."

We'd arrived home, and George walked me up to my door and fitted the key into the lock.

"Why don't you come in for a bit. It's early, and I'm sure Aunt Hetty isn't home yet."

While he sent his driver off to retire for the night, I turned on the lights in the drawing room, remembering too late about the busybody butler across the street. For goodness' sake, George and I were betrothed. Why couldn't I entertain him at my own home at whatever time I chose? Besides, Hetty would be home soon. I chuckled at the thought of her as my chaperone and opened the drinks cabinet, in search of brandy. We were a bit thin, but wasn't there a decanter in the library? I was heading in that direction just as George came through the front door.

"Make yourself comfortable. I'm just checking the library for brandy."

I didn't bother lighting the lamp when I entered the room but slipped through the darkness to the shelf behind the desk. I was right. My hand landed on the neck of a bottle of something Hetty had purchased a few days ago. I hoped it wasn't rare or special, as I fully intended to drink it. As I moved around the desk, the bottle cradled in one arm, I caught sight of a shadow moving across the moonlight that shone through the glass door. I pressed my hand to my mouth to silence my gasp.

Something or someone was moving around in my garden.

My hands shook as I set down the bottle. Should I have set it down? It might make a good weapon. What to do? Should I open the door, startle the person, if it was a person, and hit him with the bottle?

Instead, I turned to fetch George and nearly ran him down in the doorway. I let out a squeak as he steadied me on my feet.

"Sorry. Just came to see what was keeping you."

"There's someone out there," I hissed and pointed to the door.

He was instantly alert. "Stay here," he whispered and padded quietly to the door.

Instead I followed him, slipped around the desk and positioned myself next to the door. He glared. "I told you to stay back."

"What if it's just Hetty and Gilliam?"

"His motorcar would be in the street. Now, please." He put a finger to his lips and pushed me behind the desk.

I bit my lip while he released the bolt, then turned the handle. I picked up the discarded brandy bottle as a weapon. Before I could swing it at anyone, he'd inched open the door and thrown himself outside. Something landed with an oomph.

Peeking around the door, I saw George sprawled on top of another person. A very large person. "Who is it?"

George came to his knees, and the other man sat up.

It was Igor Petrov.

Chapter Eighteen

George gestured for Petrov to precede him into the library. The Russian shuffled inside, his head bowed. I lit the desk lamp and retrieved the bottle of brandy. Since we hadn't needed it as a weapon, we might as well put it to better use. With a quick trip to the drawing room, I had three glasses and was pouring one for each of us when Igor settled into a chair. George remained on his feet, pacing and trying to calm down.

I handed a glass to Petrov. "What on earth were you doing in my garden?" On seeing his blank stare, I corrected myself and asked again in French.

"Were you attempting to break in here?" George stopped pacing and glared at the man.

"I called on both of you earlier this evening and was told you were away from home. I couldn't wait out front, or a constable would move me along, so I went around the back and climbed over your wall, my lady."

"Why didn't you just come back in the morning?" I asked. "Is there something urgent you need to relay to us?"

From the way George was clenching his hands into fists, I

knew he was at the end of his tether with Petrov, Irena, and all this business. I'd hoped the brandy, his pacing, or just the even tone of my voice would calm him down, but so far, nothing had had that effect.

Petrov was eyeing him, too. Not out of any fear, since the sheer weight and volume of the man would put all of George's strength to the test, and to his credit, the Russian wasn't flaunting that. No, he was just being cautious, calculating.

Finally, Petrov spread his hands. "I had nowhere to go. I can't pay for the hotel room, so they asked me to leave. Alexei has sent me no instructions. He may not even know yet that his daughter is dead. And I don't want to leave until I know who murdered Irena and the police have him in custody." He twisted his lips downward as he lifted his shoulder. "Since you want to learn the same things, I came to you."

"You came here looking for somewhere to stay?" George looked incredulous. "Why wouldn't you go to the grand duke? Surely he would help you."

Petrov raised his shoulders in one of those maddening shrugs Irena had used so often. "Possibly, but Michael Mikhailovich isn't looking for the truth. He doesn't care what happened to his cousin."

George studied Petrov for a moment. I was just about to suggest we pay for the hotel accommodations when he made a different decision. "Get your things. You can stay with me."

Mr. Petrov lumbered out to the garden to collect his belongings, and I turned to George. "What are you thinking? The man might be a murderer. Why would you want him to stay with you?"

"I'll have to keep a close eye on him, to be sure, but something tells me he knows more than he's revealing to us. We want to talk with him, anyway. He says he wants the truth. Perhaps if I can convince him to let loose with a little more information about Irena, we'll all get to it faster."

* * *

The next morning, I woke with a vague sense of unease. As Bridget pulled open the drapes, I recalled the reason—Petrov, an extraordinary and suspicious man, if not an actual killer, was residing in one of George's guest rooms. I certainly hoped he'd survived the night. George, that is, not Petrov.

Then there was Aunt Hetty. Bridget placed the coffee tray on the bedside table. I sat up and swung my legs over the side of the bed. "Do you know if my aunt ever made it home last night?"

Bridget flashed me a grin before she moved on to the other window. "She did, my lady. Were you worried about her?"

"Of course I was. She was with a strange man, driving about in a motorcar. Why would I not worry? I'm also worried about Mr. Hazelton. Would you ask Jenny to nip next door and inquire of his valet if he's—" *If he's what? Alive?* "If he'd call on me at his earliest convenience?"

"Of course, my lady."

When Bridget left on her errand, I picked up my coffee and saw the telegram on the tray. Mother didn't have this much to say to me when we were in the same room. I broke the seal and unfolded the page.

> *My dear, you can't imagine the excitement here. Mr. Bradmore has been arrested! And not by the Prefecture of Police, but by an English inspector named Delaney. For the police to arrest a British aristocrat, he must have committed a particularly heinous crime. Thank goodness you weren't drawn in by him. Fortunately, I've heard no new gossip about your Mr. Hazelton. Has that quieted down?*

She signed off with a promise they'd be back home in a few days. For my mother, the telegram was positively economical. I set it aside when Bridget returned to help me dress.

George still hadn't called by the time I went downstairs, but Jenny had spoken to his valet, who'd told her George was up and about. It had been a late night, so I ought to give him a little more time before stalking over there and knocking on his window.

To my surprise, Hetty was already at the dining table, as bright and cheerful as if she hadn't been out most of the night.

"How was your evening?" I asked.

She lowered her newspaper to reveal a rather dreamy expression. "Quite enjoyable, thank you."

I dropped into the chair next to hers and leaned in close. "Is that all you have to say?"

She pushed me away. "We drove out of town a bit so he could take the motor through its paces." She shuddered. "It's very fast. I'm not entirely sure I'd care to do that again. Then we came back to town and had dinner at the Savoy."

"You were out quite late."

"We had a little difficulty starting the engine after dinner. Gilliam tried adjusting a few things, but it was too awkward for him to tinker with it on the street and in the dark, so he brought me home in a cab. I suppose he'll return to check on it today."

"But will he check on you today?"

She gave me a level look. "Don't be silly. Or perhaps he will. He might keep up his attentions to me until he realizes I won't be investing in his theater."

Mrs. Thompson came in with eggs and toast. I helped myself to both. "I thought you planned to tell him that last night."

"That was my intention, but the subject of the theater never came up. Odd, don't you think?"

Hardly. I was certain the man was interested in Hetty, not her money. Was her resistance to the idea because she still harbored some suspicion of him? Bradmore's arrest should provide more information about Irena's murder. Perhaps we'd learn Gilliam was completely innocent. I hoped so, for Hetty's sake.

"Why are you looking at me like that?"

I smiled. "I just wonder if Mr. Gilliam is worthy of you."

"Frances." She scowled at me. "I won't make a fool of my-self over such a young man."

"He's not that young."

"He's young enough. Too young. I would look ridiculous. What would people say?"

Before I could answer, Jenny slipped into the room. "Mrs. Stoke-Whitney is here, ma'am. She apologizes for the early hour, but she's asking to see you."

I immediately recalled that I hadn't written the promised note to her husband, and felt a stab of guilt. I ought to have said something to him last night about Harriet's season, but it would have been awkward if he'd turned me down. "I'll be with her in a moment, Jenny."

With a nod, the girl left.

I took a bite of toast to keep my stomach from growling, while Hetty let out a tsk. "You should at least make her wait until you've finished your breakfast."

I washed down the toast with some coffee and shook my head. "Actually, I'm very interested in what Alicia has to say to me." After dabbing my lips with a napkin, I stood and headed for the door, then turned back and watched my aunt as she returned to her newspaper. Last night hadn't been easy. In fact, I'd been anxious the whole time, but I was also proud that I'd taken the risk. "Aunt Hetty, do you really care?"

She raised her gaze from the paper to me, her brow furrowed in confusion. "Care about what?"

"What people will say. Before you rule out any possibility of a romance with Gilliam, you should ask yourself if it really matters to you what society thinks."

She still looked puzzled when I left, but I thought it best to let her mull things over on her own.

Alicia awaited me in the drawing room. When I entered, she was pacing back and forth in front of the window.

"Good morning, Alicia. Such a lovely gathering you had last night."

She turned to face me, a pout on her lips. "I noticed you managed to use it to your advantage." She gave me a grudging smile. "Well done."

"I hope we changed a few minds. Even your husband greeted us warmly."

She looked surprised. "I'm very pleased to hear that. I was afraid because of this Teskey business, he'd reject you as a sponsor for Harriet. I've been trying to work myself back into his good graces." She raised her hands, then let them fall to her sides. "I even helped him with his speech for the Ladies' Society for Morality and all that rot. And it's all been for nothing."

"Mrs. Chiswick belongs to that group. I understand she was spreading rumors last night. Do you suppose that's her idea of moral behavior?"

"I daresay it is, and Arthur's, too, for that matter, but you know how he is. Not a breath of scandal can touch his family."

"Yes, I do know how he is. But one wonders if you do."

"I usually have no trouble managing him, but I admit I overstepped this time. His first wife was careless, and that makes him rather prickly if I am ever less than discreet."

Good heavens, what a marriage. "Would you care for tea?"

"Thank you, no. I am on my way to the country now and only stopped to ask if you would please remember to write to Arthur? If he understood this issue would be resolved in a matter of days, I'm sure he'd consent to your sponsorship."

"You are leaving now?" Stoke-Whitney's justice was swift. And somewhat ridiculous, considering he wasn't punishing Alicia for her actions, but for the fact that they'd become public. And what kind of ogre punishes his wife? Yes, the man could be pleasant, but this high-handedness with his wife quite put me off the idea. "It might be safer to ask someone else. Perhaps Lady Fiona?"

She boggled her eyes. "Hazelton's sister? I don't see how that will be any better."

"Right. I'd forgotten about the connection. Isn't there anyone else?"

"You know I have few female friends, and how can I contact anyone while I'm buried in the country?"

"You could write to them. And you're hardly to be buried in the country when you're only an hour from London by rail."

She pouted. "I believe my stay will be of some duration, and I can't come back to make arrangements. I'm depending on you, Frances."

I'd likely regret conceding to her request, but I'd run out of arguments. "Fine. I'll send him a note, but I can guarantee he won't accept my offer until we've resolved this case."

"And I'm sure you will. Thank you so much." She took my hand. "I'm in your debt."

"I'll be sure to remind you of that."

The bell rang as I walked her to the door. I opened it to find George on the other side.

After greeting him, Alicia heaved a sigh. "Perhaps I should have been more selective," she said and strode down the walk to her carriage.

He frowned. "What did she mean by that?"

I drew him into the hall and handed his hat and coat to Mrs. Thompson, who'd come to answer the door. "She's just wondering what might have been if she hadn't married a sanctimonious man twenty-five years her senior."

"A little late for regrets."

I nodded. "It's good to see you alive and well."

"Yes, Petrov has been the perfect houseguest. I assume your aunt also came to no harm last night."

"You assume correctly."

I gestured to the drawing room, but he shook his head. "I've sent Petrov on an errand, and I have a spot of business myself.

I'm to meet Lord Vellefort for luncheon, and I wondered if you'd care to join me?"

"I'm happy to join you anywhere, but why is meeting Lord Vellefort for luncheon a spot of business rather than just a pleasure?"

"He's the man the Home Office put me in touch with regarding the Romanovs. He has a lengthy history with them, and with any luck, he may be able to shed some light on Irena."

I could not have been more shocked. Vellefort, who'd only recently taken his seat in the Lords, was a bald, gaunt sexagenarian. A happy-go-lucky man, who took nothing seriously except his meals. Those, he took very seriously indeed. Was everyone in London involved in espionage? Well, I had no intention of missing this visit. The letter to Arthur Stoke-Whitney would have to wait.

"Do I have time to change my gown?" The one I wore was definitely unsuitable for paying calls.

He cocked a brow. "Can you do it in under thirty minutes?"

"Don't be absurd. Of course I can."

"Then I'll order the carriage while you do." He turned to go, but I caught his arm.

"Wait, I have news for you. Delaney caught up with Bradmore. He has him in custody."

He grinned. "Your mother?"

"She'd make a wonderful spy, wouldn't she?"

It was one of the best meals I'd ever had the pleasure to enjoy. Light and delicate, every morsel simply melted in the mouth.

"Lady Vellefort, how is it that no one has stolen your chef away? He is a culinary master," I said.

Lady Vellefort smiled, the action bringing the apples of her cheeks high enough to turn her dark eyes into crescents. In every other way, she was a formidable woman—stately and square of form. Even her steel-gray curls looked as if they wouldn't dare budge in a gale. But when she smiled, she transformed into a jolly old soul. "It's all Vellefort's doing."

"Our chef is indeed a master," he said. "And a female. She came to us when we were first assigned to Paris. It took a great deal of encouragement to convince her to return to London with us. Many of our so-called friends have attempted to lure her away, but fortunately, she is very loyal."

"She revels in Oscar's praise," Lady Vellefort added. "I fear he would simply waste away if we ever let her leave."

Indeed, Lord Vellefort didn't seem far from wasting away as it was, though he ate just as much as the rest of us. He pushed his chair back a bit, and I suspected he wanted to pat his stomach in satisfaction. Instead, he shot George a look. "You have some questions for me, I understand. Should we leave the ladies and adjourn to the library?"

George dabbed his lips with his napkin and turned to the older man. "As long as the topic doesn't disturb Lady Vellefort, I see no reason for us to discuss this in private."

The lady flapped a hand. "You need not concern yourself with my sensibilities, young man."

George glanced at Vellefort, who gave him an almost imperceptible nod. "No doubt you've heard about our sticky situation with Irena Teskey. Please accept my assurances that I neither married nor murdered her. We are, however, having a difficult time determining who did. I hoped with your knowledge of the Romanov family, you might be able to shed some light on her situation within the family. My only experience with her was short and happened a number of years ago. Lady Harleigh has spent time with her in more recent days, but Irena revealed nothing about her relationship with her father or his family."

Vellefort studied George above the rim of his wineglass. "You think the Romanovs had something to do with her death?"

"A strange group of people," Lady Vellefort said. "I suppose it comes from living such an isolated existence."

"Russia is somewhat cut off from the rest of the world," I said.

"It's more than that," she said. "They live in this rarefied sphere, where their every wish is accommodated. They have more money than anyone could estimate and absolute power over a vast expanse of territory. Yet they spare no thought for their own people or consider how they manage to live. It's no wonder the Duke of Teck would not allow a match between Michael and his daughter, Mary."

"I heard he said the Romanov men make bad husbands," I said. "But Michael and Sophie seem to be quite happy."

"That's because they're cut off from the family and banished from Russia. They should count themselves fortunate," Lady Vellefort said with a firm nod.

"Since the czar didn't cut off Michael's income," I added. "I must agree with you."

"There you have it. The best possible outcome. I should think all the cousins not immediately in line to rule the empire wish they'd had the foresight to marry without the czar's permission."

"When examined in that light," Lord Vellefort said, "Miss Teskey should also have considered herself fortunate. She reaped the benefits of the czar's generosity without having to suffer his whims, rules, and rages."

George frowned. "You think the czar funded Irena's living, not Alexei?"

"Alexei would have gone to his brother and arranged for an allowance and caretakers." He shrugged. "I'm sure the czar found it convenient to have the Teskeys placed in France to provide him with intelligence. Fostering Alexei's child was the perfect cover for them."

"Cover?" This came as a surprise. "Are you saying Alexei did not just find a French family to raise his child?"

Vellefort gave me a pitying look. "I spent twenty years in the diplomatic service for Her Majesty. Ten in Saint Petersburg and ten in Paris."

"Paris was much more to my liking," Lady Vellefort murmured.

"I had several interactions with Monsieur Teskey. He is in service to the czar, and so is his wife. As I said, Alexei's daughter was just a good cover for them. For that, Alexander, and now Nicholas, rewarded her. And the Teskeys."

"What of Petrov?" George asked.

"Petrov was Alexei's doing. He wanted to put an end to all the abductions. I don't know where he found the man. He may have been in the Russian Navy. As soon as they were in port, Alexei gave Petrov a new assignment—protect his daughter, or at least keep anyone from making off with her."

"So to your knowledge, he isn't actually in service to the czar?" George asked.

Vellefort reeled back in his chair. "My good man, if they are Russian, they are in service to the czar. There's nothing else to be."

George looked down at his plate and let out a sigh. "What I'm trying to determine is if Alexei or the czar or any other Romanov might have been responsible for Irena's murder, perhaps using Petrov for the actual dirty work."

Vellefort put a hand to his chin and stroked his short beard. "When she left France, she was of no real value to them anymore, but I can't see how she'd be a detriment, either. I don't know why they might want to have her killed, but I can ask a few questions. See if I can come up with an answer for you."

"That's all I can ask." George raised his glass to the man.

"I can ask one more thing, if I may?" The two men directed their gazes at me. "Miss Teskey was half English. Do you have any idea who her mother was? I understand she died when her daughter was born."

"That would have been before my time in the diplomatic

corps. The mother died, did she? That's a shame, but I suppose that's what set everything in motion." Lord Vellefort gave me a nod. "I'll add that to my list of questions, but you might do better asking around here if you really want to know." He frowned. "Why do you want to know?"

"Before her death, Miss Teskey received threatening letters, telling her to leave London. She told me her mother had been married." I glanced at the two older people. Neither appeared particularly shocked. "Obviously, not to Alexei. I can't help but wonder if the husband is still alive and in London. If so, this is the last place he'd want that child to live."

George turned to me with a look of amazement. "You see now, Vellefort, why I wanted Lady Harleigh here. She brings an altogether different perspective."

Vellefort let out a snort. "Just as well, you're learning that now, as you two are to be married. Took me ten years of marriage to realize women are far smarter than we men."

"Hear! Hear!" Lady Vellefort raised her glass.

Chapter Nineteen

Since the day was fair—or as fair as November in London can be, I convinced George to walk the few blocks from the Velleforts' Mayfair residence back home.

"After all, we attended the reception together last night," I said. "What would be the point of hiding now?"

He agreed and sent the carriage on without us. The temperature was on the brisk side, so there were few others on foot. This should have allowed us to discuss the details we'd learned about Irena's family, if one were to call it that, but George had grown rather pensive.

I gave his arm a nudge. "What are you pondering so intently?"

"Nothing really. I'm mentally kicking myself. We should have spoken to Vellefort sooner."

"Don't kick yourself too hard. We may still find that Bradmore is our murderer." That had the desired effect of making him smile.

"My sense is you don't hold Bradmore in much esteem."

"Your senses are correct. I didn't think very highly of him

when I met him back in Hampshire. Now that I know how he treated Miss Teskey, he has fallen even lower in my esteem. He used her. Married her when he thought she'd provide him with a fat dowry, then wanted to divorce her when he no longer needed it. He is the worst sort of man."

"We don't know the circumstances that led to their marriage. You know yourself how difficult Irena could be, and once she'd made up her mind, he'd have had the devil's own time changing it."

"That doesn't excuse Bradmore. Six years ago, she would have been only eighteen. One doesn't make the best decisions at that age."

"Then, by all means, we won't excuse him, and of course he's still a suspect, but I have to wonder about the others in her life—the Teskeys, Petrov. I can't believe it never occurred to me to consider the husband of her mother."

"Of those choices, the only one we know anything about is Petrov." I tilted my head forward to see his face around the brim of my hat. "Can you imagine a military man's reaction to such an assignment? Go to France and watch after my daughter." I boggled my eyes.

"It's a far less risky occupation, so I'd imagine Petrov was delighted with the task. If he came along sometime after the Velleforts left France, he's been with her about five years. That's long enough to have developed a close friendship."

"It's also long enough to develop a strong distaste for someone. Do you think he might have murdered her?"

"Only if so ordered. Otherwise, he'd have the wrath of the Romanovs to face." He stared off into the distance. "The same is true of the Teskeys, which is why I wish we'd met with Vellefort sooner. We really need to know if there's some reason Alexei would want to be rid of her."

"I don't see it. The Romanovs are an old dynasty. They have so much power and so much wealth. How could one young woman living in another country cause them any trouble?" At George's look of derision, I corrected myself. "Enough trouble to have her murdered? I doubt they took any notice of her at all. On the other hand, both the Teskeys and Petrov might have been tired of this assignment. They might have thought they'd be done with her once she gained her majority. But no, they still had to act as her loyal retainers, while spying for the czar. Perhaps they came up with a plot to have Petrov murder her once she was out of the country."

We'd just turned the corner onto Chester Street, putting the cool wind at our backs and the sun on our faces, or perhaps that warm glow was just a change in my disposition because my home was in sight. I wondered if Irena had ever felt this way or if she had ever felt that she had a home. I turned to George.

"What of her mother's husband?"

He sighed. "Another person we don't know, and in his case, one we can't even identify."

"The Countess de Torby believes the woman was an aristo-crat. There must have been some sort of scandal at the time, don't you think?"

"Not necessarily. A woman and baby die in childbirth. Sadly, that's not very unusual."

"But the child didn't die."

"No, but she was ushered away as soon as possible. Chances are all reports were that both died."

I couldn't give up my point. "Reports, yes. But someone had to attend the mother and deliver the child. If even one person knew the truth, then word might have leaked out."

I pondered this until we arrived at my door.

"If there was any gossip, even the hushed-up variety, there is someone who might be aware of it, and she could be convinced to tell me what she knows," I said.

George had opened the door, but with an amused glance, he now blocked my entrance with his arm. "Do tell."

"Bradmore's aunt. Lady Esther. She was the Fiona of her day, always aware of the latest on-dit about everyone. If there was even a whisper of a scandal, she'd know about it. Perhaps I'll pay her a visit this afternoon."

Upon arriving home, I immediately sent out two notes. One to Lady Esther, asking if I could call on her, and one to Arthur Stoke-Whitney, assuring him this case would be resolved within the next few days. Thus, the scandal would no longer hang over my head. I didn't expect him to jump at my offer to sponsor his daughter, but I had promised Alicia.

Good fortune was with me as to the first note. Lady Esther replied promptly and in the affirmative. She'd be delighted to receive me for tea and a nice coze. How nice she'd consider the topic of our conversation remained to be seen.

George and I discussed just how much I should tell her. He thought I should only hint around the edges of Bradmore's dilemma, while I felt Lady Esther should be told everything. After all, she was his aunt. There was no danger she'd spread the story. Besides, Bradmore was at this moment on his way home, under arrest and escorted by the police. She'd find out soon enough.

Ultimately, he gave in, and since Petrov was still out on George's assignment, he thought this an excellent opportunity to go through the man's belongings. I left him to it and took the carriage back to Mayfair, to Lady Esther's residence.

The older woman and I were not particularly close friends— or friendly at all, for that matter. She'd been much more a fixture in society when I first arrived in London ten years ago. I could still recall her words when I'd been introduced to her as Reggie's fiancée. She'd cringed upon hearing my American accent. "Another one?" she'd said in tones of utter contempt. "What is wrong with our Englishmen these days?"

The only reason I hadn't curled up into a ball and cried was that it was hardly the first time an older matron had insulted me to my face for something over which I had no control. For the sake of my own pride, I had had to take the stance that if she didn't like Americans marrying Englishmen, she could just avoid us.

As it turned out, Reggie dropped me off at the old manor in the country, and I was the one who stayed out of society, except for a few weeks during the season. Apparently, these small exposures made her more tolerant of my Americanness, and I became more tolerant of her crankiness.

Of course, we pretended we held one another in high esteem.

Thus, when she greeted me in her drawing room, I took the bony hand she offered and smiled, as if seeing her was the highlight of my day. On this occasion, it might prove true.

"It's been far too long, Lady Esther," I said.

"Can't blame me for that," she replied, leaning on my arm. "I've been here. You haven't been by." She pointed with her walking stick to two very uncomfortable-looking Queen Anne chairs next to a tea table. They were the only surfaces not draped with fringed cloths or filled with various ornaments and trinkets.

"Once the weather turns, I don't get out much," she continued as we seated ourselves. "The damp makes my very bones ache. That's why I don't spend much time at Fairview. Can't keep that place warm enough." With a flitting of her hand, she indicated I should pour the tea. "I understand congratulations are in order. For you and Hazelton, that is."

"Yes, I managed to catch another Englishman. But I believe it's appropriate to convey congratulations to the groom, and good luck for the bride."

Her lips compressed as I handed over her tea. She muttered something under her breath that sounded like he would need all the luck.

"It may not be public knowledge just yet, but my nephew will soon be asking for your congratulations." She gave me a smug smile. "An Englishwoman."

"I had heard something of that, but I wasn't aware he'd actually proposed." I took a sip of my tea. Barely tepid. "Is it a settled matter now?"

"He has proposed, and it's all but settled." She gave me an insolent glare and tapped her stick on the floor. "How did you hear of it?"

"Bradmore mentioned it himself just a few days ago."

She narrowed her eyes. "Did he now? I wasn't aware the two of you were so well acquainted."

"Not all that well acquainted, but his wife was at my house, and for obvious reasons, he needed to ask her for a divorce."

Her teacup froze on its way to her lips, then slowly reversed course. "I beg your pardon? His what?"

I felt the tiniest twinge of guilt at shocking her in this way, but I had to tell her somehow, and if I'd wanted to be evil, I could have led off with the fact that Bradmore had been arrested for murder. I glanced at her stony expression. "His wife," I repeated. "Bradmore was married."

"*Was*? Do you mean to say he managed to obtain a divorce in a matter of days?" She set her cup on the table with such force, I was astonished it didn't shatter. "Don't string me along with tiny bits and bobs. I insist you tell me the whole story immediately."

While I complied, her eyes grew larger, and her fingers squeezed the walking stick so tightly, I expected the silver head to pop off. The one thing I didn't mention was how Bradmore came to meet Irena in the first place. His work for the Crown wasn't relevant to this discussion and wasn't something Lady Esther was likely to learn of, unless Bradmore chose to tell her. It wasn't my place to do so.

"Then that young woman I read about, the one who was murdered, she was my nephew's wife? Not Hazelton's?" She heaved a sigh. "You may as well tell me. Is he suspected of killing her?"

I actually began to feel some remorse about giving her this information. She was taking it far better than I'd expected, and I had to admire her for that. "I'm afraid he is a suspect. It didn't help that immediately following the crime, he left for Paris."

She let out a groan. "Idiots," she said, shaking her head. "Men are complete idiots."

"Inspector Delaney of the Metropolitan Police followed him there. I understand he has arrested your nephew and is return-ing with him to London. Even so, it is not at all certain that Bradmore will be charged with this crime. There are other sus-pects."

"If that is an attempt to jolly me out of my present distress, you may save your breath. I don't for one minute believe he murdered the chit. I'm just annoyed he allowed himself to come under suspicion." She pressed her lips into a thin line. "Then, to make it worse by running away. His actions defy logic. But this is good for you, I suppose. Your Mr. Hazelton must be absolved of the crime if my nephew was the poor fool married to her."

"I must admit that revelation brought me some relief, but as I said, Bradmore may not be charged with the crime. I'd like to discuss one of the other suspects with you, if I may. Miss Tes-key had received at least two threatening letters since coming to London."

"You cannot imagine they came from me. I had no knowl-edge of the girl until her name appeared in the papers."

"We don't yet know who sent the letters. I don't mean to suggest you had anything to do with them, but I did hope you had some prior knowledge of Miss Teskey. She was the offspring of Alexei Alexandrovich Romanov and a married British woman of the upper classes. It was twenty-four years ago, and I would imagine there were some whisperings among the ton."

She raised her brows. "And you assume I had some role in those whispers?"

I took a sip of tea. "Only on the receiving end, of course."

"How does this signify in the matter of the girl's murder?"

"I don't know that it does, but whoever wrote the letters told her to leave London. I'm sure the husband of her mother would have been distressed to see Miss Teskey in London. After all, he thought he'd rid himself of her long ago."

"Of course." She pursed her lips as she studied me. "I may have heard something about Alexei, but I'm afraid you're about to be disappointed if you think I can tell you who the woman was."

"Your nephew will be even more disappointed."

Her eyes flashed. "You mistake me. I am not dissembling. Something of this nature is almost impossible to keep secret. It would be whispered about still if the mother were alive. But when a woman dies giving birth, one keeps those little barbs to oneself. Even the worst gossips have some decency. I'm afraid you are also asking me to stretch my memory back too far. I do recall he visited here, whether that was twenty-four years ago, or more or less, I couldn't say. Many women flirted with him. He was an attractive man, and had one conducted an affair with him, it would hardly be of note, you know."

She was right. I was terribly disappointed. I had underestimated the discretion of society at large. Yes, they could keep a secret, but I didn't think they could prevent someone like Lady Esther from finding it out.

"There is one thing." She held up a finger as she stared through me, focused on a memory. "Again, I couldn't tell you if the timing is right or not, but there was a delegation to Saint Petersburg somewhere around that time. In addition to the prince, several MPs made up the group, and of course, they took their wives." She held up a hand before I could ask my questions. "I have no idea who they were, my dear. All I know is I wasn't part of the delegation."

I filed the information away for later discussion with George. It was a good lead, but I had no idea how to go about following it. As it seemed I'd exhausted her store of information, I took my leave. Perhaps Mr. Petrov had returned with some news by now.

Petrov stepped through George's door as the carriage pulled up before my house. Once Jack had helped me down, I'd have scurried over there myself if I hadn't spotted Mrs. Chiswick walking down the street in my direction. Instead, I let myself into my own house and made straight for the library and the door to the garden. When I reached the back of George's house, I spied him and Petrov speaking in his study and quickened my step. Both men glanced out the window as I sped by. George was opening the door to his drawing room just as I arrived.

"Your timing is perfect," he said, taking my hand and leading me into the study. "Petrov is just giving me his report on the alibis of the theater folk."

I stopped at the doorway. "That's the errand you sent him on? A man who barely speaks English?"

"He seemed to think he could do it." He lowered his voice. "And I needed to get him out of the house."

"That's right. You planned to check his belongings. Did you find anything?"

"Nothing of importance." He gestured to the doorway. "Shall we?"

The large Russian gave me a nod as I seated myself beside him in one of the club chairs near the window. George leaned against the desk.

"Good afternoon, Mr. Petrov," I said in French. "I understand you've been to the theater. Did you happen to speak to Sally Cooper?"

"Not to her, no. She only speaks English, but one of the other actresses spoke to me."

"She spoke French?"

He shook his head, and his expression brightened. "Olga is Russian. We've spoken many times when I came to fetch Irena. She came here many years ago, but she still remembers the old language."

I gained the impression Petrov had enjoyed many talks with Olga. Well, good for him.

"I told her Sally gave two different stories about where she was during the break in rehearsal that day, and asked if she knew where the woman really was. Olga didn't want to tell me, but I reminded her how much Sally hated Irena. Olga, she has a soft heart. She didn't want me to blame Sally when she didn't do it."

"Ah, so she knew where Sally was," George said.

"She tells me Sally decided she'd had enough of Gilliam and the Hanover Theater. She was at another theater—for an audition."

And there went another suspect.

"I suppose I can understand why she didn't want to risk that information getting out," I conceded. "She wouldn't want Gilliam to hear of it."

"I checked with the other theater. She was there. Miss Cooper didn't like Irena, but she didn't kill her. She just had a secret. This is why she lied to you."

"Perhaps you can clear up a few things about yourself for us," George said. "Like why a military man was saddled with the task of watching after a headstrong young woman. That couldn't have been how you imagined your career turning out."

Petrov looked surprised. "I wasn't a military man. I was

bodyguard to Alexei. He wasn't really a military man, either. He was a sloppy commander with no interest in the navy or military campaigns, or anything that distracted from his own amusement. Since I was to protect him, both his poor command and his amusements often put me at risk. When he asked me to watch after Irena, I was glad to do it." He shrugged. "It had to be the safer of the two assignments."

George stared absently past us, stroking his chin, as he weighed the man's words. "I've heard he's known for slow ships and fast women, neither of which is without peril."

"As his bodyguard, you must always have been by Alexei's side," I said. "Did he ever confide in you about Miss Teskey's mother?"

"He never talked about her."

My shoulders slumped. If Petrov couldn't tell us, we'd have to wait for word from Alexei. That could take weeks.

Igor released a heavy sigh. "He took Irena because it was the honorable thing to do. It was also easy for him to do. He was always demanding allowances from the czar for this woman or that woman. Why not his child? But he also took her because her mother's husband demanded it. And Alexei swore he'd never tell Irena or anyone else who her mother was."

"Why would he make such a promise?" I asked.

Igor curled his lip. "He detested the man. Said he never wanted Irena near him."

"She told me her mother was murdered by her own husband," I said. "She claimed Mrs. Teskey told her."

"I never heard that, but the man couldn't wait to rid himself of his wife's baby. Gave it to the man who cuckolded him." He lifted his arms at his sides. "With that kind of anger, who knows?"

Who knows, indeed? How angry would he be if he learned Irena had moved to London? I glanced at George, wondering if he was satisfied with Petrov's explanation. Before I could ask him, there was a knock at the door, and his butler stepped into the room with a note.

George read the note and glanced up, startled to see both Petrov and me leaning forward. "It's from Delaney," he said. "He's returned from Paris and has Bradmore in custody. We can visit him in the morning."

Chapter Twenty

I'd never had a reason to call on Inspector Delaney at his precinct, and I had no idea what to expect. I was surprised by how open the interior of the building was. A constable sat behind a long barrier just past the entry. Behind him, a wood-paneled wall, about a quarter of the width of the room, divided this section from the rest of the large warehouse-type area. Small offices lined one side wall. Desks and tables, long and short, were lined up across the floor, each positioned under a lamp that hung from the high wood-paneled ceiling, which echoed the general hum from a dozen or so conversations. Many of the desks were occupied by uniformed police officers and other men and women, not in uniform. Were they criminals?

I had no chance to ask George, as the constable stationed at the barrier, really a chest-high counter, pointed to the door we'd just entered through. "Lost property office is around the corner," he said.

"I'll file that bit of elucidation away for another time," George said. "Today we are here to meet with Inspector Delaney."

The officer looked us over. "Name?"

George provided his, and the man sent a boy off to notify Delaney, then returned to some documents he was filing, leaving us to cool our heels. Though I was a bit put off by his brusque manner, I reminded myself I wasn't a customer or a patron here. This was a different type of business than I might typically visit in my daily pursuits.

The boy returned and solemnly escorted us to one of the offices along the wall. In addition to a battered desk, a cabinet, three wooden chairs, and a coatrack, it contained Delaney and Bradmore. The latter was seated in one of the chairs against the wall and wore manacles, his hair and clothing were dirty and disheveled, yet he still managed to appear relaxed.

Delaney looked anything but as he jerked to his feet. "What are you doing, bringing Lady Harleigh in here? This is no place for her."

"If you think she'd allow me to leave her at home, Inspector, you greatly overrate my influence."

"Of course I came," I said. "We were both eager to see Mr. Bradmore and hear what he has to say for himself."

"Well, I hope it comes as no surprise that what I have to say is, 'Not guilty.'"

"No surprise whatso—"

"Hold up." Delaney raised a hand, interrupting George. "This man is my prisoner in a case of murder. I still have to take his statement and have him moved to Newgate. Once that's done, you can visit him there."

"Come now, Inspector," George said. "You sent me a note, telling me you'd returned with him and that I could call this morning. Surely you expected me to do so."

"I did, but only because I had news for you." He rifled through the papers on his desk and pulled one out. He handed it to George with something of a flourish. "Here. This is all that should concern you at the moment."

I leaned across the desk to see for myself. "It's the infamous marriage certificate." And Bradmore's name was listed, along with Miss Teskey's.

"My reason for going to Paris. I could hardly start divorce proceedings if I couldn't prove we were actually married." Bradmore glared at Delaney. "And that's the only thing I wanted from her. I had no reason to kill her."

I ignored Bradmore and pursued my own interests. "Now that you have proof Hazelton was not Miss Teskey's husband, is he no longer under suspicion?"

"He's moved much farther down the list." Delaney reached out and snatched the document from George's hand.

"Wait," I said. "I need that. Right now, everyone believes Hazelton was married to Miss Teskey. I'd like to set the record straight."

"I'm afraid that will have to wait, Lady Harleigh." His glower told me he was in no mood to argue. "This is evidence." He tucked the evidence back among the assorted documents on his desk, along with my last hope of ever escaping this scandal.

"Will you at least let Bradmore write a statement for the press?" I asked.

"He's not making statements to anyone, not the press and not the two of you."

"What about legal counsel?" George said. "Surely he has the right to legal advice before making his official statement to you."

Delaney looked exhausted as he jerked his head toward Bradmore. "He's been offered a chance to speak to legal counsel. He turned it down."

Bradmore parted his lips to speak, but George was faster. "Well, he's changed his mind. I'm here to act as such counsel."

This elicited a bark of laughter from Delaney. "You can't represent the man when you're a suspect in the same case."

"But I'm barely a suspect. You said so yourself. The probability of my being the murderer is far lower than Bradmore's."

"If he's fool enough to accept such counsel, he deserves you."

"I accept," Bradmore said. "I'd like to confer with my counsel."

George gave Delaney a sheepish grin. "I gather he's fool enough."

"If they're both agreeable to this, Inspector, it must show you that neither of them believes the other committed the crime." At least it seemed so to me.

Delaney stacked the papers on his desk, perhaps in an attempt to calm his temper. "Don't fool yourself. They're just comrades willing to back one another up." He drew in a breath and expelled it in something of a growl. "You have ten minutes, and I'll be right outside the door. After that, he will be processed for transfer to Newgate, and you will leave before I arrest you for interfering with an investigation."

The inspector left the door open, but he did step outside.

George drew up two chairs near Bradmore, and the three of us gathered close. "Did you kill her?" he asked.

Bradmore's expression changed from wary to angry. "No, and if you're only doing this so that you can set me up for her murder, I'll dismiss you now."

"It wouldn't be necessary or worth my time," George said. "You set yourself up by running off to Paris. Between that and your sudden move to new lodgings, with nothing but the essentials. I can see why you're Delaney's prime suspect."

"I went to Paris to get proof of our marriage. As to my lodgings, I had been letting a furnished flat in the city. Now that I'm entering an engagement with a suitable lady, I decided I needed a more prestigious address."

"How did you know to go to Paris?" I asked. "I know you called on Miss Teskey the day she was murdered, but I understand she refused to see you."

Bradmore nodded. "That's what your housekeeper told me, but before I even left your doorstep, Irena threw open an upper window and said she'd meet me in the garden."

"She called down at you from the window, and none of the neighbors witnessed it? Jackson must have been napping."

"Timing is everything, I suppose. By the time I walked around the corner and found your gate, she was already there and let me in." He cast his gaze between George and me. "You must believe me. All we did was talk. She'd calmed down a great deal since breakfast." He shook his head. "And before you say it, I suppose I could have handled that better. When we spoke in the garden, she admitted she really had no interest in being married to me and was willing to allow me to file for a divorce. We decided I should go back to her flat in Paris and retrieve the marriage certificate."

He held up his manacled hands. "I swear by all that's holy, she was both alive and reasonably calm when I left her."

"Did she lock the gate behind you?" I asked.

"Irena doesn't bother with things like locking up, and I was too pleased with the result of our conversation to think of reminding her. She was still on the bench when I closed the gate. Someone must have come in after I left." He shifted his gaze to George. "The inspector said she was strangled?"

"She was." George stood and moved to Delaney's desk. "I'm afraid we're running low on suspects at this point." He turned and went about his usual pacing. "Did you see anyone on the street when you left the garden?"

"I took no notice. I was eager to be off and headed straight to Grosvenor Street to find a hack. If anyone was lurking about, I didn't see him."

"What kind of spy are you, Bradmore?" I tsked.

"This wasn't a covert assignment, madam," he snapped. "When I'm not working, I can be as oblivious as the next chap."

George stopped pacing and leveled his gaze at Bradmore. "Have you had any communication with the Romanovs or Irena's bodyguard, Igor Petrov?"

"She had a bodyguard?" His eyes widened. "A bodyguard named Igor?"

George cocked a brow. "You didn't know?"

"No, and I can only wish she'd had one sooner, though for all the good he did her, I suppose it doesn't matter. As to the Romanovs or the Teskeys, I've had no contact with them. Do you think they might have something to do with her murder?" He looked doubtful.

George came up behind me and placed his hands on my shoulders. "As I said, we're running low on suspects."

"Did Miss Teskey ever speak to you about her mother?" I asked.

Bradmore raised his brows. "Her mother? No." With a sigh, he turned away. "Seeing you two like that while I'm like this"—he raised his hands, jiggling the manacles—"reminds me that I'm likely to lose my fiancée once she hears of my arrest."

I bit my lip. I did feel some sympathy for the man, but he'd had no right to become engaged while still married to another woman. "Your aunt will pay her a visit, I should think. Perhaps she can salvage your engagement."

Bradmore's shoulders sagged. "Aunt Esther knows?"

At that point, our time ran out, and Delaney returned. "Mr. Bradmore's transport is here." He turned deliberately to George. "Time's up."

George offered Delaney his hand. "Thank you for allowing us a few moments." He turned back to Bradmore. "I'll meet up with you at Newgate."

With that, we left the office and made our way out of the building. "Do you believe him?" I asked.

He ran a hand through his hair. "Well, now that I'm representing him, I'd like to, but as no one has come forward to say they saw her alive after he left her, it doesn't look good for him."

I sighed. "What will you do now?"

"I'll report in to the Home Office, just in case they want to step in to aid Bradmore, and then I'll meet with him at Newgate and work on some sort of defense. You should not come with me. The precinct was one thing, but Newgate really is no place for a lady. Perhaps you should go to the *Observer* and give them the news that Bradmore is in custody and that he was Irena's husband."

"I wish Delaney had let me take that marriage certificate. Mosley would respond better with proof."

We'd reached the carriage, and George helped me in. "You take the carriage. I'll find a cab and go about my business. Oh, and you might want to check your bag before you talk to Mosley. I borrowed something for him. But please remember, it's only borrowed."

I frowned in confusion as he withdrew and headed up the street. With a jolt, the carriage pulled away. I opened the strings of my bag and looked in it. George had slipped the marriage certificate inside. Delaney was likely to throw him in a cell with Bradmore for this, but my heart swelled with gratitude.

In George's absence, I needed a companion for this trip, so I stopped at home to see if Hetty was willing to accompany me. Fortunately, she was both home and willing, and before long, we were on our way to Fleet Street and the *Daily Observer*. I told her of our progress with regard to Bradmore, and she repeated how she simply couldn't believe Gilliam would have murdered Irena. Neither of us knew what to think of Igor Petrov.

I relayed the details of my visit with Lady Esther and recalled that I hadn't mentioned it to George. "As we seem to keep exonerating our original suspects, I can't help but wonder about the person who wrote the threatening letters to her. If he was following her, he might have known to find her at my house."

Hetty squinted at me. "You think it might be the husband of her mother? After all these years, why would he trouble himself with her now?"

"Because she'd moved to London. What if Alexei told her who her mother was? Though people seem to think the mother died giving birth to her, Miss Teskey said she was murdered—by her own husband. If you were that man, wouldn't you be worried about what she might know or, worse, reveal?"

The carriage pulled up in front of the newspaper office, and Hetty and I stepped out. I was as surprised to see the young and lanky Mr. Ryan still at the front desk as he was to see me.

"Lady Harleigh, have you come back to write for us?"

"No, Mr. Ryan. I haven't come to do any writing, but I am here to see Mr. Mosley. I do hope he's in."

"If you give me just a moment, I'll go and check." He slipped through the door to the back offices, allowing the sound of raised voices and the clacking of typewriters to flow through until the door swung shut behind him. I took note of his new confidence. This job was doing him good. I wondered if he was getting along any better with Mosley just as I heard the man bellowing—even through the closed door. Some things never changed.

Mr. Ryan returned to the front desk and guided us around to Mosley's office.

"Lady Harleigh." Mosley stood behind his desk and indicated we should be seated. Ryan closed the door as he left. "I hope you've come with some news, ma'am. I'll lose readers if I don't print something new soon."

"I'm afraid I don't have an actual culprit for you, Mr. Mosley, but I do have something to report." I pulled the marriage certificate from my bag and handed it to him. "Proof that Miss

Teskey was married to Mr. Bradmore. He had it in his possession when Delaney brought him back from France." I told him about our visit to the police station this morning. "I brought this so you can see for yourself, but I must return it to Delaney as soon as may be."

Mosley studied the document. "Then you do have a culprit for me. This Bradmore fellow is the killer."

"Killer? No, no. You are being far too hasty, Mr. Mosley. There's no proof Bradmore killed her."

"Maybe not, but the police have arrested him. If he's going to Newgate, he's to be charged with the crime. I can certainly print that, and I intend to do so immediately, before someone else does." He gave me a hard stare, taking in what must be my shocked countenance. "Isn't that what you wanted? To clear Hazelton's name?"

"Yes, of course, but it's by no means certain that Bradmore is a murderer. There are other suspects."

"Who?"

Hetty's glare dared me to say Gilliam's name, while Mosley drummed his fingers on the desk with impatience.

"There was a man who was threatening her."

Mosley heaved a sigh. "Does this man have a name?"

"You are applying a great deal of pressure, Mosley. I am working as quickly as I can."

"I've a deadline to meet, and I see no reason not to print this story."

"Well, please stop short of accusing the man of murder." I picked up the marriage certificate to return it to my bag and noticed Irena's birth date. An idea began to take form. "Mr. Mosley, how long has the *Observer* been in operation?"

"A good forty years or so. Why?"

"Do you have copies of all the old papers printed?"

"We do, and again, I'll ask, why?"

"I'm hoping some of those old papers might help me find

out who was threatening Miss Teskey. While you write your story, I'd like to do some research." I showed him Irena's birth date and asked for the papers dated around that time. "Perhaps two weeks both before and after."

"What do you hope to find?" Hetty asked.

"Miss Teskey's mother."

Mosley settled us in an office across the hall from his. Mr. Ryan brought in an armful of newspapers and swept aside the original occupant's work on the desk to make room.

"Tell me what to look for, and I'll help," Hetty said.

We were seated on opposite sides of the large desk, the papers stacked between us. "We're looking for death notices for a young woman. They may or may not mention that she died in childbirth. Society finds it unseemly to announce the reason for death under these circumstances." I opened the center drawer of the desk and found paper and pencils. "When you find one, write down the name and date."

What followed was a solid hour of studying small print until it floated before my eyes. Hetty refolded her last paper and placed it on the finished stack, then let out a shriek.

"Just look at my fingers!" She held the offending appendages in front of my face. Indeed, they were completely covered in newsprint. I cautiously examined my own, which were every bit as bad. "This never happens at home," she said.

"That's because Jenny irons the newspapers before you read them. It sets the ink." I folded my last paper and added it to the stack. Hetty had pulled out a handkerchief and was attempting to remove the ink from her fingers. "There's no point in doing that yet, Aunt."

"Aren't we finished?"

"I hope not." I reached for her notes. "How many did you find?"

"Just the one. Poor woman. She and the baby died."

"I found two myself."

I read Hetty's notes twice before I allowed myself to believe it. Jane Stoke-Whitney passed away at her home in Chelmsford on January 24. The very date Irena listed as her birth date. I forced myself to remain calm. Irena might have had no idea of her exact date of birth, since she was sent so quickly to the Teskeys. This could all be a coincidence. Then I recalled Lady Esther had mentioned a visit of dignitaries to Saint Petersburg, including some members of Parliament. I wondered when Stoke-Whitney became an MP.

Leaving Hetty staring at me, I slipped from my seat and crossed the hall to Mosley's office. The editor jumped as I pushed open the door. "I need a list of the members of Parliament from eighteen seventy-five. Is there a way to find that?"

He pointed a finger at me. "You've found something. I see it in your eyes."

"I'm not certain, but I'll know more when you find that list."

Mosley grunted as he pushed himself up from his chair and moved around me and through the doorway. After taking a breath, he let out a shout. "Ryan!"

The young man popped his head around the swinging door at the end of the hallway, leading me to believe this was their standard form of communication. Mosley told him what we were looking for and followed me into the other office, where Hetty waited.

I joined her at the desk and explained my theory about the husband of Irena's mother and why he might have wanted her to leave the country. In failing to achieve that goal, he might have murdered her. "We have three names of women who died at the time of Miss Teskey's birth. Now I want to know if any of them had husbands who were MPs at the time."

"And then what?" Hetty asked. If one of the husbands was an MP, what does that prove?" She frowned. "What I don't understand is why someone hasn't contacted Miss Teskey's real father. Surely he knows the name of her mother."

"I would certainly hope so. However, Alexei is currently out scaling the Rocky Mountains or learning how to hunt a buffalo. In other words, he is not near a telegraph office. Michael sent him word of his daughter's death. We asked him to send another cable, inquiring about Miss Teskey's mother, but I have no idea how long it will take to obtain an answer."

Ryan came in, carrying a large book. He dropped it on the desk and opened it to a marked section. "This should be the list you need."

"Wait." I reached out to stop Mr. Ryan as he was about to leave. "There's something more." I turned to Mosley. "I need any information you can find about a formal visit to Saint Petersburg. A big one. Several dignitaries would have gone, and prominent members of Parliament and their wives. I need to know if it happened around April of seventy-four and who went on this trip." I gave him a helpless look. "Would you have that information, or do I ask too much?"

"We're a newspaper, Lady Harleigh. A trip such as that would be news." Mosley gave me a wink. "We've got it."

The two men left us to retrieve the documents we needed. I checked the three women's names against the list of MPs for 1875. The only one that matched was Stoke-Whitney. He had been a member of Parliament for some time. When I looked up, Hetty was watching me.

"Come now," she said. "Tell me what you're thinking."

I shook my head. "I don't know if I'm even willing to think it. If I find this woman was part of the group who visited the Russian royal family nine months before she died giving birth, it doesn't prove she was Miss Teskey's mother, but it certainly raises my suspicions."

She patted my hand. "I suppose that means we'll have to wait to hear from her father."

"Yes, we'll simply have to verify it with him."

"Then why do you look so distressed? You are in a far better position than you were just yesterday. Hazelton is no longer under suspicion. You will soon find out if this man has anything to do with Miss Teskey's death."

"That's not true. We may find out if this man's wife was her mother, and I feel quite certain she was. But even if Alexei gives us his name, proving he murdered Miss Teskey is another matter."

Mosley and Ryan returned with a new stack of newspapers. Shuffling through them, Mosley glanced at the front pages. Finally, he stopped and pulled one out. "Here it is. Delegation travels to Saint Petersburg to visit the emperor and his family."

I stood to read over his shoulder. "There. The list of delegates." I ran my finger down the short column until I came to the name I'd been expecting. "Arthur Stoke-Whitney and his wife, Jane."

Chapter Twenty-one

⟨❧⟩

"You cannot print this, Mr. Mosley." I barely restrained myself from stomping my foot. Mosley, lacking in such discipline, slammed his palm on the desk.

"This is news, Lady Harleigh. You can't stop me from printing it."

"What we have at this point is nothing more than idle speculation, and you know it. Something like this isn't even worthy of the Miss Information column."

He pinched the bridge of his nose and seemed to be wrestling with his more responsible self. When he dropped his hand, his gaze landed on Mr. Ryan, who stood in the doorway. "What are you gaping at?" he growled. "Get yourself back to work."

Ryan fled the room, and I placed a hand on Mosley's arm. "Any insinuations you print now will only give rise to a lawsuit from Stoke-Whitney. I'll take the information to Inspector Delaney. I don't know if he'll do anything about it, but at least you and I will have done our best."

With one enormous sigh, Mosley pushed away from the desk. "I've missed the deadline for the morning edition, anyway, and I already ran the story about Bradmore." He waved a hand over the newspapers and documents spread out on the desk. "Show that to Inspector Delaney, but you tell him if he doesn't pursue an investigation into this Stoke-Whitney bloke, I'll be at his desk first thing in the morning to find out why."

"An admirable plan, Mr. Mosley."

He made me promise to send him word of Delaney's intentions regarding Stoke-Whitney. Then Hetty and I returned home, where to my surprise, Gilliam's motorcar waited in the street.

"I'd forgotten Herbert planned to call today."

"Herbert, is it?" I nudged her shoulder with mine as we stepped through the door.

Hetty was beaming. She barely paused to leave her coat with Mrs. Thompson and check her hair in the mirror before opening the doors to the drawing room in an elaborate sweep.

"A letter's come for you, my lady," Mrs. Thompson said as she took my coat.

I picked up the letter from the tray in the hall and joined Hetty and Gilliam in the drawing room.

"I hope this isn't an imposition," Gilliam said. "I told Mrs. Chesney I'd call on her today, so I thought I'd best wait for her return."

"Of course not. Shall I order refreshments, or are you planning on taking my aunt for a drive?"

I know he made some answer, as I heard his voice, but he lost my attention as soon as I looked down at the letter in my hand. It was from Arthur Stoke-Whitney. I fumbled with the paper as if I had ten thumbs, and finally revealed the message. He did not consent to my sponsorship of his daughter in light of the scandal involving my fiancé. Just a few hours ago, I might have been highly offended by his answer, but at the moment, all I could see was his handwriting.

A quick check out the window told me the carriage had already gone. I turned back to Gilliam and Hetty on the sofa, in conversation. "Mr. Gilliam, forgive me, but I must beg a favor of you."

The man had been in mid-sentence and turned a surprised gaze at me. "Of course, Lady Harleigh. Consider me at your service."

"Excellent, excellent. Give me just one moment to write a note." I waved absently, then hurried to the library to write a request for Delaney to call on me and bring the threatening letters with him just as soon as may be. In my haste, I nearly stumbled over Jenny in the hallway. I sent her to fetch George and Petrov and returned to the drawing room, where my companions waited.

I handed the note to Gilliam and asked him to take it to the inspector at his precinct. "If at all possible, I'd be grateful if you could bring Delaney back with you."

He picked up his hat and gloves and gave me a curious look. "I'll do my best to convince him."

As Hetty walked him out, I darted back to the library, where several newspapers lay on my desk. I rifled through them until I found the article about the gala for the Russians and the picture of Stoke-Whitney. It was not a great likeness, but it would have to do.

Hetty blocked my way out. "What are you doing? Why the sudden urgency?"

"Urgency? I suppose that's just in my mind, but all the pieces are coming together, Aunt Hetty, and I simply must find out if I'm right."

"About what?"

I tucked the newspaper under one arm and looped the other through hers, then led her back to the drawing room. "I'd prefer to wait to explain everything once the others arrive. I have only the slightest grasp on this theory, and if I start going over it now, I may lose even that."

Fortunately, we didn't have long to wait. George and Petrov arrived within minutes, and I waved them into the drawing room. "Thank you for coming so quickly. I was afraid you'd still be at Newgate with Bradmore."

"I've just returned," George said. "What has you so distressed? Something in that newspaper?"

"No, but there's something in here I need Mr. Petrov to look at." I held the paper out to him, folded to reveal Stoke-Whitney's picture. "Does this man look familiar to you?" Recalling I was speaking to Petrov, I asked again in French.

He studied the picture for a long time. With a frown, he glanced up at me. "Perhaps? I think you are asking if this is the man I saw following Irena." His pursed lips disappeared behind his whiskers. "It could be, but I usually saw him at the theater when it was dark. I never got a good look at him."

Bother! "Could be" was not enough, but now that I thought of it, he wasn't the only one to see the man.

George took the paper from me. "Arthur Stoke-Whitney? Why?"

I had everyone sit while I explained about our search into the archives of the *Daily Observer*. "He and his first wife, Jane, were part of a delegation to Saint Petersburg to visit the Russian royal family in seventy-four, when Alexei was still in Russia. They stayed for several weeks. Nine months later, Jane Stoke-Whitney died giving birth—right on Miss Teskey's birthday. Is that just a coincidence?"

George narrowed his eyes. "Sounds like one to me."

"I realize this is only loosely tied together," I continued, "but it does tie. Jane was in Saint Petersburg with Alexei, and she died nine months later, the very day the child was born and pressed onto Alexei. It could easily be coincidence. That's why I showed that picture to Mr. Petrov. I'd hoped he might recognize Stoke-Whitney as the man who'd been following Miss Teskey."

Petrov's brow furrowed as he tried to follow the conversation in English. "If you think this man killed Irena, I will recognize him."

Well, well. The words were slow and heavily accented, but Petrov had a better grasp of English than I'd thought.

"It doesn't work that way, old chap," George said. "We can't manufacture evidence. It's a good theory, but we have no proof."

I smiled. "Not yet, we don't. That's why I asked Inspector Delaney to come by with the threatening letters, which I will compare with the letter I just received from Stoke-Whitney." I dangled it from my fingertips.

A range of emotions passed over George's face. I was sure he was running all the bits and pieces through his mind. At least I hoped he was, because the end result was a brilliant smile. "I think you may be onto something," he said.

Aunt Hetty sat back with a smile. "Good work, Frances."

Petrov still looked confused. "Why would this man murder Irena?"

"Because she dared to come to London—his world. She made no secret about being Alexei's daughter. Somebody might recall these little scraps of information I dug up and put them together. And for all he knew, Miss Teskey knew exactly who her mother was and might be willing to make it public. After all, it would seem Stoke-Whitney sent her away in the first place to avoid a scandal. Her being in town might dredge that scandal back up to the surface. With his political ambitions, he couldn't allow that to happen."

"You are a genius, my dear," George said. "I think this calls for a toast."

I basked in the praise for only a moment. "Shouldn't we wait for Delaney?"

"Gad, no. We'll have another when he gets here." He stepped over to the drinks cabinet and returned with four glasses and a bottle of brandy. Hetty must have replenished our supply. Once the glasses were filled, we held them aloft. George frowned. "Not sure what the proper toast would be."

A good point. Irena was still dead, whether we'd solved the case or not. "To justice," I said. "That's all we can claim in this case. We didn't stop the crime, and we can't bring her back, but with any luck, the culprit will face justice."

A perfunctory knock preceded Mrs. Thompson's entrance. "Inspector Delaney and Mr. Gilliam to see you, ma'am."

I glanced at George, who placed his glass on a table and stepped forward to greet the two arrivals.

"Don't be too happy to see me, Hazelton." Delaney moved toward him and held up his hand with thumb and index finger a hair's breadth apart. "I'm this close to having you arrested."

George grimaced and backed up toward me. "Ah, yes. I suppose this is about a particular document, isn't it?"

"You know very well it is." Delaney glowered. "You've pushed the line many a time, but taking evidence right off my desk crosses that line. You may find yourself right next to your friend Bradmore."

"I have the document, Inspector."

I retrieved my bag from the hall table and handed the folded page to him. "It proved helpful in discovering some new information about the case, and when we tell you, you may find yourself releasing Bradmore rather than locking up Hazelton."

We all took a seat, and I ran through everything I knew, including the fact that Petrov had been unable to identify Stoke-Whitney as the man he'd seen following Irena.

"Might I see that picture?" Gilliam said. "I saw the fellow around the theater a few times, as well."

"Of course." I indicated the newspaper on the tea table, then watched as Gilliam wrestled with his conscience for several minutes, before tossing the paper back on the table. "I'd like to say he's the one, but the best I can say is he could be."

"This is a poor photograph, so that's understandable. That's why I asked Inspector Delaney to bring the threatening letters that were sent to Miss Teskey. I'd like to compare the handwriting on them to the letter I just received from Mr. Stoke-Whitney."

"Lady Harleigh, you never cease to surprise me." Delaney pulled the letters from his coat pocket and smoothed them out on the table. I held my breath and placed my letter beside Delaney's. The writing was as close to identical as I could hope for.

Delaney leaned back in his seat, working his jaw. "This proves he wrote these letters, but it doesn't place him in your garden at the time of her death."

I sank back in my chair. "I hadn't thought of that."

Delaney came to his feet. "It helps. It's enough to authorize an interview with the man."

"Your constable interviewed the neighbors," George said. "Did none of them report a stranger on the street?"

The inspector made his way to the hall. Unwilling to let him leave without an answer, George and I followed.

"I'll review Constable Martin's report again," he said, "but I don't believe so. Most of the residents of the street were either away from home or keep to themselves."

He paused with one hand on the door handle and the other held up to stop us. "This is a good lead, but now you two need to step back and allow us to follow it."

Chapter Twenty-two

Mrs. Thompson was just bringing in the tea service when George and I returned to the drawing room. She placed the tray on the table and, noting the increase in our numbers, left to fetch more cups. I took a seat and poured for Gilliam, Hetty, and Petrov while George paced behind the sofa.

Hetty turned her gaze first on him, then me. "Well, why aren't you two celebrating? Isn't this good news?"

"I'm not completely exonerated just yet, and neither is Bradmore," George said. "And we won't be unless Stoke-Whitney falls apart and confesses under Delaney's questioning." He stopped pacing long enough to give Hetty a doubtful look. "He's been a politician long enough to know when to speak out and when to keep quiet. Delaney is good at getting to the truth, but Stoke-Whitney is an expert at twisting it for his own means."

Hetty peered over her cup at him. "But if the inspector has the letters, Stoke-Whitney can hardly lie about having written them."

"Can't he? Even if he does admit to it, threating someone

and carrying out the act are very different things. He could have one of his assistants say he was working at his office at the time of the murder. We have no way of placing him here. No one saw him."

"Where is Jackson when we need him?" I busied my hands, refolding the newspaper. "What good is having a busybody in the neighborhood if he misses important things, like murderers lurking about?"

George leaned on the back of the sofa between Hetty and Gilliam. "I suppose even Jackson devotes part of the day to his duties."

"I suspect he considers gossip as one of his duties. Do you know he told Mrs. Chiswick about the gate connecting our gardens?"

His eyes narrowed. "How would he know that?"

"From snooping. As I said, he's a busybody."

Mrs. Thompson returned with the extra cups as George rounded the sofa. He stopped and allowed her to pass to the table but kept his eyes on me. "Jackson certainly keeps watch over the street, but he can hardly see through buildings. How would he know about the gate?"

"Somebody must have told him." I shrugged. "He visits with you from time to time, doesn't he, Mrs. Thompson?"

Mrs. Thompson straightened from her task and faced me with an expression of wounded pride. "He does, my lady, but surely you're not suggesting anyone in this house would share that kind of information with an outsider? If you and Mr. Hazelton use that gate to come and go between your houses, that's your business."

"There you have it," George said. "Your staff wouldn't have told him, so how would he know?"

"Does it matter?"

He held out a hand. "Come with me."

Intrigued by the glint in his eyes, I let him lead me through the library, out to the garden, and over to the Wilton Mews gate.

"You told me you keep this locked, correct?" he asked.

"Yes. From the outside, one needs a key, but from this side, one simply turns that knob to drive the bolt home. Mrs. Thompson opens it for deliveries. Perhaps Jackson stopped by while the coalman was here." I raised a brow. "You're still trying to determine how he managed to see our passage, aren't you?"

"Indeed." He turned me around and set my back against the gate. "Look toward my garden and tell me if you can see the gate."

I couldn't.

With a hand on my shoulders, he walked me forward. "Keep your eyes focused on the wall and stop as soon as you see the gate."

I was surprised by just how many steps I had to take. First, my house blocked the view, then the tree, then finally—

"Now I see it." I glanced around to see we were standing next to the bench where Irena was killed.

"Jackson would have had to walk more than halfway across your garden, which is usually kept locked."

"It is always locked. Petrov managed to climb over the wall, but Jackson is nowhere near his size, nor can I imagine him exerting himself to that extent. How did he get in here?"

"Shall we go find out?"

"You mean to question him?" I pressed my fingers to my temples, as if that might help to organize my thoughts. "I am completely lost now. Did Jackson have something to do with Miss Teskey's murder?"

"I don't know, but this is a loose thread, and I mean to tug at it. Are you coming?"

Within two minutes, we stood at the service entrance of Colonel Perkins's house, knocking on the door. A thin young maid in a stained apron answered, took one look at us, and ran back in, calling for Jackson. Since she'd obligingly left the door open, we stepped inside.

The short hallway led to an open area, probably the servants' lounge, where Jackson was rising from a chair at the worktable. His expression was an array of conflicting instincts. Outrage at our audacity at letting ourselves into his domain, and the ingrained manners that demanded he greet us with polite deference.

"Mrs. Chiswick is not home at present, sir, my lady." Jackson nodded at us both in turn.

"We're actually here to see you, Jackson," George said. "We'll only detain you a moment."

The butler glanced around the room and spotted the little maid hovering in the doorway. Another servant peered over her shoulder. "You may go about your business." They scattered as he intoned the words, and he returned his attention to George. "How may I be of assistance, sir?"

"It's a sticky situation, Jackson. You see, there's been an accusation made against you, and I've come to find out if it's true."

Indignation stiffened Jackson's spine. "I can't imagine what you might have heard."

"I'm afraid you've been accused of trespassing, specifically, in Lady Harleigh's garden."

The butler relaxed enough to give us a tight smile. "I don't know who told you that, sir, but it is a falsehood. I have never set foot in Lady Harleigh's garden. Perhaps you can give me the name of your informant, so I may set him to rights."

"Hmm. That's where the situation becomes ticklish, since the informant is Mrs. Chiswick. It seems you've told her something about Lady Harleigh's garden that you couldn't possibly know unless you'd been there yourself."

Jackson's hand slipped to the back of a chair. He leaned heavily against it. Something was going on behind his blank stare. George's line of questioning was beginning to make sense to him.

"Considering what so recently happened in that very garden, you must understand this leads me to wonder why you were there. And when."

"No, sir. I was never there. If you refer to a certain passage through a wall, it was Mr. Stoke-Whitney who told us about it. Actually, he told Mrs. Chiswick about it. I merely overheard."

"Why on earth were Mrs. Chiswick and Mr. Stoke-Whitney talking about my garden?" I asked.

The butler looked chagrined. "Perhaps it was somewhat indiscreet, ma'am, but Mrs. Chiswick was telling him about the man who'd been on the street a bit earlier, conversing with a woman in an upper window of your house."

So, someone had seen Bradmore and Irena.

"Mrs. Chiswick was shocked to have seen that because she considers that you conduct yourself with great propriety," he continued. "She said as much to Mr. Stoke-Whitney. That's when he gave her a wink and mentioned there was a convenient gate in the wall separating your garden from Mr. Hazelton's."

I parted my lips, but before I could speak, George squeezed my hand.

"When and where did he convey this information?" His tone was sharp enough to make me wince.

Jackson, who had clearly begun to add everything up, was shaking, though he clung to the chair. "The day the woman was murdered. Mr. Stoke-Whitney called on Mrs. Chiswick."

"Why?"

"She's a constituent and chairs a committee in which he takes an interest."

"And to give himself an alibi," I added. "In case anyone noted his carriage on the street."

"This is terribly disturbing," Jackson said. "Are you suggesting Mr. Stoke-Whitney entered your garden to murder that woman?"

"I'm saying you must tell this story to the police," George said. "Terribly sorry, Jackson, but I'm afraid you'll have to come to the Chelsea police precinct with me and give your statement to the inspector in charge of this case."

Jackson looked completely shattered. "I'll just go and get my coat." He shuffled away, presumably to inform the maid of his imminent departure.

"I never thought I'd say this, but thank heaven Jackson was eavesdropping."

George released a heavy sigh. "Delaney's probably still at the precinct, obtaining his warrant. I daresay Jackson's statement will make it a little easier for him to do so."

I leaned back against the wall. "I know the evidence was pointing this way, but it's just now sinking in that Arthur Stoke-Whitney killed her. Will Jackson's statement be enough for Delaney to arrest him?"

"Undoubtedly. I don't think Stoke-Whitney stands a chance. That means we can get on with our lives." He drew my hand to his lips, and I leaned into his shoulder.

"You should return home," he said. "Once I deal with Jackson, I'll come by to let you know what happened."

I nodded and would have left, but he held on to my arms.

"It's over, Frances. I know it's been exhausting and upsetting. I can't tell you how grateful I am that you stayed by my side."

I stepped back and touched his face. "There's nowhere else I'd rather be."

*   *   *

Petrov had abandoned us to return to George's home, but Hetty and Gilliam still waited in the drawing room when I entered, eager to find out what had transpired. I ignored the now cold tea and poured a glass of brandy instead before taking a seat and telling them about Jackson.

"You must be so relieved this situation is over and the truth will come out at last." Aunt Hetty reached over and patted my hand.

"It will be a relief not to have to worry someone will leave a room when I enter it or cross the street to avoid me. But I have to admit I'm disappointed in several people I thought were my friends. How quickly they turned their backs on me."

"Well, if they are anything like Arthur Stoke-Whitney, I hope they keep their backs turned." Hetty tsked in disgust. "It's ironic that he ever worried about his wife causing a scandal. Not that she's a model of propriety, mind you."

"Now that I know more about her husband, I understand her choices a little better. And you're right. The most sanctimonious man in London turns out to be a murderer." I let out a bitter laugh. "After he's charged, she'll need more than my help in bringing out her daughter. She might do better to take Harriet to Paris for the season."

Once I stopped to consider Alicia, I realized she'd suffer far more than George and I had. This scandal would ruin her and her daughter. And, heavens, she was in the country and didn't even know yet. I stood up and returned my glass to the table. "I really should write to her. It would be too awful for her to find out from the papers."

"Honestly, Frances, after all that woman and her husband put you through, I can't believe you are worried about her feelings. Besides, reading about Stoke-Whitney's crimes in a letter is hardly better than reading it in the papers."

"I'll be kinder, and she'll find out ahead of everyone else. It would be better in person, but I'm not up to checking the train schedules at the moment."

"Where is her country home?" Gilliam asked.

"Not far, actually. It's in Chelmsford," I replied.

"Well, that's less than an hour away, and on a good road, too. I could have you there and back before nightfall if you'd let me drive you."

I felt a sudden chill. "In your motorcar? No, I don't think that's a good idea."

"Why, it's a splendid idea." Aunt Hetty had suddenly become all smiles. "Though I don't know why you wish to trouble yourself with her, I think a drive to the country is just the ticket. The perfect way to blow off the cobwebs."

I was afraid it would blow off more than that. "This seems like a great deal more trouble than just writing a letter."

"No trouble at all," he said. "I'm delighted to provide some assistance. As Mrs. Chesney says, you've been through a difficult time, and a drive is just the thing to remind you that you are still alive."

"But for how long?"

"Don't be such a stick in the mud, Frances. Gilliam hasn't lost a passenger yet. We'll all go." Hetty got to her feet, as if the discussion was over. "You'll love it."

I did not love it.

Once the novelty of the first twenty minutes of breathtaking motion had worn off, all I noticed was the discomfort. Hetty sat in the front seat, as, of course, did Gilliam. I could forgive him, as he had to drive the contraption, which he explained to me was called a Daimler. This arrangement left me clinging to the seat directly behind and slightly above them. My breath was not the only thing taken away by the wind. It took my hairpins, even though my hat was secured with a scarf. It took every drop of moisture from my eyes, possibly a layer of skin from my cheeks, and every word from my lips—most of which were calls to stop or at least slow down.

This might have been an amusing occupation in May or June, but this was November, and despite my thick coat, I was thoroughly chilled. There could be no conversation, as nothing could be heard over the rushing wind. Why did this thing not have a roof? Had anyone tried this motorcar on the open road before manufacturing and selling them to the public? This machine would never catch on as a mode of transportation.

While I stewed in my discomfort, we did manage to pass a few more miles and slowed down to enter a village. We stopped briefly at the inn for directions to the Stoke-Whitney home, and for me to stuff my hair back up into my hat. We were on the road again far too soon, with Gilliam's assurance the manor was only a few miles ahead. I should have insisted on sending a letter.

Blow off the cobwebs, indeed.

Fortunately, he had not exaggerated. Within minutes, we turned off the road and into the drive leading to our destination. He turned off the engine, and I pried my fingers from the back of Hetty's seat, while he came around the front of the vehicle to help us both down. My legs felt as wobbly as if I'd been aboard a ship.

The Stoke-Whitney butler met us at the door. "Good afternoon, ladies, sir." He backed away from the entrance to allow us into the hall.

"Good afternoon," I said once inside. "I am Lady Harleigh." I withdrew a calling card and handed it to him. "My aunt, her friend, and I are here to pay a call on Mrs. Stoke-Whitney. I'm afraid it's rather urgent, so I do hope she's at home."

"I am grieved to disappoint you, my lady." Indeed, he did look distressed. "But Mrs. Stoke-Whitney is unable to receive callers at this time."

Through sheer force of will, I didn't roll my eyes. Knowing Alicia, "unable to receive callers" could mean she was in bed with the underbutler or some neighbor's husband. "Perhaps you could check with her? We've just come from town, with a message of the utmost urgency. I am certain she will want to see me."

"I'm afraid it's not possible to disturb her at the moment, as she's quite unwell."

"Unwell? That's unfortunate. Didn't she just arrive yesterday?"

"She did, madam. And she seemed in good health at the time, though a bit out of sorts. It seems she fell ill overnight and telephoned Mr. Stoke-Whitney. He arrived early this morning and has been faithfully caring for her."

"Mr. Stoke-Whitney is here?" What was he doing here? Something about this story sent a chill through me. He wouldn't care if Alicia was ill. He certainly wouldn't come running to her aid. And nursing her? Something was just wrong about this situation.

"Yes, he is in residence, but he asked very specifically not to be disturbed. I'm terribly sorry you've made the trip for nothing."

Gilliam replaced his hat and moved toward the door. It was clear we'd been dismissed, and under normal circumstances, we'd return to the village and inform a constable or the magistrate that the Metropolitan Police was looking for Stoke-Whitney. But I couldn't make myself leave. Something odd was going on here, and I couldn't help but think Alicia was in danger.

Still, what could I do? Insist upon staying or demand to see

Stoke-Whitney? No, actually, I had no desire to see him. An idea occurred to me, and as much as I hated to do it, I saw no other choice.

"If you would indulge me," I said. "Before we take the long drive back to town, would it be possible to refresh myself?" Under normal circumstances, a lady would never acknowledge such a need. Indeed, I had the man flustered, but after a scant hesitation, he recovered his composure.

"Of course, my lady. If your companions would care to wait in the blue salon." He waved a hand, indicating an anteroom to the left of the hall.

Hetty pulled me aside before following Gilliam into the room. I didn't wait for her question.

"I have to find Alicia and see if she's all right. Then we'll fetch the police. If I don't return in a timely manner, go without me."

I turned away from her horrified face to find the butler waiting. "If you'll come this way, ma'am."

As I'd expected, he led me up the stairs, past the main rooms, to the family area of the house, which was where I hoped to find Alicia. He came to an abrupt halt and indicated a door along the hallway. "You should find everything you need in here, ma'am."

"Thank you." I looked around. "I should be able to find my way back on my own." Heaven knew what I'd do if he insisted on waiting.

"Of course." With a bow, he turned and headed down the hall.

I stepped inside the small room and closed the door behind me, just in case he looked back. I counted to five and slowly eased the door open, then peeked out with one eye. He was gone. Now, where was Alicia?

There were six doors between me and the turning in the hallway. We'd come up the central staircase, a very elaborate affair. Where would the master suite be? Near the stairs, for convenience, or farther down the hall, for privacy? My guess was convenience, and as my gaze traveled the hallway, I noticed a key in one of the closest doors. Odd, unless Stoke-Whitney had locked Alicia in. Was that a crazy idea? I reminded myself he was a murderer. Nothing was crazy, but this could be terribly embarrassing.

I turned the key as quietly as possible, but it made a click, and I heard someone stir inside the room. I pushed the door open and poked my head in.

And came face-to-face with Alicia.

We both started, but she was first to recover and pressed her fingers against my lips, her other hand pulling me inside. Once my heart returned from its leap to my throat, I complied, then closed the door behind me and took in the luxurious appointments in the very feminine room.

"I don't know what you're doing here," Alicia whispered, "but thank goodness you've come. Arthur arrived this morning in a foul mood." She gestured to the key still in my hand. "He found that from who knows where and, without so much as a word, locked me in here."

"Then you didn't send for him? You didn't know he was coming?"

"Send for him? Why would I do that?"

"He told your butler that you are ill, that you sent for him, and that he came here to care for you."

She flung out her arms. "You can see how he's caring for me, and I'm not ill. What is he up to?" She stepped back and gave me a look. "Why are you here?"

"It's rather a long story. First, tell me, why are we whispering? Is your husband nearby?"

"Just on the other side of the dressing room. I've heard him moving around. I know he's angry. The last thing I want to do is disturb him."

Bother. But then I supposed it was good to know where he was. I placed a hand on Alicia's shoulder. "I shall have to give you the abbreviated explanation, and you will simply have to trust me. Arthur is in trouble back in London. Now that he's here, I'm afraid he wants to hurt you. I think you need to come away with me." I finally realized she was still in her night-clothes. "It's the middle of the afternoon. Why are you not dressed?"

She ignored my question. "Why would he want to hurt me?"

"I don't have time for questions, Alicia. Did you miss the part where I said to trust me? We have to leave quickly, before the butler tells your husband I'm here."

Too late. I heard a key scratch in a lock. The dressing room door. We had mere seconds.

"Get in bed and pretend to sleep." I gave Alicia a shove toward the bed and looked for somewhere to hide, finally opting for the heavy draperies over the window. With any luck, Stoke-Whitney would see his wife sleeping and would come back later—after we were long gone.

I heard him step into the room and pause. Now, if only he'd turn around and go away. A floorboard squeaked as he advanced toward the bed. *Bother!* I'd counted on him to behave like a gentleman and let her sleep. If he decided to quarrel with her now, I could be stuck here for hours, while Hetty and Gilliam attempted to distract the butler. At least he wasn't likely to look for me in Alicia's room. And he could hardly report my trespass to his master, so I supposed things could be worse.

Things became worse quickly. The bedsprings creaked. Alicia groaned softly, as if she didn't want to wake up. Then she groaned again, this time with a bit more enthusiasm. Were they doing what I thought they were doing? Was I really to be stuck behind these draperies while they made love not a dozen feet away from me? I looked out the window and wondered how much damage I'd sustain if I jumped.

Another noise. Was that a squeal?

"Are you begging for mercy, Alicia? What a shame I can't quite understand you."

His silky voice made me shiver. And those hardly sounded like words of love. I moved the edge of the drape ever so slightly, just enough to peer out, and blanched at the sight on the bed. Stoke-Whitney knelt over Alicia, pressing a pillow against her face, while her right arm flailed helplessly in the air.

Heavens, he was killing her before my eyes!

I don't even recall moving, but I did see the man's expression of utter shock as I ran from the window and launched myself at him with enough force to take us both across the bed and onto the floor in a tangle of sheets and counterpane. Before I could catch my breath, he pushed to his knees with me clinging to his back, a very precarious position.

Stoke-Whitney managed to come to his feet, though he was covered with a sheet. I still hung from his neck while kicking at his legs and screaming for all I was worth. As he spun this way and that, I caught a glimpse of Alicia, struggling to sit up. I'd find no assistance from her.

Just as my grip grew lax, the door burst open, and a maid rushed in, followed by the butler. How must this look to them? Before they could decide I was the problem in this situation, I took charge.

"You, go and help your mistress. And you . . ." I nodded at the butler as my grip gave way and I slid from Stoke-Whitney's back to the floor. "Help me with him. He was trying to murder her."

The maid ran to Alicia, but the butler stood in the doorway, his eyes wide and jaw slack. Fortunately, Hetty and Gilliam pushed past him. Just as Stoke-Whitney fought himself loose from the bedsheet, Gilliam pinned him down.

"Whoever you are, you have this backward." Stoke-Whitney struggled in Gilliam's hold. "It was her. I came in to find Lady Harleigh smothering Alicia. I attacked her to save my wife."

I pushed myself to my feet as the butler weighed the veracity of his master's statements. We were three strangers, after all.

"Send for the magistrate," I told him.

"No." Stoke-Whitney's face was a mask of impotent rage. "I am master here, and this woman was trying to murder your mistress." His eyes pleaded with his wife. After what he'd done, he still thought she'd lie for him?

Clinging to the maid, she stared at him as if he were crazy, but he made one more plea.

"Think of my children."

She turned away from him. "It was as Lady Harleigh said. He tried to kill me. Call for the magistrate."

"Aunt Hetty, go with him. Tell the magistrate to contact Inspector Delaney at the Chelsea division." I took custody of Alicia, who was shivering and limp in my arms, and sent the maid in search of a wrapper.

Hetty and the butler left, and with the departure of his only ally, Stoke-Whitney ceased struggling and simply stood, with Gilliam holding his arms behind him.

"Inspector Delaney is already looking for you in London," I told him. "He has enough evidence to charge you with the murder of Irena Teskey."

Alicia's eyes rounded in horror. "You? What have you to do with that woman?"

"Nothing. I never had anything to do with her."

"His first wife, Jane, was Irena's mother," I told her.

As Alicia put all the pieces together, her face reflected her revulsion.

Stoke-Whitney saw it, too. Trapped in Gilliam's grip, he released a growl of frustration. "Jane was just like you. The two of you did your best to bring shame to this family."

"Yet, ironically, it was you who succeeded in doing so." Alicia sank to the bed, and I sat beside her, wrapping a protective arm around her shoulders. She lifted her gaze to her husband. "You tried to kill me because you thought I disgraced the family name." Her voice dropped to a breathy whisper. "Did you murder Jane?"

Stoke-Whitney snapped his jaw shut and gave her a look of contempt that chilled me.

Alicia ignored it and continued in a soft monotone. "It would have been so easy for you to do. She was here. She'd just given birth, probably weak as a baby herself. All you had to do was put a pillow over her face, as you did with me. I was just fortunate someone was here to stop you."

"Be quiet," he snapped. "Aren't things bad enough?"

"Then you just sent the child on to her father, like so much useless property."

"I said, be quiet!" His eyes bulged. A bit of spittle wobbled on his lip.

Gilliam and I exchanged a glance. This was far more than either of us had expected.

Alicia was in no mood to be quiet. It was as if she needed to pay him back for all his years of bullying. "Why should I? Your silver tongue won't save you from this mess, Arthur. There's no question you tried to murder me. The police seem to have evidence to prove you murdered that young woman." She let out a strangled laugh. Tears filled her eyes as she began to shiver. "It doesn't even matter if you killed Jane, too, at least not to any judge. After all, they can hang you only once."

From the expression on his face, this was the first time he'd considered the punishment for his crimes. Once again, he struggled and failed to break free.

"What will your boys think, Arthur? You murdered their mother."

"She was planning to leave them." His voice was a low growl. "She couldn't just have an affair. She had to fall in love with the man. She was willing to leave me and the boys for him—let the world know it was his child she carried. I couldn't let that happen."

"Now the world will know you're a murderer." Alicia bowed her head and released a sob. "I know you don't care about Harriet or me, but you have ruined your sons' lives, too."

"For their sake, you must help me," he said.

I was stunned. Despite the blatant fear in his eyes, it was clear he still held out hope of Alicia helping him.

"You're beyond my help, Arthur." She nodded to the bedside table, where the Book of Common Prayer lay—just as pristine and untouched as one might expect. "There's your salvation." She stood and wobbled on her feet. "Frances, will you help me to Arthur's room? I'll wait for the police in there."

I caught her as she stumbled. The maid had already disappeared through the dressing room, and Alicia clung to me. I glanced at Gilliam. He still held Stoke-Whitney's arms behind his back, though the man had ceased struggling and seemed almost resigned to his fate—his face blank and eyes lifeless.

Gilliam gave me a nod. "Go with her. I'll be fine here."

"I'll get her settled and return to wait with you."

Alicia leaned on my arm and let me guide her through the dressing room and into Arthur's bedchamber, where I helped her into a chair. When I turned to leave, she caught my arm.

"Wait. He needs some time."

Before I could make sense of her comment, I heard a scuffle in the other room. I pulled away from her grasp and was starting toward the dressing room when a shot rang out. Surging forward, I stumbled into Gilliam, who caught me up in the doorway and pushed me back.

"Don't go in there," he said, turning me around.

I looked him over for signs of injury. "What happened? Are you hurt?"

He shook his head. "It's Stoke-Whitney. He's dead."

Chapter Twenty-three

❧

We had a great deal of explaining to do once the local authorities arrived, which they did within ten minutes of Stoke-Whitney taking his life. Alicia managed to answer a few questions and confirm her husband had attempted to smother her before she broke down into sobs. By then, the coroner had arrived, and I was allowed to take her away from the grisly scene and its attendant activities. Stoke-Whitney's room was far too close. The drawing room was exposed to everyone coming and going. I finally took her to the library at the back of the house, where we found a quiet spot, privacy, and a tantalus filled with spirits. After pouring from a decanter of something amber, I joined her on a leather sofa and pressed the glass into her hand.

"This might help with the shock."

She stared absently into the glass. "I'm not certain I want help with that. Right now, I simply can't grasp what happened up there. My husband tried to kill me." She glanced from the glass to me, her eyes wide. "I think I prefer shock for the moment. I'm not ready to come to terms with this—or the lie he lived that led up to all this."

"You didn't know about Jane or Irena?"

She looked at me as if I were daft. "Do you honestly think I'd have married him if I'd known he murdered his first wife?"

"I see your point."

"Arthur and I had more of an arrangement than a marriage. But he held all the power and kept changing the terms. I wasn't just supposed to be his hostess. I had to help push forward his political policies and support his charities. If I made a mistake or, heaven forbid, embarrassed him, he treated me like a dim-witted child. I always thought I was the bad one, and he was so good."

She took a healthy swig from her glass and shuddered as the alcohol burned its way down her throat. "I think that's what has me so bewildered. Regardless of how he treated me, I'd have wagered good money that he really was the virtuous, honorable man he presented to the world." She turned her confused face to me. "But it was all for show. How did he get away with that?"

I wouldn't say he got away with anything, considering his present condition, but I knew what she meant. What I wanted to understand was that final exchange between Alicia and her husband. "Were you giving him a signal? Did you know he would take his life if given a chance?" I paused. "And why on earth do you keep a pistol next to your bed?"

"That was Arthur's idea. He was a public figure, after all, and not always a popular one. I guess I did know one thing about my husband after all these years. He'd rather die than publicly fall from grace." She shook her head and took another drink. "It seemed to me it was his decision to make, but I regret it now. I'm relieved none of us, not me or the children, will have to go through the circus of a public trial, but part of me still wants the truth to come out."

"But the truth will come out, not in so public a way, but it must come out."

Alicia gave me a twisted smile. "You're clearly not familiar with politics. Just wait and see. His cronies and colleagues in the house will contrive a new story. Money will change hands, and all Arthur's misdeeds will be buried with him. They'll remind everyone what a respected member of Parliament he was and garner sympathy to push his morality bill through."

I stared at her in horror. Could they do this? Could they rewrite the history of Arthur Stoke-Whitney into something good and honorable? Would they practice such a deceit on the public?

"I suppose it's for the best," she said. "Still, it seems wrong that nothing will be brought to light."

I studied her for a moment, wondering, if given a choice, what she'd do. "Something must be brought to light, or Bradmore, Hazelton, and even I may lose our reputations. We must be cleared of Miss Teskey's murder. I won't be a casualty of your husband's lies."

Alicia slumped against the back of the leather sofa and turned her gaze toward me. "How *do* you tolerate me? I'd forgotten how Arthur's misdeeds affected you. What can we do?"

"We tell the story first. And it just so happens, I have a friend in the newspaper business."

At some point in the evening, George arrived with Delaney, who consulted with Alicia and tied up loose ends with the local authorities. I stayed the night with Alicia, and together we devised the story for Mr. Mosley's paper. In our version, Stoke-Whitney fell in love with the actress Irena Teskey. She wanted nothing to do with him, and in a fit of passion, he strangled her. Caught in the grip of remorse and grief, he took his own life a few days later. It was a paltry tale, but no one seemed to notice. The actors from the Hanover Theater gave it credence by recalling they'd seen Stoke-Whitney backstage. Whether they really had, we'd never know.

Nothing was mentioned about Jane Stoke-Whitney or her relation to Irena, though Michael did finally receive a cable from Alexei confirming Jane was Irena's mother.

Nor did we reveal Stoke-Whitney's attempt to murder Alicia. I'm sure it's something the village magistrate wouldn't soon forget, but he was instructed not to breathe a word. Alicia planned to leave for the Continent with her daughter immediately after the funeral. Perhaps they'd return once the scandal died down.

The story had the benefit of putting a chink in Stoke-Whitney's falsely gilded reputation without bringing the truth of Irena's parentage to light, something Alexei was still dead set against. It also cleared both Bradmore and George. And as there was no longer any scandal attached to George, I was no longer guilty by association. The timing could not have been more perfect, as my mother and Rose returned the day after the story ran in the *Observer*, which was also a mere two days before our engagement party. Those who had sent their regrets earlier in the week suddenly found their schedules cleared and were able to attend, after all.

What a surprise.

However, allowing them to attend the party did not mean I had to forgive or forget. As I watched our guests dancing across the ballroom floor at Robert and Fiona's home, I felt my resentment dissolve. George and I had opened the dancing, and now I stood beside him on the perimeter of the dance floor. Strains of a waltz flowed around us as dancers streamed past, including Aunt Hetty and Gilliam. I took George's hand and leaned into his side. This was one of the few times it was acceptable to show affection in public, and I aimed to take full advantage of that.

He smiled down at me. "Do you have any idea what a wonder you are?"

"I haven't the foggiest. You'll have to tell me."

With a laugh, he obliged. "Not only were you instrumental in solving Irena's murder, but you also caught the culprit and saved a woman's life."

"Oh, that. I thought you were marveling at how I brought society to heel." I waved my hand at the dance floor, filled with glittering aristocrats.

"Quite an accomplishment. I might be intimidated by you if I weren't secure in the fact that you love me beyond all measure."

The image of bliss on his face had me chuckling. "Do I?"

"You must. A woman from my past shows up, claiming to be my wife. I saddle you with that woman, nearly ruin your reputation, and get you banned from polite society, and not only do you take it all in stride, but you also forgive me."

I held up a finger. "Only if it never happens again. Once, I can tolerate, but you cannot make a habit of this."

George promised and stepped away, in search of champagne, which might have been nothing more than an excuse, as my mother was headed our way, looking surprisingly pleased for once.

"I believe this party is an unqualified success," she said when she reached my side. "How fortunate that silly gossip about Hazelton died down. I worried it might keep some people away, but this is quite the crush."

"It was an absurd story. No one should ever have given it any credence." I raised a brow. "You never believed it, did you?"

Her cheeks reddened. "Well, perhaps. For just a moment, you understand." She raised her chin a notch. "It doesn't hurt to be suspicious."

"No, I suppose it doesn't."

"After all, you wouldn't be the first woman to fall under the spell of a handsome rascal."

I smiled. "So, you think George handsome, do you?"

She raised her brows.

"But a rascal?" I let out a tsk.

"I haven't completely formed my opinion of him yet, but I intend to stay nearby. In the event he does exhibit rascally tendencies, I'll be on hand to nip them in the bud."

I heard only one word of that statement, and my playful mood dissolved rapidly. "Nearby?"

"In your house, dear, or should I say Hetty's? She does take ownership at the end of the month, I believe. I'm sure she won't mind if I stay on for a bit."

Good heavens, how long was a bit?

"And I do so enjoy spending time with Rose. Your sister will be back in town soon, and of course, I love being near you."

"And we love having you, but won't Father expect you back in New York soon?"

She made a dismissive gesture. "He certainly doesn't expect me to leave before your wedding. A few more months won't hurt."

A few more months? She expected to stay with me for a few more months? Where was George with that champagne?

"Now that we've had the engagement party, we simply must start planning your wedding. I have so many ideas. Of course, it must be an elaborate affair, something appropriate to your status." She placed a hand on my arm. "I've spoken to your brother-in-law, by the way. Do you know he told me you don't have to give up your title? You can remain, Frances, Countess of Harleigh, even after you marry Hazelton. I think that would help with Rose's prospects once she starts thinking of marriage, don't you?"

I flicked open my fan and applied it to cool my face. Rose was eight. Just how long was my mother planning to stay?

"We could have arrangements in place by spring, don't you think?"

Somehow, I'd lost the thread of our conversation. "Arrangements?"

"For your wedding. What do you think of spring?"

I thought of living with my mother's "arranging" for another four months or so and made a quick decision. Hopefully, George would forgive me. "I'm afraid there won't be time for an elaborate wedding, Mother. We plan to marry much sooner than that."

She narrowed her eyes. "Indeed? How soon?"

"Almost immediately. Sooner will be better, don't you think? You and Hetty will have more room in the house, and Rose and I will be just next door." I felt better as soon as I spoke the words. I loved having my mother in my life, but having her in my house would certainly try my patience. A speedy wedding would bring everything back into balance. I'd be married to George. That was a plus. I'd also gain some distance from my mother. Plus, plus. And . . .

Well, perhaps this particular equation didn't have a negative.

Author's Note

This novel is a work of fiction, not of biography or history. The thoughts, words, and motivations of the "real" people in this book are as much a product of the author's imagination as those of the fictional characters are.

Some of the events mentioned in this work did happen but not necessarily in this time frame. Grand Duke Alexei Alexandrovich took an extensive tour the United States, but it was in the 1870s not 1899. The actress Fanny Moody played Tatiana in Eugene Onegin, but not in 1899. However, Grand Duke Michael Mikhailovich and Sophie, Countess de Torby did visit London in November of 1899. That visit was the inspiration for this story.

Acknowledgments

A special thanks to all you readers who have enjoyed the Countess of Harleigh mysteries and to the librarians and booksellers who have championed the series.

While writers write alone, there are many people who help bring a book to life. Thanks go to my fellow historical fiction writers and beta readers, Heather Redmond and Clarissa Harwood for their considered comments and suggestions. And to my critique partner, Mary Keliikoa, who shares all my writerly ups and downs. To the many people at Kensington Books who play a role in the final product and its success, particularly Robin Cook, Rosemary Silva, and Larissa Ackerman.

Writing is a joy for me and I will always be grateful to my agent, Melissa Edwards and my editor, John Scognamiglio for taking a chance on me. And to my family and friends for all your love and support especially my husband, Dan, who I love even more than writing.

Frances Wynn, the American-born Countess of Harleigh, returns in Dianne Freeman's charming, lighthearted mystery series set in Victorian England, and finds her wedding day overshadowed by murder . . .

On the eve of her marriage to George Hazelton, Frances has a great deal more on her mind than flowers and seating arrangements. The Connors and the Doyles, two families of American robber barons, have taken up residence in London, and their bitter rivalry is spilling over into the highest social circles. At the request of her brother, Alonzo, who is quite taken with Miss Madeline Connor, Frances has invited the Connor family to her wedding. Meanwhile, Frances's mother has invited Mr. Doyle, and Frances fears the wedding may end up being newspaper-worthy for all the wrong reasons.

On the day itself, Frances is relieved to note that Madeline's father is *not* among the guests assembled at the church. The reason for his absence, however, turns out to be most unfortunate: Mr. Connor is found murdered in his home. More shocking still, Alonzo is caught at the scene, holding the murder weapon.

Powerful and ruthless, Connor appears to have amassed a wealth of enemies alongside his fortune. Frances and George agree to put their wedding trip on hold to try and clear Alonzo's name. But there are secrets to sift through, not just in the Doyle and Connor families, but also in their own. And with a killer determined to evade discovery at any cost—even if it means taking another life—Frances's first days as a newlywed will be perilous indeed . . .

Please turn the page for an exciting sneak peek of Dianne Freeman's next Countess of Harleigh mystery A BRIDE'S GUIDE TO MARRIAGE AND MURDER coming soon wherever print and e-books are sold!

Chapter One

London, February 1900

Family, like a rich dessert, is a treat best enjoyed in small portions. One may love it and want to indulge in great quantities, but too much of either can lead to such a noxious experience one might be prompted to avoid it—or them—forever.

Well. Perhaps just my family.

My mother invaded—I mean, arrived—at my home four months ago for my sister's wedding, then stayed on to plan mine. Since that time, I'd gone from considering elopement to contemplating a move to the Outer Hebrides, but since the Gaelic language eluded me, I stayed home and endured the invasion—I mean, visit—for four months. Four. Long. Months.

The single refuge left to me were my thoughts. Daydreaming had become my escape. It might appear that I was enjoying breakfast with Mother and Aunt Hetty while they reviewed the final—please let it be the final—list of wedding details, but in my head, I was in the church, saying my vows.

I smiled. The dream would be a reality in a little more than twenty-four hours.

I Frances Helena do take thee, George—

"Ahem!"

And just like that, the dining room came back into focus. The altar transformed into the table, draped with a white cloth and littered with handwritten notes and forgotten breakfast plates. The candles that had glowed in my daydream were replaced with the gas chandelier, and the choir turned into rattling china as Mrs. Thompson, my housekeeper, brought in fresh plates.

The reverend's voice was replaced with my mother's.

"Do you intend to drink that coffee, Frances, or simply admire it?"

It took another moment before her ice blue stare came into focus. "I beg your pardon?"

"You've been gazing into that cup for at least ten minutes now and haven't heard a word I've said."

That was rather the point.

She drew her brows together. "What's wrong with you?"

Where to begin? I had a house full of relatives. My mother was organizing my wedding like a military campaign, while I attempted to coordinate a move to my new home during the coldest February in my recollection. And now I'd been distracted from a lovely daydream. Of course, I could tell her none of that.

"Nothing's wrong." I pasted on a smile. "What were you saying?"

"I've just heard from the florist." She tossed a note card onto the table. "He can't manage the pure white roses for the wedding. Now what am I to do?"

I shuddered to think. It was quite possible that poor florist's head would roll.

Aunt Hetty sought refuge behind the morning paper. I took a long drink of my coffee for fortification. "If they're the pinkish color, they should be just fine," I offered. "Rose is wearing

pink." Rose was my eight-year-old daughter and only attendant. She was also the one person Mother didn't argue with. To
her, Rose could do no wrong.

She sighed and sank back into her chair. "I can't risk the
flowers being the wrong shade of white. I'll have to call at the
shop and have a look at them myself." She gave me a pointed
look. "That means I shan't be able to accompany you to your
dress fitting."

Somewhere in the heavens, a choir of angels sang.

I covered my grin with my cup. An afternoon without
Mother's harping was akin to a miracle. For a few hours, I'd be
in control of my own life while she scoured London for the
perfect white flowers.

This was my second marriage, so I don't know that white
everything was appropriate, but neither was it worth the argument. Besides, I'd prefer to forget my first marriage. Ten years
ago, my mother had orchestrated that one, too. She had even
chosen the groom. I'd gone along with her plan, so I can't really
lay all the blame at her door. But Reggie Wynn had been a poor
choice. At the time, he was the heir to the Earl of Harleigh and
was experiencing financial distress. Thus, he met Mother's cri-
teria: a man who needed my money and could give me a title.
For my part, I was relieved he wasn't in his dotage, as were
many of the eligible aristocrats. At thirty-three, he was fifteen
years older than I'd been, but he was dashing, and his devil-
may-care attitude made him seem much younger.

Rose was the only positive result of that marriage. I'm actually surprised by my willingness to try it again, but I have an
excellent inducement in George Hazelton. He was the farthest
thing possible from Reggie. First and foremost, George loved
me, not my money—a good thing since I had very little of it
left. He loved my daughter, and we loved him. More impor-
tantly, I trusted him. He had a very progressive attitude about
women, or at least me. Though George occasionally practiced

law, his true profession involved a variety of clandestine assignments for the Crown. That he never spurned my assistance told me I needn't worry about being left at a crumbling country estate like some unwanted baggage, which was an apt summary of my first marriage.

"Good morning, ladies," my father said, joining us in the dining room. He and my brother Alonzo had arrived from New York the previous evening. "Alonzo's still sleeping, is he?" He rounded the table and bussed my cheek before slipping between the back of Mother's chair and the sideboard to pour himself a cup of coffee.

"Good morning, Franklin," Mother said, still studying her wedding notes. "You've been up for hours. Where were you?"

"In Frankie's library," he replied. "I had some cables to send. Your kitchen boy took them to the telegraph office for me. I hope you don't mind the liberty."

"This is Aunt Hetty's house now," I pointed out. "He works for her." Since Rose and I were moving to George's home next door, Hetty had offered to purchase the lease on this snug little house. I couldn't imagine a better neighbor and was delighted to sell it to her.

Hetty waved a dismissive hand at my father. "Please, make yourself at home."

"But you are meant to be on holiday, Frankie," I replied. "Can't your business wait?" To my siblings, Franklin Price was Father or Papa, but I had never called him anything but Frankie, and he called me the same. After all, I was named for him. It was clear to both of us, we were the only ones who had not grown weary of the affectionate moniker, but it was one of the few things I shared with him. Perhaps the only thing. As a child, I knew the back of his head better than his face since that was my view of him as he left for his office. The last time I saw Frankie was at my previous wedding. I hoped I wouldn't have to marry a third time in order to see him again.

He pulled out a chair and seated himself between Mother and Aunt Hetty. "Business never waits, my dear."

Hetty lowered the paper, and I was struck by the image of brother and sister side by side. They could not have looked more alike—thick, dark hair, brown eyes, tall, sturdy build. Frankie now sported a few more lines than I remembered and a face full of whiskers. Aunt Hetty, happily, had neither of those things. Nor did she wear spectacles. Alonzo and I both looked more like our father—tall, regular features, and dark hair, though there was some of my mother's pertness to my nose and I had her blue eyes.

"Now, remind me," Frankie continued. "Why won't Lily be at the wedding? I thought she lived here now." He took a sip from his coffee and sighed in satisfaction.

Mother gave him a long look, cocking her brow before deigning to answer. "Lily's father-in-law sent them to France. Her husband is working on," she waved a hand, "something or other."

"It's business, Franklin," Hetty added. "Since you missed her wedding due to your business, I would have thought you'd approve of her keeping Leo's nose to the grindstone."

"I don't disapprove, but France is not that far away. Just a short trip to attend her sister's wedding."

Mother placed a hand over his. "It's too far for my daughter to travel when she's with child."

In truth, Lily had been with child when she married Leo four months ago. Her decision not to attend my wedding was so no one would see that her pregnancy was perhaps a bit farther along than expected. Once the babe was born, she could claim it was early. I wasn't sure if my mother was aware of the circumstances. I certainly hadn't the nerve to tell her.

"You'd know better than I about that, but I'd hoped to see her. Imagine, Daisy. Our youngest is soon to give us another grandchild." He pulled off his spectacles to wipe them with the napkin while he studied Mother's profile. "You look far too young to be a grandmother."

"Why, thank you, Franklin." Mother looked positively flustered. Was that a blush?

"I suppose you'll want to go to her and stay until the child is born," he added, taking another sip of his coffee and fogging his spectacles once more.

Mother's smile faded. "Perhaps I will," she snapped. My gaze flitted between Frankie and Mother. That went wrong quickly.

Aunt Hetty folded down the corner of her newspaper to glance at my father. "Do you know Peter Bainbridge, Franklin?"

Frankie tapped his index finger against the cup he held. "One of the Bonanza Barons. Made his fortune in silver. Now he has a financial interest in nearly everything west of the Mississippi."

Hetty released a tsk. "I meant personally."

"I might have met him at a business dinner back in New York," Frankie said. "Why do you ask?"

"He arrived a few days ago for a visit to his London home. Yesterday someone broke in and vandalized his office."

"I'll give you three guesses as to who is responsible for that, and the first two don't count," Frankie said. "Does the article lay blame on anyone?"

Hetty lowered the paper. "No, but who else could it be but James Connor? He's also residing in London at the moment, and I can't imagine a better suspect."

"Why James Connor?" I asked.

They both threw me a look of scorn. "Because of the feud," Hetty said. "Haven't you heard of it?"

I'd have to be dead not to have heard of it. Both men immigrated to America—Connor from Ireland, Bainbridge from England—many years ago. They had been business partners early in their careers, but had fallen out. Since that time, they'd gone to great lengths to spread shocking and scandalous stories about one another, using the newspapers.

"It's not by chance they're both in London. Word is, they're interested in purchasing the same company," Frankie said. "Connor is trying to scare Bainbridge off, I'd wager."

"His office was the only part of the home damaged and nothing was stolen," Hetty added. "It's the type of petty act they've both participated in. From what little I've heard of him, petty describes Connor quite well."

The truth of her last statement was disheartening. Mrs. Connor was a friend. Her husband, whose fortune was also founded on silver, had a lamentable personality. He was loud, vulgar, and his humor was always at someone else's expense. As much as I enjoyed Willa Connor's company, I avoided Mr. Connor whenever possible. Fortunately, he didn't care for society, so that wasn't difficult.

"Petty, you call it? It's a criminal act." Mother tutted in disgust. "This feud of theirs has everyone in London believing Americans are daft. It's an embarrassment, and I blame Mr. Connor. The Bainbridges wish to put an end to this constant baiting of one another, but Connor refuses to cease."

All three of our heads swiveled in her direction. She turned her round, blue eyes on each of us and held up her hands. "What did I say?" She looked as innocent as a china doll, and even more lovely. Her flaxen hair was drawn back from a perfect oval face, devoid of a single wrinkle, blemish, or freckle. She worked very hard to keep it that way. Maintaining her beauty was part of Mother's very being. Having such intimate knowledge about robber barons like Connor and Bainbridge was not.

"How are you so familiar with the matter?" Hetty asked.

Mother wavered. "I don't suppose I am, really. The Bainbridges are friends of mine. What I know about this so-called feud, I have from them." She shrugged. "One-sided, I suppose, but they have told me they'd like to call it a draw and have an end to this nonsense."

My father chuckled and rose to fill a plate at the sideboard. "I imagine they do. That way, Gladys Bainbridge can offer to buy up all the prominent landmarks of Paris and no one will be the wiser."

Mother gave him a quelling glare. "That was years ago, Franklin. She is not such a rube anymore. I think it's horrible of Connor to have someone spying on her and reporting her every move to the papers."

"Everything they do to one another is horrible," I said. "The newspapers are the sole beneficiaries of this feud. Mr. Connor pays them to publish every foolish thing Mrs. Bainbridge does, while Mr. Bainbridge digs up unsavory details of the Connors' lives. It wasn't long ago I read a story about Mrs. Connor's humble origins. They have a daughter making her debut this season. A story like that might ruin her chances for a good match." I let out a tsk. "What do these men have against one another?"

Hetty shook her head as she moved to the sideboard for more coffee. I tried my father. "Frankie, do you know?"

"No idea," he said. "As long as I've been aware of their existence, I've been aware of the feud. I barely know the men except by reputation, and Connor's isn't good. An enormous fortune and a lack of principles is a dangerous combination. I've done no business with him and hope I never have to."

"It may not be business, but you will have to put up with him for one day, at least." At his inquiring gaze, I continued, "The Connor family is coming to the wedding."

Hetty, having returned to the table and her newspapers, looked up in surprise. Mother gasped. "You've added someone to the guest list? Without consulting me?"

I'd given up reminding Mother this was my wedding. Judging from the look on her face, she saw my inviting the Connors as an egregious act of defiance.

"I added the Connors two weeks ago at Alonzo's request. You must have missed their names on the guest list."

"Why on earth would he want them at your wedding?" My mother's eyes narrowed as suspicion formed. I wished Alonzo had dragged himself out of bed to deliver the news himself.

"I think he's quite taken with Miss Madeline Connor. They met in New York. She told him she'd be here for the upcoming social season." I picked up my fork and returned to my now-cold eggs, hoping I'd sounded casual.

"I thought she was here to catch a duke or an earl," Hetty said. "Someone with a distinguished title."

"That's certainly possible. Her father could provide an enormous dowry for some lucky lord. However, as with the Bainbridges, you can't believe everything you read about the Connors." I shrugged. "They accepted the invitation."

Mother grumbled as she rifled through the wedding notes. Probably looking for the seating chart.

My father returned to the table with a full plate and a grim expression. "I must have a chat with Alonzo," he said. "The girl may have the face of an angel, but her father would be the devil to deal with. He'd do better to find someone else. I don't even like the idea of that man at your wedding."

"If you don't like it now," Mother said, scribbling on the seating chart, "you'll positively hate it when I tell you Mr. Bainbridge will be there as well."

"You invited the Bainbridges?" It must have been after she'd taken over the guest list. It was one thing for me to add to the numbers, but quite another when Mother did. This was my wedding, after all. "This was meant to be a small affair, with close family and friends. I don't even know them."

"I suppose you are close friends with the Connors?"

"I'm well acquainted with Willa Connor. Alonzo must have

a friendship with Miss Connor. And Graham is hosting the wedding reception at Harleigh House, which happens to be next door to their home. Thus, they are neighbors to my brother-in-law."

"As if that counts for anything." Mother lifted her chin. "The Bainbridges are my friends. With Gladys in Paris, Mr. Bainbridge is alone, so I invited him. And a good thing too since you've invited an extra lady. Now the numbers will be even."

"But he doesn't know the Connors are also attending, does he?" I asked.

"Of course not. I just found out myself."

My father grinned as he glanced around the table. "Two parties to a feud at your wedding. You may well end up with fireworks, Frankie."

I set off for my errands that afternoon with a lighter step and my maid, Bridget, cheered by the thought that in one more day, I'd be sailing off to the south of France on a wedding trip with my husband. Ten days alone with George at the luxurious Villa Kasbeck. The owners of the villa, Russian grand duke Michael Mikhailovich Romanov and his wife Sophie, Countess de Torby, were involved in our last investigation. They felt George and I had done them a service, and I suppose we had, but I was stunned when they'd offered us the use of their home.

Upon our return, I'd live next door to my former house with George. Mother would stay with Aunt Hetty, or return to New York with Frankie and Alonzo, or travel to France as Frankie had suggested, to be with Lily. Whatever her decision, we'd be in separate houses, making for a much better relationship.

Bridget and I alighted from the cab on Bond Street, where despite the heavy gray sky, ladies and gentlemen crowded the pavement, moving briskly from shop to shop while ragged boys with brooms rushed ahead of them to clear their paths of slush, mud, or any other unpleasantries. Our destination was just a few steps away—one of the most expensive dress shops I'd dared to enter since becoming a widow. I'll confess that while I've never been the reckless spendthrift my late husband was, I paid little attention to the price of anything until he was gone, and the bills landed on my desk. That was a gasp-inducing surprise. From that point on, I became utterly parsimonious when replenishing my wardrobe—having gowns restyled, hats refurbished, and only buying new when it was absolutely necessary.

Until now, such a purchase had not been necessary. But Mother had bought my wedding gown, so I felt emboldened to splurge on my going away dress. I wanted something special. Something new to start my new life. Madame Arquette's clothing was nothing if not special. I couldn't wait for this final fitting.

A bell jingled when Bridget opened the door, causing two ladies to glance our way as we stepped inside the cozy receiving room of the shop. Of all people to meet here! Mrs. and Miss Connor. Bridget took my coat and slipped away to join another maid in one of the chairs against the wall, while I approached the ladies with a smile and a "good day."

"Such a surprise to see you here, Lady Harleigh." Mrs. Connor spoke with the slow, lilting accent that placed her origins somewhere in America's South. I'd always wondered where, but then the embarrassing gossip about her background had come out, marking her as working class before her marriage to Connor ten or so years ago. Though my own family had solid middle-class beginnings, I sensed asking about her past might cause her pain, something I was loath to do. She was a bright, handsome, middle-aged woman, small of stature with dark hair and eyes and currently dressed in a fashionable red suit. Regardless of her history, she seemed to have landed on her feet.

Yet she always had a tense look about her, as if she were waiting for the other penny to drop.

"I would have thought you'd be busy preparing for the wedding tomorrow," she said. "Are there not a hundred things to do?"

"Ah, but this is one of those many things, the final fitting of my going away gown."

Madeline Connor perked up at this. "Where are you spending your wedding trip, Lady Harleigh?"

"Cannes, primarily. But I hope to see a bit of the French countryside too."

"That sounds lovely." Mrs. Connor's face took on a dreamy look. "I'm afraid we're here for the rest of the winter. Mr. Connor has some business to take care of, and we need to outfit Madeline for the upcoming season."

"Assuming Papa allows me to have one." The young woman's tight lips and the glint in her eye warned of rebellion.

Mrs. Connor, easily four inches shorter than her step-daughter, reached up to stroke her cascading brown curls. "Your father would not deprive you of a debut. But the season is not all about parties and dancing, you know." She turned back to me and smiled. "Madeline has a new suitor, and Mr. Connor seems to think he's prepared to offer for her hand."

That would be bad news for Alonzo. I schooled my expression so as not to show my disappointment. "Perhaps you should make him wait for an answer, Miss Connor. You may have many suitors once the season begins."

Mrs. Connor's brow furrowed as she twisted her fingers together. "Madeline wouldn't want to cause him any anxiety, would you, dear?"

Before the girl could answer, Madame Arquette stepped up to fetch Mrs. Connor. "I will be with you in the briefest of moments, Lady Harleigh. We are a bit short of staff this morning."

"I could not have better company," I said. Linking my arm

through Madeline's, we moved to a comfortable settee hidden by a table piled high with bolts of sumptuous fabrics. Never one to pry into another's personal business, I dearly wished to learn the name of her new suitor—for Alonzo's sake, of course. At eighteen years of age, she looked impossibly young to me, but I tried to see her through my brother's eyes—heart-shaped face, rosebud lips, half-moon eyes that tipped up at the corners. About average height, she'd come up to Lon's shoulder and glance up at him through her long eyelashes. Oh, yes, Lon would be lost.

While I struggled for a suitable way to return to the subject of her suitor, Miss Connor took charge of the conversation. "Has your brother arrived in town yet, Lady Harleigh?"

"Yes, he and my father arrived yesterday."

"Yesterday?" Her eyes rounded. "Golly, a spot of foul weather, and they might have missed the wedding altogether. I assumed they'd been here for days now."

Despite her professed concern, I noticed a small smile. Had she thought Alonzo was in town for days now and not called on her? "Not even one day yet," I said. "My father was up and about this morning, but Alonzo was still sleeping off the effects of travel."

"I see." She turned on her end of the settee, facing forward. Then, with a tip of her head, she glanced at me from under the brim of her hat. "May I speak in confidence?" she asked. "I don't wish to impose, but because my step-mother mentioned a suitor, I'd like to explain."

It was as if she'd read my mind. I nodded my encouragement.

"It's Daniel Fitzwalter."

Heavens! Her family was aiming high. Viscount Fitzwalter was the first-born son, and heir, of the Marquis of Sudly, a powerful and influential member of the House of Lords. His was an old and lofty title. The only one higher would be that of duke. To top it off, Fitzwalter was young. He'd recently finished his studies at Oxford, so barely over twenty. If she were title hunting, I'd have offered her a "well done," but her expression told me she was not pleased with this outcome. Her unhappy face was turned to me. Waiting for a reaction.

"I sense you are less than thrilled with the potential match," I offered.

She heaved an exaggerated sigh. "I'm so pleased you understand."

I blinked. Understand what? She'd told me nothing. "I'm afraid I don't."

"My father is overjoyed at the mere possibility of such a match, but I have no interest in titles or pomp and circumstance. I hardly know Fitzwalter, but my father is bribing him with an enormous dowry, and I'm worried the viscount will propose to me. If he does, I don't see how I can turn him down.

As I listened to her lament, I realized she wasn't looking for advice so much as a messenger. I was meant to deliver this information to Alonzo, which I would, but I wished he had told me what his intentions were toward Madeline. Did he care enough to fight for her, or would he give her up to Fitzwalter? Without that knowledge, I had no idea what to say.

"If you object to Fitzwalter," I ventured, "but you don't want to reject him, why not tell your father, or Willa, how you feel?"

"My father would be furious with me, and I don't believe my step mother would try to sway him. I'd much rather speak to your brother."

That's what I'd feared. She wanted Alonzo to rescue her. That almost never worked. Not to mention that any assistance he provided Madeline might bring on the wrath of her father. And none of us wanted that. "I'm sure the two of you will speak soon, Miss Connor."

A motion at the back of the shop caught my eye. Willa Connor had finished her business and was coming our way along with Madame. "At some point, you will have to make your preference known to your father," I continued. "Though you fear he won't like your decision, in time he may adjust his opinion. You might gain that time by discouraging Fitzwalter's suit. In delicate matters such as this, it's best to proceed with caution."

I rose as Madame beckoned to me. After saying goodbye to Mrs. Connor, I turned to bid Madeline a good day and was struck by the bleakness of her gaze. There was clearly something she hadn't told me, and now I doubted my advice would be sufficient for her needs. I hoped she and Alonzo wouldn't do anything rash.

Connect with Us

Visit us online at
KensingtonBooks.com
to read more from your favorite authors, see books
by series, view reading group guides, and more.

for sneak peeks, chances to win books and prize packs,
and to share your thoughts with other readers.

facebook.com/kensingtonpublishing
twitter.com/kensingtonbooks

Tell us what you think!

To share your thoughts, submit a review,
or sign up for our eNewsletters, please visit:
KensingtonBooks.com/TellUs.